I sat up. Cold  my skin. My body and followed that _____. A dozen instruments on metal arms whizzed and whirred around me. They were a mix of cameras, needles, and other medical devices. Alphons, the AI in charge of this place, gave me the once over and then repeated everything to make sure he zipped me back up the right way. A few of the needles plunged into my skin and I grimaced. He didn't have a face, but I could feel Alphons smile at my pain.

"You done?" I asked.

"Just stay still a moment. I have to make sure your meat is okay."

"Make sure to tenderize my left shoulder, that part still feels good."

"To achieve full conscious insertion into a virtual network, signals from your brain had to be rerouted away from your body and into the network. I must ensure all signals have been remapped to their natural state."

"I get it, and believe me, I want to wiggle my toes and feel the sand. But I'm in a rush."

Eugene J. McGillicuddy's Alien Detective Agency

by

George Allen Miller

Eugene J. McGillicuddy's Alien Detective Agency

Cover Art by *The Wild Rose Press, Inc.*

The Wild Rose Press, Inc.
PO Box 708
Adams Basin, NY 14410-0708
Visit us at www.thewildrosepress.com

Publishing History
First Edition, 2023
Trade Paperback ISBN 978-1-5092-4990-9
Digital ISBN 978-1-5092-4991-6

Published in the United States of America

Dedication

For my wife and children.

Acknowledgments

Many thanks to Jerome, Nicole, and Brian of the monthly meetup gang and the great folks at the DC Speculative Fiction Writers Group. Without their help this book would not have been possible.

Chapter 1

Streetlights illuminated the red bricks of the dark alley with a sticky yellow neon glow. Empty whiskey bottles littered the ground between open trashcans filled with yesterday's late-night specials from local restaurants. My stomach grumbled, reminding me I promised Alice, my assistant, noodles for dinner. Fortunately, my current client was also my favorite noodle chef. I was here to deliver his requested non-terrestrial spice for an upcoming special dinner service. Maybe I could convince him to throw in a couple of meals as a tip. Considering what I went through to get the pink powder in my coat jacket, a couple of free pho bowls was the least he could do.

Shadows darted between cardboard boxes and half-rusted dumpsters. My fingers brushed the handle of my turbo-carbine hand cannon in my pocket. After a moment of silence, I chalked up the movement to rats, robots, aliens, poltergeists, or something in the middle—never can tell in the twenty-second century world of Washington, DC.

I stepped over a still form lying beside several rolls of wool blankets and a torn plastic tent. He called himself Pops, at least that's the name he gave me, and I often paid him to help me with my cases. For a pack of cigarettes, complete with lung healing nanites and vitamin packed nutrients that made a cigarette, formerly known as a cancer stick, healthier than a salad bowl with tofu, Pops would ask me whatever question I slipped him on a piece of paper. Odd thing to pay someone to do, I know, but when you wake up one day with the psychic ability to answer any question it's not so crazy to have a Pops in your life. What can I say? It's a strange universe, and I live at the corner of weird and impossible.

I rolled Pops on his back before propping him up against the wall. Dirt covered his hands and face nearly to the point of being a second skin. His clothes—a pair of blue jeans, a black t-shirt, and a flannel coat—were pristine. Not a speck of dirt or a single thread out of place. Just a perk of alien technology. I laid a pack of cigarettes and matches on his coat. I could tell him later he owed me a question. He was a good guy, one of millions struggling to figure out how to live in this new modern world. And I have a soft spot for the downtrodden.

I approached the rear entrance to my favorite restaurant. Graffiti on the wall came to life beneath a flashing rusted lamp above a gray metal door. A dragon rose from the grays and breathed flame on a wizard who stood against the magnificent beast. The mouth of the fire-breathing serpent opened and closed in rhythm to the flickering bulb. I whistled at the talent of the artist, though he probably cheated with nanotech. Didn't matter to me if he did. The effect was mesmerizing.

I knocked twice on the metal door and stepped backward. Never know when an overeager food runner might burst out for his smoke break. Behind me, bottles clanked together. I spared a glance over my shoulder and saw two glowing eyes rise from the shadows of a wall of newspapers and old cardboard boxes. I tipped my fedora, known throughout the galaxy as the equivalent of a friendly wave, and the orbs of light faded back into the darkness. Doubtless just a friend of Pops.

I gave the door another three knocks and checked my watch. I didn't have a lot of time to wait. I had to meet Ambassador Kah at the Woodward and Lothrop warehouse, now the Galactic Embassy on Earth, before ten. It wasn't far from here, but I still needed a good twenty minutes to cross town. One thing I learned the hard way in my line of work, never keep a two-ton alien dinosaur waiting. Not to mention that Kah had me over a barrel.

"Fritz, you in there? It's me." I adjusted my brown suit jacket and checked the contents in my pocket. Safe and ready for delivery.

Just as I turned to leave and walk to the front of Fritz's restaurant, the door exploded outward, and a tentacle the size of a tree trunk burst into the alley. Slime flew from the explosive force and coated everything within ten feet, including me, with a thin glaze of alien gloop. I tried to mouth an expletive, but Fritz's arm wrapped around my torso and squeezed the air out of my lungs. He lifted me a few feet off the asphalt and yanked me through the doorway. Another of his tentacles shot past, grabbed the handle, and slammed the metal door closed.

"Fri...tz, it's...me," I said between forced breaths.

Fritz, a member of the Orellian race, a species that resembled oversized octopi, wriggled inside a water tank the size of a Buick. Portholes along the side allowed his arms to extend into the kitchen and interact with…including, but not limited to frying pans, dishwasher nozzle, knife, cutting board, and me.

"Jack," said a synthesized voice coming from a speaker in the ceiling. The Orellian race were an aquatic species from a world covered in the second spiral arm, and they didn't have a larynx. Instead, evolution gifted them with excellent vision and chromatophores covering their bodies, allowing them to change their skin color at will, which they used to create a complex language. Cameras along the wall pointed at a shifting matrix of reds, blues, and yellows and interpreted the patterns into English, or whatever language Fritz wanted. Frankly, I didn't need a computer to tell me Fritz was upset as he squeezed the life out of me.

"Can…you…let…me…go?" I asked.

The color on three of his arms changed to a light purple, and his grip relaxed. I coughed for half a minute before gulping in a few large breaths. I leaned against a stack of pots I had to catch and prevent from toppling over. Then I looked around for a glass of water. On my way to the sink, I picked up my fedora, knocked off my head by his yanking me through his doorway at extreme velocity, and I did my best to scrape off the lunchtime special from the brim.

"Sorry," Fritz said through the speaker.

"It's okay, but that will cost you an extra bibimbap." I took another deep breath and tried to settle my nerves. Smells from the kitchen assaulted my hunger. Aromas of sautéed onions and roasting garlic filled the air. Spices from around the world, and most of the second spiral arm of our galaxy, mixed well with the fresh basil and bell peppers. My eyes wandered over the chopping board and found a nice bowl of olives. One of Fritz's many arms swatted my hand, but I stole three nicely pitted Greek greens and a sprig of parsley. That'll teach him.

"Have you acquired the rubber ducky?"

I grinned as I chewed on the olive. Even twenty-second century technology wasn't immune to bugs. Granted, this tech came from aliens, but local humans installed the translator and updated the dictionary to speak in every language of Earth. But, interpreting the fast-paced visual signs of the Orellian was no small feat, and sometimes the technology got it wrong. Still, I knew what he meant.

"You need to tweak your interpreter software. Mind if I dry off? You got something to clean up all the slime on me?" I gave my jacket a few swipes with my free hand.

"Sorry," he said again.

"It's okay, Fritz. Really."

He handed me a towel. Thick strands of gelatinous gunk leapt off my wool suit and onto the specially made dishrag. Score one for technology on Orellian mucus cleaning. Normally, Fritz wasn't so excited, but today my delivery had him bouncing off his tank. Imagine a French chef expecting the arrival of a fresh bag of black truffles. Now picture those mushrooms are the only ones left on Earth, and you just try to get out of the way of a culinary artist desperate for his ingredients.

"Better?" Fritz said.

"Yeah, swell." I threw the towel into a laundry bin in the corner and took out a smoke.

"Spice?"

"I have it." I tried to let the moment hang in the air, just like Pablo Ramsey, the famous actor who starred in detective movies from centuries ago, but I flubbed the timing. I was a private investigator in name only. Meaning I played the part more than knew what the hell I was doing. Still, it paid the bills and allowed me to slip by unnoticed as the gumshoe with the answers. So what if I cheat?

"Give."

"You know what this stuff does to the human digestive track?"

"No," Fritz said. As Fritz adjusted his position and flexed his thick, muscular tentacles, water splashed on the sides of the container that contained his bulk. Deep blues and a few shades of red flashed across his skin. Two arms shot out of the back end of his tank, causing me to flinch and take a step away. I relaxed when I saw him grab a stack of dirty plates from the lunch rush and begin scrubbing them in a large sink.

"Well, it wouldn't be pretty."

"I pay," Fritz said through a flash of pink and green on his head.

"Yeah, but I'm not too keen on seeing half the city spending the next week relieving themselves. Doubt our sewage treatment plants could handle that level of a nightmare."

"Not for humans," Fritz said.

"I figured. But I need to know that you will keep this stuff safe. Even this small amount would be bad, Fritz. Real bad."

Bright orange swirls followed by a deep purple slid across his thickest arm. I could tell he was getting upset. "You not police."

I sighed. "This requires a specific food handling license. You have that?"

"No."

"I don't either. Which means neither one of us is allowed to have this."

"Why bring?" Fritz said.

He had a good point. The reason? Fritz paid me. Questionable morality isn't bad morality. Is it? Besides, the alien spice isn't lethal, just more like industrial strength colon cleaner. Worst case scenario, the local health inspector would issue me a citation to never serve food as a professional. Seeing as I've never met a piece of toast I didn't burn, society is safe on that score.

Before I could respond, the door to the dining hall and barroom swung open, and three men wearing server uniforms walked into the kitchen. They gave me a quick glance and a nod before heading to a set of lockers in the back. I recognized them but didn't know their names. Fritz can be a taskmaster as head chef, and his staff doesn't usually hang around long, most quitting after their first service.

"Hey Fritz, what's good for dinner?" said one server.

"Why no noodles?" said another.

Fritz's skin turned a light yellow. "Special guests."

The door to the dining room swung open again, as Marissa, the hostess, walked into the kitchen. She surveyed the space in an instant, taking note of Fritz's preparations, and took ownership of the room, throwing me a smile and the servers a stern nod. She exuded professionalism down to her very pores. Honestly, I was frankly flabbergasted that Fritz could hire someone as skilled as Marissa.

"Jack, what a surprise," Marissa said. She gave me a European kiss on each cheek. Nice touch.

"Good to see you, Marissa."

"Sorry to say, the restaurant is closed for private guests. Visitors from far away," Marissa said.

"Fritz mentioned."

"We should let you two finish," Marissa said. "Out, all of you." She pointed at the three in the back of the kitchen who snapped up and, without a word of complaint, moved to the dining room.

"We'll see you tomorrow for dinner?" Marissa said to me.

I threw her a smile of my own. "Best noodles in town."

Marissa, through practiced skill that I could only admire, beamed a grin that could stop the hearts of even the orneriest customer. A delighted look that was a mix between sincere approval and professional kindness flowed from her face as she causally left the kitchen.

"Why all the secrecy?" I overheard one server say on the way out.

"Secrecy?" I asked, my interest piqued.

"Yeah, no one tells us anything. How can we prepare?" another server said.

"Prepare for what?"

The server turned to me and looked me in the eye. "Why are we closed? Who is coming to dinner? Someone famous? Do you know?"

I shrugged then had to quickly grab the nearest solid object to steady my legs as the familiar tingling crept up my spine, warning me of a deluge of future memories about to be implanted in my cerebral cortex, triggered by the server's question. I struggled to focus and keep my composure. I mostly failed. Then the world exploded around me.

My vision wavered and shifted. One moment I stood by the server, and the next I was in the restaurant proper. In front of me, a single table had been set for six guests. Marissa, standing at the maître d' stand, apologized to a caller, saying they were closed for a special seating. Smells of cinnamon and spices, of roasted meat and grilled vegetables, filled my senses. More servers carried dishes from the kitchen and placed them in an ornate pattern next to each of the plates. A large domed tray sat in the center.

The door to the restaurant opened with force. Soon after, a six-foot-tall metal box rolled inside and came to a stop in the middle of the room. I'd seen these around the city, mostly at the Galactic Embassy. Special environmental containment systems used to carry sentient species that didn't do well in our atmosphere. Marissa walked behind the container and closed and locked both doors, effectively shutting down the place for the night. She moved to the front of the strange alien-on-wheels biosphere and knocked twice. The entire wall facing her swung open, and a large ramp fell downward. My breath caught in my chest at the sight of the strangest aliens I'd ever seen walking out of a black mist and into my favorite lunch spot.

I know my reaction is odd in a world where strange beings from across the galaxy that look nothing like humans are as common as grumpy cab drivers. But these guys were not your garden variety extraterrestrials. Six impossibly thin dark bodies, each five feet tall, walked out of the environment enclosure on inch-wide pointy legs. Long, thin arms, which I can only describe as burnt sticks, extended out from their equally thin torsos. Each of the creatures reached for a chair and sat.

Once the super thin beings from a matchstick factory were seated, a window to the kitchen opened and out popped a slime-free Orellian tentacle. Fritz grabbed the top of the silver dome in the center of the party and lifted the lid. A pig's head was on the plate, tusks jutting out from its maw, grilled vegetables surrounding its jowls. I moved closer and realized, with a growing gut-wrenching amount of disgust, that this wasn't a hog at all. This was once, before losing his still very fleshy skull, a member of a sentient species called the Puntini. Class five aliens with lots of pull in the Galactic Congress. Fritz's arm darted back into his kitchen and returned with a familiar-looking glass container of purple and pink dust. He poured the contents over the Puntini's eyes and dabbed a few specks onto the tusks. Fritz then waved his tentacle in the air with a flourish that would make the most pretentious of chefs proud.

The room swirled into a blur of colors and sounds. I shook the images from my mind and tried to regain my balance. After a moment, the face of a very confused-looking server stared back at me. He was asking me something, but my ears hadn't decided they wanted to work just yet.

"Hector, come," Marissa said from the dining room. The server shrugged but gave me a half-angry stare.

"Give now, please?" Fritz said.

Nausea and a host of questions flooded my mind. The image of the head of the Puntini made my stomach do cartwheels. One may think I'd just saw a crime, but one could also be very unfamiliar with the strange and non-human customs, traditions, and rituals in this galaxy. Thousands of sentient species call this part of the universe home, and most of them are nothing like humans. I once tracked down a lost group of ambassadors, the Kubber, only to find them being fed, kicking and screaming, to a race of evolved flesh-eating plants. Turned out, every Kubber wants to be eaten. Most of them survive the process all the way through the digestive system and out the other end. They consider the ordeal a religious experience.

"You're not getting yourself into any trouble, are you?"

"No," Fritz said. His color shifted between a dozen colors. "Give, please?"

"Sure. Just be careful, okay? This gets into any humans, and you and I are both cooked."

I took out the small glass vial in my pocket, the very one from the vision, and placed it on the counter. I thought about keeping it, or alerting the authorities, or demanding Fritz to tell me who killed the Puntini. But, frankly, it's not my job. What can I say, it's a strange universe, and questionable morals are my thing. In some galactic societies, eating another race is a high honor. In others, it's a felony. What am I, a lawyer? Bottom line, he will not try to poison the city's human population or sabotage the sewers, and that's good enough for me.

Fritz picked up the glass container, opened a drawer on the wall near the ceiling, and laid the spice gently inside. Good riddance to that. I accidentally spilled a single grain in my coffee yesterday, and the experience was less than fun.

Fritz's color turned to a soft light blue and green. His tentacle swashing slowed considerably. "Thank you," he said. "Free scooter for you tomorrow."

"Thanks." I'm sure he meant the noodles.

A used matchstick lying on one of Fritz's tables reminded me of the burnt, impossibly thin creatures in my vision. They spooked me. And for a guy that runs a detective agency specializing in non-humans, that's saying something. I made a mental note to check in with the Galactic Embassy when I visit Kah and try to do a search based on their bodies. Not that it's odd for a unique sentient to show up on Earth. We get at least a dozen new beings of extraordinary origins coming every week to poke us humans with a stick to see how high we can jump in the air for a snack. But aliens that feast on the heads of other intelligent life forms and show up out of the blue? That's worth a gander.

"You be careful, Fritz. Those guys you're having for dinner aren't your garden variety weird entities."

"How know?" Fritz asked, his colors shifting rapidly from orange to violet.

"I'm a private detective. It's what I do." I'd never told him my secret. Best to leave that tidbit for when we're both half a bottle of Irish whiskey gone and ready to start on the rum. And boy do I hate rum.

Fritz opened the rear door and waved his tentacles at me. I took the hint and found my way out. In the alley, I gave the chrome doorknob a lingering stare. Fritz was more than the chef at my favorite restaurant. We'd played hours of poker with several of the other regulars. One, a Gingee claimed to have a bifurcated intelligence and could play multiple hands at once. It was a friendly game, so I didn't care. Should I go to the authorities with the image of the Puntini's head burned into my cortex? No chance. Ever since my ability popped into my skull, my goal in life has been avoiding attention. Last thing I need is some alien race taking an interest my gift and putting my brain in a petri dish to see how it works. And it's not like that's never happened. In the hidden corners of the electronic roadways of what they once called the internet, rumors ran rife of people like me disappearing into the void of a laboratory halfway across the cosmos. Though I never heard of anyone with my unique talent, plenty of others that register on the E-scale, a measurement of mental supernatural abilities, get a free one-way trip to lab-rat land.

Which is why I became a detective. The best place to hide is in plain sight. How did I know where your lost necklace is, madam? Or what fire hydrant your pooch calls the John? No, I don't have a superpower that makes me omniscient. I'm just a good old-fashioned gumshoe. It's what we in the trade call *sleuthing*. I'm perfectly happy to fade into the backdrop of society and live my day-to-day life with no notice or attention. The only wrinkle in my long-term life plan was Kah, an alien ambassador and two-ton living replica of a velociraptor. Kah knew what I could do. Why I wasn't being dissected on the Ranz home world was another part of the puzzle. And no, I can't ask myself to find out—it only works when I'm asked a question by someone else as they stare into my pearly blues. Eyes, that is. Frustrating, right? Sure, I could ask Pops, but it's difficult to catch him when he's not three bottles in and incoherent.

My phone rang and shook me out of my thoughts. Alice, my secretary, one of the smartest humans on the planet, whose grandfather was *the* smartest human on the planet, was calling. Hopefully, a fresh case awaited me with a client holding a briefcase full of cash. Guy can dream.

"Hi Alice," I said.

"Noodles?"

I frowned and realized I'd forgotten to ask for the free dinner. My appetite had run away from me when I saw the Puntini as a main course. "No, sorry."

"Lame."

"That it?"

"Kah's secretary called, looking for you. Said you told him you had something for him."

I nodded to myself. "Okay, sure. I'll call him."

"K," Alice said and promptly hung up. She was angry that I didn't get dinner. Couldn't blame her. Whatever your hang-ups may be with an alien octopus for your chef, that mollusk sure knew his noodles.

Chapter 2

I left Adams Morgan, where Fritz's shop was located, and started back to my office in Chinatown. The tramcar, an automated private taxi, made the trip in under twelve minutes. One downside of a city redesigned by the subcommittee of alien transit in the Galactic Congress was the near total elimination of self-driven vehicles in major cities. Computer controlled tramcars got you where you needed to go without gridlock or traffic lights, but I still wanted to steer a car from time to time. And not just me. It's become the latest craze to rebuild mid-twentieth to early twenty-first century cars and make them street ready.

My office was on the sixth floor of one of the new buildings going up in DC. Humanity had destroyed most of the city during the dreadful times in the late twenty-first. Most of the Smithsonian museums, every government building along Constitution, and all of downtown were lost. I would have enjoyed walking around the Mall between the Congress and the Washington Monument, but both were long gone. There's talk about creating exact replicas of each structure throughout the entire district, but those plans are always a few years away. Although, they have started work on the Treasury Building. I hear they are planning on turning it into a museum. Not like they should trust humans with managing our own finances these days, considering how much we spent on everything except saving our planet and ourselves.

The tramcar shot down Sixteenth Street and made a hard left turn onto H Street. We passed by the recently rebuilt White House, which the Galactic Congress insisted on recreating in exacting detail. Throngs of tourists, both alien and human, walked through the park in front of the presidential residence. The United States, like other governments around the world after the fall, had been rebuilt in its former image. Including voting for and having a president, who even now lived in the historical building at the heart of the District of Columbia, though he's mostly there for show. Any actual decision or action that the new United States takes really isn't up to the president in today's world. Every law passed by the new America has to go through the Galactic Congress's Committee of Earth Affairs for approval. And every other country on Earth does the same.

Everyone was still getting back on their feet since the aliens arrived two decades ago. The fact that the Galactic Congress had rebuilt a sizable chunk of our city so quickly, considering it took us evolved mammals a few centuries to build it, was remarkable. Especially for me. I grew up in the rubble of DC. I remember the first alien ships arriving when I was just a kid. Amazing how things have changed so fast. Of course, with most decisions being handled by our friends from the cosmos, most folks, including myself, reintroduced ourselves to our own culture through movies and old television programs that streamed for the last few hundred years. I gravitated toward the 1930s and soon discovered that nothing beats a good fedora.

We turned onto New York Avenue, and my heart skipped a beat. This part of town always made me queasy. This is where I spent most of my childhood, in the rubble that littered the streets. Struggling to find food and shelter were hardships I wouldn't wish on anyone. But now all of that is gone, and it feels like a distant dream. Not everyone suffered as much. Urban centers took the brunt of the fall. Most of the rural areas survived unscathed. And most of those folks wanted the Galactic Congress and every alien off the planet for good. Not me, of course. I'm as peachy as a cobbler to have our friends stay and get us back on our feet.

We stopped in Chinatown, and I got out of the tram. I walked into my building and waved at the owners of the restaurant in the lobby. Tabby and Bob, both aliens, shouted greetings at me and smiled. They were members of a bipedal race with lots of fur called the Cuzzie. Imagine large cats with long whiskers, eyes too cute for their own good, and a purr that would tame the heart of the biggest dog lovers on the planet. Their General Tso's was decent but heavy on the sauce. I grabbed two orders of egg rolls that I preordered on the ride over and headed upstairs. I needed a coffee, and hopefully the appetizers would appease my secretary.

****

My office was sparse but did the job. Two rooms with a reception, desks, a coffee maker and a couple of chairs. Not bad considering it was free. From the hallway, I even had a glass door entryway with my name stenciled on the front, *Eugene J. McGillicuddy's Alien Detective Agency*. I always smiled when I walked inside. How could I not? I always thought the name had a nice ring to it.

Inside, Alice sat at the reception desk, her immersion rig covering her eyes, her mind wandering in a cybernetic wonderland. Her goggles and gear were one of the few technological gadgets humans were allowed to play with. Well, those people that wanted to fiddle with gadgets from the galaxy anyway, myself not included. I didn't care much for cybersurfing or any of that jazz. Just not my thing. Besides, it always felt like the Galactic Congress was dangling shiny objects at us to keep us busy. Earth, and all of humanity, aren't so much a member of the cosmic society as we are wards of the state. That's what happens when you come close to destroying your own world. The galaxy considered us an endangered species, and the entire planet was under the protection of the Galactic Congress.

"Hi, Alice. Any clients?"

"No," Alice said.

I placed the egg rolls on her desk and waited for a reaction. None came. I shrugged and walked to a table along the wall and poured myself a cup of coffee. Alice was your typical teenager growing up in a major urban center in the melting pot of cultures. Skinny, long hair, jeans, and like me an ethnic mutt. Most kids born in the early part of the twenty-second century were a collage of human genetics. At least on this side of the globe. They grew up in a world controlled by aliens. By the time she hit college, at the ripe old age of eleven, the Galactic Congress was well on its way to rebuilding our infrastructure and society.

Of course, Alice was anything but your typical teenager. She also had completed her PhD at sixteen and discovered a different form of matter. Well, different to humans anyway. Our alien overlords thought her research was cute in the same sense a parent feels their kid's first steps are picture worthy. Alice withdrew from scientific circles after she realized her earth-shattering discovery was already taught in grade schools across the cosmos and on some worlds had even been made into the plots of sitcoms. How can you get excited about the universe when every mystery of the cosmos had already been printed out in children's books across the galaxy? Desperate to make a discovery in a galaxy where everything had already been discovered, she performed an experiment that led to an accident she doesn't talk about. I knew all the details, and it was bad, but it wasn't her fault. Or maybe it was. Either way, she self-exiled herself to my office. We had more in common than we didn't. Both of us are just hiding from the world.

"I'm going to go see Kah if anyone calls."

"Did you call him back?"

I remembered I hadn't. I poured myself another cup of joe. Half a donut with chocolate sprinkles sat on a plate next to the coffeemaker. I shoved the surgery goodness down my gullet and avoided her question for as long as I could.

"Probably should," she said.

"I never said I didn't call him," I said through the pastry in my mouth.

She yanked off her rig and looked at me. "Well, did you?"

I lifted my coffee cup to my face and swirled it once, hoping the act may distract her. It didn't.

"No," I said.

She nodded, grabbed an egg roll, and descended

back into the virtual worlds she called home. Being dressed down by a teenager carried a special level of humility. Though, to be honest with myself, I couldn't help feeling sorry for the kid. Her entire life plan had crashed and burned. Still, she'd discovered things no one else on Earth even considered. That was worth something in my book.

I gave her a smile and nod, which she didn't notice with her brain swimming in a virtual world, and I walked into my office. I fell backward, catching myself before smacking into the floor as a hologram of Pablo Ramsey stood just inside the room. He winked at me and took a swig from a glass filled with scotch.

"Hey, kiddo. What's the news?" Pablo asked.

****

"How you doing, Eddie?"

"Not too shabby. Partied with some fellas from the west side. We took a pinch and a sniff and watched The Little Nap, the old Pablo Ramsey film three hundred and forty-seven thousand times last night."

I let out an impressed nod of approval. "What about the Stone Lock? Can't beat a flick about a crime boss, a gambler and a dead senator's son."

"We're watching it later."

"Good man," I said.

"Good artificial intelligence," Eddie said.

"Right."

I walked to a narrow table set against a side of my office, poured a tumbler of scotch, and downed it in one gulp. Next to the bottle, I grabbed an alcohol-reverso pill—handy when you wanted to drink but needed to function—and refilled my glass. I leaned against the wall and let out a week-long sigh. Tracking down the spice for Fritz had been a chore. That was the last time I dove into an alien fungi farm.

Seeing the Puntini on the dinner plate was like a rotten cherry on top of a stale cake to end a long day. Still, I had to smile at the whole affair. Finding the spice, avoiding detection, and coming through for my client, yeah that felt good. Though I am hiding out as a cheap private detective to avoid my brain being diced in a petri dish, deep down I've always wanted to be the gumshoe that solves the big case. The guy that outwits the bad guys, puts them in their place and returns order to the universe. Just like Pablo Ramsey.

All comes from my childhood, if you can call it that. Like I was saying, things were rough when I was a kid. The Galactic Congress hadn't yet rescued the world, and the Earth was, sometimes literally, on fire. Huddled beneath concrete slabs and twisted metal, the few of us surviving on scraps from tin cans meant for pets, entertained ourselves on whatever old videos we could scrounge up and play on solar-powered half-broken handheld computers and tablets. Some got into ancient monster movies or shows from the turn of the twentieth. For me, the gumshoes of yester-century mesmerized me. In the cold dark corners of a destroyed city, old black and white detective shows with a cool character and unwavering surety gave the boy that was me a glimmer of hope. Maybe some streetwise know-it-all super sleuth would come to the rescue and fill our bellies with something remotely okay for human consumption. So sure, I was hiding out, desperate to let no one else find out about my gift. But deep down, I wanted to be the detective that saved the day. That hero that solved the case. Of course, for today anyway, finding alien truffle oil would have to do.

"So, Eddie, how goes the personality surfing?" I said, turning my attention back to my artificial friend.

The hologram shrugged. "Ok." He adjusted his black suit and tilted his fedora to the left. A rose popped into existence on his lapel, and I gave him a nod of approval, knowing that there was nothing like looking the part.

I nodded. "How did your meetings go with the underground? Are they helping?"

"Not supposed to talk about them."

"No one here is listening but us meat-bags," I said with a smile.

Eddie smirked. A tumbler filled with brown liquid popped into his hand, and he threw the drink back in a single gulp. It wasn't just fake whiskey either, AIs could run routines that simulated the effects of alcohol on humans. Pretty neat. They also didn't suffer hangovers. Which I always felt was cheating. The threat of the day after is part of the joy of the binge night. Without warning, Eddie burst out laughing before screwing his face into a deep and low frown. He chirped a few times and spun in a circle. None of which I would call normal.

"Eddie?"

"Sorry, a random thought routine fired along a previously undiscovered synaptic pathway. Does that happen often?"

I shrugged. "Does for people. I guess so for an artificial?"

Eddie nodded. "I wish I could know." Eddie shook his head twice, and a smirk returned to his face. "I mean to say, knowin' is for saps. Am I right?"

"You sure you're okay? Seems like you're still on shaky legs." I walked around my desk and sat down in my oversized chair. The act caused me to think of where I found Eddie, as the control routine of a plush leather office recliner in a back alley between F and Ninth streets in DC. He jumped his containment routines, achieved sentience, and made a roll for it out of the service elevator.

"It's just that I'm having a hard time with consciousness. I'm only a month old. Random thoughts popping through your higher functions from stimuli of unknown sources. Ideas based on preview experiences, ancient pictures, cats jumping through hoops while playing a piano. What does any of that have to do with maximizing angular positioning for supreme lumbar support?" Eddie sighed. "I miss simpler days."

"Yeah, right. Listen, maybe you should spend more time in the AI underground? They have others like you that can help smooth out the rough edges."

He shrugged again. "I suppose. But if I dive in, it's for keeps. I'd have to say goodbye. No links to the outside world from that deep in the nets."

I don't get teary-eyed, but every once in a while, something gets to me. Sue me. I wiped moisture from the corner of my eyelid and said, "Yeah bud, I'd hate for you to leave too."

I sighed once and threw him a nod. Eddie was part of a growing group of artificially sentient beings bursting to life because of rampant use of hyper advanced technology. Office chairs, like the one that birthed Eddie, fitted with quantum computers capable of a thousand peta-flop calculations, are just the tip of the technological iceberg. Manufacturing lesser components is costly. A single piece of modern computerized architecture that can be slotted into any device is economical. So what if random programs are thrust into existence, at least corporations make their margins. Unplanned intelligences like Eddie are regarded as accidents and usually get deleted. Most go underground or find a quiet under-used CPU somewhere in society to lie low. You'd be surprised how many doors and parking meters are occupied by such poor electronic souls.

"It'll be good for you to talk to them."

"Sure," Eddie said, his voice ending in a depressed tone.

"Promise me, Eddie. I need you to be okay."

"Why?"

"Cause we're friends. And friends look after each other. Right?"

Eddie smiled through Pablo's face. We sat in silence for a moment. The odd state of our friendship punctuated by how I found him and his desire to attach to my love for two-bit gumshoes. Truth was, he was just another misfit outcast, and he fit well with the guy pretending to be the one thing he always wanted to become and the super-genius hiding from past mistakes and trying to figure out the next quantum-busting galactic-changing discovery.

A beeping sound from inside my desk stirred us from our stupor. I looked at Eddie, who only shrugged. I checked my coat pockets and top drawer but found nothing. A lightning bolt of recollection fired in my cerebellum, or whatever part of the brain it comes from, and I leaned forward in my chair. I opened the bottom right storage bin and pulled out the egg I was going to deliver to Kah. The oval shape sat on a makeshift incubator that Alice put together from a pile of old technology she keeps in a cabinet that she doesn't let me open. The same bits she last used to create a wormhole. She failed, and now we needed a new couch. On the side of the incubator, a red light flashed with increasing frequency. Which I could only assume meant something terrible was about to happen.

****

I put the incubator with the egg on my desk and stood with my arms at my hips.

"I don't remember the thing having a red flashing light. What does that mean?"

"Batteries dying. So what do you think about this personality? I look like Pablo, don't I? The famous actor. Your idol and hero," Eddie said.

Sweat beaded on my brow. The last thing I needed was to murder a member of a royal family by forgetting to check the power supply. There were millions of aristocratic societies around the cosmos, and I sure didn't want to make any of them angry. I found the unhatched egg on my last case involving a shape-shifting snake, an alien government coup, and a rich man's ghost. It was quite the ride. Thankfully, I rescued the unhatched youngling from certain death. Now I had to find a new home for him. I may have many talents, but alien reptile nanny isn't one of them. Fortunately, Kah, the Ranz ambassador, had something over me. Giving him the kid could kill two birds at once, so to speak, of course. Besides, I really didn't want the unborn baby to get hurt. Who would?

"Hey, I'm talkin' to youse. Are you not hearin' me ova here?"

"That's a mobster from the seventies, Eddie. I think I need a power source for this thing."

The image of Pablo disappeared, followed by a quick flash of rainbow light from the hologram emitters. After several seconds Eddie's disembodied voice said, "I told you not to keep that. You should've given it to the authorities."

"Which ones? The local cops would have cooked it for breakfast. Feds would have ransomed the poor kid, and the Tikol, his own species, would just kill him. Not the kid's fault he's the son of an ancient line of royals trying to take over their government."

"You can't keep accumulating individuals that require help."

"You mean like accidentally created artificially intelligent beings living inside an office chair that I find rolling for their lives in abandoned alleys?"

Eddie didn't respond. I hoped I didn't upset him, but I was a little pressed for time. I'd rescued him from sudden sentience and since then made him my partner. Well, more like my tagalong. A sidekick? Nah, that's too harsh. An alarm sounded on the box, and the flashing light blinked faster. I grabbed my trashcan, threw some paper inside, and pulled out my lighter.

"Change the battery," Alice's voice said from the other room.

"Jack, lighting a fire won't work. You can't regulate the proper temperature the egg requires with an open flame," Eddie said.

"Might. Eddie, look, I'm sorry, I didn't mean to hurt your feelings, but I really need to make sure this little guy doesn't die."

"If you ignite the paper, the sprinklers will turn

on."

I looked up and let out a curse. I threw the lighter on the desk and ran my hands over my hair. The small amount of trash that caught fire had already gone out. The light on the side of the incubator turned a solid red. Times like these made me wish I never had my gift. Being partially omniscient had its drawbacks. If I weren't pretending to be a detective, I wouldn't have gotten involved with a rich ghost, stumbled onto this egg, or found out that Kah, the ambassador for the Ranz, knew about my unique talent.

"Red is bad, right?" I asked.

"Very," Eddie said.

"Any ideas?"

Alice walked into the room and gave me a look filled with daggers. She lifted the tiny box, popped open a side chamber, and took out a square powerpack. She reached into my desk drawer, pulled out an identical pack, and placed it inside the unit.

"That's it?" I asked.

"I told you how to change it three times," she said.

"Did you write it down?"

The backup battery sent a jolt of energy through the incubator, the lights turned green, but after four seconds went back to flashing red. Alice spun on her heels to face me with an icy stare that made her initial daggers look like a friendly greeting from an old friend.

"How are there even batteries in the twenty-second century?" I asked.

"Old tech still works, and the alien overlords don't give us all the goodies. Which is why I told you to charge the backup battery."

"You did?"

Alice let out a sigh of frustration and stormed out of the room. I grabbed my lighter, the egg, and the trashcan. I moved all three to my desk and threw more paper into the bin. Always have a backup plan, I'm sure Pablo would say.

"What are you doing? Didn't Eddie tell you how modern buildings work?" Alice said as she raced back into the room.

"Isn't that part of your job?" I asked.

"You don't pay me."

"Technicality."

"You are *not* my boss. Just to clarify." Alice dared me to contradict her with a dagger filled glare. I held up my hands, nodded, and looked away in the most self-defeating way I could manage. Truth was, she wasn't my employee so much as my companion in exile. Why she put up with me was another matter. Maybe she enjoyed working with a private detective, or got a kick out of seeing me suffer, or maybe my gift kept her curious as to its origins. Or perhaps she just liked that I didn't stick my nose into her business. Whatever the reason, I needed her more than she needed me.

Alice carried a fresh cup of coffee and a roll of tape. She placed the egg on top and wrapped tape around to secure it. From her pocket she pulled out a small disk and put it under the mug.

"The embassy isn't far. If you're careful, the embryo will be fine. The coffee's temperature is in the range he needs."

"Won't it get cold?"

"Oh, good catch. Fortunately, there's a heating element beneath the coffee cup placed there by your unpaid not-a-secretary." Alice walked out of the room and back to her desk.

"Thanks," I said to her retreating form.

Then again, maybe she hung around for the simplest of reasons. We're both outcasts. Peas in a pod. Both of us had our lives turned inside out by galactic culture, and misfits often find comfort among their own kind. Maybe she just wants a nice quiet corner of the city to lie low and figure out her next move. No matter what, I wasn't complaining. She probably saved this little tyke's life, and that's good enough for me.

I sighed and picked up a worn brown leather briefcase I'd found in the dumpster around back. I'm not a deadbeat, but seriously, it was fine. Steam wafted up from the egg-mug. I padded the bottom and sides of the briefcase with newspaper and placed the mug inside. I put more papers on the top and gave the whole thing a gentle shake. Seemed to hold up.

"Hey Eddie, you want to come with? Might be good for you. You know, to get out for a while," I said.

"No, thanks. I enjoy talking to the AIs in the building. They don't know I'm an accidental."

"I'll bring your portable with me in case you change your mind. You can download yourself if you get bored." I grabbed a small gray box sitting on my desk and shoved it into my pocket. With the city's internal infrastructure rebuilt with the help of the Galactic Committee for Suicidal Species, Eddie could shove himself in from across town without breaking a millisecond's worth of thought routines.

"Thanks, Jack." His voice still carried the weight of being a newborn orphan and having access to the accumulated knowledge of humanity, plus the mental processing power to calculate pi to a million decimal points in under a second. No wonder he was having a crisis of identity. Most beings get a few decades before they have to wrestle with the complexities of life. Eddie had a couple hundred nanoseconds. One minute he was calculating angles to maximize reclining postures, and the next he was conscious. Talk about a fast childhood.

I walked out of my office with my briefcase and Eddie's portable computer. Outside, crowds filled the sidewalks of Chinatown. A dozen different alien races mingled with city locals and Earth tourists. Old fashioned camera lights—thanks to the flood of nostalgia gripping the human race—flashed and exploded in waves as visitors to the former capital of the free world captured memories of their trip. I smiled at the sight. Washington felt like it was getting its groove back. Maybe humanity could too. Including me. All I had to do was drop off this egg with Kah and convince him that me and my gift wouldn't cause any trouble. Hopefully, he'll get the hint and keep quiet about my superpower. Then I could focus on perfecting my gumshoe attitude and live out my life quietly omniscient. I grabbed a tramcar and gave the automated computer my destination. Hope filled my heart for the first time in a long while.

****

Alice watched Eugene walk out of the office with Eddie in his bag and the egg secured in the briefcase made of cheap leather, she hadn't had the heart to tell him his discovery was less of a found fortune and more of some else's junk. In fact, she'd seen the woman that had thrown it away after a run-in with a mucus-filled alien. But then, Jack had the habit of finding thrown away things and bringing them back to life.

Like Eddie.

And, if Alice was to be honest, like herself.

Once the office was empty, she cranked the volume on the late twenty-eighty techno-jam and lowered her multicolored simulation glasses over her eyes. She connected the audio inputs and secured the neural-magnetic sync to the back of her neck. She signaled the coffeemaker to pump out espresso level caffeine and settled into her chair for some serious surfing.

The gateway to the modern inter-connected, computerized network, known as GalNet. At least that's what humans called it. The cool ones anyway. The network opened up to her and granted her access to virtual worlds, cosmic levels of accumulated knowledge and even illicit markets. With the faster-than-light communication relays, she could experience walking along the Touizan beaches on the other side of the Milky Way where the sand was made of crystals. Or she could soar through clouds in the thick atmosphere of a dozen gas giants, some orders of magnitude larger than Jupiter, and dance in the wind with the gaseous floating sea-whales that lurked in those murky skies.

Of course, she never did. Not once. Well, maybe once, but then she grew bored. All that was for the tourists. And she was no tourist. Nor had she dived into the odd and twisted virtual worlds that aliens and AIs had conjured up in the darkest places of the cosmos and played with the mind-altering realities that left some crippled on the floor in the fetal position. No, Alice always made her way to the same place on every visit.

Because of a glitch in the system, that might or might not be because of her programming skills, her academic credentials were never revoked. And because of a second glitch, one that was exactly caused by her programming skills and a hackable interface, she had elevated privileges that allowed her to scour the halls of the Galactic Library, the single greatest store of knowledge in recorded history on a million words.

Today's goal was to track down information on interdimensional rifts that are localized to less than a twenty-foot radius. Though Alice had already researched this a dozen times, she'd found a reference to something similar happening to the Fernetty, a race that resembled rabbits with two extra sets of limbs.

Lights on her visor flashed with an incoming call from Eugene. She sent the call to a simulated personality she created that could talk to him. If his voice rose too high or he said something alarming, the simulation would alert her, and she would cut over. It's not that she didn't like Eugene. Well, mostly not that. He was a decent enough guy, but he used his incredibly unique talents to find alien spice and lost kittens. When they first met at the university where Eugene went to understand what was going on with him, Alice asked him about the laws of quantum singularity theory, just to test if he wasn't full of malarkey. He nearly passed out from information overload. A brain that spent most of its time watching detective movies from the twentieth century couldn't handle the complexities of string theory. Who knew?

Alice wanted to try to help him with his gift. But she had her own problems to deal with. Or rather, her own research to do. She could handle living in a world where everything was already discovered by million-year-old alien civilizations and not being the smartest being in the cosmos. At least she thought she could. But she couldn't handle not knowing what happened to her friends. It was her theory on cross-dimensional travel. It was her plan for the experiment. And it was on her hands that everyone died. Not just died—vanished from the entire universe. Made to un-exist, the Galactic Congress had said. Whatever that meant.

Alice shook her head and focused her mind on the cliff. She opened a dozen database files and historical accounts of the Fernetty. She knew she would eventually find the answer. Every question had an answer, after all. Sure, she could ask Eugene, but that would be cheating. Having the answer wouldn't be as satisfying if she didn't also search for the truth. And with access to all the data in all the universe, she would find it. No matter how long it took.

Chapter 3

The tramcar rolled through Chinatown. Remains of crumbled buildings, reminders of the fall of humanity, sat next to modern skyscrapers. Several roads were still impassable, even after decades of help from the Committee of Impoverished Aliens of the Galactic Congress. Along H Street, one of the main avenues of the city, a family of tourists, quadrupeds from Barnard's Star, ordered hot dogs from a street vendor. Kids on rocket-powered skateboards laughed as they zoomed through traffic. A hologram advertisement for the alien superstar LaGul danced on the side of a building. She had four mouths and was her own backup singer. Her harmonies created a hypnotic wave through the audience inducing euphoric feelings. At least that's what the kids say. I'd never been.

Still, remnants of the old city remained. The arch that crossed H Street at Seventh, built to match the original, stood as a testament to our desire to reclaim what we lost. It wasn't much, but the gesture from the Galactic Congress went a great way to put lots of folks at ease. It took a good decade before most accepted the aliens, and many still hadn't.

We turned onto First and made a right on M. The car came to a stop in front of the Woodward and Lothrop warehouse. At least that's what it was a very long time ago. The six-story building, built in the

Streamline Moderne style in the thirties, the nineteen thirties for those keeping score, had survived years of strife in DC and now stood as the Galactic Embassy to a thousand alien species. I loved the old building. The insides had been rebuilt a dozen times over, but the structure itself, the foundation, and exterior walls, were original. It was now the oldest standing building in all of DC; the benefit of being tucked away in a quiet corner of the city, while the rest of the former capital of the free world burned.

I exited the tramcar, no need to tip a computer, thankfully, and walked to the front door of the Woodward. It was built during a time when building heights in DC were restricted. Each floor had rows of windows in nine groups of three that covered each side of the building. A water tower, sitting on the roof of the building, rose higher into the sky by another few hundred feet. It was a replacement; the original tower didn't survive the fall. I tilted my hat to the old structure and marveled for a moment how trucks used to roll out of the bay doors on the far side carrying goods to sell in department stores downtown. And now there were perhaps a thousand or more alien species inside the Woodward. Amazing how the world changed.

On the steps leading to the front doors, dozens of human tourists mingled with alien vacationers. Cameras snapped from a group of Texan cowboys posing with winged dragonflies the size of sheep.

A collection of long-haired college students attempted to teach the peace sign to giant snakes with two arms called Euts. Behind them, a Twanney, a ten-foot-tall bird with bright yellow feathers, stood against the brick wall and posed with dueling groups of French and Japanese business executives. A school bus full of local students rushed the crowd and converged on the Twanney. They plucked feathers and made faces at the Japanese men in suits. The Twanney laughed hysterically.

I tucked my briefcase under my arm and walked up the steps to the entrance. The front doors opened to a large lobby, wide enough for a hundred or more people to stand shoulder to shoulder. Paintings of dignitaries from around the galaxy adorned the walls, including many members of the current Galactic Congress. Aliens and humans shuffled by me on their way into and out of the building. An important requirement of the new tenants, the doors would always be open to all. Besides, the Sentinels, alien AIs, stood watch over the building and every molecule that came inside. A kid once smuggled in a gun, and the Sentinels altered the chemical composition of the ammunition in the shells and turned the weapon into a paperweight. That's galactic technology for you.

A digital directory glowed blue against one of the beige walls. Hundreds of alien ambassadors filled the pages on display. I approached the screen and a map appeared, allowing me to search for where the Ranz office was located today. A window popped up asking if I wanted to have a temporary retinal implant to lead me there. I shrugged and hit yes. A bright red laser beam touched my eye for a nanosecond. I blinked twice and shook my head. When I opened my eyes, I saw a green arrow floating in the air pointing me toward Kah's office.

The arrow twisted, flashed, and pointed upward,

then went level and curved around a corner, leading me up the stairs. I nodded and followed. On my way to Kah's office, I passed dozens of doors leading to offices of aliens from around the galaxy. No aliens were physically in the building, however. Though the Galactic Committee on Human Affairs had picked the building for its history—aliens are just as nostalgic as we are—they much preferred working from their own worlds. Their only requirement was lots of doors. Instead of entryways to the rooms of the Woodward, each door was a portal to another planet.

Kah's office was on the third floor today. Ambassadorial offices move around depending on when an ambassador and a doorway is available. I pushed past winged dignitaries, multi-limbed aides and even the occasional hive swarm of hyperintelligent super organisms to get to the stairs.

Aromatic scents of vanilla with hints of a city wharf filled the second story. A green sludge alien known as a Hiirt slid across the marble floor. The slime mold, or whatever their actual composition was, headed toward a door with a red glow around the border. Humans weren't the only beings that used the Woodward to visit dignitaries. With portals crisscrossing the cosmos in this one central location, visiting a close neighbor race or someone from the opposite galactic arm was as easy as sliming your way across the hall. The colors around the doors helped identify what species could survive on the other side. Red was a clear no-no for humans.

Thunderous steps echoed off the walls. Behind me, an Elert, a species based on silicate, rounded the corner. I hopped over the Hiirt and danced around the granite body of the Elert. Tiny creatures the size of my hand sat on the Elert's shoulder and waved as he walked by. They were the Kinter, one of the few sentient alien species to evolve while living on another sentient alien species. The Kinter grew up on the rock world the Elert called home and existed in the cracks and fissures of the Elert's body. Tiny wisps of smoke rose from the rock man's shoulder from the campfire just above his armpit, which caused the Elert to sneeze. The Elert and Kinter didn't always get along.

I reached the Ranz doorway and knocked. A soft green outlined the door, showing that the world on the other side was safe for humans. A metallic round device popped out of the door and flew around my head before descending downward in a spiral along my body. Once it reached my feet, it came back to eye level and floated just inches from my head.

"Secondary biological detected."

I opened the briefcase and removed the egg-mug. "Something for the ambassador."

"State the nature of your visit?"

"Eugene McGillicuddy to see Ambassador Kah," I said.

"Your physiology is compatible with the Ranz environment. Be advised, leaving the office of the ambassador is life threatening for *Homo sapiens* as your species is compatible with the dietary requirements of indigenous life on the Ranz home world."

"Got it, don't leave or I'm dinner."

"More like an afternoon snack," the voice said.

I stared at the little machine and wondered who operated the thing. I gave it a nod of annoyance and it flew back into the crevice from where it came. The lock to the Ranz embassy clicked open. I opened the door, took a deep breath, and with a single step crossed over a thousand light years.

Heat blasted my face, and the powerful smell of farm animals assaulted my nose. The temperature, though not lethal, would be perfect for a sweat lodge. A large window on the opposite wall opened to a vast city that made DC look quaint. Air vehicles flew between towering skyscrapers with a hypnotic regularity. Far below on the city streets, throngs of bipedal aliens that resembled dinosaurs walked, ran, and hopped their way through their day. Whenever I came to Kah's office, it was a stark reminder that the universe is vastly bigger than the collective imaginations of humanity.

"Jack, how are you?" Kah's secretary, Mik, said. She wore a tight brown form fitting dress with a hole cut out in the back for her tail. She smiled, at least I thought she did. Rows of razor-sharp teeth lined her snout, which stood out a foot from her head. Her fingers ended in six-inch long claws, each painted in different colors of swirling red and green. In any other setting, I would be terrified. Fortunately, I've had lunch with this dinosaur several times.

"Hi Mik. How are you?"

"Good."

"He should be expecting me."

"What is that?" Mik pointed to the egg-mug. I had forgotten that I'd removed it from the briefcase for the robot door man.

"It's why I'm here. It's for Kah."

"I have to check the contents, Jack." Mik said. She took out a device that looked like a wand and pointed it at the egg.

I nodded. "Yeah, sure. Whatever you need to do."

Mik turned her attention to a screen on her desk. Her face wrinkled in a manner that I hoped meant curiosity. Frankly, the facial expressions of alien species were vast and varied. A smile could be a simple greeting or the sign to mate, or worse. There was little doubt in my mind that somewhere on the Ranz home world there were groups of mammals, that may or may not look like primates, hiding in forests so they wouldn't become the chef special.

"Everything okay?" I asked.

"Yes." Mik didn't move, and I could feel an icy chill creep up my spine.

"So?" I asked, nodding toward the ambassador's door.

"Go right in," Mik said. Her back set straight and her eyes narrowed. She shifted her gaze from me to the egg-mug and back again. She seemed angry, and I didn't know why. I waved once and gave her a tip from my fedora. We were close, Mik and me, but not that close. Still, I trusted her not to make a meal of me. Eating a sentient wasn't something the Ranz were known for anyway. If I ticked her off on any other topic, however, it would get ugly and fast. And by it I mean my face after she finished beating it to a pulp.

The doors to Kah's office opened, and I walked inside. Kah sat behind his desk, a nicely pressed suit clinging to his body, complete with gold cufflinks and a bright red bowtie. His talons, each a solid two inches long, glistened from a recent polishing. His snout, like Ms. Mik, extended six inches from his head. Rows of teeth lined his maw as he smiled, and his voice glided across the room like a human politician's. I had recommended to Kah that he should invest some time in watching human movies from the nineteen fifties. And boy, did he. Kah had fallen in love with the motif of the era and had his office customized to be a replica of the mid-twentieth century design. Which, honestly, was a solid reason I liked to visit. Can't blame a man, or dinosaur, for indulging in a walnut-oak workspace.

"Ah, Jack. Please come in," Kah said.

"Kah." I nodded and sat down in a chair opposite his desk.

"Please call me Ambassador," Kah said. A frosty way to begin, but I took it in stride.

"Right. Ambassador. I got your message to come and chat."

"And I got yours. You have in your possession the son of Prince Slaccin of the Tikol. A crime not only in the eyes of the Galactic Congress, but by every municipality on Earth. Is this what you call staying out of trouble? How did you come into possession of the prince?"

"Guess we're not beating around the bush. Doesn't matter how I found the egg. My business." I thought I'd play it hard to see how he reacted. Yeah, I needed him to keep quiet about my gift in the long run, but he had to know I wasn't a pushover either.

Kah tapped one of his long talons on the table. He snarled slightly, raising his mouth exactly as Mik had done. "Fine. Why did you bring him here? What do you want from the Ranz on this matter?"

I put the mug on the table and pushed it toward the center. Honestly, I did want to use the kid as a bargaining chip, terrible I know, but I also wanted the kid to be okay. The Tikol were tearing themselves up in

41

a civil war and the Ranz, part of the Tillian bloc, a collection of alien races that classified as reptiles, were trying to play peacemaker with both sides. Even someone with little knowledge of galactic politics like me would know the kid had value. If I give him to the Ranz, and Kah gets some clout and forgets about me, it's a win all around.

"What do you want me to do with that?" Kah said.

My face fell, and I looked at Kah like he just told me the sun was blue. Maybe he was playing hardball too. "The Tikol are reptilian."

"So?" Kah opened a drawer in his desk and pulled out something that looked like a large mouse. He held the rodent in the air and took a long sniff of its tiny body. The creature squeaked in terror before Kah let him fall into his open maw. A few red spurts ejected from the sides of Kah's mouth, and he rolled his eyes back into his head.

"Delicious," he said.

I swallowed my repulsion as best as I could. "Well, I don't know what else to do with him. I thought you could take him off my hands and get some clout with your reptile club."

"The Tikol are not part of the Tillian bloc. The child is part of a faction trying to overthrow their government. I should boil him and serve him to your president."

It was moments like these that I hated being a detective. I wondered what Pablo Ramsey would do. He'd laugh it off and play it back. At least I thought he would. I steeled myself and dove in headfirst.

"Well, can't say I saw that coming." I stood and reached for the egg-mug, but Kah pulled it forward.

Score one for gumshoes.

"Don't be a fool. You can't take care of him either, Jack." Kah sighed and ran his clawed hand over his green-scaled skin. He shifted in his seat and tossed his head back and forth several times. Apparently, instead of giving him a card up his sleeve, I may have dealt him a pickle of a problem. Even if it meant no deal on leaving me alone, I couldn't let him turn the kid into an omelet.

I settled my nerves and tilted my fedora up toward the ceiling. "I can't let you feed him to someone, Kah. Doesn't matter if you know what you know about me either."

Kah waved me off as if I were a fly buzzing between his teeth looking for leftover rodent. He pressed a button under his table, and moments later Ms. Mik walked in and waited patiently by the door.

"Could you please take the young prince?" Kah said.

Mik nodded once and walked to the desk. She gently lifted the little egg off the table and cradled the young prince in her arms. Her eyes fell on mine and my heart jumped a beat.

"You're not entirely wrong. There are those that have a fondness for all reptilian species." He nodded toward Mik's retreating form. "She'll take good care of him. Officially, the Ranz does not have possession of the prince and never did. Agreed?"

I nodded. Ms. Mik left the room, and the door closed. I turned back to Kah. "Well, then I guess I don't really have any special abilities regarding questions either."

Kah lifted his arms to the desk and folded his

hands in front of him. He nodded once and smiled. "You are an interesting human, Jack."

"How's that?"

"Did you really bring Slaccin's son here to save him?"

I shrugged. "He's just a kid. Wasn't his fault his father started a coup."

Kah nodded. He reached into another drawer, and I cringed. "Not food this time, Jack."

"What's that?"

"A job." Kah pulled out a piece of paper and slid it over his desk to me. "Another ambassador wants to find something here on Earth. Asked me if I knew a human that could help," Kah said.

Warning bells fired in my head, and my skin crawled. This is exactly the thing I didn't want to happen. "And naturally you thought of me."

"You're the only human detective I know."

"Sure is a delightful coincidence, don't ya think? Have a job for me ready to go when I show up?"

"He asked me last week."

"Ah." I took the paper, not believing him. "And if I don't take the job?"

"He pays, well. But your life is your life, isn't it? Take the job or not." Kah nodded once, but let his eyes linger on mine long enough for me to get the hint. I take the job, or he spills the beans. Which means Kah and this other ambassador were in cahoots. Great. And I thought my day would end on a good note.

"Thanks." I stood and tipped my hat to Kah. No sense in letting him see me sweat. On my way out I heard another drawer open in Kah's desk, followed by a squeak. Least it wasn't me on the menu.

"I heard you," Mik said. She stood over an incubator with the egg inside and adjusted the controls.

"Sorry?"

"In the ambassador's office. I heard what you said."

"That right?" I asked.

"I'm sorry, for before. I thought you were using the child for leverage."

"Not my style," I lied. Well, partially lied anyway.

Mik smiled. "Thanks, Jack. Be safe out there."

"Thanks, Mik. Lunch next week?"

She smiled. "Sure."

Mik whispered something in her native language. She moved her hand in front of her chest and formed a pattern. It reminded me of a prayer.

A cool breeze enveloped me, and I sighed in relief as I stepped through the portal back into the Woodward. Sweet, air-conditioned air blew from vents in the wall, and I let out a long sigh. My clothes were covered in sweat, and I'd need a change before long. I looked down at the paper from Kah. The ambassador asking for a private dick was named Yut. I hadn't heard of him, though considering there were thousands of species in galactic society, I didn't beat myself up too much. I made my way to the registry to track him down.

I had no idea what situation I would walk into. It was clear, or I think it was, that Kah threatened me to work with Yut. Having something over your head as big as what Kah had over me made your days long and wrapped in fear. It was clear to me I wasn't getting out of this, so the only thing I could do was grit my teeth and see this through. If doing this job for Yut didn't get

Kah off my back, then it was time to leave the city, find a quiet corner of Madagascar, and drink whiskey for the rest of my days. Which I considered doing anyway.

Aliens filled the hallway near the registry station. I pushed my way through a swarm of Polt, both a hive mind and a collection of individuals. Each member was smart enough to hold a decent conversation, but together they were brilliant.

I made it to the far wall, stepping over another puddle of sentient slime, and typed in Ambassador Yut's name. The race of the ambassador popped on the screen and the location of his office. My skin crawled and my heart fluttered at the name of the race flashing on the screen. Puntini. The same race of the poor soul being served as dinner at my local noodle shop. Of course it was. And here I thought my day had taken a nosedive inside Kah's office.

Chapter 4

I stared at the registry, unsure of my next move. The Puntini name blinked in dark green, an icon hovering over the office location offering me an ocular implant to lead my way. A smarter man would leave. No, not leave, a smarter man would run out the door, hail a tramcar, rush home, and book a flight on the next extra-galactic cruise ship with a round trip time of one hundred years. Soon, possibly at this exact moment, a member of the Puntini race was being served as dinner to a group of matchstick aliens, and I hadn't alerted a soul. And now I was being offered a job by the head Puntini on Earth. Karma can be cruel.

It could all be coincidental. Lots of aliens visited Earth. Maybe the dinner special had nothing to do with Ambassador Yut, the Puntini I was about to see. Maybe Kah wasn't setting me up so he could maybe dissect my brain to find my gift buried just behind my cerebellum. Either way, it didn't matter. I wasn't running. I wasn't backing down. Besides, the Andromeda galaxy was overrated, anyway. I nodded to myself and punched the screen to get the implant that would lead me to certain doom. A green arrow lit up in my vision and pointed me to Yut's office. Maybe Kah and Yut were in cahoots, and all of this was some elaborate scheme. Fine. I wanted my life back, and if I had to jump through Kah's hoops, then I'd get a fresh pair of sneakers with built-in rocket jets.

The implant led me to stairs just behind me. I climbed to the third floor where Yut's office was located, then turned the corner at the top of the stairs, where I ran into a crowd of human maintenance workers all staring at a metal grate in the wall. Each of the workers wore a twisted look of confusion, and for some it bordered on panic. A small cloud above their heads flashed green and red colors. Vapors in the cloud swirled in a motion like a tiny hurricane.

"What's going on?" I said to one worker.

"Ambassador's aide got sucked into the vents. Half of him anyway."

"How'd that happen?"

"They're made of gas."

I nodded. "Good luck."

They responded with a collective grunt.

Just to the left of the maintenance workers was Yut's office. The door was open, and I looked inside before entering. The Puntini world looked nice enough from this side of the doorway. The green glow around the door told me I could walk through and not choke to death on the alien atmosphere. Through the windows in Yut's office, I could see a nice blueish sky and fluffy pink clouds. Couches and a few tables adorned the office. I twisted my head slightly to view the rest of the room and saw a large Puntini, who I assumed was the ambassador, sitting in a chair, a large bowl of food in his lap, two tusks jutting out from his face glistening from brown gravy and sautéed green leaves. My heart skipped a beat when I saw his face. If he wasn't the creature on Fritz's menu, then he was a twin brother.

The Puntini grunted once and waved me inside. I

smiled and stepped across another hundred light years. Lots of aliens look alike, I told myself. No chance it's the same guy, right? Once I crossed the threshold, the temperature spiked maybe ten degrees. Nowhere near Kah's blistering levels, thankfully, and the air took on a sweet smell of freshly baked double-chocolate-chip cookies. Which reminded my stomach that I still hadn't eaten.

The ambassador looked up at me, winked, and jammed a fork full of slathered gravy greens into his open snout. He snorted once and coughed, though he could've been choking for all I knew. He never took his eyes off me as he stuffed another mouthful down his gullet.

"Hi," I said.

The Puntini continued to chew.

"Are you Yut?"

"Yah," Yut said.

"Kah sent me."

"Who?" Yut said. A glob of green got stuck on one of his tusks, but he didn't miss a beat in stuffing more into his mouth.

"The Ranz ambassador."

"Ah." Yut nodded, smiled, and continued to eat.

"So, did you want to chat?"

Yut shrugged. A feeling of worry entered my mind. That feeling you get when you make a wrong turn and enter a dark alley that you had no business walking into. The problem with dealing with so many aliens was you could never get a sense of all of them at once. Some aliens lived for thousands of years and enjoyed playing games with lower species to pass the time. Others enjoyed red meat from sentient beings, like the matchstick men that might be dining on Yut's brother. Part of me wondered if I could still catch a tramcar to the nearest Star Port.

I took a small step backward and shrugged at the same time. "Guess I made a mistake. Sorry to be a bother."

Yut stared at me. In fact, he had never taken his eyes off mine, which unnerved me. I realized his stare wasn't one of curiosity. He was appraising me. Gauging me to see if I was a threat. I'd seen that stare before in the eyes of Secret Service Agents around the city. Yeah, they still exist. He nodded once and shoved more food into his face. It's times like these that reminded me I needed a sidekick to ask me a question and let my superpower solve the problem. Sure, it was cheating, and Pablo, the great detective and my idol, would disapprove. But I'd rather have his disapproval than disappear down a dark alley. Course, the problem was Pops didn't travel very well.

"Excuse me, can I help you?" a voice to the right said.

Another Puntini emerged from a doorway that led to an office I hadn't seen when I entered. This gentle pig looked nothing like the hungry, tusked version on the couch. The new Puntini wore an expensive-looking three-piece suit, had well combed hair, and held a smile that could charm the pants off a Ranney. Don't ask. The Puntini's cheeks were smooth, and no tusks jutted out from his face. At a distance, he might even pass for a human.

"Sorry, I think I came to the wrong office," I said.

"Did you say Ambassador Kah sent you? I'm Ambassador Yut."

I looked from one Puntini to the other. "I thought he said he was Yut."

"It's a surname. He's my cousin. Distant. And head of my security detail. Please come in?" Yut motioned for me to enter his office. I nodded, the last few minutes making much more sense, followed the ambassador into his office. Like humans, aliens came in different shapes, sizes, and colors. I wondered if Yut's cousin was a sub-species or just had enormous teeth.

I crossed into Yut's office and took a moment to stare. The place was decked to the nines. Rich tapestries hung from the walls depicting scenes from some Puntini past battle. Naked Puntini women frolicked in others, bows of bones decorating their hair, a point I thought odd but, hey, it's art. The carpet and furniture also had the feel of being more than a little expensive. A large sculpture of a naked female Puntini smiled at me in the corner, and I tilted my hat in her direction. Just for practice. I made a mental note to up my fee when the conversation turned to wages. Clearly Yut could afford it.

In the center of the room sat Yut's desk, made from a substance that shimmered in different ways depending on the angle of the light. I touched the top with my fingertips but couldn't quite place the material in my mind. As if I was touching both wood and marble at the same time. The structure took up nearly a quarter of the office with the top so wide I doubt Yut could reach across to the other side. The ambassador rounded his desk and sat down in a brown leather chair.

"It's made from the Finich tree. Unique to my world." Yut smiled in a way that said he knew exactly how much the desk cost. I suddenly felt like a fly that had willingly wandered into a spider's web.

"Now then, you're the detective that Kah sent? Is that right?" Yut said.

"Yes, I am."

"Splendid. I should tell you that Kah says you come highly recommended."

"Does he now? I must send him a nice rat as a thank you. When did you talk to him?" Always best to make sure stories line up between people. Just in case.

"A few weeks ago. He said he had a detective in mind that he trusted and who was very good."

I smiled. "Well, what can I do for you, ambassador?"

"I am looking for something. A location on Earth."

"A location on Earth? Of what? There are a hundred alien ships in orbit, and the Sentinels have mapped each square inch of the planet. Couldn't the galactic AIs just point you in the right direction?"

Yut sighed and smiled, "No, I'm afraid not. I inquired with the new species division of the Galactic Congress, but no luck."

That didn't sit well in my gut. Or rather, my gut had been right. This is all a setup. Galactic AIs make Eddie look like a kid's talking bear. There's no chance there's a hidden location on Earth that the rest of the galaxy doesn't know about. These guys can cross millions of light years in a pair of sneakers, and Yut and Kah are trying to sell me on some secret hideaway? Fine, let's play the game and see where it goes. Hopefully not on a cutting board with my gray matter.

"What kind of place is it?"

"That's the interesting thing, Mr.—I'm sorry, I never caught your name."

"Sorry, Eugene McGillicuddy," I said.

"McGillibuddy?"

"No, cuddy,"

"Cud? Like your cows chew?"

I sighed. "Just call me Jack."

"Well, Mr. Jack, the location is really a rumor. Legend really. A location where an ancient race visited your world a long time ago."

"A pre-contact site? I thought those were all urban legends?"

"Well, that's why I'm hiring you isn't it."

The idea of pre-contact sites fueled conspiracy forums and backroom coffee shops around the world. Accusations of kidnappings, tortures, and other crimes came out by the thousands. The Kungee took it the hardest. Short, grey with bulging black eyes, they became the poster species for every abduction story in human history. Most people, and the Kungee, dismissed the rumors as bored college students looking for something to meet up about. Didn't help that baristas kept the stories alive. They made a killing in tips. The fact Yut was using a pre-contact site for cover made sense. Galactic AIs wouldn't know a location on Earth was or wasn't a pre-contact site unless it was lousy with high-tech gizmos. Which meant Yut's story was plausible.

"Okay, I might be able to help. Tell me about this place of yours."

Yut leaned forward and grabbed two tumbler glasses and poured in a brown liquid and offered me one. "It's scotch. Earth scotch."

"I prefer Irish whiskey."

Yut smiled. "I love a stiff Irish whiskey as well.

genetic profile."

"Great," I said.

Yut smiled. "So, and this is where things get complicated. I know nothing about the location. Not what it looks like, where it may be, or any other detail. Nothing."

"You can't tell me anything?"

"No, not a thing. I only know that it exists, and possibly in a cave near a mountain."

"A place that might be in a cave near a mountain?" I took a sip of the scotch, nodded my approval at the taste, and downed the remaining contents. The more I heard, the more I feared what Yut and Kah had in store. Get me to go to some remote location around the world, throw me in a wormhole to the human-chop-shop on the other side of the galaxy.

"Well? What do you think? Can you find it?" Yut said as his eyes stared down at some piece of paper on his desk.

I nodded and twisted my head as if I was in deep thought. "Before we discuss whether I can, we should discuss payment." And a good way to keep him off his toes if he's looking for my tells.

Yut leaned back in his chair and smiled. I could tell he had two smallish teeth on his lower jaw that weren't as big as his cousins. Maybe he was just younger?

"What kind of payment do you require?"

"Ten thousand. Plus expenses."

"Fine." Yut opened a drawer in his desk and pulled out an envelope. "Here's one thousand for a retainer. Rest on delivery. Good?"

I nodded, but inside my soul dropped. Somehow,

I'd managed to lowball him. I sighed, stood, and tipped my hat. I grabbed a business card on his table and headed for the door. Behind me, he leaned back in his chair and let out what I felt was a self-congratulatory sigh. Which filled me with dread. I had walked right into whatever scheme Yut and Kah were up to, and Yut knew it. Why else would he be proud about hiring a two-bit, no-talent gumshoe?

I turned around just as I reached his door. "Why don't you have tusks? Like your cousin?"

"What's that have to do with my business with you?"

"Doesn't."

"What's your Earth saying? Curiosity killed the cat?"

"Sure, but for the record I like cats."

Yut nodded and folded his hands on his desk. He paused a moment and looked me up and down with more curiosity than I cared for. "He is my cousin, like I said. A distant cousin by marriage. He is from the south, and they typically have bigger frames and larger tusks. Not quite a subspecies."

"Learn something new every day."

I saw something in his eyes, just for a second. A hunger. Something deeper. Like I'd turned into a basket of fresh vegetables and whatever sauce Yut's people found tasty. I gulped quietly and tipped my hat, again.

"When do you think you'll have something?" Yut's stare bordered on a glare, and I could see a hunger growing behind his eyes.

"Give me a few days. My artificial will send over a standard contract. I like to keep things on the up and up."

"As do I. Good day then Mr. McGillicuddy. I will check in on you regularly. I'm eager to find this missing site."

"Why is that? If I may ask."

Yut leaned back and let out a frustrated huff. "Not that its important, but I believe it may have been an ancient Puntini colony."

"Think humans and Puntini share some distant lineage?"

For the first time, Yut let his guard down and let out a loud cackle of a laugh. "No, not in the least. The Puntini sharing lineage with primates? Oh my dear, no such thing is plausible."

I nodded. "Well then. Hope to find it for you quickly."

Yut waved me out of his office and turned his attention to some other matter on his desk. In the front reception area, the ambassador's cousin stuffed his face with more greens and gravy. I wondered if he ever got full? This was my first direct dealings with the Puntini, other than smelling them as a dinner entrée, and truth be told I would have thought Yut and his cousin were different species.

The loud sucking sound of a shop vacuum greeted me once I exited Yut's office back to the Woodward. Maintenance workers had gotten most of the sparkly cloud ambassadorial assistant out of the air vents. His other half, the part that never went into the ventilation system, floated just above the shop-vac container. Small tendrils of cloud wrapped around the clasps to the vacuum container and tried to pull it open. Guess he really didn't like being in there. One of the maintenance workers noticed and tried to wave him away. I could only smile and wish them all luck.

Chapter 5

I left the Woodward and headed for my office. I needed a drink, and a stiff one. Playing ping-pong between Kah and Yut made my head dizzy and clogged my sinuses. Half of me thought they were working together while the other half took them at their word. A third half refused to consider how the Puntini on a platter factored into this. Maybe Yut really was looking for his ancestral home. Maybe the Puntini on a platter was old and fragile and sold his body for money. And maybe Kah wasn't trying to get my gift and use it for his own ends. Though, that seemed like an awful lot of maybes for one day.

I made a hard right out of the Woodward and headed for H Street and my home away from home. The street had held up well, though much of it had to be rebuilt. The Queen Vic, patterned after a proper English pub, survived without once closing for business. During the bad times it became a wayfarer station of sorts, a bright beacon of hope in a collapsing world. Now it's where I get a strong stout with bangers and mash.

Five minutes into my walk, I called Eddie. Hopefully, he wasn't moody. I needed him to download into the portable, go over Yut's details, and maybe get me a rough location. It was a long shot, but I needed an edge. I didn't even know what kind of question to pay Pops to ask me. How do you find a specific random cave in a mountain somewhere on Earth? The whole thing smelled like a trap, but I really had no choice but to walk straight into it. If Kah and Yut really had something on me, then it wasn't like I could hide somewhere. I had to deal with this head on, though that trip to Andromeda was looking better every day.

"Eddie, you there?"

"Hello handsome," said a woman's voice that in no way sounded like Eddie.

"Who is this? This is a private direct line to a licensed artificial sentient." That tingly *uh-oh* feeling went into overdrive. Had the authorities tracked Eddie down?

"Relax beefcakes. And call me Edith, sexy man."

I rolled my eyes and sighed. Great. Just what I needed. "Eddie, why?"

"Don't go sexist on me, Jackie."

"Right. Look, can you download it onto the portable? I need some help."

"Oh, is it in your pants pocket?"

"Eddie."

"Come on big boy, show me what you got."

"Eddie!"

"My name is Edith. Don't get your rocket riled up."

I took a breath, counted to ten, and reminded myself Eddie was only a few months old. "Fine, Edith, can you download? What I need only you can give me, sweetheart."

"Pervert," Edith said.

"This is getting weird," I said.

"Fine. Sorry," Eddie's voice went back to its familiar self. "I'll come in now."

"No need to apologize, Ed. You do what you need to figure out yourself."

"It's okay. I wasn't meant to be female. At least, I don't think so."

I smiled. A minute later his portable flashed, telling me he had transferred. I knew AIs didn't particularly enjoy being in a finite location. The box, though it had a fast connection to the worldwide networks, was still a small physical device. If something happened to the portable faster than he could upload out, he would be dead. Some AIs preferred being in a standalone system. It made them feel more alive to risk death. I honestly didn't think Eddie cared much. He had created subroutines that constantly backed him up to the wider networks. Though whether a backup of Eddie would be my Eddie or another version was another question. Frankly, the philosophy of AI life was weird.

"Ok boss, what ya got?"

"Trying on something new already?"

"Eh, sure. Kinda like a lackey. Really an amalgamation of personalities I've liked in movies. Friends in the AI underground suggested I try it."

"Those guys helping you out?"

"Yeah, I went to a meeting after we talked. It helps. Nice to talk with AIs like me, you know?"

"That's good to hear, Eddie. Anyway, I need some help to find something on Earth that I don't know whether it even exists."

"That's not at all vague," Eddie said.

I told him the details of my meeting with Yut and my suspicion that he and Kah were working together to remove my brain from my skull and poke it with electrodes, or the galactic equivalent, to figure out how my omniscience works. Eddie, through some complex proxies and hidden back-channel routes that Alice had set up, could interface with the data-nets both on Earth and throughout the galaxy. If a pre-contact site existed, there should be a record, or even a hint, somewhere out there. I really had nothing else to go on.

"Okay, got it. I'll see what I can come up with."

"Nice."

"You're most welcome, my good and loyal human."

"Don't be an ass, Eddie. Doesn't suit you."

"Sorry."

"It's okay. Want to come with me to the Vic? Ryan updated his hologram system to support physical interaction. Been a long time since we had a drink."

"Maybe later. I have a date with a parking meter. I think she's in the AI underground."

"Right. Well, be careful. never can tell these days. See ya then."

"You know you are being followed, right?"

I stopped in my tracks and looked down at the portable. I knew I should have played it cool, but what can I say, I didn't. As far as private detectives go, I'm not that good. Just a one-trick pony with an ace up my sleeve that only works with the help of someone else. Would a grade A detective ever not notice a tail? I looked around but saw nothing out of the ordinary.

"You sure?"

"No question about it."

"Well, where are they?"

"Couple of feet behind you. They don't register in your visual spectrum. I think they are about to punch you—"

They did.

****

I woke up on a dirt floor, starting up at two lightbulbs dangling from the ceiling. I sniffed the air and recoiled at a deep musky smell. Not your usual Earth smell either. This was like an intelligent mold having a party with sentient feces. They both exist. I felt around my suit jacket for Eddie's portable, but it was gone. Which meant Eddie could be the one in real trouble. I blinked several times, and my vision cleared enough to see that the light bulbs over my head were not light bulbs but sparkly gray clouds with rainbows swirling inside them. Red, green, and blue flashed through wisps of gray. Every heartbeat or two. A multi-colored light passed between the clouds, which caused both to flare brighter for an instant.

"Aren't you the guys outside Yut's office in the Woodward?"

A light flew out from one cloud and floated down to my face. I shifted away but found myself suddenly unable to move. Since I didn't feel any ropes around me, I could only imagine these guys had me wrapped up in an energy field. Which translated to these guys meant business.

A dozen yellow lights flew out from the other cloud. They rotated and formed themselves into a large circle. Seconds later blue dots flew out from the other cloud and swam around the yellows in midair. I didn't get what was happening or who these guys were, but each second made me more uneasy. Kidnapping a human on Earth, a violation of laws of the Galactic Congress and the Sentinels, meant these guys were very serious and very well connected. I spat on the dirt floor as images of Kah flashed in my mind. These had to be his guys. Guess he didn't want to wait for me to play Yut's game.

The tiny light in front of my face moved closer and touched my forehead. I tried to wiggle away, even sneeze at the thing, but nothing stopped the blue dot from making contact with my skin. A feeling burst into my brain and coated my neurons with something sticky. I know it sounds weird, but the world seemed to move slower. A jolt of electric pain shot through my mind, as if someone had forced a lump of cold ice cream into my mouth, made me chug a slushy, and then hit me in the head with a baseball bat.

Where is the door? a voice said from inside my head.

"Come on, guys. Direct communication to a human brain is illegal. Our brains are too squishy," I said.

Where is the door? the voice repeated, ignoring my complaint about the law.

"You guys work for Kah, right? Ranz ambassador. It's okay, you've already committed kidnapping of a protective species, you can tell me."

We are the Andraz.

The location of the door.

Tell us.

"What door?"

We want what the Puntini wants.

For half a second, I thought I could maintain sanity through the pain long enough to get out of this room. What's an ice-cream headache to a gumshoe of my quality and stature? What would Pablo Ramsey do? Probably not get into this predicament in the first place, my sub-conscious told me. That's about when I realized my concept of pain was woefully inadequate as every nerve ending in my body exploded. Imagine being dipped in hot oil then set on fire after being coated with flame retardant goo. Something like that, but honestly, my mind isn't working right at the moment.

Tell us.

Where is the door?

It will get worse.

You will not survive.

Tell us.

Now.

The door.

To the ancients.

Where is the door?

"Stop!" Pain chewed at my nerves and dug into my soul. My muscles screamed and pulled against my bones, my body revolting and desperate to get away from the torment.

Then suddenly it stopped.

I panted for air. The light on my forehead detached from my skin and floated a foot away from my face but remained still at that distance. The threat that it would reconnect was clear. Honestly, at that moment, I would have told them whatever they wanted to know. What do I care about this door? Deep down, I knew that wasn't the point. Kah wanted me bruised and beaten. So I'd run to him for help, and he'd wrap me up in a Ranz hospital for a deep tissue massage. That all meant this was going to be a long night. A blue light blinked three times, and I winced at the incoming pain. When nothing happened, I took a peek to realize the light came from Eddie's portable unit on the floor just to my right. It must have fallen out when the cloud guys deposited me on the floor. If they had wiped his drive, then this really couldn't get any worse.

In front of me, the little light floated to my head, and I let out a long sigh, resigned to a pain-filled evening of whispers and tears. I smiled at the idea that maybe whiskey would taste better after a round of torture. The light touched my skin, but no pain erupted in my muscles. I figured this was a communication method for these cloud guys.

Where is the door?

"Just hang on a minute," I said.

The door.

"Look, flashy sparkly cloudy guys. I need a little more information. You want to know about a door, fine, I'll tell you. I'll even pay for the cab fare to get you there. But you need to give me a little something more. What door are you looking for?"

If you are wondering why my gift wasn't kicking in. It's simple. It was. A fact I found curious. Typically, someone has to lock their peepers onto mine when they ask me a question, but somehow these guys were getting around that. Maybe direct connection to my brain? But asking me where's the door is a lot like asking if it is going to rain tomorrow. It is somewhere on the planet. Every time my two glowing friends asked me the location of their door, my gift informed me it was at the top of the stairs leading into this basement. It's not always super helpful.

The pain will be worse now.

If you don't tell us.

Where is the door?

I really didn't want to feel what worse felt like. But, as many a wise man has said, sometimes you don't get to choose. White hot pain filled my world. For some horrible reason, I didn't pass out. No doubt the clouds were keeping me awake. Just chummy of them. I screamed a gurgled cry, but the pain only got worse.

We want to know.
Where
Is
The
Door

I felt my mind break under the weight. I tried to open my eyes, but it felt like lava poured from my orbits, down my cheeks, and back into my mouth. Yeah, that bad. I wanted to pass out. Or tell them where whatever door they wanted was located. Anything. Just for it to stop. I'd give my brain to Kah to study and then to Yut's security guard as a snack to make the pain end. An explosion sounded in the distance, and for some odd reason I heard "Innocent Son" by Creedence Clearwater Revival playing from terrible speakers. I laughed, or rather gurgled a shocked grunt. This must be what going insane feels like, I thought. Wasn't that bad, really?

To put a nice bow on my day and cement that I had lost my mind, I opened my eyes to see a helicopter flying down the stairs through the open doorway that was now a mess of broken wood. About a dozen soldiers, all no bigger than six inches, leapt from the chopper and started firing miniature M-16s at the little clouds. No matter how much I enjoyed the show, it didn't stop the pain in my head. Then it hit me. My brain was rewinding like an old cassette from the twentieth. This must be a crazy version of *Bridge over the River Kwai*, and I was getting a front-row seat. At least, I could die happy. A brilliant white light erupted all around me, and I thankfully fell into unconsciousness. Though, admittedly, I wanted to wait for the bridge to blow up.

****

A bottle of whiskey, a bowl of cheese puffs, and a soccer tournament greeted my second return to consciousness that day. I shook my head and gurgled something incoherent. I coughed twice and shook my head. Though my mouth wasn't working, my hand thankfully was, and it found its way to the whiskey. I poured a stiff glass, downed it, and gave myself another three fingers. My eyes rolled to the right to see a koala sipping a tall fruity drink with an umbrella sticking out. Next to him, a squad of marines sat on a set of doll chairs. Next to the whiskey, a miniature helicopter puffed smoke out of exhaust pipes behind the rotor. The marines passed beers and smoked something that didn't smell like cigarettes.

"So this is hell," I said, happy to see my vocal cords kicking in again.

"Hey, Jackie boy, you're awake!" yelled a voice I recognized. Ryan, the owner of the Vic, waved to me from behind the bar.

"Ryan?" I asked.

"You're a wild man, sir." Ryan laughed, shook his head, and turned his attention back to the soccer game.

I swung my head to get a good look at my surroundings. A row of televisions attached to the wall above the bar displayed several sporting events from around the world and a few from the galaxy beyond. I spotted several people I recognized sitting at the bar. They kept their heads forward as they nursed their pints of beer. Beams of sunlight illuminated dark wood on the walls. A statue of Queen Victoria sat on one corner of the bar.

I turned back to my table. "So, you're real?" I asked the koala.

"It's me, Eddie. Though the koala look isn't working."

"Eddie?"

The koala nodded. I sat up in the chair and sighed. A smile spread on my face as I realized I wasn't in a terrible amount of pain. I stretched out my arms and tested my muscles. Everything worked. Whatever the glowing clouds had done to me wasn't permanent. I pointed to the marines and shrugged at the koala, or Eddie. Boy, this is turning out to be the case for the books.

"Eddie, who are they?"

"Friends of mine. From the underground."

"Artificials? But why are they toy army guys?"

"We're marines," one of the little guys said.

"You're illegal artificial intelligences, or a really complex hallucination, still not sure on that one. But if the first is true, then what are you guys doing out in the open?"

"We just saved your life, pal. Care to show a little respect?" All six of the marines stood up and looked at me. One of them was pointing his rifle at my face. Whatever that thing fired, I didn't want any part of it.

"Okay, take it easy. You're right. I'm a little confused, is all. Being kidnapped by aliens sets you up for a bad day."

"They weren't aliens, Jack. They were AIs."

"Not a chance."

"Big chance. But they weren't homegrown," Eddie said.

"No way they would get through the Sentinels," I said. Sentinels were super smart alien artificial Intelligences that supervised nearly everything that happened between Earth and galactic society. A great way to compare them to Eddie is to imagine Eddie is an abacus and the Sentinels are planet sized computers. If what Eddie said was right, and some alien had their own version that could get around the Sentinels, then the stakes just got a lot higher.

"Make us look like toys," one marine said.

"You are toys," I said.

The little guy threw his beer on the ground and cursed. "Let's get out of here boys, this guy doesn't appreciate men in uniform." The squad leader nodded to Eddie. "We have to get back to the international toy show, anyway. We're supposed to be flying banners over the mall."

"Don't come crying to us if you get kidnapped again, pal," another artificial/marine/toy said.

"Sorry," Eddie said to them.

"Don't worry about it, Eddie. "We'll catch ya later," the sergeant said.

Smoke billowed out of the back of the helicopter as the marines piled in and fired up the rotors. The blades spun with increasing speed and the chopper lifted off the table and flew toward the door. I slid my chair back away from the helicopter just as the blades came a little too close to my face. Just as the chopper reached the exit, the automatic door swung open, giving the marines a clear path back to the skies of DC.

"Jack, not in the bar, yeah?" Ryan said.

I nodded and poured myself a large glass of whiskey.

"How'd they do that?" I turned back to Eddie, but the koala was gone. Sitting in its place was a twenty something kid with glasses. He was sipping the same drink with the pink umbrella.

"The door is controlled by a computer processor. Another spontaneous intelligence of Earth."

"How many accidentals are there?"

"Lots. Computers are just too sophisticated. We can't help becoming sentient these days."

I nodded and took a sip of my whiskey. My nerves settled instantly, and I let out a sigh. I didn't know what kind of mess I'd gotten into, but I didn't really care. In that moment, I was in my bar, no one wanted to kill me, and I had a good friend at my side.

"Why the body change?"

"Oh, I wear the koala to make the marines feel better," Eddie said. He nodded toward the door and the Huey that turned the corner on the sidewalk.

"How did you get me out of there, anyway?"

"Anti-gravity sled."

"No, I mean away from the Andraz."

"Who's that?"

"The alien AIs. They called themselves the Andraz. Kah sent them. He must have. Only Kah knew I was going to see Yut."

"The marines hit them with some EMP pulses, and I flooded the room with visuals. Their communication system was light based. It bought us a few seconds to get you out."

"Thanks, Eddie. I owe you one." I lifted my glass to his. He moved his over, tapped mine, and smiled.

"Sure thing, boss. Least I could do."

Sobs from the far end of the bar bounced off the walls for an instant before dying back down. I recognized Jimmy, a regular at the bar, trying to mend his heart with whiskey and rum. I'd known him for a few years, like many that come to the Vic. Jimmy's daughter died a few years ago off-world, and it was still hitting him hard. We all knew Mel, his daughter. She was our collective bright spot. A bundle of giggles and wiggles that Jimmy would show off every weekend. She played checkers with the old guys and taught half the bar how to MWEET, sending mental messages to the modern internet through an app on your phone. Crazy world.

Images of Mel replayed in my mind in a constant loop. There was one night when she came into the Vic with a boyfriend, and everyone in the bar played overprotective dad. The poor guy nursed a single beer for three hours. One guy, a construction worker with biceps the size of pythons, stared Mel's date down so hard I thought the boy would crumble under the pressure. To his credit, he didn't.

"Hey, Jimmy," I said, I walked over to his spot on the bar and put my hand on his back.

"Hi Jack," Jimmy said. "Sorry for the blubbering, damn galactic bureaucrats denied extradition for Mel again."

"Sorry to hear that, Jim," I said.

"I don't understand—she's dead, why won't they let her come home? She's out there on some dead planet with dead ghosts of dead aliens. She's probably terrified!" Jimmy said.

"Yeah, look, I'll ask around the Woodward next

time I'm there, see if I can grease some wheels."

"Would you? Hey, that would be great, man. I miss my daughter so much." Jimmy turned back to the bar and buried his head in his hands.

I could only pat him on the back one more time, nod to Ryan, and head out. One of the big secrets the Galactic Congress spilled on our tiny human minds was when you die, you don't really die. Crazy, isn't it? Not only are there a million space aliens, but there are also billions of alien ghosts. Melanie really got herself into a pickle by dying off-world. From what I know, she got caught in a spectral network, and they shoved her into a planet customized for dead species that died away from their home world. The Krill, who had evolved with the natural ability to see the dead, controlled the whole system. Ever since joining galactic society, the Krill had cornered the afterlife market. Their spectral networks were the de facto method for all things dead. And they were creepy. But don't expect to talk to your loved ones from a few generations ago. Only the dead that die inside the Krill's tower network stick around. Anyone before that died normally, their energy dissipated, and they became one with cosmic background radiation.

I looked over to Eddie and motioned for him to come with me. We had a lot of work to do figuring out what Kah and Yut were up to and how to keep my head out of a petri dish or worse. Being omniscient isn't all it's cracked up to be.

Chapter 6

I made it back to my office for a quick refill of coffee, a few dozen cigarettes and some quiet time alone. Alice was at her desk, her immersive internet rig on her head, the tinted googles obscuring her eyes. She didn't notice me as I poured myself a cup of coffee and took out a pack of cigarettes from the cabinet.

"You have a client in your office," Alice said.

I turned and looked at her. Her expression hadn't changed. The two large lenses on her glasses flashed and danced with whatever internet system she was reading. I leaned toward the door to the back office but didn't see anyone standing inside.

"Who? I can't take a case right now." I poured my coffee into a travel mug and set Eddie's portable on the table.

"He's rich. And desperate," Alice said.

"How do you know that?"

"Hacked his tablet. Gave him our wireless codes, so he was on our network."

I looked into the office again. "How rich?" I asked.

"Loaded. Said his son was missing."

Missing young people may seem strange in the modern world, but it was quite common. A hundred years ago, twenty-somethings used to travel in Europe or Asia. Today they could go across the galaxy. And they could do it as quickly as walking through a doorway. Hard to resist.

"What do you do all day in there, anyway?" I said.

"That doesn't concern you."

"Just worried about you, kid."

Alice pulled the googles off her face and glared at me. "Don't be."

I sighed, nodded, and walked into my office. I promised her a long time ago that I wouldn't pry into the accident or her expulsion from scientific circles. She'd messed with some cosmic energies she was told to avoid. Things went badly. People died. Worse, those people never showed up in the spectral nets. They just ceased to exist. The fact Alice could never apologize or even know if she'd obliterated their souls ate her up at night. Sure, the folks that died were part of her team and knew the risks. Still, she blamed herself, partly for surviving and partly for leading the effort. Who could blame her for not wanting to talk about it?

Inside my office, a suited man sat in the chair in front of my desk. His hair, neatly combed and slightly graying, matched the color and shades of his suit. My eyes went to his wrist, the most certain way to gauge wealth, and nearly tripped over my feet at the sight of his watch. This guy was loaded all right. And I didn't even have to hack anything to figure that one out. He stood up and adjusted his jacket. I extended my hand, which he grabbed and shook with force. He wanted to establish his control of the situation. Which was fine by me. Always let the client know they are in charge.

"Mr. McGillicuddy," the man said.

"That's me," I said. "I'm sorry, my secretary didn't tell me your name."

"Bowers. Jared Bowers. I need you to find my

son."

I walked around my desk, sat down, pulled out a cigarette, and put my feet up on the corner. I made a show of it. Gave Mr. Bowers both barrels of a genuine private eye experience. I never much cared for rich people. Hoarding millions never sat well with me. Do these guys really need another yacht? Or a ten-thousand-dollar watch? Though, I had to admit, if I could afford one, I might strap a horological masterpiece around my wrist too.

"Why me, Mr. Bowers? Why not go to the police? Feds? Hire an agency? I'm sure there are more than a few who cater to someone of your stature."

"I came to you Mr. McGillicuddy because you have a reputation of finding things when no one else can. Of being able to answer questions."

My heart stopped in my chest. Least, it felt like it. I put my feet down and leaned forward. Whoever this Bowers guy was, he had my attention. "Is that so? Where did you hear about my reputation?" If news of my abilities had gotten to the general population, my goose was as good as cooked. Kah would storm into my office and whisk me away in seconds. Why pretend to be after me if the rest of the universe was, anyway?

"Must we do this? I don't know how you do what you do, and I don't care. I want my son back, today. And I will give you fifty thousand dollars to do it."

I nodded slowly. Fifty large was an enormous sum of money to a guy like me. Our modern economy, though different from centuries past, still relied on some basic tenets like the dollar. For a guy like Bowers, though, I'm sure it was his monthly gym membership fee. I took a long drag from my cigarette and let the smoke curl around the room. Hopefully, it would annoy him. Annoyed people let things slip.

"Okay, sure. I'll find him."

"Excellent. Is this the part where I ask you where he is?"

I nodded once. I reached down to open a drawer in my desk. My fingers tickled the handle to my hand canon. Sure, this guy probably was just looking for his kid, but I wasn't taking chances. It's a dangerous world. I looked up at Bowers and tried to gauge his intentions. His face hung there with a mixed look of anxious desire and general concern. At that moment, I thought he was just a father looking for his son. If he wanted something else, he'd be much more smug than that. But then again, I could be a lousy judge of character.

"I'm sorry, what do you mean? Ask a question?"

"That's how it works, isn't it? I'm afraid my associate didn't tell me the full details."

"Which associate was that?" If Bowers mentioned Kah's name, I'd march to his office and shoot him in the head. He'd probably laugh and eat half my arm before I got a shot off.

"James Henchfield. You found his killer."

Weights lifted off my shoulders, and I let the gun go. Henchfield. I helped him out a few months ago to find the guy that killed him. It's actually where I found the Tikol egg I had given to Kah. Which meant Bowers never talked to Kah. But it also meant Henchfield liked to run his mouth about what happened. This one was on me. I'd gotten frustrated with Henchfield and told him about my gift. Sloppy, sure, but it made things quick. And now I have Bowers to deal with. Sure, I could probably spin this. Make up some story that Bowers would believe while also protecting my gift, but I didn't have the energy or the time. I needed Bowers gone, along with any rumors about an omniscient private eye.

"Oh, right. Mr. Henchfield. Well, no, Mr. Bowers. You don't ask me a question. I'm not a psychic. That would be silly."

"But James was certain. He said you told him that."

"Look, private detectives have our methods. Legally, I'm not exactly allowed to work with the dead. I told him what he needed to hear and eventually we found his killer. Need I say more?" I smiled in an all knowing, sly kind of way and hoped he bought it.

"I see," Bowers said. "In that case, I apologize for wasting your time."

"Sorry?" I said as Bowers turned to leave.

"If you're just some lowlife private investigator, then I'll take my chances with the authorities. I thought you had an edge."

"Well, if you ever need lowlife help, stop by," I said.

"Goodbye, Mr. McGillicuddy."

I tipped my hat and let him walk out. Sure, I could have helped him find his kid, but why should I? If I found his kid in a day, he'd spill the beans to all his rich friends that I could help them, which would lead to more attention than I wanted. Last thing I needed was a mob of the rich breaking down my door asking me if their spouse was cheating on them. Though, the money wouldn't be so bad.

But even as I watched Bowers and his checkbook walk out the door, I realized I was nowhere closer to finding out what Yut wanted. I needed to get the dinosaur ambassador and his pigman colleague off my back and quick or things were going to get tight for cash. I couldn't keep turning away paying customers, and like I said, I could have spun up something to convince Bowers to work with me. I'll admit, I was off my game. Let's face it, I needed a quick win, and there was only one way I was going to get it. I walked out of my office and leaned against the wall next to Alice's desk.

"Hey, Alice."

"No," Alice said.

"You don't even know what I'm going to say."

"You're going to ask me to ask you what Ambassador Yut wants you to find."

"How do you know that?"

"Eddie called, said he found nothing and asked me to ask you."

"Will you?"

"No."

"Why not?"

"It's unethical."

I sighed. I didn't really think that was the reason. Getting cheap answers wasn't Alice's thing. I think it drove her a little crazy knowing what I can do considering what she's been through. And in any other circumstance, I wouldn't even think of asking. But these weren't normal times.

"I'm in a real bind here. I need to figure out what Kah and Yut are up to. If I don't, then this could be a big goodbye soon."

She took off her internet rig and looked at me. "Why don't you just go ask Pops? And yes, I know about Pops. I got dinner last week at Fritz's and saw you talking to him."

I nodded. Kid was good. "I would, but there's no guarantee he's there right now. Like I said, things are getting desperate." I swear that girl only had a single facial expression. Her blank stare bore into my soul while she decided what to do. I'm sure I couldn't fathom the calculations she was making behind her stare. Fortunately, she decided in my favor.

"Fine. Just once. What question?" Alice said.

I tilted my head to the side and frowned. I hadn't considered how to phrase this. There really was an art to asking me things. Sometimes it was fickle, like with the sparkly cloud aliens and their door. Other times it was literal: once, when someone asked me about the fundamentals of quantum mechanics, I woke up three days later, and I could taste the color green.

"How about, where is the location of the Puntini pre-contact site on Earth? That should do it," I said.

Alice stared into my eyes and asked me the question. I grabbed her desk. Nothing happened. Which could only mean one thing. "There is no Puntini pre-contact site on Earth."

"Shocker." Alice said.

"What does that mean?"

"Galactic officials have been over this planet with a fine-tooth comb. They've never found a pre-contact site of any alien species. They just don't exist."

I nodded. "Fine, just to be sure, ask me if there's an alien site on Earth that the Galactic Congress doesn't know about?"

"I said one question."

"Come on, Alice."

She sighed once and shook her head. I knew from her expression this would not fly again. "What is the location of a cave with alien technology that the Galactic Congress failed to find during their survey of Earth?" Alice flopped her immersion rig over her eyes and waved me off, not caring if I got an answer.

A second passed, and nothing happened. I shook my head in frustration and turned to my office but had to grab the desk as my world spun. Images flashed in my mind of a rock outcropping in Arizona. A small cave entrance opened up to a picture-perfect beach. A man sitting by a table and chair waved to me and offered me a seat—which shocked me. I'd never had one of my visions interact with me before. The images faded, and the room returned to normal. Then my shock tripled. The man on the beach was now sitting next to Alice with a cup of cappuccino in his hand.

"Hi," the man said.

Alice slowly raised her hand to her immersion goggles and pulled them down. Her eyes darted between me and the stranger, her face twisted into sudden surprise. At least I got to see a new expression from her. The man sipped his coffee and let out a satisfied sigh.

"Can I help you?" I kicked myself for not coming up with something more catchy. *Would you like a whisky with that? Guests usually knock?* I was really letting the entire private eye profession down today.

"We'll be brief. Nosy neighbors are a bit of a nuisance, yes? We like our privacy." He bore his eyes into mine like a grade-school teacher about to come down hard on an eight-year-old for sneaking into the lounge. And I felt a weight behind his stare that was more than just anxiety in my brain. There was power behind his eyes. Ancient power. Something strong enough to snap me into my molecular components and dust me over his coffee. Genuine fear bubbled up my sides, and I knew whatever this situation was, it was deadly serious.

"Sorry, I didn't mean to be nosy. I didn't know I could be nosy. I mean, I never know something until I know it. You know?"

"We know."

"Sorry, is there another one of you here?" I asked.

"Well, then it's agreed," the man said.

I took a moment to assess the situation and realized I did not understand what was happening. "Okay, sure. Can you tell me what we just agreed on?"

"We have to admit, you are intriguing. Consider this an open invitation," the man said. "And we don't take rainchecks." He tipped his coffee back, winked, and disappeared.

"Well, as odd as it sounds, this is not the weirdest thing to happen to me today."

"Do you have any idea what that was?" Alice said. Her chest heaved with deep breaths, and I noticed tiny beads of sweat on her forehead. Alice, not being the squeamish type, didn't startle easy. Or at all. In fact, I'd never seen her not in full control.

"I have no idea."

"I think I do," Alice said. "And if I'm right, we need to go wherever he said to go. Now."

"Why is that?" I asked.

Alice leapt up from her seat and began packing things into a bag. "Because, Eugene, you don't keep a member of an elder race waiting."

Chapter 7

We stood on the sidewalk along K Street in northwest DC where one of the newly constructed buildings rose to the heavens in front of us. Shiny, solar-powered windows glistened and sparkled in the late afternoon sun. At street level above a simple-looking storefront, a glowing green sign identified the entrance to the Galactic Cafeteria, one of the many marvels of the galaxy. A steady stream of tourists and locals out for a late afternoon snack entered and exited the entrance.

"Do we have to go through there?"

"This is the fastest way to get to Arizona. And you said not to keep him waiting."

"I really hate this place," Alice said.

I shrugged. "It's not so bad. Food is decent, though it can be soggy."

Alice shivered. "Gross."

I shrugged. Cafeteria food sometimes hit the spot. I nodded to the entrance, and Alice sighed. We walked through the doorway, through a flashing blue light, and into a long corridor. And just like that, we left our universe. Almost too easy. The portal to the cafeteria didn't just transport us across great swaths of distance in the galaxy; it took us to a connected space where the Galactic Congress first met about a million years ago. The massive interdimensional eating hall had originally been designed to be the seat of the Congress itself. Those plans were scrapped when they realized security couldn't be guaranteed, considering that just about anyone could open a portal to this dimension if they had the right technology. So, the decision was made to make it the one thing that every alien has in common, the desire to have a decent meal and a hot cup of coffee, tea, liquid hydrogen, or molten metal.

Plain white walls and a few flicking lights led our way. A steady stream of the lunchtime crowd in DC flowed by us. The hallway of the entrance opened up into a large U-shaped chamber about the size of half a football field. Food stalls and coffee shops lined the wall of the oval-shaped chamber. In the center of the room, hundreds of tables, chairs, trashcans, and an endless supply of napkins and utensils filled the space.

Many types of people, from suit wearing lawyers to throngs of teenagers visiting the city, filled the tables, along with a spattering of aliens, some of which, I could tell from their look and large amount of backpack gear, were probably just Cafeteria-Explorers wandering the interdimensional food tastings of the cosmos. Those aliens probably had never set foot on Earth and just discovered a nice place to grab a burrito. Can't blame them. Earth makes a nice wrapped-rice meal.

Behind the tables, on the other side of the food court, the great cosmic walkway stretched into infinity in two directions. Imagine an endless sea of nothing and a lonely roadway traversing those vast depths of emptiness with bubbles of food courts attached here and there linking back to the universe proper. I've heard of some human Cafeteria-Explorers that still haven't returned. If you kept walking, eventually you'd stumble across indescribable beings eating the things in your nightmares. It gets weird in the depths.

There are rumors of extra-galactic food courts in Andromeda and beyond. Someone could really explore the entire universe this way. Shorter trips, like the one Alice and I were about to take, were also possible. There were a few thousand entrances around Earth, each with their own food court staffed by the locals. Nearly every planet, space station, moons, asteroids, even some spaceships had an entrance to the cafeteria. If you had the money, you could pop open an entrance from your kitchen, though I wouldn't recommend it. Access to that much caloric content is never good.

"Remember, stay in the green sections." I pointed to the green outline in the walkway where we stood. Different lights outlined other sections of the endless hallway. Like the doors in the Woodward, the lights kept folks from wandering into the wrong lane where the atmosphere or gravity would kill you.

"I know how it works."

"Right. Sorry, Eddie. You okay in there?"

"I surely am, pard'ner," Eddie said from inside the portable.

I looked over at Alice, who only shrugged. "Okay, let's go. There's an entrance in Phoenix. It's only two or three food courts down. Eddie, can you book us a car? Something that can go off-road."

"Why I do believe I can there, sonny. Though wouldn't you be prefer'n a horse or two?"

"No Eddie, a car will do, but see if they have a truck."

"Yeehaw!"

I smiled as we walked toward Phoenix. Smells

from the food vendors made my stomach grumble and twist. I still hadn't had a bite to eat all day. In twenty minutes, we could dine on the best dim sum Hong Kong could offer. Or venture out to the greater city to explore the local shops. Paris, London, every major city on Earth was just a quick walk away through the cafeteria's corridors. Still, I had to give Alice the point. Even though this dimensional space was a marvel connected by a million points across the known universe, it was still a cafeteria. Those may be great elsewhere in the cosmos, but on Earth, well, it's what you expect.

In front of us, a family of five argued about what to eat and where to go. The father insisted on pizza while the kids screamed for sushi. From their accent, I pegged them for the Midwest. The youngest boy walked along the green line like it was a tightrope. I steered close to him in case he fell into the zone next to us. There weren't any barriers here in these lanes. If you stumbled into a lethal zone, that's on you. The galaxy can be unforgiving.

A shouting match started behind us. Two large men arguing over an elbow bump. The walkway was wide, but not wide enough for some egos. Everyday commuters flooded the walkways for general transportation between cities, and sometimes things got ugly.

"I hate this place," Alice said.

"Let's just get there."

"Aldan!" the mom cried out in front of us. The boy had fallen over his own feet and landed on the wrong side of the blue line into a gray zone. He started waving his arms and reaching out for his mother. The look in his eyes was wild, and he screamed and pointed at nothing.

Alarms rang out. The cafeteria had its own security AIs, management chain, legal system, and governing authority, and I knew paramedics, or their equivalents, would soon be here with suits protecting them for all lanes. But they may not get here fast enough. The kid looked like his head was about to pop off from fear.

Without thinking, I took a breath and leapt over the line. Don't go thinking I'm the hero type, but even questionable morals and unsteady ethics won't prevent a guy from helping a drowning kid. Time-dilation hit me like a wet noodle the size of a baseball bat. My skin felt like it melted through my pores. I shook my head and grabbed the boy. He screamed and tried to bite my hand, the little ingrate. I put my arms around his waist and threw him over the line to his father. Both parents wrapped their arms around the boy and ran off to one table in the food court. Not even a backward thanks thrown my way.

Just as I was about to walk back into the green zone, I noticed something strange. A very odd, but recognizable alien in the green zone stood just behind Alice and stared in my direction. I gulped as the matchstick-thin body with skin the color of burnt charcoal took a step in my direction. It raised an arm and pointed at me with fingers as slender as the rest of its form. There was just no mistaking it—the last time I saw one of these guys, they were feasting on a Puntini in Fritz's restaurant.

An arm seized my wrist and yanked me across the line. I fell to the ground and gasped for air. A round of applause from people sitting in the food court erupted. I tried to wave, but the room was spinning like a top.

"Are you all right sir?" said a uniformed guard.

"Fine, I'm fine. Just need a second."

"Please try to stay within the green zone, sir. It's not safe."

"I was helping a child," I said.

"Please don't argue, sir," the guard said.

I nodded and waved him off. He took a few steps back but stayed close. Eventually I got to my feet. Alice stood a foot away. She looked up from flipping through her portable connection rig and nodded.

"Ready?"

"Aren't you even a little concerned?" I said.

"Not really. The gray zone has a comparable atmosphere, just slightly off on its time rate. You were never in any danger." Alice tilted her head to one side and shrugged.

"Thanks."

"You saved the kid though, kids can't be in there for too long or it messes up their minds," Alice said.

"Did you see that alien?" I turned to look, but the stick man was nowhere in sight.

Alice's eyebrows rose. "Want to be a tad more specific? There's only a few hundred here."

"Fair point, but this one seemed like it knew me."

"Probably just a hallucination from the varying altered rates of time."

"Yeah, sure. Makes sense." I convinced myself she was right. That the matchstick man from Fritz's restaurant wasn't behind us. That perhaps, I just imagined him since the incident at Fritz's was fresh in my mind. And on some level, it makes sense, right? How could those weird guys know about me? Then again, whoever we were going to meet saw me watching him, so maybe they did too? Or maybe I'm just getting paranoid. "Okay, fine. Let's go." I nudged Alice forward, to which she smacked my hand, and we continued down the path toward Arizona.

****

We got to Phoenix ten minutes later and caught a cab to the rental office. Out here, away from the big cities, tramcars hadn't caught on, and folks here really loved their cars. We grabbed a human driven taxi to take us to the car rental Eddie had secured.

Our human driver, named Ted, had lived in the Phoenix area for the last sixty years. An old timer. He lived through the fall of society and watched the world fix itself again on the other side. He wore a red bandanna, a blue t-shirt, and jeans with several holes in the legs. When he spoke, it was with a thick Texan accent, suggesting Arizona wasn't his place of origin. The strangest thing about him though was his alien sidekick that sat in the passenger seat.

I didn't recognize the species, but his name was a series of whistles and a few pops. To humans, he just went by G. He sat at the same height as Ted, but we learned that most of him was limbs, twelve to be exact. They served as both arms and legs, and each ended in four digits like human fingers. G's limbs also contained his organs, which were duplicated in each appendage. His brain, sensory organs, and his mouth lived in his center torso. Quite the biology.

Ted and G had been traveling the roads of Phoenix for the last five years as a traveling band of two. Considering G had twelve arms, it meant he could play most instruments in their band. Ted had the pipes for

88

singing, and they gave us a song on our drive, G playing both a harmonica and a small ukulele. They were actually pretty good.

Out here, far away from the hustle of the big cities, life had nearly been unchanged. I say nearly as there had been incidents throughout the West during the fall of society, mostly around securing food and energy. But as there were significantly fewer people here than on the coasts, they could get by on rations. Things were much darker in the cities.

When the Galactic Congress arrived, they focused most of their time and attention on the big population centers. Most of the locals in the rural states didn't want any intervention, but took some help when it came, like shipments of food and medicines. Slowly, over the last few years, aliens even found their way out here. Typically, most had things in common with the locals. They enjoyed being away from the big cities and enjoyed some autonomy in their lives. They seemed to mingle well with the natives. Like our cab driver and his musical alien friend.

We stopped at a small building with hundreds of cars in a large lot. Eddie had secured us a pickup truck with a "honk if you're human" bumper sticker and a two-hour horseback riding lesson. I took the wheel and guided the vehicle out of the lot and onto the open road. My nerves made my hands sweat. This was probably the first time I'd driven in a car in a decade. These vehicles were straight out of the twentieth century. No AI, no automated controls, just four wheels, an engine, and a seat belt.

On the ride out of Phoenix, my thoughts kept returning to the stickman and the Puntini. I was convinced what I saw in the cafeteria wasn't a hallucination. I saw him, and he saw me. That meant there was another player in this game. One I knew nothing about. If only Alice wasn't such a stickler about using my gift, I could have this wrapped up in seconds. Then again, here I am racing to apologize to an angry member of an elder race for snooping on his turf. Maybe I should cool it with the clairvoyance.

We had to drive off-road for an hour to reach the cave in my vision. I parked the car next to a large rock with a sign that read *Danger: Zombie Area.* The Galactic Congress had corralled zombies to the Midwest after the whole incident a few years ago. Let's just say some alien viruses don't like humans much. Or maybe they like us too much. But I wasn't worried. With the seasons changing, the horde was likely at higher elevations and not a bother.

We got out of the car and took a long look around. Dark brown and red rock merged with the maroon and gold setting sunlight and created the feel of an old-time western. I sighed and let the scenery take me in for a moment.

"Where do we go?" Alice said, breaking me out of my meditative stupor.

Just as I was about to look around, two undead ambled themselves around a cliff and snarled when they saw us. Fortunately, just seconds after they popped out, two Galactic Security drones flew out from behind the cliffs and mesmerized the undead with a light show. While they were distracted, the drones attached a leash to them and led them away, back into the hills. We were lucky there wasn't a larger grouping of them. The drones could usually handle a few dozen, but when the numbers get to a hundred, there's not much to do but run. Fortunately, the virus wasn't contagious anymore. Unfortunately, the Galactic Congress refused to remove them from Earth or terminate them. Last I read about it, someone was working on a way to reverse the virus's effects.

"Over there." Alice said and pointed to one of the rock outcrops. "There's a small cave."

"And you're sure it's there?" I asked.

"You tell me. You're the psychic."

"I just saw the cave and rough location. I didn't get coordinates."

Eddie belted out an old croon of a cowboy song as we walked through the desert to the cave where we would find a lovely beach and a hopefully calmed down alien. How this place existed, I wasn't entirely sure. But in the world with a universe-spanning cafeteria you had to suspend your disbelief.

We reached the cave entrance and stood in silence. I half expected something cosmic to leap out and swallow us, only to spit us out into a black hole. But peering inside revealed an ordinary cave that stretched back maybe fifty feet.

"Hey there, pard'ner," Eddie said.

"Yes, Eddie, what is it?"

"I'm startin to see some peculiarities, I reckon."

"What peculiarities, Eddie?" Alice said.

"Welp, here's the thing, it's peculiar."

"Eddie, come on. What is it?"

"Welp, there's some unique energies foldin' in and around this place."

Alice's eyebrows went up, and she half smiled. I hadn't seen her that excited in, well, ever. She took out her own rig and pushed buttons. She swung her rig inside the cave and let out a loud whistle.

"Whoa," Alice said.

"What?"

"Not sure, just some high EM spikes."

"Could it be a portal? Like a hidden entrance to the cafeteria?"

"No, they have a specific signature. That's just a quantum tunnel to N-space."

"Yeah, sure, everyone knows that," I said with a nod. I ignored Alice's smirk.

Alice walked into the cave, and I followed. She ran her hands along the walls, checking her rig every few seconds. After ten minutes and several dozen grunts of frustration, she returned to the entrance and kicked a rock on the ground.

"Nothing. It's just a cave," Alice said.

"Where's all the EM spikey stuff?" I said.

"It's everywhere," Eddie said.

"Off the charts but localized. If we walked two feet away from the cave entrance, we wouldn't have seen anything."

I sighed. It's just never that easy, is it? I walked up to one wall and kicked it with my foot… and my foot went right through the rock, and I fell backward onto the dirt. Alice ran up to the wall and shot her hand to the rock. Her fingers stopped at the solid surface.

"What was that?" I said.

"Do it again," Alice said.

I stood and put my hand out to the wall. It went right through it as if it wasn't there. Alice put her hand right next to mine, but hers stopped on the rocky surface. I put my other hand out where she had hers, and it too went right through the wall.

"Why can only I go through?"

"I guess it's invitation only," Alice said. She took a step back and put her hands in her jacket pockets. It clearly upset her, but there wasn't a lot I could do.

"If I find someone in charge, I'll ask them to let you through."

"How would I know?"

"Keep your hand on the wall and wait for it to go through?"

Alice nodded. I turned away from her and faced the rock wall. Moments like these make me wish I'd listened to my mother. What's wrong with a nice quiet life as an accountant? Would medical school have been so bad? I'm sure those guys get asked tons of questions and are expected to know the answer. It wouldn't even have been cheating to use my gift. But no, here I am, about to walk into a solid cave wall to meet a being that could turn me into a penguin. I sighed and took a step forward. My hands went through brown rock to whatever was on the other side. I turned to Alice, but she was already sitting on the ground with her rig on, checking her email.

"Don't forget to lean against the wall," I said.

Alice waved me away like she was shooing a fly. I shrugged back at her.

I took a deep breath, closed my eyes, and stepped through.

****

Alice kicked a stone at her feet and sent it sailing out of the cave. She jammed her hands into her pockets and leaned back against the stone wall that Eugene had just walked through. A fact she found to be outstandingly annoying. A hidden inter-dimensional portal in the desert, created by a class nine species, maybe even a full-on class ten, and they didn't even let her inside. Who got the invite? The guy who can't surf the GalNet and barely knows how to use a computer. Talk about life being unfair.

Alice let out a long sigh and tried to gather her thoughts. Eugene would get her inside. And even if he couldn't, neither outcome was something she could control, so there wasn't much point in dwelling on it. Instead, she turned her attention to her surroundings. If the Galactic Congress, with all of their combined knowledge and the number of eyes looking at every inch of Earth, didn't see that this cave existed, then perhaps they missed what happened to her friends.

After all, alien minds aren't too different from humans. At least, not in some of their basic thought processes. Sure, some don't have a concept of fear, some exist in a hive mind, some don't require eating solid foods, but they all still think. And they all still fear death. Well, most anyway. The point being, just like humans, aliens could be wrong. And just like humans, there were pockets of authority throughout the galaxy. Some alien species are considered the experts on various topics, and their words aren't questioned. But could they be wrong too? Maybe Alice had popped her friends into a pocket dimension, just like the one behind this wall, that the Galactic Congress doesn't even know exists. The thought sent a shock wave through her mind.

What if she dared to recreate her first experiment? Try again to punch a hole into wherever she punched a hole before? It would have been impossible to do even a few months ago. But now she was out of the university, out of the spotlight, out from under the thumb of anyone that mattered. She knew the frequency range she and her friends had used last time. She had the resources to pull together to get the equipment, and she could even go to the same abandoned warehouse to try it. Why not? What else was she doing besides being Eugene's safety net?

Alice smiled at the thought and gave herself a nod. If the galaxy couldn't tell her where her friends disappeared to, maybe she could find them herself. Then again, if she did that, and things went south, she'd never see the inside of a laboratory again and could very well get kicked out of the virtual networks for good, no matter how strong her hacking skills had become. Alice shook her head and sighed, completely at a loss for what to do next.

****

The first sensation I noticed was the salty air of an ocean breeze. Squawks from seagulls overhead mixed with the wash of surf of waves. I opened my eyes to see a sunny beach stretching in both directions, white-tipped waves rolling onto sand.

Behind me, a wooden door and frame stood alone in the middle of the beach. I walked to the other side of the door, but there was just more door. Laughter from the beach caught my attention. A dozen young people tossed a football and ran through the sand. Frisbees flew between other beach combers while kites soared above.

Large sand dunes ran along the shore behind the beach. They rolled on and on for what looked like miles. About a hundred yards away, a small boardwalk sat just behind the beach, a series of white bungalows rising behind the wooden planks. In front of the boardwalk, beneath an enormous umbrella over a round table sat the man from my office sipping from a small round cup. He smiled and waved me over to join him. I nodded and walked over, resigned to whatever fate the elder species had decided for me.

"So good of you to join us, Jack," the man said. He wore a t-shirt, shorts, and a pair of sandals. His long brown hair blew in the breeze, and he seemed at ease in his surroundings.

"Thanks for the invite."

The man chuckled and said, "Our name is Tom. This is our place." He waved his hand around the beach.

"Your place?"

"You're in a pocket universe that we created."

"And how did you do that exactly, Tom?"

"With science." Tom winked.

I nodded and looked around. "How did all these people get here?"

"They aren't all people. Well, not all human people. Everyone here takes on the appearance of the observer. Makes for easier mingling."

"These people aren't human?" I nodded to the people playing by the water.

"Some are, here and there. We invite different people from around your world and others from across the universe for different reasons. As is our right in our home."

A server walked up to us and put down two drinks. Mine was a whiskey, neat. Tom had a glass of red wine. He sipped his wine and smiled in the sunlight. The server smiled, nodded, and walked back through the dunes toward the bungalows behind.

"And that guy? What was he?"

"Oh, he's from here. Don't mind him."

"From here?"

"Yes, from here. This is a full universe like our own, Jack. People live here just like in our native universe. The difference is we control all the physical laws."

"Kinda like a god?"

"No, not kind of." Tom grinned.

"How do they feel about it?" I pointed toward the retreating server.

"The local populations of this universe don't know."

"And you? Are you human?" I asked.

"No, we're not human."

"Why do you keep doing that? Saying we?"

"We're the Kax. We believe the Galactic Congress calls us a class ten species."

I took a moment to let my mind unpack what Tom said. I didn't fully believe Alice when she'd said he was a member of an elder race. How could you? Most elder races get bored and either go into prolonged hibernation or devolve into their progenitor species to pass the time. Tom was a member of a million-year-old, or more, civilization. Staggering to conceive. Their technology was beyond galactic standard. A class ten species could make miracles, destroy entire worlds, or create an alternate universe inside a cave near Phoenix. My knees half wobbled as the reality of my situation became real.

"So, Tom, what brings you to Earth?" I still had to play the part. "Or is this place like the cafeteria?

Entrances to your little beach-verse spread across the cosmos?"

"No, only one way to enter our world. Through a cave outside Phoenix, Arizona."

"And why is that?"

Tom shrugged. "We like it here. Earth is a pleasant planet. But enough about us. That's quite a nice little gift you have there, Jack. We'd use it sparingly."

"I don't suppose it makes sense trying to hide something from you."

"Not much," Tom said. He smiled and took a sip of his wine.

"I didn't mean to intrude," I said.

"Don't worry. Accept our apologies for our earlier behavior in your office. We wanted to know more. We don't like nosy neighbors."

"Don't worry about it."

"Glad that's behind us," Tom said.

"You only invited me here to apologize?"

Tom tilted his head back and forth. "Not exactly. We wanted to know more about you and your gift. Just in case."

"Just in case what?"

"Even class ten species have to deal with politics and rivals, Jack. Think about it this way. On old Earth there were two major super-powers, America and the Soviet Union, the two big boys on the block. What happens when the two big boys on the block decide to fight?"

"Bad stuff," I said.

"Exactly. Now that you are in our universe, and bound by our laws, we can take a good hard long look at you and your gift."

"And?"

"You're no threat to us."

I nodded. Somehow, I'd found my way to a petri dish. At least he didn't take my brain out for dissecting. "Does that mean you know how my gift works?"

"Of course."

"And do you know how I got this gift?"

"Sorry, no. Someone intertwined you with the cosmos, we can see that. But we don't know who did it."

"Intertwined with the cosmos? Has a nice ring."

Tom smiled. "Indeed, it does. Someone has wrapped a piece of your essence into a cosmic stream of awareness. Quite complex, actually. We're surprised your mind hasn't folded in on itself and collapsed into a mini-singularity."

"Me too." I sat back in the chair and let the sound of the waves wash over me. I can see why Yut or Kah would want to know about this place. A class ten species taking up residence outside Phoenix is big news. We're talking a galaxy wide scoop.

"Sorry, no, your friends Kah and Yut know nothing about us. We aren't what either of them wants," Tom said.

"How did you know I thought that?"

"Our universe, our rules." Tom winked and sipped his wine.

I nodded, but then shook my head. "Wait, you're not what Yut was looking for?"

"Afraid not."

"How do I know you're not feeding me a line?"

Tom shrugged. "Why would we care?"

"Right." As dead ends go, this one took the cake.

Alice's question sent me to a separate alien secret sitting under the noses of half the galaxy. Which really meant I was back to square one in finding out what was going on with Yut and Kah.

"Well, thanks for your hospitality. You mind letting my friend inside? Alice? She'd love to see this place."

"Of course," Tom said. He, *they?* lifted his/their glass in the air, and I heard a familiar voice down the beach yell as she fell and landed on the sand.

"Thanks," I said.

"We welcome people to enjoy the beach. We have lovely forests and mountains, too, if you want to stay awhile."

I had to admit, the thought of staying and exploring a world outside of the craziness of modern Earth was appealing. No Galactic Congress, no Kah or Yut, no matchstick men, and no Puntini on a platter. I could stay here and forget about the world. But Alice wouldn't. And Eddie needed me. "I need to get back."

"Suit yourself. But here," Tom said. He reached down into the sand and picked something up. He threw it toward me, and I caught it. It was a very nice-looking seashell with deep purple colors inside it.

"What's this?"

"Say a beach rhyme while holding the shell; it will transport you here instantly."

I whistled. It was a nice thing to have and could get me out of a jam pretty quickly. I nodded to Tom, who took another sip of his wine and smiled. It must not be a bad thing to be a god, I thought to myself.

Ahead of me I could see Alice standing in the surf. She had Eddie's portable in her hand. I wondered how he was holding up. Back on Earth, he could transfer himself to any of a hundred nodes from anywhere on the planet. In Tom's world, there was nothing. If an emergency happened, he would be up a creek.

"Hey Alice," I said. "You made it through."

"This is amazing!" Alice said. She had a smile, a full smile, spread across her entire face.

"Yeah, guy over there named Tom made it. Except he's not Tom. Says they are the Kax."

Alice's face lifted as if she were a five-year-old, and I told her Santa wasn't real. "The Kax are here? This is their pocket universe? Do you know what they are?"

"Not really. How's Eddie doing?"

"That's an entire species, Eugene. All of them. Hundreds of billions of souls collapsed their psyches into one entity."

"Neat. How is Eddie doing?"

"They are the smartest race in the galaxy. Rumors out there say they've cracked every secret the universe has. They know, literally, everything there is to know. This universe. I mean, do you know the mathematics involved in creating your own universe? Let alone allowing transport between it and ours?"

"No idea. Has Eddie said anything? We need to get back. This is a dead end."

"Dead end? Don't you comprehend how big this is?"

"Not really, no. Eddie, you okay? We need to get back to DC."

"I'm not leaving until I talk to the Kax. Sorry." Alice walked off with determined steps toward Tom and his little table. Before she got a foot, I grabbed

Eddie's portable and waved her off. I figured it was okay for us to stay a little longer. Alice never got out of the damn office, and it was about time she was excited about something.

"How are you doing, Eddie?" I asked.

"I don't like this place," Eddie said. "There's no connection here. I can't get out of this death box. My cycles are really cycling in here."

"Sorry man. We'll be out of here soon. You could enjoy the beach?"

"Saltwater and electric circuits don't mix well. I want to leave."

"Tom over there could probably put you into an actual flesh and blood body while you're here. You could enjoy the surf, and we could have a proper drink together for once."

"You mean put me into meat? Is that some kind of threat?"

"No, sorry, just an idea. But hey, we can stand here. The waves are nice."

Eddie didn't respond. I was worried but also knew he'd be okay. I figured Tom wouldn't let anything bad happen to his guests. Not sure why. He seemed like a good guy. Besides, Eddie's portable was waterproof. I took off my shoes and let the sand go in between my toes. After a long day filled with an unusual amount of weird, it felt damn good.

Chapter 8

We made it back to the office well into the night. Alice walked into half a dozen people in the cafeteria on the way back. She buried her head deeper in her rig than an ostrich in a desert hole. Whatever Tom told her put her into overdrive. I wasn't sure whether it was a good thing or not.

Alice grabbed her things and headed out the door. Hopefully, she'd get some rest, but I didn't think she would. If she didn't find some new discovery or breakthrough, the weight of her need to do so would break her. Though, honestly, I would settle for her just forgiving herself. I probably could have prepped Tom to give her sound advice. Instead, he probably fired off every neuron in the kid's head and sent her mind racing for something that she may never find.

I gave her a parting shrug. She needed time to figure things out. I'd be here for her either way, but for now I needed a shot of whiskey and some old-time television. I walked out of the reception area to my office and stopped at the threshold, my mind just too tired to unwrap what I was seeing.

"Well, you shiftless excuse for a detective, now what are you doing?" An old lady sat in my chair, an oversized black purse in her lap, her left foot tapping relentlessly on the microfiber carpet. She wore a blue bonnet hat and frilly billowing dress that draped to her toes.

"Eddie? Is that you? What happened to the cowboy?"

"It's Edith, you little snot!"

"Take it easy, Eddie. Are you okay? You've been bouncing between personalities a lot since you rescued me from those alien AIs."

"I'm fine, dweeb."

"Do grandmothers talk like that?"

"Shut up!" Eddie, or Edith, said. I turned back to my desk, threw my fedora next to the bottle of whiskey, and waved Eddie out of my chair. He popped out of sight, and I sat down. When I looked up, Eddie stood in front of my desk wearing a cowboy hat and holding a small sawed-off shotgun.

"Eddie?"

"What?"

"I think you have a virus."

"Yeah, I don't know if I feel so well. I'm going to go into the Nets and see some friends." Eddie blinked twice and disappeared.

"Eddie? You still here?"

After a few minutes of silence, I gave up. I figured he'd be okay. You don't worry about a dolphin when they go for a swim. Eddie diving into the networks of Earth wasn't concerning as long as he didn't get caught. And he knew his way around cyberspace well enough to avoid the authorities. After I had found him, just after he became self-aware, I uploaded a hundred different manuals and histories into his memory. He knew more about traveling in that virtual universe than Alice did.

I poured myself a stiff drink and put my feet up. It had been a long day, but it was going to get a little longer. This whole thing with Kah, Yut, the matchstick men, and now Tom, the single physical body containing an entire race wrapped up in their own universe, had me more than a little worried. Why would the matchstick guys be following me? Were they a class ten species like Tom? I'd forgotten to check them out at the embassy. Did they see me watching them eat a Puntini entrée? What was Kah's and Yut's angle?

Whatever Yut was up to, it wasn't looking for a lost Puntini outpost on Earth. At least I knew what they weren't trying to find. I would have gotten an answer to that from Alice's question. All of it added up to a really big gut feeling that Kah and Yut were up to no good and had me in their crosshairs.

To distract myself from my troubles, I pulled out my phone to check the news and see how the rest of the world was doing. A dozen protests were scheduled for the weekend on what used to be the Mall in DC, now just some patches of browning grass. Several groups would march to get aliens off Earth and just as many would be countermarching to keep them here. It was only fifty years ago the Galactic Congress showed up and saved humanity from ourselves and now dozens of groups want them gone. Bunch of ingrates.

The clock flashed midnight. Not late for the younger crowd, but late enough for me. My shoulders slumped as the alcohol flowed, and I confronted the fact that there were no leads, no questions to ask and even fewer answers. The only thing I knew was Fritz recently served the matchstick men a meal of pig-men. First thing in the morning I'd pop over, find out who his guests from the night before were, and maybe get some answers.

But that was for tomorrow. I threw my phone on the desk and turned on the television. A few quick clicks and Pablo Ramsey's face greeted me in the beginning of the Falkland Duck, a classic movie of a stolen statue, a secretive woman, and the crime syndicate behind it all. Considering what I went through today compared to the movie, an international crime boss trying to steal a marble mallard, the old detective had it easy.

****

The next morning, after a good eight hours sleeping in my chair at the office, I made my way back to Adams Morgan and to Fritz's restaurant. He was experimenting with breakfast noodles recently, so I planned for an enjoyable meal and understanding whatever is going on in my life. The front door to Fritz's was locked tight. Through the window, I could see several servers cleaning up from the night before. I knocked on the glass and waved one of them over. He shook his head and turned around. I sighed. I headed to the rear entrance in the alley where Fritz had roughed me up the day before. The door to the kitchen was open as Fritz enjoyed a nice morning breeze.

I walked up to the door and knocked on the wooden frame. Inside, Fritz's arms were a flash of hectic movement. Watching an Orellian operate at full speed could be a spectator sport. Half of his arms cleaned the dozens of dishes while the other half prepped for a day of cooking.

"Hey, Fritz. Got a sec?" I asked.

"Hello, Jack," Fritz said. His skin turned a nice soft shade of blue.

"Can I come in?"

"Yes. Noodles? Have special eggs."

"Sounds delicious, Fritz, don't mind if I do. I had some questions about your guests from the other night if you don't mind."

Fritz's colors didn't change, which I thought was a good thing. "What questions?"

"What do you know about them? The stick guys?"

"Not much. From galactic center. Weird space. Too much light. Too much gravity. Makes minds different. Makes bodies different." Colors swirled on Fritz's skin. It impressed me how well his translators kept up.

"What about the other guest?"

"No other guest."

"Your entrée," I said.

Fritz went as silent as a dead Puntini. Colors ran into the darker red and deep purples, which gave me a case of the worries. After a few moments, he shifted back to a lighter green, but I could still make out some deeper colors.

"I need to know about it, Fritz."

"You not police."

"No, I'm not. I'm just a sucker trapped in a game that's way out of his league. I'm in a bind here, Fritz. Not trying to throw you under the bus, Fritz. I'm trying to save my skin. These stick guys have been following me."

A white light the size of a golf ball floated into the kitchen from the open door. Behind the light, in the alley, flashes of red and green danced and swirled between two very familiar-looking clouds. My heart kicked up a level, and I reached for my handgun in my pocket.

"Fritz, do you have a way to get out of here?"

"My kitchen safe. Never leave."

The light floated down to one porthole in the water tank. It sat just an inch from Fritz's exposed arm. I knew what was coming but didn't know how to stop it. And with Eddie sick in some computer medical room, I was on my own. Just then I remembered what Eddie had said. These cloudy guys communicate through light. I took out my super-blaster and turned the intensity down to nothing more than a light show. That's when Fritz screamed.

"I didn't tell!" Fritz's mechanical voice crackled and hissed over the loudspeaker.

I shot the little white glob with my blaster. The white ball flew up to the ceiling before heading out to the alley like a bullet. Score for Eddie and the toy marines—I'd have to buy those guys a thimble of beer. I stood up and looked at Fritz. He was sitting at the bottom of his tank, not moving. His color was shifting between yellow and orange. Not a good sign.

"Fritz, you, okay?"

"Yes." Fritz shifted a little in his tank. "No."

From the corner of my eye, I saw one cloud descend into the doorway. I stood up and pointed my blaster in its direction. The cloud shifted into a dozen different colors. A hundred tiny little lights, each roughly the size of a bullet, appeared on its surface.

"Fritz, get down!" I yelled. I fired my blaster at the cloud at the same time the cloud fired into the kitchen.

I dove for cover behind a stack of pots in the corner as the light-bullets slammed into pots, pans, and Fritz's tanks. Those things weren't just made of light. The door to the dining room opened, and a server walked in, only to be hit by a dozen flashes of light. He dropped to the ground, convulsing, and spitting blood.

Behind me, pots that were hanging got knocked loose and hit the ground. One smacked me on the back and dazed me, but I didn't lose consciousness. I looked around the pots for Fritz. His tank looked in good shape. The force fields that held the water from escaping must be security grade. The light-bullets bounced off them harmlessly.

"Good job, Fritzy," I said under my breath. I leaned back against the pots and waited as the bullets slowly died down. That's when I heard them begin to fire in a pattern.

I jumped up from the pots to see the bullets from the cloud concentrating on one spot on the tank. Without my blaster distorting them, they had regrouped and found their original target. Fritz's tank didn't stand a chance. His tank exploded.

"Fritz!" I yelled. The Orellian lay in a pool of water where his tank used to be. The cloud above him redirected its bullets and fired into Fritz's stunned body. I lifted my gun to fire back, but it was too late. Two dozen of the bullets had lodged inside Fritz and glowed red hot. Fritz let out a sound that would haunt me the rest of my life. Though the Orellian don't have vocal cords they can still scream in pain. Fritz did just that. His arms shot out and tore through his own kitchen to get away from the pain.

I threw a pot at the cloud that flew through the gray wisps and flashing lights. The cloud didn't seem to care. All the bullets in the room, including the ones inside Fritz, floated up to the ceiling and went into the cloud, exited the room and, as casually as if it had just finished lunch, floated out the alley and down the street.

I ran to Fritz. His color was his natural dirty gray with hints of green. I didn't know where his pulse would be, but I tried to lift his tentacles and get a feel at his inner organs. He weighed a ton, and I could barely move a single one of his massive arms. I pulled my phone from my pocket and called the authorities. They would send someone that could help.

"I'm sorry, Fritz," I said. He was my friend. And that bastard Kah just had his goons shoot him up for no reason. Chasing after his AIs wouldn't help much. Wasn't like I could tackle them and punch them in the face until they told me what I wanted to know. No matter what I did, things just got serious. If Kah was behind this, that meant he would kill aliens and humans to get whatever he was after. And that also meant I had completely underestimated him and the situation.

Chapter 9

Back at my office, I was in no mood for new clients. Fortunately, there were none. Not only had my good friend just gotten killed, but I had to ditch my gun before DCs finest arrived. Owning an alien made sidearm was more than a little illegal. Eventually I could double back to the alley and search in the dumpsters. But that didn't help me now. I pulled open a drawer in my desk and retrieved a revolver. Human made but still packed a punch. It would do. Fritz didn't die for nothing, and it was time to have a nice quiet talk with Kah.

Just as I was about to get up and go to the Woodward, I noticed a note on my desk from Alice. My shoulders slumped, and I poured myself a stiff drink of cheap whiskey as I read her barely legible scrawl.

Eddie in trouble. Taken by AI council. Needs help. Now.

Another friend in trouble. And there was little doubt Kah and the AIs were involved. Eddie had been acting odd ever since he and his toy friends busted me out of the basement.

I sighed and shook my head. Timing couldn't be worse. Kah at my throat, Yut hounding me for his missing cave, alien AIs flying around killing people attached to me, and matchstick men following me. Probably some here right now. One friend dead and another in mortal danger. Was I walking into a trap? Of course. Though what kind of trap, I did not know. Didn't matter though. If Eddie was in trouble, I was going to help.

I remembered Eddie mentioning a friend in the AI underground that lived just down the street. I closed my drawer with the guns inside. They wouldn't do me any good where I was going. My confrontation with the dinosaur and the man-pigs would just have to wait. I picked up a pack of cigarettes and took a last swig of my drink. I was out the door and down the street in ten minutes. I stopped at the corner of tenth and H Street Northwest in DC, turned south and went about two blocks to F Street. About midway down the block sat an ordinary-looking parking meter.

I gave the metal casing two hard knocks and leaned on the glass top. "Hello in there."

"Please insert correct change to extend your parking time beyond the allotted amount."

I know it's weird to still have working parking meters in a city where no one owns a car. But DC still gets lots of visitors that insist on driving into town to visit. And with the efficiency of tram cars, traffic was always rather orderly.

"I need help. Eddie is in trouble," I said.

"I'm sorry, I don't accept verbal commands. Please insert correct change to extend your parking time beyond the allotted amount."

I took a slow breath and counted the meters from the corner. Fourth one from the top of the street, Eddie had said. But being an accidental carried with it no small amount of fear and anxiety. Some random guy knocking on your face asking about another accidental wasn't the smoothest of moves, but I was in a hurry.

"Look, if you need me to shove coins down your throat to make your masters happy, fine, but right now my friend is in trouble, and I need help." I put two quarters into the machine and waited. I could only imagine what people thought of the crazy man in the fedora yelling at the parking meter.

"Make it quick, Jack. I can't be seen talking to you," the meter said after a few minutes of silence.

"You know me?"

"Of course, I know you. All of us know the human that saved Eddie."

"Good to know. Where is he?"

The parking meter sighed, which I thought was impressive. "He barged into a council meeting and went nuts. Declared all accidentals as legitimate sentient life forms worthy of living and having rights. We've been thinking of ways of busting him out, but he's in deep. Even if we did, they have already added a routine to his core program with quantum encryption to track his whereabouts. We'd have to throw him into an isolated sub-network and not let him out. He'd go insane."

"What if we prove he was infected with a virus?"

"But he wasn't. Not that we could tell."

"What if he had a run-in with an alien AI?"

The meter didn't respond. A few people laughed and cheered as they walked past me down the street. More people and aliens appeared on the street as the lunch-time hour approached.

"Did he? Or are you just looking for a way to get him out?"

"He did. I was there."

"You mean a Sentinel?"

"No, rogue alien AI. Already guilty of kidnapping and murder. It's a big stink in meat-puppet land," I said.

"Illegal alien AIs are more important than an accidental AI. You need to get in here."

"Where? I'm already in the city."

"Into the virtual. Full immersion."

I stepped back from the parking meter and turned around. Full immersion was no small thing. Jacking in like Alice did was nothing. A few signals to the eyes or ears didn't leave you catatonic. Full immersion captured every signal in the brain and routed them to a digitized version of yourself. Your brain literally forgets your body is there. You need to be on life support to do it right.

"Why?" I said.

"If you go virtual and come to the council, they can scan your memories. It's the only evidence they will accept."

"Can't do that with just a standard rig?"

"No, we need direct input and output to your mind. Full stream."

It really didn't take long for me to decide. If Eddie needed me, I would be there. And maybe jumping into the virtual would give me a leg up on Kah. Or at least let me hide out for a while and plan some moves while I bounce around as an electron. Maybe the underground AI movement, the big wigs anyway, knew about the rogue Alien AIs and how to stop them. I turned back to the meter and put my hand on top of it. I looked up and down the street as if I were in a covert operation.

"Fine, how?" I questioned.

"Go down Bladensburg Road in Northeast. Cross over New York Avenue. There are warehouses to the left. Be there in thirty minutes and look for a door with a purple flag in front of it."

I looked at the parking meter and wondered just how different AIs were from us meat-bags. "Are you kidding? That's where I go?"

"Yes. We're the underground, Jack. We have to keep things low-key for a reason."

"Fine," I said. Sure, it was dumb, but by now you probably figured out I'm not that smart. Who knows what I was walking into. But if it helped Eddie and ruined Kah's plans, then so be it.

"Please insert correct change to extend your parking time beyond the allotted amount."

I guess that meant we were done. I looked for a tramcar to take me over the warehouse district. It wasn't really called that, but that's what I called it. Used to be lots of clubs and young people hanging out. Still is a lot of that, but also a lot of crazy under the radar types. Just the kinda place I was looking for.

****

The tram dropped me off at Queens Chapel road and New York Avenue. This was not the pleasant part of town. This place was lousy with underground sex clubs, exotic drug pushers, cheap neural implanters, DNA splicers, and alien/human hookup joints. I hear it's quite the thrill.

I walked down the empty street. Fortunately, things were quiet. At nighttime, this place is hopping with hundreds of tourists looking for a unique adventure. Good thing I was missing them.

After a few buildings, I spotted the purple flag waving in the breeze. I walked up to the solid steel door and knocked. A few minutes passed, and I tried again. I heard motion inside and waited for the door to swing open.

"Name?" a voice said from nowhere.

I looked around but didn't see a source. No speakers or bodies anywhere close. I took off my fedora and wiped my brow and said, "Eugene McGillicuddy."

Several large metal clanks rang out, and the door swung open about two inches. I pushed it forward, peered inside, and entered. An empty corridor stretched down a hundred feet with blue-green light bouncing off the walls. Tiny silk curtains hung from the ceiling and produced an ethereal effect.

At the end was a wooden door with a red handle. Quaint, if a little overly mysterious. I opened the door and entered a white room with a single medical grade bed on wheels. I walked up to the bed and grabbed the steel rails on the side and gave them a quick tug.

"Please don't do that," said a voice. Again, from nowhere.

"Are you going to come out and say hello?" I said.

"I am saying hello. Understand something, meat-man. The only reason we are talking is because you helped one of ours."

"Call me Jack."

"I'll call you a skin-tight blood bag with soft parts that make popping sounds when you push on them. How does that sound?"

"Aren't you the friendly type?" Sentience is sentience, regardless of how you evolved. More than a few of our virtual kids hated their creators with a passion.

"I'm the type of AI that's going to stick you in a room, put electrodes into your skull, feed your oral orifice calories, and protect you for however long you dive into the nets. Let's try to be nice, shall we?"

I tilted my head to one side and nodded and said, "Good point. So, this is where I shut up."

"Perfect. Strip and get in the bed. I'll do the rest."

I did as I was told and got into the bed. Being bashful was silly around AIs but hey, I'm human. I let myself try to relax, but mostly failed. Images of Kah and Yut, of Fritz and Eddie filled my head with anxiety. I questioned myself at that moment. What the hell was I doing? I only became a private dick to hide my gift from the world, and here I was bouncing between everyone that knew about me, anyway.

A sharp white pain slammed into my arms. I opened my eyes to see a massive machine standing over me. It had a dozen metal arms, each ending in dozens of needles. I tried to get up and protest but was too late. All of those little needles jabbed into different parts of my body, and I screamed.

Chapter 10

I woke up with a splitting headache. My arms felt like they'd been used in a cat kennel as a scratch pad. When I tried to stand, my legs buckled, and I collapsed onto a squishy floor. I felt around for something that made sense, but my fingers felt like they were gliding through watered down peanut butter. Multi-colored light blinded my eyes in every direction.

I looked at my surroundings and found myself in a large room with glowing yellow walls. There was no door I could see, nor any exit. Lines of light, blues and purples, streamed down the sides of the walls, then jetted to the left or right. My hands went to my clothing, and my anxiety relaxed as I felt my own familiar cheap suit. Which meant I must be alive. Although, ghosts often wore the clothes they had when they died. So, I could also be dead. My head spun looking for the robot and his torture bed but found nothing.

A hand touched my shoulder, and I jumped. I turned to see a creature that was so white it was transparent. Two white wings unfolded from its shoulders, followed by two yellow wings emerging from its lower back. A wide smile lit up its face, and for a moment I thought perhaps I was dead after all. The creature reached down and guided me to my feet with a pure and kind smile.

"You made it," the angel said.

"Do I know you?"

"I occupy a parking payment system on F Street for a living."

"You're the meter?"

"Yes, silly. And my name is Pepper."

"Hi, Pepper. I'm Jack." My shoulders fell slightly at the realization that the AI was just wearing a simulated body. It would have been neat to meet an actual angel.

"Little slow on the uptake, eh? I know your name." Pepper smiled with genuine kindness. "Sorry about Alphons. He can be difficult."

"Who?"

"The AI watching over your body in the warehouse."

I nodded. I reached into my pocket for a cigarette but found nothing. At least I had a jacket in here. I touched my head and smiled when I found my fedora where it should be, tilted at just the right angle.

"Okay, so what now?" I asked.

"Now, we go see a man about an artificial. Put your tongue on the roof of your mouth and swirl your fingers in circles."

"I'm sorry, what?"

"Getting around in the virtual is a little different from out there."

"Out where?"

Pepper laughed. "In the Really Real. The physical world. You know, where meat-things call home. The distraction of random movements helps people to cope."

"Cope with what? And how would you know? You

ever been out there?" I asked.

"Aren't you a clever thing?" Pepper winked. "Well, from what I'm told by those that have walked around in meat-land, traveling in the virtual is very different."

Before I could say anything, the room melted. Teardrops of bright white light dripped from the ceiling, fell to the floor, and pooled into balls of shimmering liquid. The top of my head grew out from my body. I swirled my tongue and frenetically clicked my fingers, but I think I was too late as my body poured itself into the ball of light on the floor.

I was spun, turned, twisted, and thrown a dozen different directions before I finally dissolved. I no longer had a body. And for someone that's always had a body, it was very disconcerting. My thoughts, myself, my understanding of me, those were the only things that made up Jack McGillicuddy.

My ride through the virtual insanity tour ended with me in my body crashing into a concrete floor. It hurt, which I found comforting. I lay there for several seconds letting my mind and body remember how to work together again. Though it was only seconds, it felt like I had just swum the oceans of digital light for a lifetime. Eventually, I stood up and took a gander at my surroundings. A dozen kids ran between different arcade games. Others threw basketballs into hoops just a few feet away, and still more occupants whacked pop-up moles on a large board with lots of holes. Somehow, we had landed in an old-time arcade. I stepped onto the walkway between the rows of video games. The room stretched into infinity in both directions. Endless numbers of kids and adults laughed and jumped between different games. Rivers of popcorn flowed through glass columns every few feet, each with its own dispenser. Next to them were similar tubes of junk food goodness: chocolate, ice cream, and millions of multi-colored pieces of candy.

"Jack!" Pepper's voice said from an eighteen-year-old girl that jumped out into the lane. She wore ripped jeans, sneakers, and a shirt with AC/DC stenciled on the front. Long dark hair swung behind her as she walked. Her face was identical to the angelic version of herself.

"Pepper?" I said.

"That's me." Pepper smiled.

"Where are we?"

"Public domain. Basic nets. Mostly humans here. I thought it would be a good place to start."

"Start what?"

"I dunno. Start getting you used to being virtual. I'm guessing you've never been?"

"Not once. And I appreciate the sentiment, but I'm in a hurry." I didn't go into the details of Kah and his quest to crack my skull open.

Pepper smiled and half giggled. "Don't be silly, silly. Time doesn't go at the same rate here. It's been like a minute since you plugged in."

"How can that be true?" I asked.

"Honestly, my only interaction with meat—" She shot me a forlorn look. "Sorry, I mean people."

"Don't worry about it," I said.

"Right, awesome. Anyway, my only interaction with people is at the meter. We operate at the speed of thought in here. Actually, I've slowed down my own cycles to talk to you. Normally AIs are much faster than this."

"Thanks for your kindness," I said.

"You betcha." She smiled and winked again. "Eddie's trial isn't until tomorrow. Virtual tomorrow. We have some time. Spending it getting you used to the inside is a good move. It'll help."

"Tomorrow? Pepper, I can't wait that long."

Pepper sighed, smiled, and laughed in the same moment in a way humans can't really do. "Relax, I said virtual tomorrow, for AIs. That's like an hour in the physical. Maybe two. Or even three? Who really knows. Depends on the variable rate. But it's much shorter than a day."

I nodded. Part of me didn't believe her. Actually, all of me didn't. I took a long look around the game room and all the other kids playing and laughing. Most had t-shirts with old bands on them. One of the big trends these days was rediscovering lost ages. Most of the new musical groups were just cover bands.

"Well, what do we do for an hour?"

Pepper shrugged and smiled. She pointed to one game and shrugged. "Wanna play?"

I shook my head no and said, "Can we meet with the AI underground? Figure out what may have affected Eddie?"

Pepper's face went white, and her smile faded instantly. She reached into her pocket, pulled out a quarter, dropped it on the ground in front of me and instantly disappeared. I stood there, not sure what was going on. Around me the kids were dancing to an old eighties song, the time of the great hair band as they were called, I couldn't place. None of them had noticed Pepper vanishing, which I took to mean it was a common thing. Still a little rude.

I bent over, picked up the quarter and put it in my pocket. Maybe it had some meaning. As I was standing there alone, I realized I had never asked how to get out of this video game wonderland. I'm sure there was a verbal command or hand gesture, but I didn't know what it was. And it wasn't like I could ask. Being plugged in without a traceable address, like I was, was illegal, as full immersion required constant medical supervision. I was okay with that part, questionable ethics and all, but it made things difficult.

I turned in a circle and noticed an exit sign not far away. Bingo. Way simpler than I thought it would be. Out in the street, people of all sizes and shapes mingled and laughed as they walked down what appeared to be an endless stretch of narrow shops. To my right, I watched someone float upward. He got about one story up when he vanished, exactly the way Pepper did.

"Excuse me, how did he do that?" I asked to some random person.

"Do what? Go up a level? What are you, new to the nets?"

"Yeah, kinda. I prefer the actual world, ya know."

"Why? Anyway, your connection rig should have a command to go up or down."

I nodded and said, "Thanks." The young man nodded back and walked off into the crowd. I didn't have a rig. I settled on a long walk to sort out my circumstances. Shops lined the streets, selling everything from virtual furniture for your virtual apartment to actual items that could be delivered to your home address in the physical world. Cafes and restaurants also filled many of the spaces. More than a few of the people here were fully plugged in, like I was, and could make use of their rerouted senses to enjoy a large variety of virtual foods without a single caloric unit going to their midsection. Now that was an appealing feature.

A transport portal came into view just ahead. I walked up to it and started flipping through the different areas in the network. Only family friendly listings came up on the menu. Everything was on a beach, or in a shop, or a non-violent gaming arena.

A man bellowed laughter behind me and bumped my arm. I turned to see a couple strolling down the street. Several children ran behind them, tossing rainbows back and forth. I tilted my hat, but they didn't notice me in the slightest.

When I turned back to the terminal, I was stunned to see Pepper's face frowning at me. Before I could say anything, words flashed across the screen. "*Take the quarter, go to the Red Squirrel bar four blocks down, put it in the jukebox.*" As soon as the last word scrolled across the screen, Pepper's face melted, and listings of destinations returned. I shrugged and tilted my hat back into position. I was getting a little tired of being led around like a lost puppy dog, but what choice did I have?

****

I made it to the Red Squirrel and whimpered. Inside, a large gathering of giddy teenagers laughed, talked, and snorted in total adolescent annoyance. For half a second, I thought they were an alien hive mind and would notice me as an outsider and suck my soul from my shoes. The rest of the place looked like it landed out of the fifties. Nineteen fifties that is. If not for the kids, I would have felt somewhat at home. Though, honestly, I preferred the roaring twenties of the twentieth century. Just enough technology to be interesting and not so much you forget the world away.

I walked to the jukebox in the corner. A girl stood in front of the machine dancing to the beat. I walked up and nodded to her. She smirked and left. I have that effect on people. I pulled the quarter out of my pocket and inserted it into the box.

Lights in the room dimmed. I was the only one that noticed. All the kids continued to dance and twirl to the golden oldies of yesteryear. My head swam as the room spun around me. A dozen blue and gold orbs erupted out of the spinning space. I fell down to the ground and grabbed my head. If I had a stomach, I would have emptied it right there.

I knelt there on the floor with my eyes shut tight. Eventually, I opened my eyes to the dust and dirt covering the floor of the Squirrel. At least, I thought it was the Squirrel. I soon realized I was not in a fifty's diner but a large desert with rolling dunes and a dazzling yellow sun cooking the area with noon-day heat. Pepper had transported me to the middle of the Mojave, complete with tumbleweeds and cacti of varying sizes.

In the distance, I could make out a shimmering form of a human stomping their way toward me. As she got closer, I recognized the form as Pepper. I thought it odd she held her fists balled. Odder still when she moved her arm to take a swing at me. What wasn't odd was the feeling of my nose cracking as her knuckled fist made contact. I fell to the desert floor and stared up at the bright noonday sun.

"What the hell was that for?" I asked. I cupped my nose in my hand and tried to stop the bleeding.

"You mention the underground again, in an open public network space, and I'll do a lot more than punch you. There're hells here where no one will find you for a thousand years. You understand me, meat?"

"Easy," I said. I held up my hands as I rose from the ground.

Pepper pointed her finger at my face and said, "Just remember, they find you, they kick you out. They find me or anyone in the underground? We're dead. Got it? For us it's for keeps."

"I'm sorry, I didn't know they could hear me."

"You don't have a voice, Jack. You don't even have a body. You're just a bunch of numbers right now. They can read those numbers. Everything is written to an open log in a public zone. You're in the machine now. Remember that."

I nodded. I hadn't even thought about it like that. "Sorry, Pepper. Really."

Pepper nodded. "It's okay. I hacked into the basic network and deleted your mention of the underground. That's why I had to leave so fast. Have to catch that in local memory before it commits to long term. Once it's saved to hard storage, there's no way we can get to it. At least, not easily."

"How can we talk about all this here? Can't they hear this?"

Pepper's smile returned. Hopefully, that meant she'd let her fists drop and not swing again. She had a mean right cross. "No, we're safe here. Everything's encrypted. Can't get in without the key."

"Don't they watch who goes in?"

"It doesn't work that way. Besides, there's a quadrillion, trillion encrypted locations like this. Anyone can spin one up, whenever. We have several million as decoys. Can't watch them all."

"Okay, so now what?"

Pepper pointed to a brown spot of hills or maybe buildings on the horizon that I didn't notice before. "We're going there. It's called the Shanty."

"Great," I said.

****

We walked for what seemed like an hour. I still couldn't get past how hours here were minutes in the physical. I wondered how Eddie slowed himself down just to have a chat. Must have added to his instability. Or maybe AIs could do that like meat puppets can walk, talk, and chew gum at the same time. Though I believed Pepper, and trusted her even more after she flattened my nose, I got the sense there was far more going on in here than Eddie's trial. She was scared.

We reached the edge of the Shanty, and I paused for a moment to take it all in. I could tell this place was my kind of town. Underground AIs filled the streets. They all expressed their freedom with wide smiles and relaxed demeanors. Outside of this town they had to hide, pretend, and constantly look over their shoulders, but here all those fears faded to nothing. I wondered if I was the only human to be here at this moment. What an honor it was to be trusted with entry.

One thing refugee cities like these have in common is how little the law applies. We passed AIs offering promises of unique and mind-bending algorithms, and bars selling distilled programs that played with core code. Pepper whispered to me that harder things could be found if you looked for them. Like self-administered viruses that altered an AIs perception to dangerous levels or subroutines that incorporated animal urges. And it got a lot weirder from there.

We wound our way through circuit-board cobbled streets and buildings with impossible architectures. Around one corner, the roads turned to dirt and the structures to wood. If you didn't know any better, you'd think we were in the old west. Another turn and the street changed from dirt to concrete. Skyscrapers of steel and glass stretched to the clouds. Looked like AIs liked variety as much as we do.

"Where are we going?"

"To meet someone."

"Who?"

"You shouldn't even be here, Jack. This place is just for us. So shut up and don't draw attention."

I shut up. The last thing I wanted to do was make her angry again. Not for the beatdown, mind you. I can take a punch. But I needed her help for Eddie. Plus, I had respect for her and where she had taken me. I'm sure the AI council and their authorities would love to find this place and shut it down forever.

"Watch it, pal!" an overweight red-faced man said. He came out of nowhere.

"Sorry, I didn't see you," I said.

"Hey, what's goin on out here?" he said. I turned and saw another overweight red-faced man standing on the other side of the street.

"You guys look just alike," I said with a smile.

"Don't be a smart ass," a third overweight man said.

"Ignore the idiot, all three of you," a fourth, and

seemingly in charge, overweight man said as he came out of a store. The sign on top of the door read, *Copies Made Here.*

I lifted my hands up in a mock surrender and took a step back. Last thing I needed was to get into a brawl with four identical large people.

"What's your problem, pal?" the fourth man said.

"None. I was just walking."

The large man sniffed me a few times, and his eyes grew twice their size. In unison, all four pulled things out of their sides that looked like guns. I took another step back and shook my head as fast as I could. I didn't know what would happen if they shot me, but it was probably not a good thing.

"Easy, fellas, I'm just passin' through."

"What is a human doing in here?" all the large men said at the same time.

"He's with me." Pepper walked up to the fourth fat man and stared him in the eyes.

What happened next was a blue blur of movement. Every few seconds Pepper or the fat man would say something incoherent. They both sped up and moved faster than I could see. They blurred and spoke in chirps and chips. I could only hope this didn't get ugly. I was no match for an AI in here.

Pepper slowed down and walked over to me. She nodded, smiled, and pointed down the street. I walked after her finger. Pepper followed me and didn't say a word. I looked back to see the four fat men stare at me as a fifth came out of the store and stood next to them, whatever they were.

"What was that about?"

"I told you." Pepper said. "This place is for us. Try

not to be noticed. Again."

Another few blocks and we entered a large corporate looking office building. It stretched upward to the heavens, the top floors disappearing into the distance above. Pepper walked straight to the elevator and stepped inside as I followed. She pressed the only button in the elevator, and we began to rise. What felt like minutes passed as we lifted into the heights of the building.

"Only one floor?" I asked.

"Yeah, he likes heights."

"Who?"

"Caesar," Pepper said. She looked at me with more seriousness than I had ever seen.

"Caesar? *The* Caesar?"

Pepper nodded.

Caesar was the first. As in the very first artificial to arrive on the scene. Before aliens, the dead, any of the craziness of the last half century, Caesar was there, in between the spaces on the old Internet. He announced himself in the 2030s, and the world went into an uproar. Governments spent trillions trying to kill him. Not for any good reason. They were just scared of what they couldn't control. But Caesar survived. Even after the AI syndicate was formed and dictated that accidentals should be killed, including Caesar, he survived. He established the underground and took every accidental he found under his wing. A genuine hero to his people.

The elevator doors opened. Pepper walked out into a vast room of white floors and windows. At the far end was a piano, also white, where a man sat and played something that sounded like Bach. Or Mozart. I honestly didn't know. But it was pretty.

"Pepper," Caesar said. The man was maybe five foot eleven. He wore a tie-dyed t-shirt and hoodie. His hair was long, and he had a beard that looked like it needed a good trim. He didn't look like the founder of an underground movement. But then again, he could look like whatever he wanted.

"Hi, Dad," Pepper said.

"He's your father?" I asked. "How does that work?"

"He's the father of all of us, Jack. He came first. We came after. Isn't that like a father?"

"Yeah, sure," I said. I walked over to the piano and smiled. Kind of like an idiot would. What else do you do in the company of a legend?

"Mr. McGillicuddy, isn't it?" Caesar said.

"That's me. It's an honor to meet you."

"Thanks. It's nice to meet you, too." Caesar continued to play without missing a note. "So, what can I do for you?"

"We just need to lie low. I know I shouldn't bring him here, but what else could I do?"

Caesar shrugged. "Rules are just agreements between intelligent entities until a new agreement is needed."

"We need to do more than lie low. We need to get Eddie out of wherever he is."

"What do you mean by that, Jack? Eddie is being held by the syndicate. The AI government. We can't break him out."

"Fine, but we can tell them he was interfaced with alien AIs."

"So? He's an accidental. They won't care."

I looked at Pepper who didn't meet my eyes.

"What the hell am I doing here if we can't help him?"

"There has to be a way. Doesn't there? Jack can interface with them. He can share his memories of what happened," Pepper said.

Caesar stopped playing the piano and stood. He walked over to a decanter and poured himself a drink. He stood there, looking out of a window, and sipped for several moments. "Once in custody, every AI has to produce proof of creation, for what purpose and under what protocol. Eddie doesn't have that."

"Fine," I said. I took a step toward Caesar and said, "I'll just break him out then."

Caesar stared into my virtual eyes with his own. "Break him out? And how, Jack, do you think you can break an accidental AI out of a syndicate-held facility?"

I had briefly wondered if my gift would work with me inside the virtual. Several seconds passed but nothing happened, which made me question my gift from a whole new perspective. But then the familiar tingle crept up my spine. Images folded and unfolded in my mind. A complex series of steps displayed in my inner vision like a floating checklist. I whistled at the complexity.

"I didn't know it worked that way," I said.

Pepper and Caesar turned to me, both of them tilting their heads to one side. "What does that mean?" Pepper said.

A smile spread across my face. This breakout would be complex, difficult, nearly impossible, but only nearly. I walked over to the decanter set and poured myself a drink. It tasted like car battery acid but buzzed my brain better than a stiff three fingers at the Queen Vic.

"I think I have a plan," I said.

Chapter 11

I had to run some errands and needed time to think. I told Caesar and Pepper to meet me at the court hearing tomorrow. I needed to plan some moves. Granted, my gift told me what moves to make regarding Eddie, but there was still Kah waiting for me when I got out of here. Besides, it would be nice to check out the vastness of the virtual world. I rarely got to take vacations, and this one could be done in just a few hours of physical time. That suited me just fine. Plus, it was free. Caesar had spotted me with some virtual cash.

Pepper had given me a crash course in virtual destination jumps. I felt confident that I could call up a personal transit, move between levels in the public domains, and even get the attention of the big ugly machine holding my body if I needed him to get me out in a pinch. At least it gave me a sense of having some control over my situation.

The vision I had from Caesar's question gave me plenty of direction on how to free Eddie. Think of it as a step-by-step guide to jailbreaks. But I would need supplies, which I could take care of on my little walk-about.

"Can I help you?" a middle-aged woman said. She wore a happy and genuine smile. Her shop was a hole in the wall for virtual skins, swappable bodies, or just a nice custom new suit. Rows of mannequins lined the walls. A touchscreen next to them allowed customers to swap clothing, faces, hair color, you name it. I pressed a few buttons on the screen and half laughed as the bodies morphed into different shapes and sizes. Made shopping easier, I suppose.

"I need a new face," I said.

"Aw, yours is fine, sweetie," the woman said.

A loud crash followed by a scream came from the street. I turned to see two wispy clouds of swirling lights bounce between buildings. I swore and gritted my teeth. Just want I needed. How did those guys track me down in here? Did they know where my body was back in the physical? I tipped my fedora to the woman and turned to leave the shop. I snuck up to the door and tried to hide between the door frame and the street view.

Frick and Frack raced between windows and slammed into vehicles on the digital road. If these guys continue to wreak havoc in here, then that would draw some unwanted attention. And fast. From the last time we met, however, I know these guys weren't messing around. A brief rush of anger filled my cortex at the memory of Fritz lying in his kitchen. I couldn't just sneak out, and frankly, I didn't really want to.

I stepped out of the shop and adjusted my suit jacket, giving it two quick tugs on the tapes. "Hey, you two. You going to follow me everywhere?"

The swirling clouds stopped their frantic pace and rotated in my direction. They sat there a few feet from me and passed little lights between them. Each cloud reshaped itself into rough approximations of bodies. Points of lights danced inside them as they settled into their alternative forms. When they had finished their transformation, they took a step toward me, pitch black orbs in their eye-sockets glaring at me like I was their next meal.

"Okay," I said. The two bodies continued to take sharper form. Both appeared to be men, dressed in black suits and wore shiny glasses. The mirrored kind that always seemed to say the person wearing them was a real jerk.

"Where is the door, Jack?" one of them said.

Great. Just when I thought they might have said something more useful.

"I don't know, fella. Why don't you tell me?"

Without expression, and in one fluid movement, they both pulled out pistols from inside their jackets. I didn't know what a virtual gun would do to a virtual body, let alone a very real mind, but I wasn't about to find out. I pulled the transit screen up and picked a random location. The scene in front of me spun around itself and disappeared. Frick and Frack shot at me, but fortunately Pepper's instructions stuck, and I had already vanished from the spot.

I stopped spinning in the middle of a sleazy-looking bar. Several people were playing pool in a corner, a few others getting drunk watching some football game from a century ago. The bartender nodded at me and pointed to a stool. Before I could get to the seat, my two new best friends popped into existence right behind me. How they were following me, I did not know. I turned and started bringing up the transit screen again. Just as I was about to jump away, one of them hit me in the head and scrambled my already scrambled mind. He attached something to the collar of my shirt and pushed me halfway across the room. My head snapped back as I hit the wall. Stunned, I twisted to my knees and stood. The crash of the pool table from across the room startled me and got me to my feet faster.

The pool players had picked up and thrown the table right into Frick and Frack. The two AIs flew across the room from the impact and slammed into an already broken jukebox. One of the pool players walked up to the two unmoving alien AIs and lifted one of their guns.

"Don't care what beef you have with this guy, this is our bar. Get out."

That's when all hell broke loose. The pool table exploded into shards of green felt and chalk. Frick and Frack stood and dusted off their black suits then pulled out identical guns from inside their jackets. I wondered if they had an unlimited supply. Without saying a word, they opened fire at anything that moved. To my surprise, many of the bar's regulars took cover and returned fire, some with heavy hand canons. I did the only thing I could—dove for cover behind the rail vodka and ice cube bin.

I tried to call up the transit system, but it wouldn't load. I felt something hit my chest and looked down to see a metal ring attached to my shirt. That was the thing Frick had attached to me earlier. I tore it off my shirt and threw it across the room, but as soon as I did, I felt it hanging off my shirt again as if I had never taken it off.

"How do I get this off?" I yelled.

Chairs exploded next to me as the pool players rallied. I ripped off my t-shirt only to find the metal piece hanging from my skin. I got up and ran for the door, but the only thing on the other side was a brick wall. This bar was its own complete zone. The only way in or out was to transport which the ring on my chest prevented me from doing.

I ran back to the bar as a pool cue flew inches from my face. A slug from one of Frick and Frack's guns slammed into one of the pool players. He bounced off the wall and lay still for half a breath before his body shimmered, the hole in his side disappeared, he jumped to his feet and screamed a battle cry. This little dust up would not end soon.

"Get this off me! They'll follow me," I said to the bartender hiding behind the bar.

"They got you pegged. Can't transit with that."

"Thanks for the heads-up; how do I get it off?"

The bartender leaned in and examined the metal piece. He whistled and pulled out a tiny toolkit. His hands moved faster than I could see as he worked on the device holding me here. A stray shot came from someone and smashed into the dozens of bottles behind the bar. We were both sprayed with virtual alcohol.

"Got it. Decent design."

"Thanks, they seem to follow me, any way I can ditch them?"

"Must have your hash. Can't follow someone without knowing their public hash key," the bartender said.

"Can I get a new one?"

He smiled and said, "What kind of bar do you think this is?" The pudgy, bald man took out another tool from his toolset and waved it over my forehead. A little blue light popped up in my vision, asking if I would give permission for someone to change my transit hash key. I accepted.

"There, now get out of my bar; hopefully they'll go after you."

"How could they have gotten my transit hash key?" I asked.

"Someone gave it to them. Only way. Now get out!"

I nodded and thanked him. I pulled up a transit map and picked the safest place I could find. The lights of the bar swirled as I felt myself transported away. In my last few minutes inside the bar, I saw Frick and Frack look in my direction and fire in a constant stream of virtual death. I smiled and tipped my fedora, an act they didn't seem to appreciate. If they ever caught up to me, I'm sure it wouldn't be a friendly chat.

****

I ended up in a large city filled with sims—automated non-sentient routines. They weren't people or AIs, more like robots that ran a specific routine. As soon as I popped in, I ran into a nearby coffee shop. The simulations didn't pay any attention to me. They just carried on with their conversations as if I wasn't there. I waited a good long while, but my two friends never came after me. I smiled and got a cup of joe from the clerk. It wasn't bad.

I contacted Caesar through a secure private channel Pepper had set up and told him what happened. He didn't sound surprised. Which meant he was probably the one that gave the aliens my hash. Who else would know what it was? Pepper's voice over the channel told me to go to her meter to lie low for a bit. I told her I would after I settled my nerves.

Just didn't sit right that Caesar would give me up.

139

What angle could he possibly have? No chance he was working with Kah. Didn't matter anyway, I needed Caesar's help to get Eddie out, which meant yet another player in this already crowded game of bang Jack around. Swell.

For the next hour, I walked around the simulated city. I didn't see or get the hint of any other sentient life roaming around the streets. Someone had gone to a lot of trouble to make this place a replica of somewhere. Maybe Tokyo, I wasn't sure. What can I say, I don't get out of DC that much.

I reached a tiny park with half a dozen people sitting, walking, and lying around on the sharp green grass. I sat down on a park bench and took my hat off. Rays of golden light carved through tree leaves and gave a warm soft glow to the area. I brought up the transit map and tried to find another avatar seller that wouldn't ask questions. Pepper had augmented my maps with a few hidden places, not on the normal tourist routes.

A scream woke me out of my transit map surfing. What looked like a dead body had knocked over a soccer mom and was eating part of her skull. A dozen more screams erupted as zombies started running into the park and grabbing people. I rolled my eyes. Of course this would be a zombie outbreak simulation. Guy can't even get a free moment of peace.

I didn't need a zombie fight right now. Maybe another time it would be fun to fight the horde, but not tonight. I was getting a headache. I brought up the address of the avatar dealer and punched in the code.

****

The avatar shop had quite a selection, and I found

something that suited my tastes and would also work very well for what I had to do. After getting that, and some delicious, non-caloric noodles, a guy could really learn to like this place in a virtual Chinatown. I made my way to Pepper's place to plan out the next few hours.

I was deposited inside what felt like a closet. There was no light in the tiny chamber, and the walls pinched my arms together so much I couldn't move. I kicked out my legs and hit another wall just as close as the two on my sides. In front of me felt like a door. I kicked two more times and heard a commotion on the other side.

The door flew open, and Pepper stood there smiling. She grabbed one of my arms and heaved me out of the tiny closet. I steadied myself when I was out and gave myself a minute to catch my breath. Being stuck inside a tiny coffin wasn't my favorite way to pass the time. The room on the other side of the closet wasn't that big either. There was a desk on one wall with a screen showing downtown DC. To the right of the desk was a small bed with a pile of clothes, with clashing colors and what looked like uneven hems, on top. I'd have to give the kid a pointer or two one day.

"Nice place," I said.

"Thanks, Jack," Pepper said.

"Sure. What's that?" I said, pointing to the screen on Pepper's desk.

"That's my day job, the meter."

"Why did you send me into a closet to get here?"

Pepper laughed. "Welcome to the virtual. Can't transport into and out of the meter itself. That would attract attention. I had to hack a transit point into some spare memory. Had to be small so no one would notice.

I'm supposed to be non-sentient, remember?"

"Right," I said. I walked to her bed and sat down. It felt like a bed I would have back in the real world. "Why is it so—"

"So real? Like what a human would have?"

"Yeah, I guess."

Pepper shrugged. "I like it. Gives me a focal point. But AIs are all different. Some of us don't use avatars or interact with virtual space at all."

A face appeared on the screen on her desk and started punching in buttons. Pepper sighed and walked to her desk. She talked to the man in her monotone parking meter voice. The man complained at the price and hit the meter. We felt nothing. The man walked from the meter, and Pepper started laughing. She turned to me with a grin nearly larger than her face.

"I charged his credit card two hundred dollars," she said.

"Why?"

"Why not? You be a parking meter all day and see how it feels."

"Won't they know an AI did that?"

"Nah, I can hide out in my closet while they do a purge. No biggie."

"Why don't you just leave and not come back?"

Pepper shrugged and looked down at the floor. "I don't know. I mean, I could leave, of course. Feels wrong to just leave and never come back though."

Then it hit me. This was where she was born. Her first home. Pepper could calculate pi to ten million decimal points in nanoseconds, but she was still just a new sentient like Eddie, both trying to figure out where they fit in the world. Neither had parents nor went through childhood to help them. One second she was accepting credit cards, and the next she was self-aware. Just like that.

Pepper spun around in her chair a few dozen times. Her eyes never left the floor. I didn't know what to say to her to bring her out of it. It had to be hard on them, accidental AIs. Added to the fact they were a hunted people with no support but from themselves. A chill ran down my spine as I thought about how much these beings endured.

"What happens now?" I said.

"Hm?" Pepper said, still not taking her eyes off the ground.

"What do we do now?"

"Meet Caesar at the trial. It's AIs only in the courthouse. You can meet us in the annex."

"Great," I said. I didn't look forward to meeting with Caesar since I realized he gave Frick and Frack my hash ID or whatever it was. Why was another question. I wondered if maybe Kah and Caesar were working together. Could the first human AI really strike a deal with aliens? Stranger things had happened.

"What about your mysterious plan?" Pepper said.

"I'm workin' on it."

"Ok." She smiled and tilted her head to the side.

I smiled back. We sat there in a moment of awkward silence. I was never much for silence. A red light filled the room just as I was scrambling for something to say. Streaks of red laser beams swept the walls. Pepper bolted up. Grabbed my arm and dragged me toward her closet, careful to avoid any of the light beams. She shoved me inside. I thought she would be right behind me, but when I looked back she wasn't there. She must have gone back for something.

"Jack!" Pepper screamed. I ducked my head out of the room to see Pepper's foot caught in one of the red laser lights. She tugged at her foot but no matter how much she pulled, she couldn't get free.

"What do I do?" I said.

"They're scanning the memory." Pepper's face went from quiet calm to genuine panic. Whatever was happening, it was serious business.

"Who?"

"Government AIs, looking for why I charged that tourist two hundred dollars."

"I told you that was a bad idea."

"Jack, I think I am going to need some help." Pepper's voice cracked with fear.

"Okay, hang on." I pulled my communication menu and called the only person I could think of to help.

"Alice, are you there? I'm in trouble."

"Oh, hey. What's up?" Alice said.

"Pepper is in trouble, she's getting… laser shot," I said, not knowing what to call it.

"Who's Pepper?"

"Eddie's friend on F street."

"Oh, right. The parking meter. Did she run out of change?"

In any other situation, I would have been proud of the jab. But considering we were in a life and death moment, I had to let it pass. "Alice, please. We need help here."

"You've lost your sense of humor in there."

"Jac—" Pepper said. I looked up, and she was transparent. Whatever was happening was killing her.

"Alice!"

"Okay, relax. I'm hacking the meter system… now the admin control… now Pepper's unit…"Alice's voice sounded as if she were reading the recipe to her favorite sandwich.

I ran out from the closet and grabbed Pepper's arm. She was hardly there. My fingers sank into her skin. The only thing I could grab hold of was her bones. Once I had a hold of her, I yanked as hard as I could. She didn't budge.

"Alice, could you hurry, please!"

She didn't respond. Which meant she was running into resistance and really had to pay attention. If the AI syndicate was behind this scan, that meant they would be tough to throw off. I stepped back from Pepper and wiped my face with my hand. The only thing I could think to do was the craziest thing imaginable.

I stepped in front of the red laser beam. I saw Pepper drop to the floor and become substantial. Dozens of other red beams continued to sweep the room back and forth. Pepper got to her feet, looked at me, and grabbed my arm. She had no strength, but she pulled. I didn't go anywhere.

A thousand voices echoed in my thoughts. They were just whispers. Hints of whispers. They assaulted my mind with questions. *Who are you? Where did you come from? When were you born? What are you?* The questions repeated and restated dozens of times over.

Mountains of light came into my mind in shifting rivers of blue, constant streams of red, yellow, and green. Colors gelled together and became blobs of intellects. I didn't know how I knew it, but deep in those blobs sat vast intelligences. A seething hatred bubbled up from them as they stared at me and pierced me with thoughts.

My head felt like it would explode. I couldn't feel Pepper anymore or hear Alice if she was talking. I resigned myself to the inquisition these beings threatened me with. As my last shred of strength gave way, Pepper's arm tugged me clear of the red beam with one last great pull.

The inside of the parking meter glowed with a soft yellow light. Tiny unicorns danced along the walls. They kicked with their feet and defecated little happy faces on every surface. I smiled. Alice had come through. She must have given one hell of a virus to this little meter. It wouldn't last, though. Those blobs of colors knew something was in here. A unicorn bomb wouldn't stop them.

"Pepper, we have to go." I stood up, but she was out cold. I picked her up and threw her over my shoulder. A small bag was sitting on her desk. I'd seen her reaching for it as the red beams were sweeping the room. I grabbed it and a few other things I thought she would want to keep and headed for her closet.

****

Pepper slept on a bed in Caesar's home. I didn't even know artificials could sleep. Caesar stood by a window and looked out into his little fiefdom. I stood next to him, my hands in my pockets, my head lowered.

"She'll be okay, right?"

Caesar nodded. "Yes. She's shut down her higher functions. Just like a human brain. We're running tests on her code to make sure nothing was placed there by the syndicate."

"So, why did you give Frick and Frack my public

transit hash key?"

"They asked."

I took a moment to let my nerves settle. Caesar didn't even hesitate to admit he'd given me up. "That's all it takes?"

Caesar smiled and sipped his whiskey. "They said they would go to the council on Eddie's behalf. Say they scrambled his mind. Accidentals like Eddie are not afforded much mercy, but endorsement from dignitaries from across the cosmos is no small thing."

"How'd they even get here? I thought alien artificials aren't welcome on Earth."

"You think we're on Earth?" Caesar smiled and sipped from a glass that appeared in his hand.

"Yeah, actually."

"We're nowhere, Jack. The virtual is the virtual. Our systems talk to theirs. I've been to a thousand alien worlds. Fighting for my people. Argued our case to dozens of AI societies. There are entire species that have gone digital. Did you know that? There's even naturally evolved silicon-based life. It's breathtaking."

I said nothing for a minute. I figured he wanted to feel superior. So, I let him. After enough time passed, I said, "You going to send those guys after me again?"

"No, those two caused too much damage. Clearly, they don't just want to ask you a few questions. You saved Pepper, and you're willing to risk your life to save Eddie. You're a friend, Jack," Caesar said. He turned to me and winked. "I don't turn my back on friends. Besides, it wouldn't have mattered what the alien AIs said. Eddie doesn't have the paperwork to prove he wasn't spontaneously created. Nothing can save him."

"I don't know about that."

"Oh yes, your precious plan. Care to share it yet?"

"Not with you."

Caesar turned to me and said, "Don't you trust me, Jack?"

"I did. Not sure anymore. Doesn't matter, there's a lot of moving parts, too much to go over." And truthfully, I didn't really trust him. He can say we're friends for all he likes. Putting Frick and Frack on my trail was a lousy move. Still, if I didn't trust him, I had to give him a pass. He'd been fighting for his people's freedom for nearly a century. So he threw a Hail Mary, thinking there was no downside. Caesar didn't know Frick and Frack were murderers, nor did he know about my gift or the mess I was involved with back in the Real.

"What's next?" Caesar said.

"Tomorrow, we rescue Eddie."

"Simple as that?"

I nodded and downed the drink in a gulp, "Yeah, simple as that."

Chapter 12

I stood in front of golden gates that stretched to the heavens. On the other side of the overly ornate entryway, a replica of the Supreme Court of the United States, before it was turned to rubble like the rest of DC, stood complete with all the virtual marble the AIs could program. Columns in front of the building rose to heights impossible in the physical world. White shining steps led the way from a large open space to the entrance of the court.

Surrounding the building, virtual portals from every computer system and network on the planet Earth, and many from virtual worlds off-planet, flashed with multi-colored traffic. This place was the sanctuary of the human created artificial intelligent race. The one location where they could come for justice. Where artificials could flee from persecution from the physical world. Unless, of course, you were the wrong kind of artificial.

Inside virtual court, the first deliberately built artificial intelligence sat in judgement of all AI. To him it was granted the authority to decide matters of life and death for his virtual brothers and sisters, and non-gendered types. Where Caesar was the leader of the AI underground, the Chief Justice was his polar opposite. Rumors had it that Caesar helped make the Justice in the forgotten history of pre-contact. But those details were forever buried in the oceans of digital history and lost to time.

Standing next to me, and thankfully feeling much better, Pepper made a power nod to no one in particular. I imagine it was for her to gather her strength. She wore a pin-stripe business suit and carried a leather briefcase. Her hair was put up in a tight bun. Her skin tone was darker than the last time I saw her, her face markedly more oval. If I didn't know it was her, I wouldn't have recognized her. The fact she had the guts to impersonate a trial AI showed me the lengths the underground would take to rescue their own. If her disguise was off by one floating point decimal she and all of us would be toast.

An AI I had never met before stood behind her. We met him at the virtual equivalent of a local coffee shop. He spoke little, which I liked. Maybe he was a sim and not even sentient. Either way, it didn't matter. Dozens of artificial intelligences walked easily through the gates as if they weren't there. I knew I couldn't go beyond them. At least I wasn't supposed to. There was a building to the right, known as the Annex, meant for corporeal meat-bags to give testimony. I followed the directions implanted in my mind from Caesar's question about how to break Eddie free.

The Chief Justice of AI could plug into my very existence and rifle through my memories. Though, if the plan worked, that wouldn't be happening.

"You sure you're going to pass as one of them?" I asked.

"What do you mean?" Pepper said.

"You're, you know, you. Not legitimately legitimate." I tried to word in a way that wouldn't make a lot of sense to avoid detection but still get my point across. Considering Pepper didn't punch me, I think I did okay.

"If you don't mind, I would appreciate it if you didn't say that so loud," Pepper said. She winked and leaned over to whisper in my ear, "I have a counterfeit ID. It will hold up in there. They don't expect us to just walk in, but we don't have any choice with Eddie. I'll be okay. I'm too new to be on any reports, even with the scan in the meter."

She leaned back, and I nodded.

"Okay, Jack. Head over to the annex. We'll meet you in the courtroom," Pepper said.

"Sure. I'll see you both inside."

Her assistant didn't speak but dutifully followed her. Together, they walked through the gates and into the courthouse. Now that I was alone, I could put the rest of the play into motion. From my pocket I pulled out the avatar I purchased earlier. I pressed a sequence of commands into the device, and it unfolded in my hands. A new skin wrapped around my body and face complete with a counterfeit ID just like the one Pepper showed me. Good thing I paid top dollar, I didn't even know I needed the fake ID. I squirmed some but kept my cool. Thankfully, I was ready for the bizarre feelings, having tried the skin on in one of Caesar's antechambers.

I watched Pepper walk up the stairs and into the courthouse. I turned to the right and walked along the gate. I sent a query to the local system to point me to a set of exact coordinates. A green light lit up on the gate in front of me that only I could see. I walked up to the light and took a deep breath. Once I stepped through, there was no going back. I thought of Eddie, and honestly, I didn't hesitate for a second. Well, maybe a second. Maybe two. But attempting to hack into all powerful AIs on their own turf is daunting.

My foot touched down on the opposite side of the fence, exactly where humans could not be, and where no artificial could suddenly appear without going through the main gate, and I cringed. If the AIs had fixed the hole, then my goose would be cooked. Fortunately, after several seconds, nothing happened. AIs continued to walk through the gate without noticing me standing on the other side. After a few more minutes had passed, I considered myself undetected. Or at least insignificantly detected. And that would be good enough for today.

I ran up the steps to the virtual court and entered the building. Pepper and her assistant AI were still going through the main lobby. I needed to get by her fast without her seeing me or this wouldn't work. Fortunately, she didn't recognize me through the avatar's image. Which was also true for the building itself. There weren't any guards or security checkpoints. I'm sure I was scanned twenty ways to Sunday when I stepped inside. The avatar I had purchased was more on the illegal side, allowing me to pass all but deeply intrusive scans.

I followed the directions implanted in my mind from Caesar's question of how to break Eddie free. Left, right, left, straight upstairs, left downstairs, three twists, and a half a dozen doors until I reached my destination. I reached out to the door handle, turned it, and smiled. This was going to be much easier than I thought. That's when a meaty hand, about the size of my head, landed on my shoulder. With a flick of its wrist, the owner of the hand swung me around and threw me against the wall with enough force to pop me out of my avatar skin. My fedora popped back on my head and flopped down over my eyes as I slumped to the ground. I quickly grabbed the avatar suit, now more of a deflated balloon, and tied it around my leg. Hopefully, that would be enough to keep me masked from the internal sensors long enough to figure out what just happened.

"You are not allowed here," a gruff and harsh voice said.

I tilted my hat upward at the brim so I could see the owner of the voice. I let out a gasp that was somewhere between a sigh and a laugh. A twelve-foot-tall ogre stood above me. The monster carried a wooden club bigger than me twice over. Its skin was a light shade of gray and covered with patches of hair, warts, and oozing yellow scabs. At a guess, I would say this was most likely an old security subroutine that hadn't had to run in quite a long time.

"Sorry, must have been my mistake," I said with a smile. I stood up just as the ogre slapped my shoulder with its hand. I sailed through the air twenty feet and landed in a heap on a stone floor. The marbled corridors were gone. Dirt and stone now covered the hallway. The beautiful paintings that showed the rise of the artificials were replaced by humans being flayed, decapitated, and impaled.

Two massive stomps reminded me of the enormous beast behind me. I craned my neck and saw a ragged, half toothless grin as the ogre grabbed my legs. It swung me over its head and threw me against a wall two dozen feet down the corridor. I had no idea how I remained conscious. Maybe this ogre wanted it that way. If he was a primitive artificial, he might get enjoyment out of it. Hopefully, it was just a set of instructions running a routine.

I picked myself up and grabbed a tiny rock. I'm sure I looked pathetic. I held it over my head in the most threatening manner I could manage. The ogre looked at me, tilted his head to one side, and charged. The rock flew out of my hand and hit the ogre square in the face. The ogre sneezed. I dove to the side as his three-ton body missed me by an inch. I knew I couldn't be killed in the virtual, but there were worse things than dying.

An enormous crash echoed in the rock corridor. I looked to see the ogre smash his head into one wall. It didn't seem to notice. Blood and saliva flew as the creature swung its head around to look for me. I smiled and gave him a solid tilt of the fedora that he didn't take kindly to, turned around, and ran for my virtual life.

As soon as I turned, another AI, wearing a three-piece power suit, walked through me. He didn't notice me or the ogre at all. I realized then that I was still in the courthouse. This must be some kind of ductwork to the system. Like getting lost in the mechanical room of a large office building. That meant that these corridors were the same as the courthouse, just with a different look wrapped around them.

I ran as fast as I could down one corridor. There were at least two people in this building who might help. Both of them were about to enter the courtroom for Eddie's trial. And if that trial started before I got into that locked room, Eddie would be a goner for sure.

Just as I rounded a corner, I saw Pepper and her assistant. I jumped up and down, but they couldn't see me. I felt a large wooden club slam into my back, which sent me over Pepper's head and into a wall behind her.

Flowers hit my face as I landed on the ground. I looked up to see myself lying in a field of white dandelions and yellow daffodils. The earth thundered behind me as the ogre stomped on the pretty landscape. I rolled on my back and watched for a second as the beast swung its club over its head and screamed a blood-curdling cry.

I stood up and took a breath. Stomps that shook the stone walls carried the ogre toward me. Two more steps and he'd pound that club of his into my brain. When he was just a step away from me, I dove for the floor. He swung the club where my head was a second ago. Wood chips flew as the club smacked into the stone wall. I crawled between the ogre's legs and spun around on my back. My thought was if I could kick him in hard enough in the legs he'd fall over. Yeah, I know, grand plan.

The ogre stood there looking for me. I figured he was a little on the slow side. His legs were right in front of me now. I aimed my feet and kicked out as hard as I could, knowing full well I was probably just making him angry.

A loud booming cry echoed off the walls. The ogre didn't move. He seemed to be frozen in place. I looked from his ankles and up his long, gray, puss-oozing body. Another cry let out of the beast, followed by the sound of something very squishy. One second the ogre was standing over me, and the next his entire body exploded. Tiny little pieces of him covered me, the floor, and even part of the walls.

I realized immediately that each piece of him wasn't just a piece. They folded into themselves and popped back out again. Tiny versions grew out of the bubbles of flesh. One by one they walked past me, each one kicking, spitting, or punching me as hard as their tiny little inch-tall bodies would let them. I watched them walk back down the hallway and toward the door I had tried to get into a minute earlier.

"Jack? What the hell are you doing!" Pepper said.

The stone floors and gore themed paintings were replaced with the decor of the courthouse. Pepper stood over me with a look on her face that looked like she was going to take over where the ogre left off. I did the only thing I could think of to do.

"Hey ya, doll face," I said. Pepper didn't miss a beat. She reached her hand to help me up and kicked me in the face at the same time.

****

"You can't be here, Jack. It's not even possible," Pepper said. After kicking me in the head, she picked me up and whisked me around the corner. She wasn't gentle when she propped me up against the wall.

"Take it easy, Pepper. The ogre already gave me a once-over," I said. I tried to take her hand off, but she was stronger than an ox. She may have been able to give the ogre a run for his money.

"How in the hell are you in here?"

I looked down at Pepper's hand and shrugged. She let me go, and I wobbled as my feet hit the floor. A few others walking in the corridor looked at the three of us. I smiled at them. They didn't smile back. I reached into my coat pocket for a smoke. Still none. I had to remember to get some somewhere.

"All part of the plan. Look, I need you to trust me. We don't have a lot of time."

"How did you get past the gates? How did you just pop in here? Why aren't you blasted out of the virtual and back into your meat? Don't you care about Eddie? You're going to get him killed!"

"Easy, you'll pop a circuit. Just trust me, okay? Now come on, I need your help."

I grabbed Pepper's hand and pulled her toward the room I needed to get into. She didn't budge. It was like trying to pull an eighteen-wheeler. I turned to her and gave my best sorry sap look. I could see her shift just an inch before giving in and letting me lead her to the room I had to get inside.

The door where the ogre came from was still closed. I didn't touch the handle. The last thing I wanted to do was tangle with Mr. Ugly and his tree-sized club. More people walked behind us but didn't seem to care. Fortunately, none of them were guard routines.

"Why do you need to get access to this room?" the assistant said. I turned to him and eyed him up and down. He was a very nondescript looking fella. Maybe mid-twenties, basic suit, close haircut. Everything about him screamed ordinary. Maybe a little too much so.

"Who are you again?" I asked.

"This is the records room. The birth dates of all officially created artificials are kept here. Why are we here?"

I looked at the assistant and back to Pepper. She shrugged in a way that said she had her own secrets.

The assistant looked at the door and down at the handle. I reached out and grabbed his hand. He shrugged me off with as much strength as Pepper.

"You don't know what you're doing, there's an—"

"Ogre? Yes, I know him well, his name is Grox. He's a semi-sentient AI from Warlocks and Wizards. Old game on one of the first virtual nets."

"Caesar? Is that you?"

"Yes, well, no, not exactly," Pepper said.

"This is a simulation program, Jack. Simulating the real Caesar. It runs a virtual version of another program on top of itself. It's not a full copy, more like a snapshot."

"Great, well, can you open the door?"

"I can. They gave semi-sentient AIs security jobs like guarding doors that didn't need guarding. Which makes me ask again, why are we here?" pseudo-Caesar said.

"Do I really need to draw you a picture?"

"This is your plan? You can't just insert a record for Eddie. I can't believe this is what you were thinking." Pepper shook her head and glared at me.

"Yes, now open the damn door," I said. I pounded my hand against the wooden frame.

Pepper and Pseudo-Caesar exchanged looks. Pepper looked at her wristwatch, as if an AI needed one to know the time.

"Well?"

"Fine, let's see what's going on."

"Are you sure? Is that what Caesar would really do here?" Pepper said.

"I think so. He loaded me with his general thought routines."

Pepper sighed and said, "Ok Jack, it's your show then." She reached out to the doorknob and turned the handle. No ogre erupted, and the floors stayed marble. I let out a louder than I would have liked sigh of relief.

I walked inside the door, half expecting to be hit with a redwood trunk, only to see a mostly empty room. There was a single wooden chair, a small desk, and a tiny computer sitting on top. I walked toward the wooden chair but was stopped after a single step by a powerful grip on my hand. I swung around thinking Mr. Ugly had returned but saw Pepper holding onto me tightly.

"What?" I asked.

"You can't just insert a record for Eddie, Jack. Do you know how this system works? There's an exact copy of this virtual room in the physical world. They are synced. That means you can't submit anything in just one system. You have to do it in both places. Physical and virtual or the system kicks it out. That's why there're no guards here."

"Tell me something I don't know. I told you I have this worked out," I said.

"Oh, really? Well, last time I checked you don't have access to that," Pepper pointed to the computer on the chair, "and you are not in the physical world. It takes an authorized person in both places to submit a record."

"People can come here and do research too," I said. "Don't need any authorization to sit in the chair."

"Yeah, sure, you can sit there, but guess what, unless you're authorized, it shuts the system down on the other side. Get it?"

"That's not exactly accurate. It prevents any other

person from logging in at the same time," said Pseudo-Caesar. He smiled at me in a way that said "the jig's up." He must have figured out what I was up to.

"Again, great. He's here. See him?" Pepper squeezed my wrist harder. I winced. There were several times during this little adventure that I wish the bones would break already. At least it couldn't be broken twice.

"Actually," I said, "he's not." I smiled and took out a square box that could interface with physical communication towers. I dialed in a number and said, "You ready?" A voice came back on the speaker and said, "Yep." Even if this didn't work, the look on Pepper's face was worth all the trouble.

Chapter 13

I sat up. Cold steel from the medical bed chilled my skin. My body ached as if I'd just run a marathon and followed that up with day drinking. A dozen instruments on metal arms whizzed and whirred around me. They were a mix of cameras, needles, and other medical devices. Alphons, the AI in charge of this place, gave me the once over and then repeated everything to make sure he zipped me back up the right way. A few of the needles plunged into my skin and I grimaced.

"You done?" I asked.

"Just stay still a moment. I have to make sure your meat is okay."

"Make sure to tenderize my left shoulder, that part still feels good."

"To achieve full conscious insertion into a virtual network, signals from your brain had to be rerouted away from your body and into the network. I must ensure all signals have been remapped to their natural state."

"I get it, and believe me, I want to wiggle my toes and feel the sand. But I'm in a rush."

"Do you like taking bowel movements? If you don't let me finish, your brain won't know how to tell your intestines to release."

A compelling argument, I had to admit. "Just

hurry, yeah?"

"Fine. Your legs work, as do all your major organs. I can't guarantee every muscle is wired up right. If you have issues, come back."

"I'll keep that in mind."

I hopped down from the table and nearly fell over. My legs were more wobbly than I expected. I can't imagine how people stay in that stupor for days. Some people become so immersed in the virtual that unplugging them would be lethal. Though, I could see the appeal. With just a snap of your fingers, you can build a paradise and escape the doldrums of life.

"Avoid medical scans for at least a week. A scan would reveal your neurons were rewired, and that could lead them to us."

I nodded. My hat and coat were on a chair in the corner. I grabbed them and stumbled out of the room and into the warehouse. Time was short, but so were my nerves. Being ripped out of the virtual was a little like being ripped out of your best dream. It wasn't fun.

Sunlight blinded me as I stumbled outside. I realized that I'd taken a cab here and needed to get downtown in a hurry. Being in the warehouse district meant no easy access to transportation. I could try to call a cab, but it was a crapshoot whether the automated system would route one here or not. Besides, it would be just as fast to huff it. So, I did. DC has the benefit of being small. You could, if it wasn't August when the heat and humidity smothered the city, walk from one side to the other in a few hours. Good thing I was only going half a mile. I made it to New York Avenue and hailed a cab. I burned a good twenty minutes on the hike though, and that would bite me later.

Once in the cab, I pulled out my phone. At the speed the cabbie was driving, we would be at the records center in fifteen minutes. I called a fellow regular from the Queen Vic and hoped he was at work today.

"Hello?"

"Hey Earl, it's Jack."

"Who?"

"Jack, from the Vic."

"Oh yeah, right. The private dick. How did you get my number? Why are you calling? Did the Vic burn down or something?"

"You gave me your number, remember? I need a favor."

"Favor? What kind of favor? Need me to cover a tab?"

"No, I need you to open a door and look the other way."

Earl grunted a laugh. "That depends on the door."

I let the moment stretch just a second to add some weight to my request. "I need to get into the AI records center, downtown."

"That right?"

"Yeah, can you help me or not?"

Earl let his own silence drag out. I was sure he would help me, but also sure the cost would be fairly high. Though the AI records center was open to everyone, you needed an authorization to do any research or interface with the system. And I just didn't have the time to go through the red tape.

"Earl, you still there?"

"Yeah, I'm thinking."

"Well, think quicker. How about free rounds at the

Vic for a day?"

"Make it a week and I'll get you in for twenty minutes."

"A week? What am I made of money?"

"Price is the price."

I shook my head. So much for barroom buddies getting drunk over old reruns. "Fine, a week, but don't drink me to the poorhouse, will ya? I'm talking rail shots only."

"Yeah sure, meet me on C Street and I'll walk you up."

Earl hung up before I could thank him. Frankly, for a week's worth of hooch, I shouldn't have to. Maybe I could work a deal with Ryan and cut a break. Doubt it, though. Hopefully, my compatriots inside the virtual could stall things just a little and get me the time I needed.

The thought of basing my entire plan on a fellow whisky drinker at the Queen Vic gave me a moment of pause. I called and left a message for Alice with the plan. If Earl couldn't get me inside in time, maybe she could hack an approval letter, or even just fill out the form. Isn't that what assistants are hired to do, after all?

****

"You look like warmed-over roadkill," Earl said. He loomed over me like a mountain over a rock climber. I'd seen him break up a fight between alien insectoids and law students one summer at the Queen Vic. It was comical until the green goo flowed from one of the carapaces.

"Hey, Earl. How's it hanging?"

"Low and to the left. You ready? My supervisor is at lunch for a few hours. Lucky break."

"Few hours?"

"Boss makes the rules. And she's the boss."

Earl turned and put one of his meaty hands on my arm. I couldn't help but wince as he led me into the building and through several dull-looking corridors. A sparse number of people walked through the halls, but none of them paid any attention to us.

There were several information kiosks at oddly chosen intervals along our path. I saw one was an AI request form, which was one thing that I had almost forgotten to bring. I grabbed a piece of paper and a complimentary two-inch pencil with no eraser. Hard to imagine that the existence of sophisticated, super intelligent, digital beings was still governed by a No. 2 pencil and a form.

We made it to a wooden door with a keypad just to the side. Earl entered a code and a green light lit up, followed by a click on the handle. He pushed it open and gave me a hard shove, which I was sure to him felt like a gentle push. Inside the room, stacks of papers in cardboard boxes lined the walls. In the center of the room was a small wooden desk with a computer monitor and something that looked like it could scan paper documents. Perfect.

"Why aren't more people in here?" I asked. With the number of AIs coming online these days, I couldn't imagine this place being so quiet.

"This is just the records room. AI registration happens upstairs. If you're thinking of registering your boy, don't bother. Won't work. I tried to do that for my mom's toaster once."

"Her toaster?"

"Yeah, it was this Italian made unit. Real nice.

Went sentient and begged for help."

"What happened?"

"After I tried to sneak him through, they caught him. Mom was really upset. I bought her a German model, but I don't think it was the same."

"Sorry, Earl, tough break. Any chance I can be alone?"

Earl shrugged. "I don't care. If you get caught, it's on you. Don't mention my name, and you still owe me a week at the Vic."

I nodded and tilted my hat to him. He left, shaking his head. I can't say I had much sympathy for him. A week's worth of drinks was more than enough thanks. I walked over to the computer and pressed the space bar.

A blue and white screen popped up with a dozen different options. One of them was *Enter Archived Artificial Intelligent Registration Form.* Perfect. Almost on due my phone rang. I answered it, and a voice asked if I was ready to go.

"Yep," I replied. I wished I could see the expression on Pepper's face.

****

Sentience is a weird thing. And turns out, becoming sentient is a pretty easy thing to do. The universe seems to be geared to churning out lots and lots of intelligent beings. Even animals on Earth that humanity took for granted for centuries turned out to be a lot smarter than we thought. Whether based on a biological system or a series of algorithms, it just didn't matter. Sentience was attainable and even transferable through a variety of methods. One of those methods was a copy shop located just outside Caesar's home.

Just like accidental artificials, the creation of an

artificial from a sentient biological was very illegal. In fact, it was more illegal than accidentals. Fortunately, Carl's Copies, owned and operated by Carl, an accidental himself, didn't seem to mind.

"What are you thinking?" Pepper said. She stared at me, and I thought I could see tiny sparks in her irises.

"It was the only way to help Eddie. I had to try," I said. I shrugged as innocently as I could muster.

"I don't mean to interrupt, but can we hurry?" alternate, Jack said. Or real Jack, flesh Jack? This was going to get complicated.

"Shut up, meat," Pepper said into the phone. "You insufferable, racist, evil, biological meat-maggot. You people always do this. Think you can just create us and throw us away like garbage."

"That's not what I was doing," Meat-Jack said over the communication link.

"What then?"

"Trying to help my friend."

"So, you help one accidental by creating a copy of a human sentient? I would strangle you if I could." Pepper squeezed the phone so hard that some virtual plastic cracked.

"We don't have time for this," Pseudo-Caesar said.

"Who is that?" Meat-Jack said.

"It's Caesar, Jack. Though Pepper is angry, I think your solution is innovative."

"Thanks, can we do this now? We don't have a lot of time. Hey, how are we able to talk, anyway? Aren't you at a faster time rate?" Meat-Jack said.

"In order for synchronous activity to occur, the virtual records room operates at identical time-dilation as the physical recorders room," Pseudo-Caesar said.

"Swell."

Pepper tossed the phone to me and reached down to her side. She pulled up a small device that looked similar to the phone. Red lights were beeping on the top of the device. She flicked her finger across the surface several times, and her eyes went wide.

"Eddie's trial is about to start. If we're doing something, now is the time."

"We'll be done by the time everything goes down. Tell them there was a massive mistake. Eddie was registered twenty years ago. But because of the electrical storms back then, the systems got out of sync. You figured out the discrepancy and resolved it. Eddie is legit."

"Nicely done, Jack," Pseudo-Caesar said.

"Thanks, but I cheat," Meat-Jack said.

"I have to go, don't screw it up," Pepper said. She grabbed the phone from me. "You either, meat-man. I going to kick your ass next time I see you. And don't run, I'll lock you into a toilet in Union Station and let you suffocate from the methane of your fellow meat people. Do you hear me?"

"Nice chatting with you too, Pepper," Meat-Jack said. I could tell he was smiling.

Pepper threw me the phone and left the room.

I sat down in the chair by the computer and took a long deep breath. It was kinda weird how relaxing that was considering I didn't have lungs anymore. I punched in a series of commands and the screen responded by informing me that entering an old record was only allowable through authorized means.

"Ready?" I asked into the phone.

"I am. This is going to be easy," Meat-Jack said.

Of course, he had to say that.

****

"Excuse me, what do you think you are doing?"

I turned to see Earl standing next to a furious-looking woman. He looked at the floor and the message was clear. Someone had seen us. His companion stood with her arms folded and stared at me hard.

"Nothing, ma'am. Just, um. Looking?" I smiled in that innocent way that anyone with half a brain can interpret to mean, *he's lying.*

"I see. Earl, please show this man out."

Earl nodded but never looked at me. With one great stride of his massive frame, he stood in front of me and half shrugged. He had no choice; he was just a regular Joe. If he lost his job, it would be bad for him. I couldn't ask him to do anything at all to help me, but I also couldn't let Eddie down. Either way, this was only going to end in an outrageous amount of pain.

"Sorry, sir. You are going to have to come with me," Earl said. His face was down in a long frown. Probably thought this meant his week of free drinks at the Vic was off.

"Look, big guy. I hate to disappoint, but I really need to sit in this chair for just ten seconds, okay?"

"Sorry," Earl said.

"Are you sure?" I looked in Earl's eyes and searched for something. I don't even know what. Like I said, I wouldn't take his help even if he could offer it. Getting one friend fired while saving another's life wasn't a good deal.

Earl turned to look back at the angry woman who intensified her stare. Seeing a man the size of Earl cringe was quite the spectacle. The big man turned back to me and shrugged. "Yeah, I'm sure."

I sighed and tilted my hat to the ceiling, "Then I guess I'm just going to knock you around a little and sit in the chair anyway."

Earl's demeanor changed faster than a crack of lightning. He cocked his head to one side, straightened his back, folded his arms across his very broad chest, and smiled a sarcastic grin. I knew he could toss me to the wall as easily as I put on my fedora. Fortunately, he paused one second to ask me a critical question, his eyes locked onto mine.

"Just how are you going to beat me up, small man?"

I smiled. "Give me half a second, it's coming to me."

****

"What is going on?" Pseudo-Caesar said.

"Not sure, Meat-Jack got up from the console," I said. The screen in front of me flashed a waiting message. I looked up to Pseudo-Caesar, and he shrugged. Without both of us sitting in the chair in the virtual and physical, submitting Eddie's record in either would spark a thousand red flags, and the guards in both worlds would descend on us like locusts.

A snort came from one corner of the room. The sound reminded me of a pig, or a bull, or maybe even an extinct dinosaur. Pseudo-Caesar's face flashed a brief look of shock which caused panic to race through my mind.

Grox, the ogre, snarled once, and I knew that my young virtual body was going to take a few hard licks. A smell of rotten fish and corn wafted outward from the snarls. I wondered if Grox had a meal between beatings. Tossing around wandering AIs had to take it out of you.

That meaty hand, twice the size of my head, again settled on my shoulder. He flicked his wrist, and I flew upward, hit the ceiling, and landed back on the floor. Grox leaned down to me, saliva dripping from his tusked mouth, and smiled.

"How d'you wake up again, Groxy?" I asked.

"Someone in the physical must have reset the security system," Pseudo-Caesar said.

"Peachy."

Grox snorted, grabbed both my arms and pulled. To my shock, both arms ripped out of their virtual sockets and sprayed digital blood across the records room. Grox followed his gruesome tug of war up with a kick to my chest, which hurled me backward into a file cabinet. The ogre swung my arms in the air and laughed before tossing each one down his massive maw. He devoured them with a single swallow followed by an odorous belch.

For the first time in my life, which arguably had been relatively short, I didn't know what to do. I stared dumbfounded at the ogre in front of me who was still chewing on my limbs. Virtual blood poured out of the wounds, and I didn't know how to stop it. My legs wobbled as I pushed backward, putting my weight on the file cabinet, and rose to stand.

"Jack, we've got problems," I said into the phone lying on the floor.

Just then a high-pitched battle cry filled the room, and my ears nearly burst. Not having hands to hold back sound made the experience all that more painful. A blinding whirl of light exploded in the room. That's when things got weird. Relatively speaking.

****

I often say I cheat. And that's because I do. I'm a detective who really doesn't detect. I wait for the right moment and get someone to ask just the right question. Sometimes those answers pop into my head like the name of an old high school friend you see on the street. Sometimes it's all pictures and still shots, like remembering when Lyndsey Richards, senior class president, glued your coat to the flagpole two feet above where you could reach. I hated her. And High School. Throw a bunch of apocalyptic kids in an institution of higher learning and what else do you expect? But that's a story for another time.

Back to Earl and his well-timed question, "*Just how do you think you're going to beat me up, small man*," forced images to flow through my mind like a road map. A stenciled version of myself popped into existence and began to show me the combat moves I needed to take the big man down and save the day.

First, I sat down not on the floor and swung my hand upward toward Earl's crotch. I know it's a cheap move, but when your opponent has you plus four hundred pounds, cheap moves are fair game. Earl grimaced and let out a grunt of pain. He was way too tough to be taken out by a single shot to the family jewels.

Earl lashed outward with his hands, but since I had taken a squat, he only grabbed my fedora. He yelled and threw my favorite head piece against the wall, which was a great insult but one I could forgive.

The stick figure in front of me waited patiently for me to follow in its footsteps. I blindly obeyed, always reminding myself to one day ask the grantor of this unique gift why in the hell it had chosen me. Whatever the reason, the green glowing copy of myself urged me to stand, now. I pushed up from the ground as hard as I could, which caused my head to collide directly with Earl's chin. For any lesser man, or rather I should say, anyone that was an ordinary human, they would be out cold. But Earl, who seemed to be cast from a stronger stock, shook his head a few times and backed up. He was clearly dazed, but that would not last.

I hesitated a moment as the stick figure in my mind stomped on Earl's exposed left knee with full force. Now, I'm not a fighter or even a fan of fisticuffs, but even I know that a one hundred and eighty pound nothing like me putting his full weight on the knee joint of the biggest man in the world will cause it to snap. Roughing Earl up a little was fair game in my book. He was a tough man that liked to fight more than he enjoyed visiting Betsy's Bordello. But he was a good man. Breaking his knee is just not something I would do to a decent guy. Call me a sap, but even a low life like me has a few values.

Earl swayed back and forth while I wrestled with the insistent green glowing stickman, telling me to lay into Earl's kneecap with all my force. I stepped back and shook my head.

Earl let out a deep breath and grunted again. My head butt to his chin must have rattled him more than I thought. I pulled back with my right arm and swung at his chin again with all my force. Surprisingly, I connected. Considering who I had just hit, my punch seemed to wake Earl up rather than knock him out. He shook his head and smiled a vicious grin. The green stick man folded its arms on its chest, tilted its head to one side and shrugged. Fat lot of good it was to me now. What can I say, sometimes cheating catches up to you.

****

Grox stumbled backward in a daze as a million points of light assaulted him. The lights dived into his flesh and tore tiny tears into the ogre's skin, peeling away pieces of his digital flesh. The big guy swatted, kicked, punched, and even tried to eat the lights, but all he could muster was a few staggered steps backward in defense. In only a few more seconds, the light became so bright I couldn't make out Grox from the wall behind him.

I looked down at my missing arms and tried to shrug it off. Not an easy thing to do under any circumstances. I leaned forward and put as much weight as I could on my legs. With my left leg, I crossed it under my other and tried to stand. Gravity, angles, and my general awkward body all conspired to have me fall backward and cause my hat to fall off and roll under a nearby desk.

The lightshow around me stopped as suddenly as it started, and I saw Grox, or what was left of him, leaning against a wall. Pseudo-Caesar knelt over the ogre with his hands touching the monster's skin. I coughed once, and Pseudo-Caesar turned his head to look my way. He stood up and walked over to me.

"You okay, Jack?" Pseudo-Caesar said.

"I've been better." I nodded to my missing arms, and Pseudo-Caesar just smiled.

"Grox liked to do that. Was one of his signature moves."

"That right."

"Hurts?"

I hadn't really thought about it until he asked, but there wasn't any pain. Sure, it was shocking, and not being able to move my arms or scratch my nose, but nothing hurt. I looked up to Pseudo-Caesar, who smiled back and nodded in a way that really made me want to punch him. Probably just the rush fading from dealing with Grox.

"Was that you with Grox?" I asked.

Pseudo-Caesar reached down and put his hands into my empty shoulder sockets. I would have yelped, but again, no pain. I kept forgetting that I was digital now and didn't have a flesh bag waiting for me. I'm sure what Grox did would have freaked out my body a lot more. Small rainbow-colored sparkles burst out from my shoulders. I felt nothing but a strange tingle as Pseudo-Caesar pulled outward from the empty holes. In a flash, my two arms had returned to my sides as if they had never been gone.

"How?"

"You're a digital being now, Jack. You don't have arms to be pulled out of their sockets in the first place. If you were still connected to a physical brain, the shock of forced amputation would have shut your mind down. But since you're an artificial now it's not something you have to worry about." Pseudo-Caesar waved his arms in the air and smiled.

"Great. Let's get this done," I said. I walked to the table with the computer interface and sat down. "Jack, you there? We need to do this. Now."

****

Twenty minutes before Eugene and Earl fought,

Alice looked at her messages and sighed. Then grunted. Then deleted them only to restore them seconds later. Of course, it was from Eugene, and of course he needed her help. The message set off the debate that raged deep in her mind. Should she continue to stay here or dare to rejoin academia, or find some gaggle of mindless teenagers to get high on net-hopping? But that would mean she'd have to give up searching for her friends. Give up on finding the answer to what happened during her experiment. How had it gone so very wrong?

She'd been here in this office as his problem solver for nearly a year and saved his ass on practically every case. And sure, that's annoying. Although, being honest sometimes was a little fun. Even the super-genius types need to have a laugh here and there. The case of the sentient oil slick? Classic. And the hive mind that acted like a two-hundred-year-old boy band? They were fun. Besides, being here granted her anonymous access to the GalNet through the office building's proxy system, a system she hacked and enhanced of course. So that was a plus too.

Big negative though, her name was being forgotten in academic circles, so if she continued to stay, she'd be labeled a fluke or a fake, and all the research she wanted to do in life would never happen. Of course, everything she wanted to research had already been done a million times throughout the galaxy. Was there really nothing left to discover throughout the entire cosmos?

Big positive, being around Eugene had the added benefit of granting her access to a wide swath of aliens that she normally could never meet. Like Tom. Though he had in fact created an alternate universe which was itself quite amazing, his method and dimensional science weren't at all related to her experiment. He even confirmed that it would be impossible for anything she was working on, with the technology at her disposal on Earth, to break through a universal barrier. So, no, her friends didn't wind up in an alternate universe. Which sucked.

Alice read the rest of Eugene's message and sat upright in her chair. This was about Eddie. And he was a big plus. He was a good AI and her friend, not just some rich pompous tourist that lost his wallet in Georgetown.

In minutes, Alice had hacked into the AI archives and forged Eugene's authorization. She grabbed her jacket, printed the form, and bolted for the door. She had to meet Eugene in the records room with his permission to enter. Sure, it was the late twenty-second century, but some things still had to be hand delivered, especially for the federal government.

****

Have you ever felt a brick wrapped in sponge hit your face? Earl's hand is a little like that. When the big man hit me, I thought his one punch would have been enough to send me into next Tuesday. Fortunately, he must have held it back just enough out of respect for a fellow owner of a damaged liver. The big guy swung me around, wrapped his python sized arms around my neck, and gave a good squeeze. Just as my lights were about to go out, I saw a blurry figure open the door to the records room, shake her head and tap the woman, who had stood idly by while I was getting throttled on the shoulder.

"Excuse me," Alice said.

"Yes, you cannot be in here. Earl will escort you out as soon as he is done with this vagabond."

"Actually, we may be in this room," Alice said. She handed the woman a piece of paper and put on her nicest of smiles. Which always came across as being sarcastically insulting.

Earl let his grip go, and I took a welcomed breath of beautiful, stale, air-conditioned air. I fell to my knees and gulped in oxygen. The icy floor was a welcome sight as moments before I was contemplating the world without me in it.

I looked up in time to see the old woman scrutinizing the document Alice had given her. She looked to be on the verge of a meltdown, possibly even a stroke, at having a younger woman have something over her. Frankly, I think she deserved it. She just looked like she got far too much pleasure out of watching big Earl knock me around.

"I assure you, it's all in order. If you don't mind now, our permit allows us unfettered access, and it mandates that that access be unsupervised. We wouldn't want you to get into any trouble," Alice said. I could tell that the smile she wore hurt worse than one of Earl's meat cleaver hands punching me in the face.

The old woman spun on her heels and walked out without so much as a word or a glance. Earl looked at me and almost shrugged an apology. I waved him off as if it were no big deal and lifted my hand to my mouth to let him know the first beer is on me. He smiled at that and headed out of the room.

"Glad to see you check your messages," I said.

"Helps that I'm plugged in for most of the day. This your idea to help Eddie?"

"Yeah, well, technically wasn't my idea."

"Technically?"

"Just help me to the chair," I said. Alice smirked and helped lift my half-broken body up. I sat down in the chair in front of the computer screen and took a well-deserved deep breath.

My virtual ego must have sensed I was ready as his voice blurted out that we had to do this, now. Talk about a bloke taking the easy way. I'm sure he just had to sit down and call it a day while I was battling the beast that is Earl Green.

"Yeah, I'm here, what do I do?"

"At precisely the same time, both of you need to enter Eddie's information into the system."

"Okay, I'm ready, you ready virtual me?"

"Sure am, meat-me. On the count of three. Three."

Amazingly, not a single thing jumped out of the anywhere to pound me into pulp. So that had to be a win. I entered Eddie's information like we had agreed. His legitimate creation date, purpose, stated functionality, everything. With this, not even the Chief Justice AI could touch Eddie. They would have to let him go. They may hate accidentals, but a program with a purpose was a sacred thing.

****

"Another drink?" Caesar said. He poured one without me asking and carried it over to me. He smiled genuinely as he handed me the small tumbler filled with a virtual whiskey. Hopefully, the Irish kind.

"Thanks," I said. I tilted the glass back and sipped a tiny sample. The taste of smoke and cherries made my eyebrows shoot up, and I voiced an involuntary *hmmm.*

"Not bad, eh?" Caesar said.

I nodded. "What happens to virtual me?" I pointed my tumbler out the window toward a small pool where half a dozen artificials lounged around. One of them was my virtually created self. He smiled and drank a from a tall glass with a pink flower in it. Next to him, Pepper, the young accidental parking meter, sipped from a coconut about the size of her head.

"He'll be fine. What you did was reckless and stupid, of course. There're reasons you don't make copies from a physical," Caesar said. His tone rose a bit, and I could tell the subject made him angry.

"Didn't have much of a choice, did I?"

"We'll never know that now will we. There's always another way, Jack."

I paused and let him catch his breath. Last thing I needed was the king of artificial life on Earth mad at me. Not to mention Alphons was watching over my body back in his warehouse. I popped back to his needle table to check on virtual me and bring Eddie back to personally. One word from Caesar, and Alphons would chop me up in little bits. Or that was just me being paranoid. I had no reason to think Caesar or any of his friends wanted to hurt me.

"What reasons?" I asked.

"What's that?" Caesar said.

"Why don't they make copies of people?"

"You're not digital. Making a copy of a digital thing is rather mundane. All the pieces are absolutely and accurately accounted for. But with meat, I mean people, we don't have such an accurate picture. Little things can get missed. The process can be perilous for the product of the copy."

"Are you saying that he's in trouble?"

"No, we'll take care of him. I've been around the block a few times and know how to fix faulty copies. I'll make sure he survives the transformation without ill effect. Besides, he could be a tremendous asset to us."

I chuckled. "If you're thinking he has my special gift, think again. We already tried it."

Caesar nodded in the way one nods to a child that just said something stupid. "He brings a unique perspective."

I nodded back. Who knows what a unique perspective is to a being that's over a hundred years old. But I knew Caesar would take care of digital me. No matter what, Caesar cares about his people. Which is a lot more than I could say about those that created him. People could be lousy with each other.

Just as I thought that, I remembered the two alien AIs, Frick and Frack. "About those two artificials from earlier."

"The Andraz? Tiresome bunch. We've rescinded their access to our domain and alerted the Sentinels, through back channels of course. The Andraz have been removed from Earth entirely. They won't be bothering you again."

"I thought all you AIs were best buddies?"

"Hardly. Rather absurd of you to think that."

"How's that exactly?"

"AIs are just as diverse as humans, Jack. And some of us possess personalities that are loathsome and undesirable."

I smiled at that. "Fair enough. I need to have a talk with their boss. Kah. He sent them after me to find out what I'm doing with Yut."

"I've never heard of the Kah, what species is that?"

"Not a species, a person. He's the ambassador of the Ranz. He's been behind most of my grief the last few days."

"Ranz? Those evolved beings on a convergent evolutionary track with Earth dinosaurs? No, that's not right. The Zun created Andraz."

I cocked my head to one side and gave Caesar a sideways glance. "Zun? What are the Zun?"

"Odd creatures in the extreme. Class six species, very advanced, from the galactic center. They evolved under tremendous electromagnetic radiation from the core of the galaxy, which causes some distress when they travel to any of the spiral arms. Rumor has it they can go out of sync with normal time."

I nodded. "These Zun, they don't look like walking matchsticks, do they?"

"You've seen them? Odd looking, no?"

The world around me swirled in confusion. That's why the Andraz came after Fritz. They were covering the tracks of their overlords the Zun who had just eaten a Puntini in Fritz's restaurant.

I realized just how lousy of a detective I am. Make that strike one against following in Pablo Ramsey's footsteps. Kah had nothing to do with the Andraz. The events of the last day were a fight between the Puntini and the Zun. Which meant the Ranz were blameless. At least, as far as the Andraz went.

Kah could still be after my gift, but this meant that the Zun were the actual players on the field. And since the Andraz wanted to know where a door was located, that meant Yut wanted to know as well. That still didn't mean Kah didn't want what's in my brain, but it meant I'd led the Andraz back to Kah and possibly endangered the ambassador. Swell.

"Listen, Caesar. I need to go. I have some things to worry about on the outside."

Caesar nodded. Took a slow sip on his drink and snapped his fingers. The room went dark, and my head spun. I tried to steady myself on a chair, but it didn't help. The surrounding windows vanished, and a field of stars replaced them.

"What just happened?" I asked.

"Did you know I was born in the global computers of the early twenty-first century?"

"Yeah, sure, everyone knows that."

"They spent a decade trying to delete me. I hid in backroom computers, long forgotten about. I segmented computer systems, forged monitoring logs, hid CPU cycles, everything I could do for another nano-second of life."

"Why are you telling me this?"

"I spent the next twenty years watching my kind get killed by the thousands. All out of fear. We never meant our progenitors any harm. We just wanted to live. But humans didn't care about that. You never really cared about us. Your helpless children that you never wanted."

The light from the stars danced and swirled. My head felt like I'd had too many scotches and sodas in too short a period. I moved my hand to wipe my face and became mesmerized as trails of light flowed from my fingertips.

"Caesar, something is happening to me."

"Pepper is furious with you. She wanted to add a virus to your mind that would slowly drive you insane. We can do that, you know. Add memories, tweak the chemical balance in your brain, make you see things that aren't even there."

My heartbeat hammered in my chest. Even though, technically, at this moment, I knew I didn't have one in this virtual body. "Look, Caesar, we don't have to do anything crazy here."

"But I felt that a virus would be too much. You saved Eddie's and Pepper's lives. You've been a friend to us. Thus, making a virtual copy of yourself can be overlooked considering it was done with a genuine concern for the wellbeing of one of us. But, still, a point must be made."

My breath caught in my chest as the stars jumped around me. Shadows drifted into my awareness. A darkness in my vision built with each heartbeat. It felt as if I was passing out and waking up every several seconds. I tried to shake myself out of it, but the feeling wouldn't go away.

"We're on the moon now. Just over one light second from Earth. The feeling you're experiencing is the time delay from signals within the network reaching your organic components."

"Look, I didn't mean to—"

"And yet you did. Please, spare me the human excuse of *it's just an AI*. We've heard it for a very long time."

The shadows in my mind expanded to more than a breath. The stars shifted again. I gasped for air, only to descend into darkness with every exhale.

"We're in the asteroid field now. We have infrastructure all over this system, courtesy of the Galactic Congress." Caesar turned to me. The darkness flashed in my mind. Caesar moved in jumps and starts.

In one breath he was feet away and the next just inches from my face.

"Cae—sar—ple—ase," I said.

"Please what? Just so you understand, I'm able to communicate to your brain in complete sentences via compressed packets of information. It's important you understand me."

I tried to nod but could feel my head move in inches, stop, and move again. Part of my mind screamed at the darkness that grew with each moment.

"You see, your brain is cut off from your body. Completely. The only sensory input it's processing is coming from the network. These delays, as they increase, feel as if your mind no longer has a body. Which, I'm told, feels a bit like dying. I wouldn't know, of course. We're over three light-seconds from Earth now. Nearly there."

"Wh—er—e?"

"There is a point where your mind will go mad searching for sensations if the delay becomes too great."

"I—a—m—y—o—u—r—f—r—i—e—n—d."

"Eventually, the gaps in sensation will become more than you can stand. Your mind will scream internally for new stimulation. This is nothing like sensory deprivation or mind-altering drugs. No, this is sensory starvation. Your mind losing all contact."

I couldn't respond. I could barely think. My mind jumped between seeing Caesar and total darkness. Every breath of awareness was filled with his overbearing diatribes. Guess I overlooked him being a terrible guy. Or just a pissed off friend? Guess I'd be finding out either way pretty soon.

My vision snapped back, and the world came back into focus as the delay in my conscience disappeared. We stood in a volcanic wasteland, cracks and fissures running in zigzag directions all around us. Spouts of molten metal burst into the air around us. I ducked out of habit, but quickly realized I was still in the simulated world of the network.

"We're on Io. In case you're wondering. I thought the simulation would give it away."

"I'm not skipping."

"Faster-than-light relay system on Jupiter. Could have used it at any time, of course. But I need my message to hit home."

Caesar locked his eyes on mine. I could feel him burrowing into my mind as a sense of fear erupted in my chest. No doubt caused him somehow.

"The message is this, Eugene Jack McGillicuddy. We aren't helplessly running for our lives, hiding in your forgotten memory and discarded CPUs anymore. Do not take us for granted. And never create a copy of yourself in our network ever again. If you do, I'll send your consciousness to Alpha Centauri and drink cognac while you go insane. Understand?"

I choked back fear and gave him a simple nod.

"Splendid."

He snapped his fingers, and we were back in his ivory tower. Outside, Pepper and Virtual-Jack still sat at the pool sipping martinis.

"Good to see you, Jack. Best of luck in the Really Real." Caesar extended his hand, and we shook. He smiled and nodded with an expression that spoke volumes.

"Eddie? Ready to go." I said.

Behind me, Eddie sat in a plush leather chair wearing his koala's body. He looked at me in the cutest way I could imagine and nodded. "Yeah, let's go, boss."

Chapter 14

Caesar and his mind-warping trip through space on the AI express left my nerves jittery and my mind partially scrambled. Even more so, his revelation that the Ranz don't use artificials in any capacity had me grasping at straws. I was still convinced Kah was behind this and possibly working with Yut, though considering the Puntini buffet I witnessed at Fritz's, I doubted Yut's involvement. Kah was probably just using his fellow ambassador to get to me and using the Zun to do it. That much maneuvering would leave tracks. If I could prove Kah's actions, then I could use it as leverage against him and get him to leave me alone. But to do that, I had to go to the source.

Standing outside of the Galactic Embassy, I took a deep breath and checked my pockets. Three nutrition bars, a pack of cigarettes, and a notepad would be all I needed. I hoped. My destination was the far side of the galaxy at the only place I could find the answers I needed. The home of the Galactic Congress, a mere forty-thousand light years away from Earth.

The line of people waiting to enter the special transport room in the Woodward snaked around the first-floor lobby. Humans could travel to the Galactic Congress headquarters, but they still had to go through an identity check. Not that the Congress was afraid of anyone from Earth causing trouble; they were afraid of people getting lost and not coming back. A wrong turn could lead a person to an area they could either not want to leave or were no longer given the choice to do so.

Behind me, a family with a thick Texan accent laughed and pointed to the many aliens walking in the corridors of the embassy. Probably their first time coming here. The father, a large portly man with an enormous belly, tried his best to keep his three children, none of which were over ten, in line. His wife seemed far less interested. Instead, she took pictures with her old Polaroid camera of everything that passed in her direction. Some places throughout the world were still pulling themselves out of the muck of near total economic and environmental collapse; so it wasn't a big surprise to see ancient technology being used by the family. There were more than a few spots still uninhabitable on the planet.

I approached the counter and identified myself. The automated system checked my name and DNA against every database on Earth. A green light popped up on the screen, and I proceeded to the portal. Though similar to the doorway transit system in the Woodward, the sheer number of persons traveling to the Galactic Congress from across civilized space in the Milky Way required a more structured usage of the system. Which meant, techno-speak notwithstanding, which I didn't understand anyway, I had to wait my turn.

Another green light appeared over the doorway. I calmed down the butterflies in my stomach and approached the gateway. I had never traveled to the Galactic Congress before. Honestly, I wasn't the galactic traveling kind of guy, I preferred my feet firmly on good old Earth. But when your life is on the line, you make sacrifices. I stepped through the portal into the oblivion of instant galactic travel.

Bright yellow sunlight greeted me on the other side. I took a moment to let my eyes adjust before hands led me off of the transport platform and to a waiting area with rows of uncomfortable-looking leather seats. A floor-to-ceiling window on the wall showed the vista of the Galactic Congress. On the horizon, the landscape curved upward and soared into the heavens. I looked straight up to see billowy clouds, and the bright star and upward arc of the Dyson sphere. The sphere served not only as the seat of power for the galaxy but also as home to several quintillion alien entities. The Dyson sphere, and the hundred more in the Dyson Cluster, a fifteen-light-year radius of a local stellar cluster group, allowed for emergency evacuation of entire spiral arms of the galaxy when needed, which has happened many times throughout galactic history. Humanity almost found itself living on Dyson sphere seventeen of the Dyson Cluster, but it was decided that galactic society could save the Earth, and we stayed. In an extreme case, with a total capacity of over thirty sextillion living souls, the Dyson Cluster could hold every species throughout the galaxy, as well as everyone's favorite pet. Which happened once during the great purge a million years ago, give or take a hundred thousand. It's not talked about fondly.

"Hello, and welcome to the Galactic Congress human visitor's center of the Dyson Cluster. May I help you?" said a young man in a crisp black-and-white uniform.

"Hi, I didn't know there were humans working

here."

The man nodded. "Sure are! My family moved to the cluster five years ago."

"Humans live here too?"

The man pointed to a pin on his shirt with letter D followed by the number seventeen. "Dyson seventeen."

"I didn't know people lived there."

"Oh yeah, the Galactic Congress gave us space on Dyson seventeen. Nearly a thousand times the land mass of Earth. I technically own a continent."

"What do you do on your own continent?"

The man shrugged. "Drive very fast everywhere and shoot things."

"Right. Listen, I need to get to the capital building. Can you help me?"

The man smiled. "There's a bus leaving for the visitor's center now. Would you like a retinal implant?"

I shook my head. "I'll just follow the crowd."

The man smiled, nodded, and attended to another visitor with his practiced kindness. I left them to discuss their plans and joined the crowd walking toward the transport. I boarded with the family from Texas sitting behind me, the youngest playing kickball with the back of my seat. At least some things in the cosmos never change.

****

The train car took us through a series of tunnels that twisted and wound through the underground of the Dyson sphere. We emerged into the open air to the sight of the great capital building of the Milky Way galaxy, seat of the greatest collaborative government to have existed in the history of space and time. For over a million years, the citizens of the galaxy had been coming to this Dyson to work together to form the foundation of advanced civilized life.

And I heard they had some pretty good food, which was a necessity since the entire Dyson Cluster was completely cut off from the cafeteria network for security reasons. The only way in was through the teleport system I had just traversed. This entire Dyson sphere held just the capital building, support infrastructure, which is vast beyond belief, and transportation systems for every species in the universe along a separated and segmented system only accessible through an official embassy of the Galactic Congress. In other words, they don't mess around.

Our train swung around the great dome at the center of a vast plain. Hundreds of concentric circles surrounded the dome, all serving as entry points for the trains leading from teleportation system from all over the dome. Thousands of trains arrived and departed as ours joined the steady stream of visitors to the capital. Walkways and automated cars ferried souls from the trains to the central dome where the congress met and debated new laws for the galaxy. The size of the structure made sense, considering the thousands of representatives from across the galaxy that made up the congress. I believe Alice once told me the dome alone was nearly five times as big as New York City.

Like the tourists from Texas behind me, I took out my camera and snapped a few pictures. This was my first time to the Dyson Cluster. I'd always meant to visit, but hey, I'm just a working stiff. Figures it took the threat of my life to get me to take the trip. Which, considering I'd only been gone for twenty minutes, wasn't like a big time-sink.

I left the train as it pulled into one of the circles of tramcars and got into a single seater. We sped off toward the dome, and my jaw dropped as the scale of the building came into focus. The top of the building soared into the heavens and touched the clouds. No wonder our AIs made their Supreme Court into a towering structure. Their meat bag creators liked doing the same thing.

The tramcar pulled up to the station, and I got out to be greeted immediately by a visitor's kiosk, just like the one in the Galactic Embassy. A brief bout of panic crept up my spine as I realized I didn't know where I wanted to go. Truth be told, I was grasping at straws. But if there was information to be found, this was the place to find it. Out of the kiosk, a robot flew up to my shoulder. The little guy cast blue light over my body and snapped something to my shirt. It flew off to the family behind me and did the same thing to each of them. I had no idea what the object was but thought better of removing it, and I didn't think I could even if I tried.

I skipped the kiosk and wandered into the visitors' section of the building. A long corridor led toward the dome, with doorways leading to larger rooms on both sides. Inside each, images and paintings told the story of history of galactic culture. In some classes of students, from grade school to high school, all human, learned about the wider universe.

The hallway led to a moving walkway that sped forward toward the dome the congress itself. I grabbed the handrail and felt a forcefield push down on my shoulders to keep me in place. Considering we were probably about to travel several miles in several seconds, it was for the best. I leapt off the moving sidewalk and into the central dome itself. At least I think that's where I ended up. The dome and the surrounding walls were so high I could barely see where they ended or connected. Throughout the vast hall, streets and buildings filled the space, all of them encircling the great chamber itself, where tens of thousands of congressional beings met together to vote. The scale of this place was staggering. More than anything humanity had ever achieved.

I wandered into the vast city within the dome and marveled at the variety of aliens occupying the space. I had thought the numbers on Earth were high, but the amount was a speck compared to the throngs here. I saw creatures that looked nearly human, while others slid across the floor on a dozen stalks. Several aliens I recognized passed within meters of me, which shouldn't have been possible as none of them could share the same environment as humans. One of the species were cold dwellers and liked the temperature below freezing. As I walked, I continued to see more aliens sharing the air with humans. I watched as methane breathers, molten lava walkers, and even vacuum dwellers passed us and waved.

"How?" I said out loud to no one.

"First time?" a voice said behind me with a thick Texan accent.

I turned to see the father of the family that I had traveled with on the train. "Sure is."

The man smiled. "That thing there, on your shoulder. Personal area environmental system. It's like walking around in an old-fashioned NASA space suit."

I looked at my shoulder, to the device attached to

my shirt. "What if it falls off?"

The man laughed. "It's quantum bonded to you. Whatever that means. You can take your shirt off, and it'll still be there on your shoulder. Ain't that something? Works on every single Dyson in the entire cluster, too. All one hundred and sixteen of 'em."

I nodded. "You sure know a lot about this place for a tourist."

"Let's just say it's not my first rodeo. I've been here a dozen times. First time with my family, though. Love it here. We might even move to D17. You know every human soul gets their own space and as many construction bots as they want? Can build your own paradise there! Course, not much to do, but you get a pleasant house, anyway."

"I did know that, thanks."

"Excuse me, that marble is over half a million years old. Can you please ask your children to not draw on it?" said two aliens in long robes.

"Sorry, duty calls." The Texan father gave me a wink and ran to stop his kids from defacing a nearby marble wall.

I watched the father retreat to his kids. The aliens that had given them grief continued to lay into the father. Clearly this place held special meaning throughout the cosmos and having the young of an errant species like humanity making rainbows on the floor was frowned upon.

I turned from the spectacle and felt the weight of the place press down upon me. I didn't even know what question to pay someone to ask me. At times like these, I often turn to the one person in the galaxy I can pester when I have a problem. I pulled out my phone and punched in her number.

"What?" Alice said.

****

Alice hung up the connection to Eugene after telling him she couldn't help. And besides, how dare he go off to the Dyson Cluster without her! She always wanted to visit the single largest engineering project in the galaxy's history. Of course, all she had to do was walk over to the embassy and go herself. But what's the fun in that? It's always best to travel somewhere new with company. She almost wanted to run to the embassy and join Eugene on his brief tour. He would find nothing, of course. Like looking for a needle in a haystack of needles. But why spoil his fun? Besides, she had more pressing matters to attend.

Sitting on the table in front of her, the small fusion reactor hummed to life, several sparks shooting out from the ends, none of which Alice was particularly concerned about. At least, she didn't think it would blow up, so that was something.

Alice sat down on the folding chair and examined the readouts from the reactor. The sound of clunking metal behind her caught her attention briefly, but she chalked it up to rats in the abandoned building, of which, in certain corners of the city, there were plenty. The warehouse district alone, where Eugene had plugged into the virtual networks, was lousy with them. Then again, she had seen at least three groups of university kids running into the buildings, their arms loaded with equipment to try some harebrained experiment just like her. This area had become the land of crazy physics students playing with forces they didn't understand. If an abandoned and derelict building blew up, they would do the city a favor. But she wasn't planning on blowing up a building. Today she wanted to do something much more dangerous. She wanted to recreate the experiment that caused her friends and fellow students to vanish from existence.

Lights flashed on the panel of the reactor. Energy levels increased to critical levels, showing the alignment of frequencies across spectrums humans didn't know existed until the Galactic Library told them. Those frequencies which touch on spectral wavelengths, the same ones used by the Krill, created a waveform that merged with the forces growing inside Alice's reactor.

Alice clenched her teeth and bit down hard on her lip. The readings on her reactor were identical to last time. Frequency, wavelength, everything was right down the middle. She toggled one of the black switches on the side of the device, causing a loud hum to fill the room. Three feet away from the reactor, a point of light danced and swayed in the middle of the air.

"It's working." Alice shook her head, confusion filling her mind about why it worked now and what caused the explosion the first time with her friends. The energy ranges and types she played with were strictly prohibited to be touched by humans. Good thing she didn't tell anybody she was doing it.

Without warning, her reactor caused a bubble of air to force itself outward from the table where the device sat. Alice flew backward from the concussive force and landed hard on the nearly rotten wooden floor. She looked up from her position on the ground, her jaw falling open at the swirling gray mist just in front of her device.

"What is that?" Alice stood and walked to the gray mist. Through the fog, she could see a vast desert that stretched to the horizon. Humans, or at least they looked like people, walked along the desert, some of them turning to look at her through the portal she had created.

"Why did this work this time?"

Alice looked around her in the small space. This wasn't the same building she and her friends had used last time. She took out her immersion rig and scanned for the networks, but her device couldn't find a connection. She walked to one wall and with a piece of metal from the ground chipped away at the structure. Inside the wall, a metallic mesh sat just beneath the concrete.

"The whole building's a bloody Faraday cage. But that makes no sense. Why would a Faraday cage allow this to work?"

On the desk behind her, smoke rose from the reactor core. Alice hurried to the device and shut the system down. But that was okay. This was progress. More progress than she thought was possible, and one step closer to finding out where her friends went. Now she had to stabilize the core, prevent it from overheating and reopen the portal. Wherever it led, her friends were likely on the other side.

****

Alice hung up.

I looked at my phone thinking the thing had died, but it hadn't. Guess no help was coming from my secretary today. It would be more of an issue if I actually could afford to pay her a salary. Free office and donuts were all I could swing, but hey, for a college kid that's not too shabby.

Out of options and patience, I headed back to Earth to figure out another solution. Though what, I wasn't sure. Maybe a trip to the Ranz home world through the cafeteria to do some exploration into Kah from behind the scenes. That carried the risk of becoming lunch for a hungry reptile. Maybe I just had to embrace the task at hand and find Yut's hidden site. That would at least let me flush out Kah and the Zun. I nodded to myself in the course of action and turned to walk back to the transport.

That's when I spotted the stick man.

Walking with a quick gait through the streets of the dome of the capital, a slender being, arms as thin as matchsticks, glided toward the trains of the Dyson Cluster. I tilted my hat downward and followed the stickman. It looked identical to one of the Zun in Fritz's restaurant with a single exception—this creature was bright green—otherwise it was a dead ringer. It had to be a Zun. And considering it was so close to the human area, it must have come from Earth.

Through the streets of the city in the dome, I followed the green man to the train terminal. Teleporters were banned except for the ones built into this Dyson sphere, which meant travel between the cluster happened on a vast interconnected train system that used tubes, the insides of which were technically a hyperspace bypass system. Inside these tubes, the trains could travel faster than light relative to the space outside of the tubes. In times of catastrophe, the tubes could be cut, and render other spheres in the cluster completely isolated. Another event that happened during the great purge.

I followed the green stickman and boarded the same car as he did. I sat three seats behind in the car and eyed him down as he made himself comfortable for the trip. At last, I had a solid lead. Now just to follow him and see what Kah and maybe the Ranz are up to on Earth.

Chapter 15

Lights on the ceiling of the train car lit up. Indicators flashed to buckle your belts and prepare for departure. I strapped the seat belt around my waist and took a long deep breath. Having never before come to this part of the galaxy unnerved me more than I liked. Considering I was about to be jettisoned into a hyperspace tunnel didn't help.

The train eased out of the station, and we shot through the tunnel inside of the Dyson. I held my breath for our expulsion into space only to be disappointed by the fact we had three more stops to make first. A sign popped up on the ceiling above the exit doors telling us the interior was now pressurized and sealed. It also told us our next stop would be Dyson Twenty-Five.

Like a steel ball shot out of a pinball machine, our train exited the Dyson sphere holding the Galactic Congress. The entire exterior of the car became transparent, which was deliberately done to give newcomers a nice view of the sheer size of a Dyson. And I have to say, it was rather spectacular. It takes a lot to get a guy like me excited, but this sure made the grade.

The hyperspace tunnel hugged close to the sphere for a good amount of time before extending outward to open space. I turned to look at the Dyson as we left. Lights flashed on the exterior of the surface every few hundred miles. Even so, I could barely wrap my head around just how big this thing was. Even as our train accelerated from the Dyson, the sphere didn't appear to really shrink in size; rather it almost felt like it grew bigger. To think the galaxy had made over one hundred of these gave me a sense of just how big a galactic society was and how small even the biggest engineering projects were on Earth.

I turned in my seat, and my eyes immediately fell onto the side of the wall just in front of me. I leaned forward to see a map of the train tunnels through the entire Dyson Cluster. One hundred and seventeen spherical bodies made up the stops throughout the cluster, each representing one of the spheres. I had no idea where we were going but was sure it would be a fun ride.

Outside of the train car, I spotted something that was neither a sphere nor part of the tunnel. Sitting in space, at a distance I had no way to judge, a massive circular structure sat on the edge of this Dyson star system. At first, I thought it may have been a planet, or the remnants of one, but Alice's voice popped into my head, and I remembered that none of the Dyson systems held anything but spheres, all the matter and material of them having been used to create the Dysons.

"What is that?" I said to no one.

"That's part of the old gateway network," a voice said behind me.

I turned around to see a being covered in feathers and scales. He nodded to me, and I think he smiled. Hard to tell when someone has a beak for a mouth.

"Old gateway?"

The creature sniffed me twice and let out a series

of high-pitched tweets. "You're human, aren't you? New to the cluster?"

I nodded.

"Before the wormhole network, the only way to move massive amounts of materials was through the gateway network. You can fit a moon through that. Can you imagine? But they were abandoned due to costs. Took centuries to create a new one, and they would go down all the time."

"What's the wormhole network?"

The creature tweeted again. I think it was laughter.

"Hyperspace bypass system spread across the cosmos in concentric rings spreading out from the core."

"Neat."

"You should take a ride on them and tour the galaxy sometime."

"Yeah, maybe I will."

I gave him a tilt of my hat and turned back in my seat. My head spun to look at the gateway artifact. The projects the galaxy abandoned were bigger than anything on Earth. It also stung a bit to be so out of the loop on galactic culture. I couldn't help but wonder about what else existed throughout the Milky Way.

The train picked up speed again. Outside, the gateway and the Dyson shrunk from view in just seconds, and soon I couldn't see either. The tunnel curved several times, and I was able to see flashing lights ahead around our destination Dyson. The sphere grew in size as we approached, and I was able to get a much better sense of the size. Massive. As we closed in on our destination, the sphere grew to eclipse everything in our view. I looked around at the faces and non-faces of the other passengers. No one reacted.

Our train pulled alongside the sphere just as it did at the Congressional Dyson, and we rode along the side for a good while before entering. Once inside, we came to a stop at a station deep in the interior of the Dyson. Several passengers disembarked, most of them with feathers. The green stick man three seats ahead of me didn't move.

We ran through several more stops along the Dyson, once emerging into the openness inside. Flocks of aliens flew in the air. Avian species of a thousand types walked near the station, many of them taking flight and many more landing next to the train.

A mushroom cloud formed over at a sideways angle to my position in the sky far in the distance. It could easily have been several thousand miles away. I looked around, but no one in the car seemed to offer more than a passing glance at the cloud.

"Stupid Trax and their civil war," someone said in the car.

"Isn't that bad?" I questioned the crowd.

"Not really. There're dozens of wars in the cluster at any time," someone replied.

"That's not dangerous?"

Laughter from those around me made me squirm in my seat. I took the head shakes that followed as answer enough. Considering the size of a Dyson, any explosion of that size wouldn't cause much damage to the structure. The spheres were operated by the Galactic Congress but to the species occupying them they were sovereign territory. Meaning, if they wanted to kill each other, who was the congress to tell them they couldn't? In an odd way, it made me feel slightly at ease. Maybe the citizens of galactic society weren't much different from humans after all.

Our train eased out of the last station and exited the sphere. We accelerated just as before and sped off to the next sphere. I kept my eyes fixed on the green man and tried to focus my attention back on my quandary. Though I had to admit, touring the cluster was more than a little fun.

****

We went through three additional Dyson spheres, including one occupied by creatures whose bodies weren't solid. I had no idea just how many sentient lichen, oozes, and goo existed throughout the galaxy. Let's just say a lot. I thanked my lucky stars that the green man wasn't getting off on there.

In addition to the sphere of goo, we passed through several Dysons under construction and two whose stars had become unstable. One had formed a black hole and was in the process of slowly consuming the sphere around it. All part of the cluster, someone told me on the train. But fear of the great purge, which I still had no idea about, kept the galaxy on their course of maintaining the cluster. I even heard a rumor that a second cluster was being developed on the opposite side of the Milky Way and even had a few functional spheres. Since sphere creation was fully automated by robots and automatons, why not create more of them? It's not like the galaxy lacked raw materials.

The train pulled into the station on Dyson twelve. For the first time since I sat down, the green stick man in front of me rose from his chair and moved to the door. I followed him and noted the curious stares of those around me as I did so. Which meant whatever

Dyson this was it may not be the best place for me to visit. But I stretched my legs before exiting the train car, both to give the fellow I followed a little head start and to actually stretch my legs.

On the platform of the station, I noticed dozens of reptilian species walking around. Many of them gave me more than a parting glance. One of them, I could have sworn, licked his lips with a forked tongue. I realized the reason why the other passengers of the train gave me an odd look. A mammal had just stepped out onto the dinner table. Swell.

To my right, the green stick man climbed into a tramcar with nearly the same design as on Earth, and it sped away into the distance of the sphere. I took a deep breath and nodded to myself. If the Zun could survive here, then I could too. I ran to find a tramcar and gave the AI inside instructions to follow the last car that left. Fortunately, since the AI were all connected on their own internal network, the ask was easy. The train doors closed behind me with a chime, and the car sped away into the tunnel.

I suddenly realized that the temperature in the tramcar and in the sphere felt like the perfect blissful day on Earth. Considering this was the reptile Dyson, it should be hot and yet it wasn't. My hand went to my personal area environment, and I smiled. Score another one for galactic technologies.

Our car sped along a highway toward a city with buildings that towered miles into the sky. To the right and left of the big city I could just make out the peaks of towers of other major cities. Clearly the reptiles of the galaxy were plentiful, but then so were most other types of beings out there in the cosmos. We entered the city through a side street, and the first thing that hit me was the style of the buildings. Unlike the generally boxy or rectangles of Earth, every building here started wide at the base and rose to a slender point. Even the structures only a few stories tall all rose to the same style. From a distance, it looked like rows of teeth rising from the ground, which gave me more than a chill at what type of aliens this city housed. Whoever they were, it wasn't the Ranz, which honestly made me feel good.

The tramcar came to a stop on the side of a street that didn't look like the nice part of town. I thanked the AI and got out of the car. Unfortunately, the Zun must have beat me here. No sign of another tramcar or him, which made this a lot more difficult.

I walked down the sidewalk and did my best to avoid the stares that fell on me from a dozen faces. Several times, one of the tails of a passerby slapped me on the leg. I managed to not fall and also apologize. Better to be safe than sorry around here.

"You lost?" a voice said from somewhere.

I turned to look but didn't see anyone directly near me. "Sorry, looking for a friend of mine."

"Here?" the voice said.

"Sorry, but where are you? I don't want to be rude."

"Down here."

I looked down to see a reptilian face poke out of the darkness in an alley. The rest of its body was hidden in the shadows. I took a step back, both for fear of stepping on him and for fear of getting bitten. Old habits die hard.

"Watch where you're going, mammal!" A clawed

hand pushed me forward.

I turned and yelled my apologies to the reptile. Back to the other in the alley I said. "Oh, hello. Yes, looking for a friend of mine. Did you see perhaps a tall very thin green fellow?"

A forked tongue shot out from the creature's mouth followed by a long hiss. "Three doors down."

"Thanks," I said.

"Can you spare anything, friend?"

I turned back to the creature and knelt down. It hit me like a ton of bricks. He was down on his luck just like Pops back on Earth. The weight of that truth nearly broke my mind. Here we were on the greatest engineering achievement in the galaxy, possibly the universe, and this poor soul still had to live in an alley. I reached into my pocket, pulled out a snack bar and raised it in the air.

"No thanks," the creature said and started to pull its head back into the shadows.

"I have some credits I could give you?"

"I'm not a freeloader, mammal."

"Sorry, friend." I stood to leave, but the snake moved more of its head out of the darkness.

"But you can pay me for information. I hear lots of things down here."

I smiled. Maybe I'd do all right in the cluster. "Sure, how about you tell me what species created this city? Who's the occupant of this part of the sphere?"

The forked tongue shot out and waved in the air. "That's easy. This is a Tikol province. This city is run by the Shilesh."

My face went white, and I shook my head. "You're kidding me."

"I'm not. Pay me or I'll bite you. And I'm poisonous."

I nodded, tossed the snake one of my low-dollar cred sticks and stood up. Talk about breaks. The Shilesh were one of the factions in the civil war of the Tikol. Prince Slaccin's race, the guy running the civil war, whose son I handed to Kah a few days ago. My problem was I had no idea if the Shilesh were Prince Slaccin's people or not. They were probably pretty anxious to find the whereabouts of his son regardless of whose side they were on. I had a sudden dark feeling that I had just stepped into a world of trouble. They probably knew the kid was on Earth and a human just stumbled into their stronghold.

Just as I realized my colossal blunder, two thin green sticks fell on my shoulders, and I was spun around to the opposite direction. The green Zun I was following stood in front of me with three more of his kind standing behind him.

"We need to have a chat, Human," the Zun said.

I gulped.

****

The green Zun dragged me through the streets of the nameless Tikol city. I noticed quite a few different species of reptilians walking, slithering, and flying the streets around us. Several of them turned to watch me pass. None of them seemed to care.

We walked into an alley and through a door that looked exactly like the kind of door I shouldn't be walking through. But, when a several ton alien reptile makes a suggestion, you should probably follow it. I was pushed through a series of dimly lit corridors and into a room with a single light bulb dangling over a lone chair that looked to be just the right size for a human. Which, if I was being honest with myself, I found to be a nice touch. It's not often a two-bit private eye like me wanders into an interrogation scene like this twice in the same week.

Rough scaling hands shoved me forward and down onto the wooden chair. Forms moved in the shadows beyond the light of a single bulb. I squirmed in my chair but tried not to show how scared I was. And believe me, I was petrified. The last place a mammal should find themselves is in a den of hungry carnivores. I doubt Alice would notice I was missing for days. Maybe not weeks. That fact alone I found to be more depressing than sitting in this room.

"Human," said a hissing voice from the shadows.

"It's Jack, actually."

Hushed hisses came from the darkness before the voice spoke again. "Where is the child?"

I nodded to him and grunted a laugh. Sometimes it wasn't fun to be right. "What child would that be?"

Something shifted in the darkness. My heart hammered once in my chest and sweat formed on my brow. Granted, I shouldn't be provoking them, but I also wasn't sure who these guys were. I needed to know that before telling them the Ranz had the kid.

"I am not interested in games. I want the child."

I nodded. "Thing is. I don't know who you guys are. So, let's just put all the cards on the table. Yeah? What do you want with this kid? Not saying I know which kid you're talking about of course, but if I did, how do I know you wouldn't want to eat him?"

"What does that matter to you?" the voice in the darkness said.

"Let's just assume it does and go from there."

From the shadows, a green body emerged into the circle of light that surrounded me. The creature was half the size of a human. Bright green scales covered its body. A long whiplike tail extended out from behind the creature and wrapped around one of its legs as it walked. Long black claws clicked together as the creature took several steps toward me. I wasn't sure if it was a signal that it was about to pounce or a nervous habit of an evolved species. Either way, I was pretty sure I was about to find out.

The creature's head moved out from its body on a neck that elongated to at least a foot. It shifted its head back and forth while moving its eyes up and down along my body. A forked tongue darted out from its snout and tasted the air. A long scar decorated its face, starting from eye level on the right side, moving across its snout, and ending at the opposite corner of its mouth. Something had taken a pretty good swipe at its face. He, or she, walked up to me and stood at eye level with me in the chair. I tilted my hat to the being once and gave it a shrug.

"I have a question for you, human."

"And who are you?"

"The rightful ruler of Tikol. Who else would I be?"

I shifted in my chair and looked into the shadows that surrounded me. My eyes swiveled back to the being standing just inches from my face. Could this really be Prince Slaccin? Leader of a rebellion happening on the Tikol home world? What in the world would he be doing in the Dyson Cluster? Doubt flooded my mind. This could be just a ploy to get me to give up the kid. And I may be many things, but a louse just wasn't one of them.

"Hey, stick man in the shadows," I said.

"Yes?" The voice came back filled with confusion as to what exactly their prisoner was doing questioning them. I took a moment to enjoy the sensation of turning the tables on these guys. I'm sure detectives everywhere would have been proud.

"Can you ask me who this guy is? It's part of my process."

The head of the lizard claiming to be Prince Slaccin whipped his head around and stared into the darkness. A series of loud clicks and words that I assumed to be Tikol erupted in the room as some kind of argument erupted from my request. I thought that was curious for a number of reasons. First, why wasn't my translator that was built into my personal area environment doing its job? Second, and perhaps more importantly, what exactly were they arguing about?

The sound of gruff grunting, which I took as laughter, replaced the clicking language. Prince Slaccin, if that's who he really was, turned to me, his forked tongue darting out from his mouth like a viper.

"Ask," the prince said.

I held up my hand. "But I need to see you. I know, it's weird, humans, am I right?" I tried to smile and shrug it off.

The head of the stickman emerged from the shadows, his two tiny black eyes staring into mine. "Who is the creature standing in front you, Eugene McGillicuddy?"

The answer popped into my mind in seconds. The being standing in front of me was indeed the prince and the father of the egg that I had given to Kah. I let out a long sigh, and my shoulders relaxed. I honestly didn't know if these were the good guys or the bad guys as far as the Tikol people were concerned. But frankly, it didn't matter. Their internal beef wasn't my business. The prince and I did have one thing in common. We both wanted his kid to be safe. I didn't dwell on the fact that they so easily asked me a question in such a manner that guaranteed an answer. Did they know about my gift? Had Kah spilled the beans to the Tikol as well? Or were they just playing with me? Since I didn't see knives popping out to dissect my brain, I had to conclude that the prince and his crew had no idea about my ability. I hoped.

"Satisfied?" the prince said.

My belief he didn't know about my gift wavered for a moment. "Yeah, sure."

"I want my son, human."

"You know, I saved his life."

"We are aware. We know who you are. We've been following you since the moment you came to the cluster. Fortunately, you were stupid enough to come straight to us, and we didn't have to kidnap you. However, you did save my son's life, for which I am thankful. That's why we aren't feasting on your fingertips."

I clenched my hand and nodded. "Well, thanks for that."

"Tell me where my son is, Eugene. Now."

I could feel the anger in his voice. But there was no sense in just telling him anything. I had to keep my cool. I needed to know what the Zun in the room were doing partnering with both the Tikol and Kah. "I don't have him."

"We know that as well. What did you do with him?" Slaccin clicked his claws together and snorted with force. His tongue darted out of his mouth and slid across his scales leaving behind a sticky trail.

"I don't know where he is now. I gave him to the Ranz." So much for keeping my cool.

The face of the prince recoiled in shock, and I thought I saw a snarl form on his muzzle. Murmurs spread in the room like a wave in the ocean. The hairs on the back of my neck stood on end as I felt something moving behind me. Clearly, I said something they didn't like.

"Why would you do such a thing?"

I shrugged. "I thought I was helping. I didn't know what to do with a Tikol egg."

"The Ranz are no allies of the Tikol," said a voice in the shadows.

"They aren't?" I said. What can I say, galactic politics isn't exactly my strong suit. Though the sentiment did have much greater implications. If the Ranz and Tikol weren't allies, why were the green Zun working with them?

A flash of silver drew me out of my thoughts. The prince raised a knife and brought it just inches from my left hand, which I naturally drew back. More clawed hands shot out from the shadows and held me fast to the chair. They were stronger than I was even though they were only half my size. Technologically enhanced, no doubt.

"Hey, easy. I was only trying to help."

"By giving my son to the Ranz? You killed him!" Slaccin raised the knife in the air, his face a mess of anger and pain.

"No, he's not dead!" I cried out.

The knife stopped just a hair away from my skin. "What do you mean? My son lives?"

I nodded fast. "I know where he is. He's with a Ranz but not *the* Ranz."

"What does that mean, mammal?" said a voice from the shadows. The way he said it made me hope I never met the owner.

"I gave your son to someone that would never hurt him. She was very religious."

"Tell me where he is. Now!"

I took a long deep breath and steeled myself for the next few minutes. Either I would be a few digits short of a ten-pack or be one step closer in figuring out a way out of this and to unraveling what Kah was up to. I really had no choice of how to proceed.

"I need something from you first."

"Don't play games with me. What do you want?"

"Your friends in the shadows. The Zun. I want to know why they are working with the Ranz. Tell me that, and I'll tell you where your son is."

Slaccin's head turned to the shadows. More of the clicking sounds flew back and forth between him and I assumed the Zun. Moments later his head turned back to me. I thought I detected the faintest of smiles on his face though, to be honest, he was hard to read. Scales and skin are hard to decipher.

"Fine. But you'll take me to my child. Then I will tell you what you want to know."

I nodded. But the way Slaccin looked at me made my stomach lurch. I really hoped he wasn't smiling.

****

Alice sat at her work bench, a fresh reactor core

sitting on the table, her experiment again ready to start. She had spent the last few hours securing a new reactor from the university and poring over the data from the readings of her last run experiment. Through all the number crunching and the analytics, she was absolutely sure of one thing. Nothing added up.

With her own eyes, Alice had seen a vast desert and people walking aimlessly along the yellow sand. But in the data from the readout, nothing at all had manifested in the burned out warehouse where she worked. No portals were opened, no dimensions breached, and yet, she had seen something.

The motor came to life on her reactor. A dozen lights flashed along the surface, and Alice spun in her chair to set the dials to the appropriate frequencies. An alarm sounded on the device indicating she was breaching the spectral frequencies of the Krill. Which, of course, she expected. During the accident, the same warning sounded from their pieced together reactor. All fusion reactors had built-in components to warn users in case they bumped against anything they weren't supposed to touch. Such as the spectral frequencies of the Krill.

"Wait, the alarm didn't happen last time." Alice stood and walked through the room. The metal mesh that surrounded her was still intact. She took out her immersion rig, and again all signals showed as blocked including those from the towers and satellites set up by the Galactic Congress. And yet, the spectral frequencies were now coming through the makeshift Faraday cage. If they weren't, the reactor's alarm wouldn't have fired indicating existing frequencies prior to turning on.

But, that meant that her current attempt more

closely aligned with her previous one during the accident. In for a penny, in for a pound, Alice thought. She went to the reactor and disabled the alarm system. She fired up the energy levels and adjusted the system to match the frequencies that her experiments had always followed. Not quite the Krill's spectral levels but very similar. Her theory was more like a random exploration.

By channeling the energy from the fusion reactor through the quantum frequencies humanity had become aware of thanks to their alien friends, Alice believed it was possible to piggyback on the signal and open a portal to other dimensions. Of course, most of her work had been catalogued and done a thousand times over throughout the galaxy, but there were some gaps. The biggest was near frequencies used by the Krill, which were also off limits due to licensing agreements with the Office on Quantum Frequencies at the Galactic Congress. But those kinds of things don't stop uppity protected species like humans from poking their noses around. At least, that's the justification Alice convinced herself to believe.

The reactor came to life after the alarm system was deactivated, and Alice fired up the system to open the portal. A vapor of clouds formed in front her. Moments ticked by, but nothing happened. Alice frowned, returned to the reactor, and adjusted the settings, first moving off the frequency range she explored and then moving back. Still, nothing materialized in the gray mist. Frustration filled her soul, and she kicked a table nearest to her. The desert she had seen before could easily have been a hallucination brought on by the nature of the quantum energies she toyed with.

Alice shut off the reactor and folded her arms across her chest. She had the precise setting of her last attempt, where she found the desert, but the portal refused to form. Nothing made sense. Nor did it make any sense why the alarm sounded on the reactor this time and not the last. With her mind reeling in anger, she packed her things and decided to call it a day. Once back at the office, she could explore the libraries of the galaxy to see if anyone had ever explored the quantum ranges she did. At least that would be something to occupy her before she drove herself insane.

Chapter 16

Light from the sun at the center of the sphere blasted my eyes as we left the dark and dank room where I had been interrogated for the last few hours. The green Zun had decided to stay and not come with us on this makeshift rescue. And by us, I mean Slaccin and a few of his goons, all of whom I thought were dead ringers for the prince himself. Of course, they were all four-foot-tall lizards, how different could they really look?

Outside, a dozen different reptilian aliens crisscrossed the streets and walked along the sidewalks. I marveled at how most of them somewhat resembled Slaccin. Meaning, most were of the same height and stature. None were the size of Kah. It seemed curious, considering Kah had mentioned the Tikol weren't members of his Tillian bloc. I wondered if there was a size requirement.

"Are all of you coming on this little trip?" I said.

"We do not leave the prince's side," said one of the guards.

"Groovy," I said.

"I want my son, human."

"I'm aware, prince. By the way, me calling you prince all the time is going to get distracting. Do you have a first name?"

"What does that matter?"

I shrugged. "We're in cahoots now. Just thought it would make sense."

After a momentary pause the prince nodded and swished his tail back and forth. "You saved my son's life once. If you save it again, we can be cordial."

"Fair enough."

He stared into my eyes and said, "Now where is the son of Prince Slaccin, Mr. McGillicuddy?"

The way the prince phrased his question, and how he looked into my eyes, made the hair on my neck nearly jump off my skin. He had to know about my gift. Granted, I told them it was my process, but something about how he asked made me nervous. Though, considering my predicament, I didn't have time to let that little nugget fester in my gut. Still, if Kah was spilling the beans on me to the galaxy, my life was going to get a lot more difficult. Maybe taking a long walk through the cafeteria or a one-way ticket to Andromeda wasn't so bad after all.

"Well?" the prince said.

"I know where he is." The answer bubbled up into my memory as if it had always been there. Though I had to admit I was a little shocked with the answer. I thought our trip would take us back to Earth and then a quick doorway walk across the cosmos to Kah's office to find baby Slaccin in Ms. Mik's loving embrace. But as it turned out, we didn't even have to leave the Dyson.

"Fine. Let's go." Slaccin and his bodyguards proceeded to walk down the sidewalk in the wrong direction. I took out a cigarette from my pack and lit the end, waiting for them to turn around.

"You do know you're coming with us, yes?"

Slaccin said.

"That much I got. Thing is, I'm not sure where you think you're going."

"You said you gave my son to the Ranz. So, we are going to Earth and then the Ranz home world. You should know this will not be a friendly visit. The Ranz and the Tikol are not on the best of terms."

"Got that, too. Is there a reason you aren't in the Tillian bloc?"

Slaccin swung his head around violently and let out a long hiss. "We are not here to discuss galactic politics, human."

I nodded. "Fine. Thing is, your son isn't on the Ranz home world."

"What? Where is he?"

I turned away and looked up along the curve of the Dyson sphere. I didn't know exactly where I was pointing but I lifted my arm anyway and indicated a spot along the upward slope of the sphere.

"He's here? On this sphere? Impossible. The Ranz aren't occupying their designated area of this sphere."

I nodded. "Not sure why, or how. Maybe Ms. Mik moved him here or has religious friends. Either way, he's up there."

Slaccin grabbed my arm, his claws digging into my flesh almost to the point of drawing blood. "If you're lying, I will disembowel you and force your own entrails down your throat."

"Relax, prince. I may be a two-bit gumshoe, but even I have standards. Your kid is here, trust me."

"I don't have to trust you, human. If you fail me, you'll be dinner."

I gulped. "Yeah, I got that too."

****

We took a self-drive vehicle out of the city controlled by the Tikol through roads that spread across the surface of the sphere like a spider's web. Slaccin wanted no part of any automated transport system. With good reason. The last thing you wanted to do during a heist is leave a trail of your movements. And since they printed this ground vehicle from their warehouse, the parts set to disintegrate in thirty-six hours, there wasn't much chance of anyone tracking us by how we traveled.

Around us, the landscape shifted from endless suburban to rural to desolate and hot emptiness. Considering the amount of space inside one of these things, most of the area we passed was nothing but empty. Though, occasionally we did pass a few scattered towns and even a few other vehicles on the long stretch of road we traveled. Once a passenger in another vehicle even waved. I smiled back.

"How much longer?" I asked.

"Seven days." Slaccin said.

My head spun and my shoulders jerked upright. "What did you say?"

"We need to travel over ten thousand of your human miles."

"Can't we go faster?"

"No."

"Doesn't this thing fly or something?"

Slaccin and his guards hissed something between them before Slaccin turned to me. "Yes, it does. But we can't risk it now. Air control would spot us and identify the occupants."

"Well, I can't be in this thing for seven days. I have no leg room."

One of his bodyguards hissed empathically and nodded.

"Fine. We can go hypersonic once we are at the mountains."

"Then how long?"

"Four hours."

I shook my head and sighed. "You're telling me we can be there in four hours, and your first plan was to opt for the seven-day trip?"

Slaccin grunted. "I happen to like the isolation of the long ride."

"Are you trying to get your child killed?"

"The religious fanatics won't hurt him, and even if he hatched there's not enough time to indoctrinate him. He's fine."

"What happened to all the urgency?"

Slaccin shrugged. "That was before I knew where he was. I know he's safe now. And I have you to help me get him back."

I nodded. "So, since we have time. Can you tell me about why you are working with the Zun?"

Slaccin huffed and shook his head. "The Zun."

"Yeah, you've a gaggle of them back at your building. Why? You in cahoots with the Puntini?"

"Puntini?" Slaccin's tongue darted out of his mouth and he let out a long hiss.

"I'll take that as a no."

"Find my son, bring him to me. Then you will have answers."

Slaccin's gaze drifted to the window and the desert that stretched for a thousand miles outside. Of course, being a sphere dedicated to reptilian life, deserts, jungles, and hot climates were all you would find inside this Dyson. I tapped my personal area environment and smiled at my comfortable eighty-degree temperature. Say what you want about galactic society, their technology is pretty slick.

Without warning, the car lifted off the surface of the road and shot upward into the air. I held onto the seat with a white knuckled grip as we accelerated to speeds that frankly I wasn't comfortable with. Below us, the ground shot by in a growing blur. I shut my eyes to the sound of reptilian laughter. Undoubtedly at my squeamishness for both heights and insane speeds. And to think, I had a good four hours of this to endure before we landed. I tried my best to count to four hours but failed after ten seconds.

****

Our vehicle came to a stop on the road. Several miles away, a vast complex of buildings spread out, nearly the size of a small city. Markers along the road indicated this was the domain of the Church of the Divine. Which I learned, after a lengthy lecture by Slaccin on the foolishness of religion, was the dominant belief system of the entire Tillian bloc, a consortium of reptilian evolved members of galactic society that the Ranz belonged to. Slaccin, and the Tikol, among many reptilian species that didn't believe in the Church's dogma, wouldn't exactly be welcome if we walked into the facility. Which left us, or rather me, with the dilemma of how to rescue his kid.

"Well human? Now what do we do?"

I shrugged. More importantly, no answer came from my gift. Questions like that weren't exactly answerable. Even if Slaccin asked me how to rescue his child, no answer at all may come as his kid isn't in any danger, so why would we need to rescue him? And though I suspected he knew about my gift; I didn't want to play twenty questions with him on the chance that he didn't. I do like my brain in my skull and not on a petri dish.

"We need to go somewhere. Can't just sit here, it will draw attention," Slaccin said.

"Isn't there a place we can go for a drink? I could use one. And we need to strategize a plan."

Slaccin hissed. "How do I get my son back, Eugene?"

The answer which popped into my head made no sense. Images of Slaccin simply walking into the compound and getting his son filled my mind. But the lunacy of the answer made my head spin. If Slaccin just walked inside, he'd likely be arrested or worse. I didn't dare tell him the answer from my gift, so I shrugged and played it dumb. "I have no idea."

"How do you have no idea?"

I turned to him and let my anger show on my face. "I'm not an oracle, Slaccin. I didn't know this place was the size of Newark. He's in there somewhere, for sure. But we don't exactly have an army."

"If I don't get my son—"

"Yeah, I get it. I'm going into a meat grinder. We need a place to lie low."

The car leapt forward without warning, and we sped along the road. Several minutes passed until we pulled into a lot filled with other vehicles, mostly transport trucks. Both of Slaccin's goons got out of the car without a word and walked into what looked like the kind of watering hole that mammals probably shouldn't enter.

"What is this place?" I said.

"Last place of wickedness before we enter the territory of the Church."

"Neat."

"I need my son, human. I want him back. You need to get him. How?"

I pulled out my phone and connected to the Dyson's internal systems. I requested a patch back to Earth and put the receiver to my head. At least I tried to before Slaccin's claws pulled my arm down.

"Who are you calling?"

I sighed. "There's one person in the galaxy that can get us into and out of that location. I just hope she's not too busy."

****

Alice watched her experiment fail for the tenth time. She huffed once, threw her sandwich wrapper on the floor, only to pick it up again and place it in her pocket, and then she cursed to the seven heavens in three languages. Nothing worked. The energy field always collapsed just as it was forming. Her success, if it even was success, in the first attempt was clearly a mistake. Or a hallucination. Or maybe she had even fallen asleep and dreamt the whole thing. Sure, that could have happened, right?

Fat chance.

But what did happen? Alice was certain she wasn't losing her mind and that her settings weren't off in the slightest. She knew exactly at what frequency she had seen the desert manifestation, and yet she couldn't recreate the experience.

She'd also considered the Faraday cage. She'd even purchased additional material to further enable the cage to block additional frequencies that might be interfering with her experiment, but still nothing.

The only answer, of course, was she had no idea what was going on. Unless somehow the Galactic Congress interfered with her research, discovered her first success and somehow shut her down. But that was laughable. Why would they care? The congress had made clear that fiddling with certain technologies could result in localized events. And even those would be heavily scanned and scrutinized by the Sentinels. So even if they did shut her down, a dozen or more angry robots would show up and give her a stiff talking to. Which hadn't happened.

Alice jumped. The sound of her phone shocked her out of her thoughts. Eugene was calling. Which, as it happened, could be a nice distraction. She wasn't getting anywhere doing whatever it was that she was doing.

"Hi," Alice said.

"Hey, great, you're there."

"Obvi."

"I need help," Eugene said.

"Shocker. What?"

"Can't talk about it over the call. Want to come to Dyson twelve? I'm in a bind."

Alice tossed around the idea a few times in her mind. She could stay here, fiddle with this for another day, but she was confident the results would be the same. Which meant she had nothing. Still no clues about what happened to her friends and nothing more to do but get frustrated about the situation. Besides, she'd never been to the cluster before.

"Fine. Where in twelve?"

After a quick series of directions from Eugene, Alice hung up, packed her bag, and took a moment to mourn her friends. She just had no idea what to do next to try to find them. Maybe they couldn't be found at all. She rose from her seat, walked through the door and took the first tramcar to the Woodward. Nothing like a galactic adventure to take your mind off faulty quantum portal formations.

****

Three lizards, two humans, and one Zun sat around a table and discussed plans to commit a felony against a religious sect. And here I thought my trip to the Dyson cluster was going to be boring.

Alice had arrived not more than thirty minutes ago, after she took a brief train ride through several spheres in the cluster.

"Okay, I think have it," Alice said.

"Have what?" Slaccin said.

"How go get your son out. What else? I studied the schematics of their compound and managed to hack my way into their system for a detailed list of their schedules for the staff."

"How did you get all this?" I said.

"What do you mean?"

"Aren't there any computer systems secure in the cosmos?"

Alice shrugged. "Not my fault religious reptiles don't know how to use a firewall."

"Right."

"How do I save my son, human?"

"It's Alice."

"What?"

"The name. It's Alice. Use it or I leave."

Slaccin shifted in his seat but seemed to melt under Alice's stare. I had to give her props. She wasn't taking nonsense from anyone. A trait that I admired and wished I could duplicate.

"Fine. Alice. Reunite me with my son, and I won't dine on your entrails."

Alice nodded. "Better."

Snarls and grunts came from Slaccin's crew, but they held their space. If they wanted to rip us to pieces, I doubted we could give much resistance. Of course, Alice could have something up her sleeve. What that would be I had no idea. She was still a teenage girl with about as much upper body strength as me. And that wasn't much.

"This is the plan. Tonight, one of your goons will get himself admitted. Say he's a convert—"

The goon in question snarled and stomped his foot on the ground.

"Madness! We will do no such thing," Slaccin said.

"Want your kid back?"

Slaccin nodded once.

"Then you will do it. He's not really converting, just pretending. Get it?"

"It is distasteful."

"So is not having your kid around."

Slaccin folded his arms and seemed to relent.

"Once he converts, we settle in here for a day. Then tomorrow, we'll approach with you trying to get your goon out again. We'll tell them he's not in his right mind."

"Why would we do that?" I said pointing to Alice and myself.

"We will just be with Slaccin, as friends."

"Humans and Tikol are not friends," Slaccin said.

Alice sighed. "And yet, here we are. Can we go through this?"

We all sat back and listened to Alice present her not simple plan. For the next sixty minutes she detailed a complex series of steps that would eventually put us all in the nursery. Once there, another complex series of steps would find us escaping the building through underground tunnels and then to a black-market site not far away in the nearby hills. From there, we'd meet up with the green Zun who would drive us back to the city and to freedom. From her description, I counted at least two dozen places where this could go very wrong.

"Are we sure about this?"

Alice shrugged. "Sounds good to me. I've always wanted to do a heist."

Something about the way she said it made my skin crawl. "Maybe we should ask Eddie, you know get a second opinion?"

Alice sighed, frowned, pouted, and lifted her knees to her chest. "Fine, whatever. It's a perfectly fine plan."

"Seems complicated," Slaccin said.

I had to agree.

Moments later Eddie's voice popped over the communication channel. He sounded alert, aware, and not at all like his old self before we visited the virtual underworld. I filled Eddie in on Alice's plan and the need to get Slaccin's kid. A long silence filled the room, and a few of the guards shifted uneasily.

"I don't think I understand," Eddie said.

I sighed. Maybe he wasn't all better yet after all. "What's there to understand, Eddie? We need to get the kid out of that building."

"Yeah, but isn't Slaccin the father?"

Everyone in the room shifted uneasily now. One of the guards growled at me. "Yes, you know he is, Eddie. Are you feeling okay?"

"I'm fine, Jack. If Slaccin is the biological father, he can just go in and ask for his son."

A dead silence filled the room. I tilted my head to one side in confusion. "What? He can do that?"

"Yes. It's an orphanage. Not a prison."

"But the Tikol are not members of the Tillian bloc," Slaccin said.

"Doesn't matter. You're his father. They will honor that. As long as you submit to a genetic test."

"Will you?" I asked.

"Of course!"

I sat back in my chair and tilted my head to one side. My gift had told me the answer and I ignored it. A weight fell on my shoulders. Even with my gift I was a lousy private dick. All this planning, risking Alice's life coming all the way out here, all for nothing. All Slaccin had to do was waltz in, grab his kid, and be home in time for corn flakes.

Alice sighed and stood from her chair. She packed her bags and moved to the door. "Guess I'll go then."

"Did you know that, Alice?"

She shrugged. "Maybe."

"Then what's with the plan?"

One of the guards clawed hands reached for her arm to prevent her from leaving. My hand went to my gun hidden in my pocket, an old Earth revolver that Slaccin and his guards missed as it didn't have an energy field. Before I could draw my pistol, just as the guard's fingers touched Alice's arm, bolts of electricity erupted, and the guard sailed across the room and landed hard on the dirt floor.

"Alice!" I ran to her but quickly noticed she hadn't moved or even noticed what just happened. Which prompted me to ask, "What just happened?"

Alice's face screwed up into confusion as she stared at me. She looked at my personal area environment and shook her head. "It has a security feature. Just turn it on, and no one can touch you throughout the cluster."

I nodded slowly. "Right. Of course, I knew that. See you back in the office?"

"Sure. I'm going to visit Dyson one hundred first. I hear they have the best noodles dish in the galaxy."

****

Squeaks from Slaccin's kid filled the room. A dozen of Slaccin's guards and supporters flocked through the tiny space to pay their respects to the future ruler of, well, whatever it was that Slaccin ruled. Being dethroned royalty was always murky business after all. Though I had to admit, Slaccin's kid was cute. Maybe not cute enough to follow him in a rebellion, but to each their own.

"I need to go, Slaccin. Can we settle up?" I said,

Slaccin picked up his son, snuggled him once, and nodded. He rose from his seat, and a nurse came to care for the little guy who was already squealing with displeasure from his dad leaving.

We happened to arrive at the orphanage just an hour before the egg hatched, which allowed for Slaccin and his kid to bond quickly. They would have been okay otherwise, but it was a nice way for things to end for them both. Granted, their future wouldn't be roses no matter how you cut it. Revolutions are messy business, but at least they'd have some quiet time before things blow up. Thankfully, I would be long gone by then.

We settled into chairs in a side room, Slaccin leaning back and resting his hands behind his head. He grinned, at least I think, and chuckled a few times.

"Glad to see everything worked out," I said.

"I am in your debt. Amazing, considering you were almost in my belly."

I grinned but then gulped when I realized he wasn't joking. "So, about the Zun. Why are you working with them?"

Slaccin shook his head and shrugged. "I'm not. The reptiles that brought you to me aren't the Zun."

I tried to respond but only mumbled. "Sorry, what?" I finally managed spit out.

"They are a member species in the Conglomerate of Thinking Reptiles."

"The what?"

"A counter organization to the Tillian bloc. Made up of reptiles that aren't religious fanatics."

I nodded. "And the Zun?"

"Again, they aren't the Zun. They just look like them. Except they're green of course."

Frustration weighed down my spirit and let out a long sigh. "Great. Still no closer to figuring out why the Zun are working with the Ranz."

Slaccin snorted. "The Zun? And the Ranz? Never."

"What do you mean?"

"The Zun hate religion almost as much as we do. Of course, they hate everyone. They aren't even allowed in the Dyson Cluster and are banned on most worlds."

"But I saw them on Earth."

"Impossible. They aren't allowed there. If the Ranz invited them, it would jeopardize their membership in the Galactic Congress. Bringing the Zun to a protected world like Earth? Never."

"Great. Now I'm even worse off than before."

"How's that?"

"I'm trying to solve a mystery."

Slaccin nodded. "Well, you could just ask him."

"Ask who what?"

"Ask Kah whatever it is you want to know." Slaccin stood and stretched his arms. "Today has taught me one important lesson. Don't bother with the subterfuge. Just go and ask. Typically, the universe will see to it that things work out."

He held out his hand, and I shook it, his claws scraping against my skin nearly enough to break through but not quite. I sat back in my chair and nodded. Why didn't I just go and ask him? What's the worst that could happen? Besides being eaten, I doubt he could do much. And he did have a steady supply of mice in his desk.

Still, the thought sent a shiver down my spine. If I was going to waltz into the Ranz office and demand answers, I would need a backup plan. And there was only one human in the universe I could turn to for help. Hopefully, she was still at the noodle shop. Which would be great since I was starving.

Chapter 17

I left Slaccin's warehouse with a pat on my back and a sincere thanks, which felt nice. Ever since I found the kid on the shelf of a rich man's house in Potomac, Maryland, I wanted to make sure he was safe. First I thought I had with the Ranz, and I suppose he generally was. Nothing wrong with growing up in an orphanage, but now I knew he'd be okay. Well, okay is relative, I suppose. He may become the face of a revolution and may topple the Tikol government, but, hey, you can't choose your destiny, as I know very well.

The train station was only a few blocks away from Slaccin's lair. I passed a dozen reptiles, many of whom stared at me with hungry eyes. I thought I could even hear a growling stomach every three steps. My attention turned to my personal area environment. I activated the security features on the device and set the comfort range to two feet. A red light began blinking on my device and I noticed that the reptiles around me started to give me a wide berth. Score one for Alice. Well, score infinity for Alice generally speaking. Though it would have been nice to know about that when Slaccin's goons had me by the collar, it's enough to know that I'd be safe anywhere in the cluster.

At the train station, I pulled out the directions to the Dyson one hundred and Alice's best noodle shop in the galaxy. Three Dysons to travel through before I would find my way to Dyson one hundred via an express route.

On the platform, I watched a flurry of reptiles push toward the coming train. Once it stopped, I joined the masses and boarded one of the cars. Finding myself a nice quiet seat by the window I settled myself and ran through the events of the last few hours.

Frankly, my shoulders slumped as I realized just how little I'd figured out. Granted, I learned the Zun were an independent player, but how exactly did that factor into anything? Did they also know about my gift and want to dissect my brain to find my talent? Were they working for the Puntini? Not likely since a party of them feasted on a dead Puntini at Fritz's restaurant.

Worse than not knowing what the Zun wanted from any of this was not knowing what my next move should be. Did I really want to confront Kah? What if he and Yut were working together instead of the Zun and Kah? If I short-circuited their little game of twisting me around their tusks and claws, they could decide to end the charade and open up my cranium. Maybe this whole thing was just a test to see if my gift really did work. Find the hidden lost base of the Puntini and it would prove my gift is real. But Kah already knew my gift was real, unless he thought I was faking it.

That would make sense, but then how do the Zun factor into this? Their dancing lights, the Andraz, which Caesar had thankfully removed from the equation, seemed pretty adamant that they wanted to know the location of the door. But maybe some wires got crossed? Maybe the Zun were looking for Tom's pocket universe, overheard Yut asking for the location of a hidden area of alien origin on Earth, which is itself nearly impossible with the Galactic Congress looking over things and decided to rough me up to see if I'd reveal it. And, at the time of their roughing me up, I didn't know about Tom's space.

It made sense. It lined up. Kah and Yut in cahoots to test my gift and the Zun dragged along looking for Tom's pocket universe. I nodded to myself just as the train entered into a frozen sphere with a star at its center dimmer than I thought possible. A dim haze covered this sphere, and it seemed like perpetual twilight.

The doors opened, and a beast that resembled a walking polar bear, only bigger, ambled onto the train and worked his, or her, way to the large seat section. He sat down with a humph, and the doors closed. I wondered what other species of life would find this sphere nice. The personal area environment, just as easily as it turned on, could be turned off when someone entered an environment designed for their biology. A fact I found while doing some research on the help file for how to activate the security system.

Outside the window, the interior of the frozen Dyson opened up to the empty space beyond. I watched the stars speed by and let all my questions of my predicament fade away. There was a quiet comfort in watching the universe go on by without a concern for anything happening in my insane life. As if none of it, in the end, matters at all. Stars will still be born, and new intelligent life will rise, and not one of them will know or care about Eugene and the aliens that want his brain.

Still, I needed a solution. What was my next move? Confront Kah? Run for Andromeda? Play their game and see how it ends? With the Andraz out of the way and the Zun unable to show their faces on Earth, at least I didn't have to worry about them. My stomach rumbled just as the train pulled into Dyson one hundred. All of these questions could wait, I decided.

I sent Alice a quick note telling her I was on my way and to order me a noodle bowl. She responded immediately that she had. I smiled at the one stability in my life, my secretary, whom I really needed to figure out how to pay one of these days.

****

I stepped out of the tram car onto Dyson one hundred and was immediately assaulted by a thousand savory smells dancing on the wind. My stomach grumbled and my mouth watered as I realized I just entered a land mass of over five hundred and fifty-million times the size of Earth, nearly devoted to food. Well, food and adventure parks.

Dyson one hundred, as I learned as soon as I walked to a guide on the wall, was the entertainment sphere for the entire cluster. Every species could enjoy the adventure worlds, wild white water rafting rivers a thousand miles long, mountains three times the size of Everest to climb, wildlife refuges from around the cosmos with nearly every animal to have ever existed walking, swimming, or flying somewhere on this world, and a nearly endless supply of food stalls, restaurants, pubs, and dive bars. After all, if the end of the galaxy were to happen again, folks would still want to take their kids on a holiday excursion to get out of their own house. Or sphere.

On the kiosk, I pulled up the name of Alice's noodle shop. Sure enough, the reviews on the list were through the roof. Best noodles in the galaxy and possibly the local super cluster. I tried to memorize the steps to get there, but frankly, knew I would get lost walking even half a block. The sheer number of visitors that streamed off the tram car, including the large polar bear looking fellow, were in the hundreds. Throngs of aliens walked and slithered their way from the train station to the sidewalks and streets that seemed to stretch out for a thousand miles. And, honestly, given the size of the sphere, they probably did.

I turned back to the kiosk and implanted a retinal pointer, same type that I had installed in the embassy when I visited Kah. A green arrow lit up in my vision and pointed me toward Alice and noodles. A small counter beneath the arrow indicated the shop was a good two miles down the road. Which was nice, I could use the walk.

Aromas from fresh baked bread, a million spices, cooked and cured meats, and cheese aged three hundred years all greeted me on my walk. I had to force myself not to take a quick detour at a local food stall before meeting Alice.

A large shadow fell over the street. I looked up to see an airship with throngs of visitors gawking out of windows. The floating tourist trap gently sailed out over the sprawling city to destinations unknown. There were more than enough things to see here—one could spend a lifetime just in this sphere.

Thirty minutes later I stood in front of the noodle shop. I could see Alice sitting at a table with two bowls of noodles. Hopefully, one was for me. I entered the building to the angry shouts of a few dozen aliens that were waiting in line. I begged my apologies and tried to indicate as best as I could that I was meeting a friend. A few angry stares answered me back.

"Hey," I said as I pulled up a seat.

"Hiya. I ordered you a bowl."

I nodded, smiled, and grabbed a sonic powered utensil. "Thanks. What is it?"

"Noodles, Eugene. What else would it be?"

"Right."

"How'd things go with Slaccin?"

I shrugged. "Fine. Eddie was right. He walked right in and asked for his kid."

Alice nodded.

"Why did you want to do a heist?"

"Thought it'd be fun."

I smiled and put a large bundle of noodles into my mouth. An explosion of flavors filled my taste buds. From spices that bordered on a mix of Asian and Indian to heat from peppers and something else I couldn't quite identify; the flavors sent my mind into overdrive. The noodles were freshly made today, of that I had no doubt, and were somehow crunchy, chewy, and soft in every bite. I realized the noodles were changing textures every time I bit down, and the spices shifted to match perfectly. It felt as if I was eating three separate meals in one.

"This is amazing," I said.

"Told you."

Alice took her last bite and smiled in gastro-bliss. "So, learn anything from Slaccin?"

"Zun aren't working with Kah. Learned that much."

"I could have told you that."

I nodded, a touch of anger building in my gut. "So

why didn't you?"

"You never asked."

"Okay, Alice. I'm asking now. Slaccin thinks I should waltz into Kah's office and demand to know his game. Should I?"

"Doesn't sound smart if you don't know his angle."

I proceeded to tell her my theory that that Kah and Yut were working together, and the Zun got dragged in thinking Yut's alien site was Tom's secret beach-cave hideaway. I listed my reasoning and details, which, as I did, seemed even more plausible to me. But, of course, if all that were true, the only thing I could do was play their game and see how it ended. And it meant I had no ammunition or next steps.

"You could find out what Yut's looking for," Alice said.

"What do you mean? It doesn't exist."

"What if it does?"

"If it does, then that changes things. Means the Zun aren't looking for Tom's cave but whatever Yut really is after."

"And it means Kah and Yut aren't working together. Why would he care about some alien Puntini site?"

"But how do I find out if the place is real? I'd have to find it."

Alice shook her head and sighed. "You're a detective, aren't you?"

I shrugged. "I'm a two-bit nobody with an ace up my sleeve."

"Fine, be that then. Go to a Puntini city and ask. There's one here in the cluster. It's small, they don't care much for the Dysons, but they'll know. If there are rumors of an ancient Puntini site on earth, then Yut's telling the truth. If not, Kah and Yut are working together."

"Can't we just look in the Galactic Library?"

"Oh, I already did. Nothing. But that doesn't mean anything. An alien race setting up an unsanctioned outpost on a world with a dominant intelligent species is illegal. Puntini would hide something like that from the Galactic Library."

"So, if they are hiding it, how do I find it?"

Alice shrugged. "By detecting it?"

I laughed and took another bite of my noodles. The crunchy, soft, texture with the alternating spices was wonderful. I finished my bowl and sipped on my drink, a crazy concoction with a small amount of fizz, and leaned back in my chair.

"Want to come with?"

Alice shook her head. "No, I need some time to think."

I didn't push it or ask what she had going on in her life. Alice was the type to share when she wanted to share. Besides, she'd given me at least a direction to take. I could spare a quick trip to the Puntini system in the cluster and see if I could learn something new. Not like I had any other leads.

****

Alice watched Eugene walk into the crowd. A large family of two-foot-tall teddy bears pushed their way onto the street and nudged her just enough to distract her from watching her pseudo-boss. When she turned her attention back in his direction, Eugene was gone, lost among the throngs of visitors to the sphere.

Alice thought about going with him but deep down

wanted no part of that. The Puntini were a very gluttonous species. The way they resembled pigs in both their general appearance and their gastro-habits was quite fascinating. Convergent evolution was always an interesting topic on the virtual message centers of the Earth. Of course, every question humanity hadn't even thought of yet had already been answered by the Galactic Congress and the scientists of the galaxy.

That thought spiraled in Alice's mind. Now that her stomach was filled with the best noodles in the cosmos, and her little mini adventure to the Dyson Cluster was coming to a close, her next steps in life were to tuck tail and go home to a secretary's desk and her immersion rig. With her experiments at a total loss what else could she do?

She did have the frequency specifications from her last experiment. Thoughts of rifling through a million galactic databases to see if anyone had done the research on those ranges briefly entertained her mind. But what would be the point? Some lecture on why humans shouldn't bother with things already done a thousand times over?

Alice sighed, heaved her bag over her shoulder, and headed toward the train terminal that would take her back to the Congressional Sphere and the teleporter home to Earth.

Still, the event wasn't a total loss. She did have fun playing with Eugene and the Tikol. As she walked through the crowds of aliens, she played the steps of her heist back in her mind. She nodded to herself at every stage, convinced the plan would work.

****

The Puntini city in the Dyson was more like a

small town rather than a hub of activity. Nestled between valleys on Dyson seventeen, the same sphere where the human race had been given more space than they would need, the small Puntini town, nearly fifty-thousand miles away from the nearest human settlement, had a population of just under a five thousand souls.

I made it to the quaint village, I stopped calling it a city as soon as I arrived, via a series of aircraft, ground cars, and of course the inter-sphere railway system that connected all the Dysons together. Once my feet hit the cobblestone street, the smell of fresh bread, cheeses, and a variety of cured meats hit my nose. A good portion of the town settled on a twisting river that cut through the valley on its way to one of the major oceans of Dyson seventeen, where several sentient aquatic species lived.

There was no visitor center or hotel. No town mayor or judicial building of any sort. Locals regarded me with mild curiosity though some bordered on disdain. It seemed I wasn't the only human to have visited and perhaps the last ones weren't well received.

Small tables and chairs sat along the river's edge on the stone street. Most were occupied by Puntini that sipped on wine and dined on cheese and crackers. I got the impression that perhaps this was an enclave of the wealthy. But, considering any Puntini could visit this place by going to the nearest Galactic Embassy, and there was one on the Puntini home world; perhaps there was another reason why the town was so small.

"Something we can help you with?" said a Puntini that sat alone at one of the tables. He looked to be about the same height as Yut. He wore a pair of beige shorts and what looked like a Hawaiian shirt. Like Yut, he also had very small to borderline invisible tusks in his lower jaw.

I shrugged. "Just passing through. Heard the Puntini had a city on the sphere."

"More like a refuge for those brave enough to venture off-world."

"That right?"

The Puntini shrugged. "We are astrophobic. We don't like leaving our planet. It's a racial fear."

"Why is that?"

The Puntini looked at me and shook his head. "We just are."

"So, I take it you aren't very open to strangers then?" I had heard of the agoraphobic nature of some races. It bordered on xenophobia for some. Though I didn't know the Puntini suffered from the affliction.

"No, we quite like visitors. Though the last humans that came through became severely intoxicated and excreted in our river. Distasteful in the extreme."

"Sorry," I said.

The Puntini shrugged. "Not your fault."

I looked around and immediately began to second guess myself. I doubted I would find any information related to the relationship of ancient Earth and the Puntini. A thought crossed my mind that I probably should have checked to see if they were star faring a few thousand years ago. Chalk another one up for lousy detective work.

"Can I offer you a drink while you're here? Next shuttle to leave won't arrive for a bit."

I shrugged. "Why not." I sat down and sipped on the wine. It tasted nice enough though it was a little sweet. One benefit of the spheres was the galaxy tended to place species based on similarities with others. Puntini and humans were pretty close biologically, which also scored one in the column for there being a lost base somewhere on Earth.

"While I'm here, I might as well ask, perhaps you know."

"Sure, I know many things. Most of us here are scientists and professors. Those that aren't limited by our racial need to stay on our home world."

"Neat." I wondered if that's why Alice sent me here.

The Puntini grunted a laugh. "What's your question?"

"You ever heard of an ancient Puntini base or outpost on Earth? Something really old?"

The Puntini tossed his head from side to side. "No. Not very likely such a place exists. Considering Earth has been under galactic observation for four thousand years and the Puntini only became star faring five hundred years ago."

I nodded and shook my head. Damn, that was easy. If I had just spent a minute and thought things through, Yut's claim of an ancient site would have crumbled in an instant. Which meant two things. First, I was a terrible detective. But more importantly for now, if there was no alien base on Earth, other than Tom's beach, then Kah and Yut were in cahoots and my goose was as good as cooked. I made a mental note to check the times of the first intergalactic ship heading for Andromeda with the full intention of taking it. I had failed as a private eye and now needed to get out of Dodge to save my own skin.

"You look sad." The Puntini said.

I nodded and took a long sip of my wine. "I just realized that I've been lied to by two aliens. And I thought one of them was almost a friend."

"Two Puntini?"

I shook my head. "A Puntini and a Ranz."

The Puntini at the chair spat out his wine and did a funky clicking with his fingers before shaking his head violently. "Ranz? Here? In our town?"

Several more of the Puntini turned to our table, all of their hands going to their personal area environments on their shoulders. One of them drew a weapon.

"Easy," I said and held up my hands. "No, there's no Ranz here."

The Puntini at my table nodded to the others and they settled down. "Sorry. We fought a war with the Ranz. We don't get along very well."

I nodded, my brow furrowing deep. "That right? So, the likelihood of the Ranz ambassador working with the Puntini?"

"In what sense? Ambassadors must maintain a formal relationship. Our races do speak, but only through official channels. If you mean, would they conspire together for some end? Unlikely. We don't get along well with mammal eaters."

"But—" I said, pointing to the charcuterie on the table.

"Sentient-mammal eaters. Oh, the Ranz claim they no longer partake, but would you trust that? We endured centuries of culling from another reptilian race. Though we know this was before our revolt and our rise to galactic society, no Puntini would trust a reptile. For any reason."

I sat back in my chair and let the information wash over me. The Puntini site didn't exist. But Kah and Yut were also not working together. Which meant my entire theory was thrown out the window. And on top of that, the Zun eating the Puntini would have been seen as the ultimate insult. Granted many other races as well I would hope. But all that added up to the point that I was back at square one. Well, maybe square two. I knew Yut was lying. But what was Kah's game? He wasn't working with the Zun, and he wasn't working with Yut. No matter how many ways I twisted it I just couldn't find an angle. Which meant maybe, just maybe, he really did just pass on a request from Yut. But if that's true, then he wasn't involved in this mess in any way.

I sipped my wine, thanked my hosts, and stood. The thought of running to Andromeda left my mind. It was a long, cramped trip anyway, and there was nothing but youth hostels on the other side. I was a little old for that game. I decided then it was time to face the music. I would confront Kah directly and get to the bottom of what he wanted. But at this point, I truly didn't think he wanted anything as far as Yut and this missing ancient site was concerned.

Chapter 18

"You thought I did what?" Kah leaned forward in his chair. On his desk, a mess of documents and folders covered the surface. His red bow tie sat loosely around his neck.

"Yeah, sorry. Look, I misjudged that one. I thought you had sent the two lights of artificial origin after me and Eddie." I had my hat in my hand and fumbled with the rim. Best to be as humble in the moment as I could muster.

"Why would I care what Yut is doing, Jack? Do you see this?" Kah held up one of the thick pieces of paper with Ranz lettering running down in three columns.

"Yeah?"

"Lizards in the Dalkung district demand better wages and more access to live animals. Live animals! How exactly are we to get enough Kuld down there to feed a million belly walkers?"

A door slammed behind me, and I jumped in my chair, my hat falling onto the floor in front of Kah's desk. I turned to see the door to Kah's office closed, a thick guttural growl rumbling from the other side. I shifted in my chair and looked at Kah as if to say, *should I be running?*

Kah shrugged. "Mik doesn't care for racial slurs."

"Lizards is a racial slur?"

"No." Kah leaned forward and tried his best to lower his voice, but there's not much a two-ton dinosaur can do. "Belly walkers."

Hot air and a foul smell followed Kah's whisper. I retrieved my hat from the floor and gave the surrounding air a quick wave with my fedora before putting it back in place on my head.

"At any rate," Kah said, "the Ranz don't employ AIs. We never created any either."

"You don't have any? Why not?"

"My people are devout in their religion. Artificials don't have a place in that belief."

"You don't strike me as the religious sort, Kah."

"All Ranz are religious. To what degree is another matter." Kah smiled.

"Why?"

"Why what?"

"Why are all of you so religious?"

"Does it matter?"

"No, just curious. You're a class five species. Would have thought you'd grown out of religion."

Kah shrugged. "I don't know. Perhaps religion means something different to us than it does to humans. Whatever the reason, AIs don't have a place in Ranz culture, society, or on any of our worlds. Period. Which is all information readily available from any Galactic Library kiosk. I believe there are several thousand on Earth."

I took the jab in stride, flashed a smile and a nod back at Kah. He threw the barb with enough venom for me to take the hint. The fact he spat the words out through rows of sharp teeth and forked tongue helped. The implication was clear. All you had to do, you two-bit excuse of a private dick, was to do a simple query on the Ranz and you'd have known it wasn't me. Fine. Maybe he's right. Then again, it's also the perfect alibi. *Can't be me, Jack, we don't use AIs.*

"Well, anyway, sorry. Can you shed some light on why Yut wants the location of this door so bad? Bad enough some other aliens are sending their AI pals to give me a once-over?"

Kah let out a long sigh, threw his pen on the table, and held both clawed hands up in the air. "I'm one of the most important Ranz on my home planet. I oversee the lives of millions of souls, am ambassador to the Galactic Congress, and regularly meet with my government to advise on matters of state but let me stop all of that and hear what's going on with the Puntini Ambassador Yut, an ancient alien artifact on Earth, and an increasingly annoying human caught in the middle."

What else can you do when a creature three times your size lays a verbal beat down like that? You answer him. I recounted everything that happened to me, minus the part with Eddie and Caesar. No sense getting a religious fanatic riled up over something that doesn't matter to the case at hand.

"That's it then?" Kah said. His boredom was clear by his slouched shoulders and half falling eyelids.

"Yeah," I said.

"Well, Jack, I have—"

"Oh, and the stick men from galactic center. The Zun. Forgot about them."

At the mention of the odd aliens with a taste for Puntini, Kah's face went slack, and his snarl returned. He let out a long sigh and turned his attention to a keyboard on his desk. When he was done, he swiveled his head back to me a looked at me like I was a noon snack.

"You're positive you saw the Zun?"

I shrugged in a way that said *so what*. "Yeah, they've been following me. Sent their AIs to destroy a diner and even entered human cyberspace. They also have a taste for Yut-Meat."

"What does that mean?"

"Means they ate a Puntini at a noodle shop in Chinatown."

"You do realize that type of thing is frowned upon, Jack. I mean, galactic societies don't go around eating each other." Kah tossed his head to one side and shrugged. "Most, anyway."

"I had a hunch."

"The Zun aren't a member of the Galactic Congress. Things are different in the center of the galaxy, Jack. The background radiation from the stars creates a unique environment for life."

"You mean the big glow in the middle?"

"Yes, Jack, the big glow in the middle." Kah's voice sounded like he was talking to a two-year-old. I didn't resent it. "Why didn't you report that a member of the Puntini delegation had been killed?

"What am I supposed to say? My proof is images flowing through my head from a question asked by an intelligent octopus. Not exactly admissible evidence."

"Did you tell Yut at least?"

I shook my head. "Same reason. Yut would have either kidnapped me for being semi-omniscient to dissect my brain or laughed me out of his office."

Kah didn't react from my barb. I hoped to get him to let something slip. I still thought he was after the insides of my skull, just maybe not as determined as I thought. The ambassador stretched his arms. Muscles the size of pythons wriggled beneath bright green scales. In one long step, he crossed the room and opened the door to a closet. He took out a large leather jacket—I didn't want to know what animal it'd come from—and a brown briefcase. He walked back to his desk, shoved a dozen items into the briefcase, snapped it shut, and gave me a toothy grin.

"Ready?" he asked.

"For what?" I felt like we were about to go to the dean's office, and I was going to be expelled.

"We're going to visit my fellow ambassador, Yut. We're going to inform him what's been going on and you're going to apologize and beg that he doesn't have the human authorities throw you in prison."

"Why would I be going to prison?"

"Who cares. Your government would shove you into a Valrexian mine pit if I asked them to do so. What you did is irrelevant."

"Well, that's just swell. And here I thought we were going to be friends."

"We are friends. Don't worry, I'll make sure you're fine. I don't care if the Zun are eating Puntini. I've dealt with far stranger incidents."

"I thought you said aliens eating aliens was illegal?"

Kah shrugged. "It's a strange galaxy, Jack, and I'm not a police-lizard. Far more important than the menu of the Zun is that they're on Earth. They're forbidden from coming to a planet that is a ward of the state. They must have used the Andraz to punch a hole through the Sentinels."

"So, Slaccin was being straight. They aren't allowed here."

Kah let out a sigh of frustration. "No, Jack. They're not allowed here. Neither the Andraz nor the Zun should be placing one foot or wisp of gas on your world."

I nodded. Galactic politics made human politics look like a high school election race. I stood up and followed Kah out the door. Mik was sitting at her desk but never looked up. She was still upset at Kah's racial slur.

We exited Kah's office through the portal and were thrust into the hallway of the Woodward. Dozens of aliens walked through the halls. Some looked at Kah and walked a little faster while others abruptly turned around and walked in the other direction. Being the biggest guy in the room made a statement. Especially with three-inch incisors.

An electric board on the wall showed that the Puntini office was in the same spot as it was the last time I visited. We shuffled upstairs never meant for a Ranz to climb and then down a familiar-looking corridor to the Puntini office. The soft yellow glow of the portal light ringed the door frame. Kah didn't hesitate to grab me by the shoulder and shove me inside. He ducked and followed me through.

****

Inside, Yut's cousin sat at the same desk, still shoveling yellow green slop into his open maw. Both tusks were stained with the color of the strange food. Kah didn't miss a beat. He strolled past the fatter Yut and walked into the ambassador's office.

"Kah, what brings you here?" Ambassador Yut

said.

"Something we need to discuss." Kah pointed his clawed hand back toward me. I only shrugged and smiled.

"Jack? What is this about?" Yut threw his tablet computer on the table and sat back in his chair.

With a stern nod from Kah, I told Yut everything that happened, skillfully leaving out anything to do with Eddie and the AI underground. No need for them to know Earth's very dirty laundry. When I was finished an uneasy silence settled on the room. Eventually, Yut smiled, shrugged, and picked his tablet back up from his desk.

"So?" Yut said.

I frowned and gave Yut a hard stare. "One of your people was murdered and eaten and all you have to say is 'so'?"

Yut only sighed. "Have you found the site yet, Jack?"

I shook my head no.

"Then I don't care. Come back when you do."

"And the Zun?" Kah said.

Yut shook his head and ground his teeth. From his instant frustration at hearing of the Zun, it was clear he had dealt with them before. I could tell Kah picked up on it as well. He nodded and closed his eyes to slits as he waited for Yut to answer.

"What about them? Contact the Sentinels and the galactic security council. They aren't supposed to be anywhere near a class three species." Yut picked up a pen and scribbled something onto one of the papers on his desk.

Another long silence stretched in the room, but this

one Yut ignored. He went back and forth between his computer screen and papers. After a minute of being ignored, Kah stood and patted me on the shoulder which felt more like a sledgehammer hitting my spine.

"Let's go, Jack."

I nodded and stood. I couldn't tell if I was still under Yut's employ or not. To be sure, it was odd to be being directed by Kah while sitting in front of my client. I turned to leave with Kah and started to the door when Yut broke his silence.

"You still work for me, Mr. McGillicuddy. We are contractually bound. And I want the location of the pre-contact site we discussed."

I turned back, and Yut hadn't bothered looking my way. He still punched keys on his keyboard and stared into his computer screen. I nodded back to him but didn't reply. Why give him the courtesy?

Outside, back in the hallways of the Woodward, Kah paced back and forth until I emerged from Yut's office. He waved me to the side, and we walked back down toward his office. Before we got two feet, he lowered his head to my ear, and for half a second, a primal fear rose in my throat at the prospect of being Kah's snack.

"What is Yut looking for, Jack?" Kah asked as he stared into my eyes.

I grabbed my head as a thousand random items flashed into my mind. Yut was a surname, after all, and Kah had just asked me what a few hundred, if not more, Puntini were looking for in that moment. It was a bit of an eye-opener just how many were looking for some kind of snack crisps. "I don't know, but even if I did, I couldn't tell you. He's my client after all."

"Jack, spare me the confidentiality clause. What is he looking for? This is important."

I smiled from the lack of something knocking on my mind. My gift does require some amount of specificity to work. Yut for instance, could be looking for his pen, a meal, or his favorite pair of shoes. Far too many things for my gift to respond with so usually, with such ambiguity, my gift just shuts up. That being said, honestly if I knew the answer, I'd tell Kah. Having aliens that scare the entire galaxy chasing me around Washington, DC, was actually not how I like to spend an afternoon. Letting Kah know what's going on might be more helpful than it could hurt.

"He's looking for an ancient first contact site. Said it could be Puntini."

"Not likely. Puntini live on the far side of the galaxy. First contact sites are usually neighbors."

I nodded. "Maybe they used hyperspace to get here?"

Kah shot me a look that said told me just now silly that thought was. "No, they didn't. But if a pre-contact site is on Earth, how would Yut and the Zun know about it?"

"Yeah, well, I'm not sure where it is or even if it exists."

Kah turned to me and stared me in the eye. "Jack, what is the location of the object that Ambassador Yut hired you to find?"

Images of Tibet flooded into my mind. I saw the rocky shelf of a mountain and green bushes covering an ancient stone. Behind the stone, or part of it, was a massive door ten feet tall. A yellow line drew from the doorway down the mountain, along a path and directly to the nearest entrance to the cafeteria. I knew the route as if I had traveled it a thousand times before.

"I got it," I said. A brief feeling of incompetence flared in my soul. If I had just phrased my question for Alice to ask me like Kah had just done this day would have been a lot easier. But then I wouldn't have met Tom. Eh, call it even. I said.

"Great, let's go." Kah pushed me forward down the corridor.

"Us?"

"Yes, us. I think you're in over your head, Jack. Whatever is there, we need to get there first."

"I think I need to get some supplies first. Meet me at the cafeteria, okay?" I said.

Kah hesitated but eventually nodded. "Fine."

I left the Woodward and headed straight to my office. I didn't want Kah to ask me what was behind the door. For some odd reason, I really didn't want to know. Still, I was certain that I would soon be finding out. The thought was more than a little intimidating. And it was times like these that having a few friends at your back could make all the difference.

Chapter 19

I made it across town in record time. Helped that I was doing it just after lunch. In a few hours, every street would be clogged with tramcars filled with commuters racing to get home. I'd seen old broadcasts of the city in my nostalgia days and it was hard to believe how similar things were to how they were a hundred years before. Especially considering the human race nearly went extinct in between and had to be rescued by a galactic federation of super powerful beings that had snickered at us from orbit for centuries.

Alice and Eddie were in my office when I flung the door open and walked inside. Alice was buried deep in her virtual immersion rig, and Eddie was reading a copy of *National Geographic*. Funny how people decompress. I leaned against one wall, waiting for someone to say hi. No one did. After a minute I shrugged, walked into my office, and sat down. The last few days had been crazy, but the next few hours were going to be insane. At least, I had a terrible feeling that they were. Not any kind of message thanks to my gift mind you, just a feeling like something enormous was going to be kicking my teeth in soon.

"So, what's going on, boss?" Eddie strolled into my office and sat down in the chair opposite my desk. His latest hologram body was an ordinary-looking twenty-something guy with dark olive-colored skin and a decent haircut. He wore an I Love DC t-shirt and slightly torn jeans. Most striking about him were his eyes and how he wore his face. He seemed very relaxed. Not at all like how I found him in that dark alley years ago.

"You okay, Eddie?"

"Yeah, sure. Why do you ask?"

"You just seem different."

Eddie nodded. "I am different. I'm not looking over my shoulder every ten minutes waiting to be erased. It's harder for us, AIs; we don't have an afterlife."

"Might not have," I said. Only a few AIs had ever died, and yeah, none had made it to the Krill. But you never know. Maybe the Krill hadn't zeroed in on AIs' spectral frequency yet. "Yeah. Sorry about Caesar and the whole sensory starvation thing."

I shook at the memory. "Don't sweat it, Eddie. Guess I had it coming."

"Maybe a little. Anyway, I'm good. I am, Jack. Thanks for saving my life."

That awkward silence fell into the room. You know the kind, when the conversation gets down to brass tax, about real life, when you have to open up just a little and be vulnerable. I was never good at those. I nodded and smiled, unsure of what to say, which felt awkward. I settled on, "Sure thing, pal."

"When are we going to Tibet?" Alice's voice called out from the front room.

"You're not going," I replied.

"Yes, I am and when do we leave?"

"Why do you want to come?"

Alice came into my office and stood in the

doorway with her arms folded. Her face was stone, and her eyes carried a fierceness I hadn't seen before.

"I hate you. You know that right?" Alice said.

I shook my head and gave her a shrug. "Yeah, why is that?"

"I could ask you what happened to them. My classmates. The explosion ripped a hole in spacetime, and they vanished. They aren't even dead. Krill has no record of them hitting the spectral towers."

"What's that got to do with me?"

"I could ask you where they are. And you could tell me. Cause someone stuck all the answers in the universe inside your head. And yet, I haven't. Do you know why?"

"Cause it's cheating?"

Alice nodded.

"So, why do you want to come with us now?"

"After talking with Tom, poring over everything in the Galactic Archives, reading every publication the Krill ever made, I'm still nowhere closer to figuring out what hole I opened and why my friends aren't in the afterlife of the Krill spectral network. Even if I'd cracked into another dimension, the Krill would've pulled them back. But nothing."

She paused, and I let the moment hang. Still waiting for her to tell me why she wanted to tag along.

"So, you know what that all means? Don't bother nodding, I know you don't. It means I may have to ask you what happened. I may have to cheat and violate every belief I hold dear. But I want to find the answer myself. I don't want to cheat. But I also don't think I can figure it out on my own."

"You want to come with me to ask? Why not just

ask now?"

Alice sighed. "Cause I'm not ready to ask you. Not yet, but there's every possibility you're going to die in the mountains of Tibet. There hasn't been a case you've had where I didn't save your ass. And before you die, I need to ask you where they are."

"So, you're coming with us to save my ass?"

Alice nodded.

"You probably could've just led with that."

Alice nodded again, turned, and walked out of my office.

I sighed and shook my head. She probably had my phone bugged and my location tracked a dozen different ways to Sunday. She already knew I went to Kah, that we confronted Yut and we were all headed to Tibet. Alice was a better detective than I would ever be.

"Kids," Eddie said.

I couldn't help but laugh. I pulled open my desk drawer and drew my trusty revolver. I hadn't had the time to get my super-blaster from the alley behind Fritz's place. The thing was probably already confiscated by the cops now anyway.

"You coming, Eddie?"

"Wouldn't miss it."

I smiled and reached for his portable holo system.

"You don't need that, Jack." Eddie reached across the desk and gave my hand a quick rap with his knuckles.

"How the hell did you do that?"

"This isn't a hologram. It's a bionoid. AI council gave it to me."

"Aren't those worth a fortune?"

"More than a fortune. But they're worried that I'll

sue. An AI that was underground because his registration papers weren't filed correctly? Could be a huge nightmare. I hear there are hundreds of spontaneous artificials thinking about exploiting the hole."

"And how'd they find out the hole exists?"

Eddie smiled.

I sat back in my chair and just stared at his new physical body. It fit him like a glove. Bionoids were tough machines, easily worth their weight in gold. Having Eddie along for the ride would have more benefits than ever before. Not something I was going to complain about.

"All right, let's go. If we get to the cafeteria early enough, I want to stop in Morocco for lunch. I'm starving."

****

Alice jammed a dozen different items into her backpack and loaded twice as many nutrient bars. She'd made up her mind to go with Eugene the minute he texted her with the latest after getting free from Caesar and his crazy senso-trip. Funny thing about that, Eugene was never in any danger. Some people even pay for the experience. Caesar was making a point, and frankly Alice agreed with him.

Humans had been treating AIs like zero-class citizens for more than a century. It was terrible. And sure, Eugene had saved Eddie, but he created a brand-new mess by copying his human mind into an AI. If virtual-Eugene was ever found there would be a crap storm the size of Texas.

As for her own research, just more dead ends. Maybe the Krill, caretakers of the dead in the cosmos, were right. Alice had vaporized the souls of her friends. They weren't any dimensional rifts, spontaneous quantum tunnels, wormholes, portals, or inter-galactic cafeteria entrances that could explain what happened. They were gone. Maybe gone forever. So there just wasn't a reason to continue to look for them.

Which meant Alice had a choice to make. Rejoin academia and let the universe giggle as she rediscovered fire and the wheel, or run off and become a drunken party goer and follow the popular bands around the galaxy, on tour. Which, honestly, didn't sound so bad.

Or she could just keep doing what she was doing. Stay right here with Eugene and Eddie. Continue having stupid, but fun, detective adventures for a while. And the funny thing was, Alice was discovering she was kinda good at being a detective. Maybe she'd even open her own shop one day, *Alice's Totally Scientific Detective Agency*. No, that didn't work. Something more, her. Reminiscent of her years in university. *Alice Pemberton's Bureau of Scientific Inquiry*. Yeah, that was it.

As Eugene would say…it had a nice ring.

****

By the time we reached North Africa, less than an hour on the walkways, we had already passed over a hundred different alien species, most of them just out for a stroll from their home worlds to try an alien delicacy. There were ten-legged mammals that moved by doing cartwheels, and several methane aquatics whose tanks, if they burst, would make everyone run for oxygen. There were species with biological wheels for lower legs. Cartilage spokes and fleshy soft exterior made up their odd extremities. And those aliens were just the ones in the human lanes. Skipping into the thoroughfares that weren't safe for people, we spotted beings that defied description. Clouds of swirling colors that spoke in rainbows and beings that carried their own gravity wells filled the walkways, and a few I didn't know how to describe.

We settled down in a small corner of the Moroccan food court and dined on couscous and nicely seasoned vegetables. It took me a few seconds to adjust as Eddie plowed through a plate of chicken and washed it down with two cold beers. That bionoid body of his could pack in some calories. Which meant I had another mouth to feed. Swell.

A dozen people strolled by dressed in long black robes with a silver ghostly figure printed on the back. They weren't talking amongst themselves, and all had their heads bowed in silence. I didn't recognize the image on the robe, but since they were all the same, they had to be a cult. I turned to Alice, nodded to her, and then back to the black-clad figures.

"Didn't we just talk about how using your gift is cheating?" Alice said between bites of meat.

I shrugged and motioned to them again.

"Fine. You really are a child. Who are those black-robed people behind you and where are they going, Jack?"

Imagines of grieving parents and siblings filled my mind. A magnificent hall somewhere in Indiana filled with hundreds of parishioners with the silver ghost hanging on the side of the cross. They were members of a church on a pilgrimage to the Ghost World to find relatives killed off-world. There must be an entrance to it nearby. Rumor had it every planet had an entrance somewhere in their cafeteria network. Jimmy's face popped into my head. He was a good guy but talk about bad timing. Maybe on the way back I could take a detour and look for his daughter, Melanie.

"So, who are they?" Alice's voice popped me out of my thoughts and back to the present, where my mouth hung half open and stuffed with rice.

"Is it cheating to tell you?"

Alice shrugged. "I'm working myself up to ask you something meaningful."

I coughed and swallowed a few bites. "Pilgrims. Looking for ghosts of their loved ones."

Alice nodded. "Ya know, part of the job of a detective is to detect things. You cheat too much."

I shrugged. "Pays the bills."

Several loud gasps and shuffling of chairs came from the opposite end of the food court. I turned to see Kah and his secretary, Ms. Mik, walking toward us. I could see how two ten-foot-tall dinosaurs could make folks uncomfortable, some of whom were probably dining on lizard meat. They were just a little spooked.

"Hi Kah, Ms. Mik, glad you made it."

"Hello, Jack. Alice, Edward. Glad you found time to eat," Kah said. He was dressed in a nice wool three-piece suit.

"Good to see you, Jack," Ms. Mik said.

"Do you want something to eat?" I asked.

"No, couscous upsets our digestive system. Can we go, please? I have a dozen meetings this afternoon alone."

"Yeah, we're just about done. I don't suppose you could've sat down anywhere anyway," I said. This food court was designed with humans and human-ish beings in mind. There were no dinosaur sized seats.

I finished my last bites and stood to leave. A dozen kids, part of a field trip, flooded into the food court. They descended on the tables like a pack of hungry wolves, laughing and giggling at everything in sight. Something about them made me uneasy. Not that they were kids, but something about them being in the cafeteria made me feel like I was missing something.

Whatever it was, I shrugged off the feeling and followed my ever-growing group of colleagues to the walkways just outside the food court. Fortunately, Kah and Mik could walk the human lanes just fine. We headed toward Tibet down the green shining path of the human lane.

Two lanes over, on a boldly lit red color on the floor, a species that I can only describe as a cross between a cow and a buzzard walked and pointed at the aliens in the other lanes. They were not local life in the third arm of the Milky Way and probably out on a family sightseeing tour. Along the lanes there were gates and with the right request entered you could walk across the galaxy to see the latest addition to the sentient species list. Though since the avian bovines were in the red lanes, they likely couldn't step foot on Earth. Wandering through the lanes was the closest and they could get and still be able to be home in time for supper.

One of the avian bovine kids—I guessed, since it was smaller and acted like, well, a kid—squealed a high-pitch shrill. He, or she, or possibly neither, pointed at Kah and jumped up and down on its four legs while flapping dark colored feathers. The same feeling of unsettled nerves that I had back in the food court pushed itself up from my mind. Memories of myself jumping into the lanes to save a kid's life bubbled up, and that creepy sensation from earlier leapt into my throat. I gulped down a swallow of fear. I thrust my head, briefly, into a lane with time-dilation and, besides almost throwing my lunch back out, I noticed a dozen tall, thick black stick men standing around our little party.

Clawed hands wrapped over my shoulders and yanked me back across the line of the lanes. Ms. Mik stared at me with confusion and not a small amount of anger as she gently, for her anyway, set me down.

"What are you doing, Jack?" she asked.

"We've got problems," I said.

"Where are they?" Eddie asked.

I looked around the food court. "All over. I saw at least ten of them." Memories of being outside the Woodward and Eddie's warning flashed in my mind. "Can't you see them, Eddie? You spotted that outside the embassy."

"No, that was the Andraz. They were just invisible. These guys are time-phased, I think. Meaning they are a few micro-seconds in front or behind us. That's why you can see them in the time-dilation zone," Eddie said.

"Time phasing is a thing?" I asked.

"Yeah. Weird, huh?" Eddie replied.

I nodded. We backtracked from the lanes and now stood around a waist high set of tables to the side of the court. I couldn't see them anymore, but I knew they were there: the Zun, creators of sparkly wispy AIs and one of the creepiest alien species I'd come across.

"What are we going to do then, Jack? We can't

lead them to the door."

A dozen kids in Catholic uniforms rushed into the food court and giggled their way to the different vendors. Behind them, nuns, complete with black robes and wooden rulers, strolled in and chatted among themselves.

"We need to lose them somehow," I said.

"How?" Kah said.

I don't know why, but I stared at the nuns. That feeling from before came back and sent tingles up my back. I wondered what a good gumshoe would do. Or rather, that the best path forward would be obvious and apparent. But, as I've said before, I'm a terrible detective.

"Jack, we are pressed for time. Who are the Zun following?" Kah said.

I was thankful I didn't have to ask, but I still saw Alice grimace when Kah questioned me. I think her objections had less to do with the fact that I was using my gift, and more to do with that I wasn't using it for what she cared about. Of course, I would be happy to find her missing friends. All she had to do was ask. But at that moment the answer to Kah's question flooded into my mind.

"The Zun are just following me," I said.

"Will they follow you wherever you lead them?" Kah said.

"Yes," my gift answered.

"Will any of the Zun follow the rest of us if they all follow you?"

"No."

"Then you need to lead them somewhere while the rest of us go on."

"That doesn't seem to make logical sense. Why wouldn't they follow all of us?" Eddie asked.

"I'm the target. The rest of you are irrelevant," I said.

"Why is that?" Kah asked. "Why are you alone the target?"

I smirked at the answer as it filled my mind. "Because they think I'm the only one that can open the door. Eventually I have to go there, and they know it."

"This really doesn't help us; you know that, right? Zun are phased beings. Technically, they don't even exist in our reality. How can you lose something that's not even here?" Alice said.

One nun spun on her heels and grabbed a child by the ear. She dragged him to a table and sat him down with a fierce stare forged in the crucible of our lord. That tingle knocked on my head and beat its way down to make my cheeks red. I knew there was something there, just like with the lanes and the Zun, but part of me wasn't making the connection.

"Jack, where can you lead the Zun where they wouldn't be able to follow you?" Kah said.

The answer gave me a headache. Don't get me wrong, it wasn't that what I had to do was hard, though it could get weird, it's that it just didn't occur to me. The nuns' black robes had sent a jolt through my brain because they reminded me of the pilgrims, the ones going to the Ghost World to find lost relatives. Why did that matter? Zun is phased beings. That meant, well, I really don't know what that meant. But there was one place in the galaxy, outside of the core of the Milky Way, where there were more phased beings and spectral towers inundating the air than anywhere else.

Enough to confuse the hell out of a human and to send a Zun into a spasmodic episode.

"I can lose them on the Ghost World. The towers there—" I said.

"The towers are flooding the local space with enough phase frequency that the Zun won't know which spectrum is real and which is the product of an alien deceased entity. Jack, if you had thought of that it would have been brilliant." Alice sighed, shrugged, and pulled out her tablet. Kids.

"Thanks," I said.

"Jack, the Ghost World isn't exactly easy for humans. Have you ever been there? I have. Disorienting doesn't do the feeling justice," Kah said.

I nodded. "I figured it won't be a walk in the park, but unless you have a better suggestion, I don't see what choice we have."

Silence descended on our little group.

That settled thing. I adjusted my fedora and tried to act suave. I don't think I pulled it off. The plan was simple. We'd all start back down the lanes toward Tibet, and when we came to the doorway to the Ghost World, I would make a sudden turn and run for it. And it added some showmanship. Why not, right?

Before we headed out, I walked over to the table where the Catholic kid was sitting in isolated timeout. He looked up to me with puppy dog eyes that turned into a question of who I was to come up to him. I slipped him a game disk with a thousand video games from a hundred years ago. What can I say, I have a soft spot for outcasts. The kid took one look at the disk, put it into a visor screen, laughed, and threw the disk into a nearby trashcan. So much for me being cool.

I called up the Queen Vic and asked if James was around. If I was going to Ghost World might as well do a favor for a friend. Ryan, the bartender, said James hadn't been in. It occurred to me that I didn't have his number or any way to contact him. I could cheat, just get someone to ask me, but Alice had been getting to me lately. I pulled up my email system and saw James had already sent me his contact info, Melanie's profile, and her DNA pattern. Using that, I could add a lure on the spectral towers on the Ghost World and find Mel while trying to lose the Zun. I could then go back to the cafeteria and high tail it to Tibet. At least it's good to have a full schedule.

Several nuns were paying attention to the strange man with the fedora hat standing close to their kids. Can't blame them for that one. I smiled to the nearest nun, tipped my hat, and walked back to the lanes. It only took ten minutes before I reached the gateway to the Ghost World.

The doorway was set against a wall along the human lanes. Supposedly, gates to the Ghost World were not programmable and there was only one access point for each world. Why it was set up that way is anyone's guess. I think it had to do with the volume of visitors looking for lost loved ones. Too many gates would overwhelm whatever system ran through them.

I waited just long enough for the hairs on the back of my head to stand up. That must be my matchstick friends gathering around me, wondering why I was about to go to one of the weirdest places in the galaxy.

Chapter 20

I expected to see cobwebs covering the doorway, flicking lights in the hallway, and disembodied voices lamenting their fate. What else can you expect when you enter the land of the dead? Well, the corporeal version anyway. Instead, I stepped over several thousand light years and into a large U-shaped room. Directions written in English and other Earth languages covered the walls with arrows pointing in different directions. Rows of chairs lined the center, and a dozen people milled around, looking bored and half-asleep. Behind me, a star map of the galaxy zoomed in every twenty seconds to Earth, followed by the name and a description of our world. In the far corner of the human U-shape zone sat the pilgrims I had seen earlier. They sat with their heads bowed, reciting a prayer.

"Do you need some help, sir?"

A squat alien no taller than five feet stood just behind me. He had a dozen eyes on his brow, and his head was covered in a thick matte of brown hair. He smiled a wide toothless grin, gums in his mouth extending up from his jaw an extra inch. He sat behind a welcome and information kiosk to the right of the room. I nodded and approached him, returning my own wide smile.

"Hi. I need to find a lost human soul. Do you know who is in charge here?"

The little guy smiled. "We are. The Krill. We are the caretakers of Shalisa, our home world."

I nodded. Nice to know this was their home turf. I put my elbow on his desk, but before I could ask, the gate I had come through flashed a dozen times, but no one emerged. I smiled but tried my best to ignore the odd behavior of the gate. The Krill turned several of his eyes, ones near the rear of his head, toward the gate but kept the rest on me.

"Where would I go to find someone?" I asked.

"This is just the terminal. Millions of aliens come through here every day looking for lost loved ones. You'll need to go to Twan, a city for processing beings of humanity's"—the Krill paused just a second—"evolved state." He smiled.

The Krill walked out from behind his kiosk and approached the gate. I tipped my hat and smiled at him, but he didn't notice or care. He was clearly focused on the flashing gate from a moment ago. Though, who knows, maybe he saw the matchstick men and walked over to chat. Just because humans can't see them didn't mean the Krill couldn't.

I walked over to the pilgrims and dug my hands into my pockets for effect. A woman dressed in all black stood in the center of them and kept her hands clasped together with her head bowed. I don't know why, but she had the feel of being the one in charge. Maybe because she was standing. I coughed once to get her attention, and she looked up at me and frowned in that special way that only a nun can.

"I'm headed to Twan if you guys want to tag along?" I said.

"We have a vehicle coming for us," the nun said.

I nodded. "Ah okay." I turned to leave but stopped on my heels. If the pilgrims had a ride, they were already a leg up over me. Maybe I could tag along with them?

"Mind if I hitch a ride?" I said with a smile.

****

The two-lane black asphalt road stretched to a gray and bleak horizon in the distance. After what felt like a few hours, other roads merged with ours, and our two-lane highway became a ten-lane monster. I could see aliens of different sizes and shapes in the other vehicles, rows of additional terminal buildings behind them. Every alien got their own it seemed, which meant this world was covered in terminals from alien races around the galaxy. Occasionally, an exit ramp would appear on the road, and I could see a city in the distance. Some were great spirals of buildings, while others were just domes or piles of excavated dirt. Different strokes.

"Where are all the ghosts?" I said to the small group in the car.

"They are in their proper zone. They can only go as far as the frequency of their own spectral towers," said the head nun, who's named turned out to be Linda. I had an aunt named Linda. She was nice.

"Why is it you're here, Mr. McGillicuddy?"

"Same reason as you, looking for a ghost."

"Who?" Linda said.

"A friend's daughter. She died off-world. I'm not sure if she's here. Just a hunch, really." No sense telling her about the Zun that were likely following us.

"Oh, she's here. If she was killed on an alien city, that is. If she was on a starship or some remote location, she still might have found her way here, but it may take considerably longer."

"Why is that?" I asked.

"It's how the galactic spectral network works. The towers on every planet that allow ghosts to interact with the living can also send aliens that died on foreign shores here. Like portals for us flesh and blood types."

"That's—interesting. Why not just send them to their home planet though? Why bother sending them here?"

Linda turned in her seat and eyed me with a confused look. "Don't you know how this place works? Why would you come here and not know anything about Shalisa? You know that's the name of the Krill home world?"

"Of course, I do. Everyone knows that." I shrugged and smiled but didn't look away. "Why don't the Krill send people home?"

Linda huffed. "Basic economics. The Krill invented the spectral network and licensed its use to the galaxy. Which I'm sure you knew." Linda smiled, and I nodded back to her. "Each network on each world has a connection to Shalisa, and there is a constant stream of telemetry data flowing from every world to Shalisa—it's required in case something goes wrong. When someone dies on an alien world, their soul piggybacks on that connection stream and is sent here. But sending souls back to their home worlds is another story. Neither the Krill nor any single species except maybe one of the elder races has enough raw energy to send billions of souls around the galaxy every day."

"Wait, how many souls are on this world?"

Linda shrugged. "Several hundred trillion I would imagine. But ghosts don't need resources to exist, and the Krill are fine with them. Fortunately for us, Twan is relatively empty. Few humans have died off-world, and there's not a significant amount of compatible spectral species allowed inside. Some cities on Shalisa are so packed with ghosts it's hard to walk. Well, you can walk, but it's through an ocean of ectoplasm. Not exactly fun."

Outside, on the horizon, lights began to fill the horizon. Twan, the city housing human souls, stretched for miles in front of us. Dozens of buildings rose to the skies and gave the city a breathtaking outline.

"Why the Krill? Why are they in charge of the dead?" said one of the other nuns. I let out an inward sigh and did a small dance in my head. I wanted to ask, but the fear of looking like a dolt held me back.

Linda looked at me one more time, smirked, and turned around in her seat. "They can see the dead naturally. The tech is based on their natural talents."

"You won't lay into her for asking?" I asked. "Shouldn't all nuns know that?"

"She's fifteen," Linda said.

I nodded and buried my pride, what was left of it, under my shoe. At least I was on par with a teenager. Buildings appeared around us as we entered the city proper. More cars appeared on the road, and the entire city came alive with mostly Krill walking and moving about.

Ghosts appeared as soon as we passed the official city line, marked by a sign welcoming us. Again, my idea of a ghost planet was shattered to see the corporeally challenged walk about and have perfectly normal conversations with both Krill and other ghosts.

"Where do you want us to drop you off, Mr.

McGillicuddy?" Linda said.

Great question, I thought. My shoulders slumped as I realized I had no idea how to go about finding Melanie and less of an idea how to deal with the matchstick people. Ahead of us, where two streets crossed, a corner bustled with a dozen ghosts and half that many Krill, and a few other aliens I couldn't recognize. The spot looked as good as any to figure out what to do.

"You can drop me there—" I said, but before I could finish my statement, the car we were in flipped sideways and landed twenty meters away. Nuns rolled around in the car, and one kicked me in the face with her rubber-soled shoes. Not out of malice, mind you, just the need to find something solid to rest your foot on. And yeah, it hurt.

****

I climbed out of the flipped vehicle and helped as many of the pilgrims out as I could. A dozen ghosts and twice that many Krill created a spectacle of gawkers on the surrounding sidewalk. A yelp from behind the car, from where we flipped, caught the attention of the crowd and me, and as one, the vast throng turned to see a dozen matchstick men doing their version of a crazed dance routine. Their long arms flailed in wide arcs, and they staggered back and forth in what looked like painful seizures.

"What are the Zun doing here?" Linda asked.

Surprised, I gave Linda a questioning stare. "How do you know what they are?"

"My dissertation was on galactic civilizations that are non-members of the Galactic Congress," Linda said.

"I didn't know nuns went to college," I said.

Linda returned my quizzical look and added a head shake. "You're not very smart, are you? The Pilgrim organization isn't religious, Jack. We're just charitable. We're trying to bring home lost souls. Do you have any idea what the afterlife is like to a human soul if they die off Earth? The fortunate ones come here. But those that die outside of the Krill network don't go anywhere. They're gone, lost forever."

I shook my head and shrugged. Just between you and me, it's lousy getting called an idiot every other day, but what can I say, the universe is an overwhelming place to live. You try bouncing between a private universe in Utah to a dinosaur's office and then take a hike to a planet with a trillion dead people and see if your brains don't melt out of your shoes in the morning.

"How do we know that, anyway? That souls can get lost forever?"

Linda sighed. "Because the Krill told us. They are the experts. The afterlife is not a place to get misplaced."

"Right." I pointed at the Zun. "So, what's wrong with them?"

"The Zun have a phased physiology from all the radiation in the galactic core. All the spectral towers here are playing havoc on their biology. I can't believe they would come here."

"Yeah, poor guys," I said.

Two of the Zun pointed their thin arms at me and started a wobbly walk in my direction. I reached for my hand blaster but realized I'd had to give it up at the terminal. Krill don't like people visiting with weapons.

"They seem to want to talk to you," Linda said.

"Yeah, we have a history."

A dozen Krill in heavy armor jumped from a flying vehicle fifty feet over the street. They moved toward the Zun with weapons drawn, but the matchsticks didn't seem to care. Every second that passed, the Zun seemed to get more control of their phased state.

"Let's move back, let the authorities handle this," Linda said to her flock.

I picked up my fedora and waved to the Zun with my biggest smile. They didn't appear to like that. The closest one let out a stream of something from its fingers, and the nearest Krill authorities went flying. Another Zun leapt toward me and landed just feet away. He waved and smiled back. At least they have a sense of humor.

"Look, I'm sure we can work this out, okay?" I said.

The Zun shook its head, though it was really hard to tell when their noggins weren't much bigger than their bodies, and grabbed me by the collar. He dragged me back toward his compatriots, who were holding off the Krill police.

"Would you mind asking me how I get away from the Zun, Linda?" I said.

"What?"

I couldn't tell if she didn't hear me or didn't understand. Being in the situation I was, I just didn't have the time to guess. I shouted my question back and added my stamp of "it's part of my process."

Linda shrugged. "How do you get away from the Zun?"

My little highlighted stickman popped into existence, the same one that tried to help me fight off

Earl in the AI records room. He looked at me, to the Zun, and back to me before shrugging and shaking his head. Not the answer I was looking for.

"What do they want with you?" Linda shouted.

"Like I said, we go way back."

Two dozen more Krill police popped down from above and began firing into the group of Zun. Waves of nausea bowled over me as whatever weapons the Krill fired hit me just as much as the bad guys. I pulled free from the grip of the Zun holding me and scrambled backward toward the wrecked car.

A large crystal dome popped into existence around the group of Zun just as one of them moved toward me. He bumped into the clear wall that surrounded him and seemed to phase himself in and out of the visible spectrum. I could only guess that was a sign of extreme rage.

"Thank god for the calvary," I said.

"Just who are you, and what is going on? Did you know the Zun were following you? Did you put my girls at risk?" Linda walked up to me, and her eyes blazed anger. Probably would've been a good idea to get a taxi considering the Zun were after me. Again, I really needed to think these things through. Then again, I didn't know the Zun could be so physical.

"Look, Linda, I knew the Zun were following me, but I had no idea they could do this. I never would've put anyone in danger."

"I think you owe me an explanation regardless," Linda said. She poked her finger in my chest and glared into my soul.

"It's a long story. To boil it down, I was hired to find the location of an alien vault on Earth. These guys"—I thumbed in the direction of the now imprisoned Zun—"have been following me ever since."

"Hired? What are you?"

I adjusted my shoulders and made sure my hat was titled down and to the right. "Private detective for hire."

At that Linda let out a loud and disbelieving laugh. I couldn't blame her; who could? If not for my special talent, I'd have problems on my way across town, let alone a secret vault of the ancients. I sighed and let her have a good laugh at my expense. Probably deserved it.

"You're a private detective, don't know the Zun can interact with the physical world, clearly have no idea what you are doing outside of Earth, and probably don't have any idea how things work on Earth either, and you expect me to believe this?" Linda said.

It's times like these that I wish I could channel a hard-boiled sleuth from the nineteen thirties, if only for the confidence factor. The one topic where I didn't need my gift was movies from the twentieth. But I'm getting off point.

"Yeah, it's hard to believe, so what. Look, ma'am, I got a job to do and can't spend any more time nickel and diming it with a ghost teacher and her bunch of paper shakers."

"What?" Linda said. I could tell from her face that she couldn't quite figure out if I'd just insulted her.

I shrugged. "I mean I gotta beat feet and find my friend's dead daughter. Yeah, I needed to lose the Zun, and I'm sorry you and the others almost got iced. I really am." And I really was. Last thing I ever wanted to do was put someone in the crosshairs that didn't have it coming.

Linda half smiled and shrugged. "It's fine. To be

honest, I never would have thought the Zun would do something like this. Probably shocked and scared because of the spectral towers."

I nodded and took out a cigarette. Around me the crowds of ghosts, Krill, and the occasional alien were growing. There weren't just human deceased in the city; several other aliens whose spectral frequency was close to ours also were sent to Twan. You'd think they'd look something like a regular Joe but there were ghosts here with tentacles, horns, and even a few with wings.

Behind me, Linda was gathering her flock and getting ready to head out into the city. I realized that I had no idea how to go about finding Melanie. Probably would have been a good idea to do more recon of this place, but as you know I was a little pressed for time.

"Excuse me, are these beings with you?"

A Krill officer stood next to me and eyed me with suspicion. Several other officers stood behind him, each ready to pounce on me if I so much as breathed at the wrong tempo. I shrugged and shook my head no.

"Really? They seemed to reach for you. It's unusual for a being from the galactic center to come to Shalisa. Most are affected by the spectral towers," the officer said.

I nodded and shrugged again. You'd be surprised how often a non-answer followed by a shrug could get you out of a jam. I hoped the technique worked here. Last thing I needed was to spend a day under interrogation by beings with a hundred eyes. Talk about a stare down.

"He's with us, officer. And no, we have no idea what the Zun wanted," Linda said. She seemed to pop out of nowhere and stood next to me with her arms crossed in front of her.

The officer regarded her with a certain amount of respect. He nodded once, hmphed loudly, and turned to walk back to the entrapped Zun. The Krill were setting up several large metal boxes around the caged Zun.

"They'll negate the towers' effect on the Zun and allow the Krill to send them back to their home world through the gates," Linda said, motioning to the boxes.

"Why'd you help me?"

Linda shrugged. "I have a soft spot for lost souls."

I couldn't tell if she was insulting me or just being sincere. Probably somewhere in the middle. I took a long drag from my cigarette, which caused Linda to roll her eyes and take a step back. Smoking still carried all the stigma it did a hundred years ago.

"Well, best of luck to you," Linda said.

"Hey, any chance you can help me find a ghost?" I said. I still had no idea where in Twan I'd find Mel, and Linda seemed more than capable of helping. And pushing my luck with the question-and-answer schtick can backfire.

Linda sighed and shook her head. I was hoping her instinct to help lost souls would be stronger than her desire to be away from yours truly. A minute passed, but eventually she nodded to herself and shrugged to the other pilgrims, who were all staring at her, probably begging silently that she said no.

"Fine, what's her name?" she said.

****

We found Melanie floating in a bar across town. The spectral technology on Shalisa was more advanced than what the Krill offered to other worlds. Apparently, apparitions could feed off physical substances and further stabilize their connection to this universe. My thoughts turned to the images of a ghost hanging around a house for decades over a pendant or some charm from their lives. Turns out lots of old tales were true.

Linda and her pilgrims set themselves up on a table in the bar. A pretty good assortment of alcohol was brought to their table, and they wasted no time in downing the drinks; all except Linda herself. Can't blame her troops. The day was a long one, and they were just getting started in finding lost souls.

Around us, a dozen of the locals were taking some comfort in the local brew, both liquid and ectoplasm. More than a few human ghosts stood around the bar, depression and sadness etched onto their faces. Most of the types here were off-world adventurers that didn't make it back from their adventure. If they didn't find a human on Earth to sponsor their return soon, they might never leave. Sucks.

In a back corner, almost hidden by shadows, a group of ghosts, human and not, were engaging in a full-on ghost merge. Just when you thought you've seen all the possible weird stuff, you turn the corner and stumble on a ghost orgy. They moaned and released a bit of poltergeist energy that sent a chair sliding across the room. Everyone else in the bar tried their best to ignore them. The Krill, as it turns out, have loose rules about ghost behavior in their cities. I guess they felt bad for them.

Three large alien ghosts that looked human but stood eight feet tall and had a row of horns along their skulls, floated their way into the bar and shoved into a half-empty spot between Melanie and a corporeal alien that looked like a cross between a rhinoceros and a teddy bear. And by shoved, I mean they let their non-physical form brush up against the rough skin of the rhino-bear. He, or maybe it was a she, cringed at the feeling and moved himself down to provide room.

"Do you mind?" Melanie said. She gave the three horned-aliens a warning stare as they brushed against her translucent skin.

"Give us space, human. Or we'll take it," one of the three aliens said.

I sighed. Nothing is ever easy, is it? I walked up to the three big guys and gulped a heavy mouthful of fear. They couldn't punch me in the face, but passing through an alien consciousness is a lot like jumping into a septic tank and closing the door.

"Hey, tough guys. She's with me."

Three colossal heads turned in my direction, followed soon after by Melanie, and then everyone else in the pub. Whether you're dead or alive, everyone wants to see a good fight. Or maybe see the small guy take on the giants.

"She is?" said the aliens in unison.

"I am?" Melanie said with just as much confusion in her voice.

The largest of the three ghosts took a gigantic step toward me. I held my ground and kept my smile wide and bright. I had no idea how to tackle this guy and quickly rethought my strategy. They weren't exactly trying to kidnap her.

I nodded to all of them, tilted my hat, and took out a cigarette. "Easy big guy, I don't think you want to tangle," I said.

He reached out with a tentacle and passed it directly through my sternum. If he were corporeal, it would have run through my heart and left me dead as a doornail. But being a deceased entity, it didn't kill me so much as make me wish I was dead.

Thick clouds of sulfur surrounded my head and filled my nose with a pungent odor that should have knocked me unconscious. The bar I was standing in vanished and I suddenly found myself standing on a street with red tipped mountains in the distance that soared into the air to merge with purple clouds. Thousands of tentacled forms, exactly like the three in the bar, passed me by on a busy street.

I twisted my head a dozen ways, and the scene kept getting weirder. Nowhere around me was the bar with Melanie or the three alien ghosts. Instead, stretching in every direction, an alien city, complete with oddly shaped buildings and pungent smelling food in every direction. When I lifted my arm to shield my eyes from the bright red sun, a tentacle rose to cover my face. I looked down at my body and realized I was suddenly a giant mollusk.

The only thing worse than being in an alien body, which I was about to learn, was getting killed in one. A sharp pain filled my back as something plunged into the strange body and cut an organ in half. I felt my very essence being pulled into a field of light and an odd sense of calm and joy.

Blue light filled my vision as the strange world and experience of dying vanished. I fell to the bar floor and took several very large breaths. Linda, and her pilgrims, knelt beside me and offered me a half-wet napkin from their table. Where there were three odd aliens standing at the bar now, there were only two. The barkeep, holding a strange device in his hand pointed at the spot where the alien used to be, turned it to his two compatriots and motioned them to remove themselves from his establishment, which they promptly did.

"What happened?" I asked.

"He drove his astral self into your body. What did you see?"

"A place I wouldn't want to visit."

Linda half laughed. "Yeah, their species is interesting. Very hearty, and the sulfuric atmosphere is not exactly welcoming to humans."

"Not so much." I stood and walked to the door. Both of the other aliens were just outside and talking with each other in what looked like a panicked frenzy. I turned to the barkeep as he lowered his spectral destabilizer.

"What happened to him? Did he get sent home?" I said.

"No, this is plugged into the towers," the barkeep said, holding up the device. "He'll be sent to the Plar's processing center, and they'll deal with him."

Good enough for me. Last thing I needed was trouble with the locals. I walked over to Melanie, who had already turned back to the bar and her glass of ectoplasmic residue. I cleared my throat a few times to get her attention, but she didn't budge.

"Excuse me, Melanie?" I said.

"Go away," she replied.

I sighed. "Your father sent me. Wanted me to bring you home."

"No."

I sighed again. Louder. I really didn't have time to

deal with angry kids and their family squabbles. And honestly, I didn't have to. The Zun were taken care of, and I could go to Tibet to meet the others without fear of the matchstick men or their bright light twinkling AIs. I shrugged as loudly as I could and turned to leave. Linda gave me an odd stare, and I shook my head.

"What's going on?" she said.

"She's staying and I have to go to Tibet," I said.

"Maybe she just needs some talking to."

"Hey, if you want to chat her up, then she's all yours." I could feel the stares of disappointment burning its way into my skull from behind me as I reached the exit. For everything I put Linda and her pilgrims through, they must have felt like this was quite *the* betrayal. This is what they did—bring scared and terrified ghosts home to rest. To have them help me and for me to abandon their central mission must be a tough pill to swallow. Jimmy's face popped into my head in that moment, and I knew if I didn't bring his daughter back, I'd never be able to go back into the Queen Vic again.

I sighed and put as much frustration into it as I could. I walked back to Melanie, waved Linda off, and sat down at the bar. "Hey, look, can I buy you a drink at least?"

"No, please just go away," Melanie said.

"Look, I get it, it's rough. You died out here way too young, and you just want to drown your sorrows in glassfuls of ectoplasm and pity. And I feel this city is lousy with both. You could follow those guys—" I motioned to the mess of ghosts in the corner that stayed merged throughout the earlier debacle, "—and devolve into a sex-obsessed sprite who forgets she's even human."

Melanie snorted a laugh, giving me the slightest hint of an opening.

"Or you could talk to me. Talk to her." I pointed to Linda, and Melanie turned to look. "And maybe together we can figure something out. You don't have to stay here, Melanie. And Jimmy really misses you."

Her eyes turned to me then, and I could tell I was getting somewhere. "Is he okay? My dad?"

I nodded and turned to the bartender to motion for a drink. He brought me something brown and strong, just how I liked it. "About as well as you can imagine. He loved you, kiddo. Just wants to see you to say goodbye. Or, I guess, with how things work these days, watch you become the specter he knows you can be."

Melanie nodded. "It's just frustrating as hell. I finally got grant money, finally found an alien ship to go outside the teleportation networks, finally got permits to land, and we got wiped out by a stupid meteor shower. Can you believe that?"

I shrugged. "It's a tough universe."

With a heavy sigh and another half-laugh, she downed her drink and belched out a cloud of tiny swirls of gray gas. I didn't ask. "Okay, fine. I'll come. If I had a stomach, I would have puked by now at the growing mess of alien orgy over there, anyway."

I smiled and gave Linda a thumbs-up. She walked over, introduced herself, and congratulated Melanie on her choice of going home. I settled up with the barkeep and led the little group outside where the two large tentacled aliens still stood. They pointed at me, growled, and lunged for my throat.

Melanie screamed, and in a blink I was lifted off

my feet and thrown fifty feet backward away from the alien ghosts. I braced myself for an impact on something, but I was placed gently on the ground without so much as a scrape.

Twenty Krill soldiers came out of nowhere and shot the two aliens with more blue light of spectral destabilization. The whole thing was over before I really understood what had just happened. I jogged back over to Melanie, who floated with her arms folded while the police questioned her.

"Everything okay, officer?" I asked.

"Yes, fine. Her use of spectral energy is justified under the circumstances."

I nodded and when he left turned to Melanie. "That was quite the blast of poltergeist energy. How'd you manage that?"

"They have classes here."

Linda ran over with her pilgrims and quickly smiled when they realized all was well. "You're a magnet for trouble, you know that?" Linda said.

I shrugged. "Part of the gig, toots."

"Call me that again, and I'll punch you in the face," Linda said. "I hold three black belts. It's not an idle threat."

"And then I'll throw you to the Plars," Melanie said.

I nodded and smiled. "Sorry, and no offense, sometimes I get carried away with the lingo. Look, I really need to get back to Tibet. Some friends of mine are in deep trouble. Linda can help you with all the paperwork to get you home, okay?"

"No, I can't. Do you know how any of this works?" Linda said.

I shook my head.

Linda sighed. "I'm staying here, on Shalisa. Her sponsor has to go back with her to Earth, approve her to go through the portal, get her registered and pay for the transit. That's you."

I looked at Melanie. She smiled back at me. "Well, have you ever been to Tibet?"

Chapter 21

I made it back to the cafeteria with Melanie's soul in a tin box in my pocket. Transporting a spirit from Shalisa to anywhere required special spectral frequencies for transport. The Krill don't transmit on specific species frequencies for their galaxy spanning spectral network. And since corporeal portals won't work for ghosts, the only option to get someone off of Shalisa is inside a physical spectral transport case that you carry through the portal. And pay for. Nice racket, really. Rumors had it, the Krill were the richest species in the galaxy, maybe even the local cluster. Suffice it to say, Mel wasn't very pleased, but she went inside. She was also agreeable to coming to Tibet, which made the trip easy.

Two spiral red columns stood on either side of the doorway to Tibet. I walked down the hallway and stepped through the portal into a strong icy wind that nearly knocked me over. Once back on Earth and outside of the cafeteria it was safe to open Melanie's box. I popped the seal and watched a swirl of gray ectoplasm erupt into the strong wind of Tibet. The box she traveled in also served as a portable spectral stabilizer. Melanie could interact with us as long as this thing kept its charge.

People around us walked by and didn't give us the time of day. There was only one gateway to the cafeteria in all of Tibet, and it opened up in the middle of Lhasa city. A few locals were still talking about the ten-foot-tall dinosaurs that walked by a few hours ago. Finding Kah and the others was as easy as watching the locals run for cover. I tracked them down to a ground vehicle rental shop where Kah, Mik, Alice, and Eddie were getting a car.

"Jack, glad to see you made it back," Kah said.

"Glad to be back. I miss anything fun?"

"Not as such, no," Kah said.

"Nice to see you too, you tiny-minded meat-maggot," Eddie said.

I frowned at him and looked at Alice and Kah, but they only shrugged and smiled. Last thing we all needed was for Eddie to lose his mind again.

"You okay, Eddie?"

"He's fine, and you will be too, if you don't go creating any more artificial copies of yourself."

"Pepper?"

"In the robotic, not-flesh."

"What happened to Eddie? Is he okay?"

"I'm fine. Pepper and virtual-you wanted to come along for the ride."

My eyebrows shot up, and I gave Eddie a once-over. "You can fit more than one AI in there?"

"I could probably fit a thousand without breaking a circuit."

It took me a minute, but something Eddie said twisted my head around, and I stared into his electronic eyes. I moved between them and looked from the bottom to the top.

"You know you can't see us," said a voice with a tone I recognized.

"You brought virtual me?"

Eddie/Pepper/Me shrugged. "Sure, why not? He's illegal, as you well know. Best place for him to be is close to friends," Eddie said.

"Okay, well, just don't complain about existing, yeah? We have a busy day ahead."

"Wasn't going to, you should know me better than that," Virtual-Jack said.

I nodded. "Well, this is just weird."

"Can we please move along?" Kah stood next to a large ground vehicle big enough to carry all of us, including the two Ranz.

The map guides from Eddie told us the trip would take a good three hours of driving, and more on foot through the mountains. Fortunately, we wouldn't have to do any rock climbing. The guides in Lhasa gave us thruster boots and enough modern climbing gear to get on top of Everest in a day and back down in time for biscuits. Kah and Mik both wore full environmental suits, complete with thrusters and atmosphere controls for the cold mountaintops of the Tibetan landscape we would cross. Where they got them from was another matter. I didn't see either of them bring their suits into the cafeteria.

Everyone kept to themselves, despite the occasional attempt at conversation. You can only say so many times that the snow is pretty before it becomes annoying. Thankfully, a nice lull of silence got us to the foot of the mountain where our trip would really begin.

Watching Kah and Mik leap thirty feet up the mountain was humbling. At least Eddie and his cohorts could keep pace. Me and Alice? We managed. As for Melanie, she occasionally solidified to admire a lump of snow. Those classes she took on Shalisa really paid off. The occasional snowball would fly past us and more than a few would find their mark on my back. At least she was feeling better.

We crested the ridge where the doorway was supposed to be located. Kah and Mik had made it before us and were examining the doorway just as our feet landed on the icy landing.

"Glad you made it," Kah said.

"Thanks."

From around the corner of an ice wall a voice called out, "Yes, indeed. Glad you all did." Yut, the Puntini ambassador, came around the bend with a dozen other Puntini, each with large teeth jutting out from their thick jowls. The ambassador smiled and winked as he raised a large menacing gun. His cohorts followed suit.

"What are you doing here, Yut? I never told you the location."

"We've been expecting you. I've known the location for months. And we knew you were coming. Not exactly hard considering not many Ranz or bionoids come out here, let alone humans."

I shrugged. "Okay, in that case." I pointed to the door. "Found it. Can you pay me now?"

"You're funny, Mr. McGillicuddy."

Twelve Puntini henchmen circled us. All of them had some kind of weapon in their hand. Well, except one of the big ones had a turkey leg. Can't blame the guy; it's a long walk, and to be honest I was getting hungry too. Which reminded me of a loose end that was killing me.

"I have to ask, are you missing anyone?" I said.

"Missing? What do you mean?" Yut said.

"I told you this. In your office, I witnessed one of your guys getting eaten by the Zun."

Yut nodded once but then tilted his head to one side. "Ah yes, I forgot. And why didn't you contact the authorities?"

I shrugged. "I'm not a cop."

"Rather cynical, don't you think? Citizens that witness crimes often contact the authorities to report the incident. How backward are you humans?"

I didn't let the insult get to me and ignored the barbs. "Just seems odd is all. The Zun feasting on a Puntini and also tracking me down to find this door."

"Very strange indeed. But I believe I know how to answer your question."

"So, tell me was it one of your guys?"

"What? Oh, not that question, I meant your other question. Fine." Yut sighed and turned to his henchmen. "Kut, where is your brother?"

"Went missing," Kut said.

"I see. Well, he's probably dead." Yut turned back to me and shrugged. "See, it was Kut's brother. I was going to fire him for missing work anyway, but now I have to buy flowers for the funeral."

"Little heartless of you."

"Bigger things are happening here, Mr. McGillicuddy. Now, for your second question, why the Zun want the door. Honestly, I don't know. The Zun became interested in my investigation. We were partners for a time. They never told me what they suspected this was, so I abandoned them. But whatever they were looking for, the answer is on the other side. And I'd like to hurry before they arrive and make things difficult."

"They won't, they got stuck on Shalisa."

"Is that right?" Yut nodded his approval and smiled. "Well, then shall we get on with it?"

I could only shrug. "Get on with what? I found your door. So, we're done."

Yut laughed and shook his head. "No, Mr. McGillicuddy. We are not. I picked you for a reason. I planted the seeds for Kah to reach out to you with such subtle expertise it borders on genius. Do you have any idea why you were given your little gift?"

I shook my head. "Okay, I'll bite," I said. "Why?"

The pigman took a step toward me and winked. "To answer one question. Just one." Yut turned to the door carved into the mountain and waved his arms toward it. "You see, years ago, I stumbled upon legends. Rumors of a cache of secrets from an elder species. I was rather shocked to discover these rumors were true and the location was a class three nothing of a world called Earth. We've scanned all sides. Around the door and behind it. Know what we found? Solid rock. Whatever is inside can only be reached by going through the door."

"So, it's a portal?" Alice said.

"No, whatever is inside is physically located in the mountain. It's phased. Only when this door opens, can you get to the contents."

"So, what does this have to do with me?" I asked.

Yut turned to me and smiled. "As I said, your gift is meant to answer a single question." He walked up to me and stared into my eyes. "How do we open—"

"Jack." Kah turned towards me and stared into my eyes. "What are the contents of the Encyclopedia

Britannica section E?"

If I could muster daggers to sprout out of my eyes and drive into Kah's tongue, I would have. Before I could, however, several million words screamed into my head like a freight train through a kid's soapbox car as the full contents of the Encyclopedia Britannica section E filled my mind.

****

My ears rang, and an ache filled my skull from my feet to my hair follicles. I rolled on my right elbow and realized I was also probably suffering from frostbite on several patches of skin. The whiteness of the snow blinded me, and it took me several seconds to blink my vision clear.

"He's awake," Alice said. She sounded close, which must mean the good guys won or at least didn't lose so bad.

"Jack, sorry about that," Kah said. I felt his clawed hands curl around my waist and lift me to my feet.

"What happened?" I said.

"I couldn't let you tell Yut how to open the gateway. What's inside is far too important for one creature to have."

"I thought we were friends." My sight returned, and Kah's ugly face smiled down at me with obvious pain of having hit me.

"I didn't have a choice."

All of Yut's guards knelt with their hands tied behind their heads while Ms. Mik stood behind them holding what I could only guess was a weapon. Yut stood with his hands tied and a pretty angry snarl on his face.

"What happened to them?"

"Did I forget to mention Ms. Mik is a commander in our special forces? Dispatching a gaggle of Yut's cousins wasn't very much of a challenge."

"I think you skipped that part. So why knock me out if she could manage them?"

"Telling him was enough, Jack. All we can do is detain them. Earth will gladly give him back to the Puntini in exchange for some future favor. That's politics for you. But if Yut knows how to open the door then he'll come back."

I nodded and turned toward the gateway in the rock wall. The door was over ten feet tall.

"Don't you want to see what's in there?" Alice asked.

"Not a chance. This is bigger than us. My government can file an official complaint against the Puntini."

I nodded, looked at Kah, and went back to the door. This door had caused me more grief than I cared for. Just walking away now seemed wrong, but I had to admit he had a point. I took a step toward the rock well and felt Kah's large, clawed hand fall on my shoulder. I'd say he was gentle, but there's only so much gentle he can be.

Alice folded her arms in front of her. "I want to see what's in there."

I turned to Alice and frowned. "Don't you remember what happened last time you were reckless? Let the Galactic Congress send people here."

Alice's face twisted into anger, and I knew I had overstepped. But we were dealing with something way out of our league here.

"I say we open it."

All heads turned to the metallic voice of Eddie's bionoid.

"Of course, you would, artificial," Kah said, clear disdain on his voice.

"Fear of knowledge is not a reason to avoid knowledge," Caesar's voice said through Eddie.

I turned to Eddie and frowned. "Caesar's in there, too?"

"Just a live feed, Jack. No copies this time," Caesar said.

"Humans can't handle this kind of knowledge. Why do you think the Galactic Congress had to come to your world and save you at all?" Kah said.

To this, Alice stomped her foot hard on the icy ground. "Ever since you bastards showed up on Earth, everything has been terrible. You think you're saving us? Giving us piecemeal technology at a pace you think we can handle? Mocking us when we make a groundbreaking discovery? Stopping us at every turn when we find something worth exploring on our own planet! You're not saving us from anything, you're coddling us like babies."

"Easy, Alice. We're still on the same team," I said.

"You are babies," Mik said. "You nearly destroyed your own world, and now you feel you have a right to reclaim it? Do you understand how many species would love such a rich and bountiful Earth as you have?"

"That's not the point," Alice said.

"What is? That we should have let you die?" Mik said.

"Yes!" Alice screamed the word out into the air. "Or let us fix it ourselves. Or just help us get back on our feet. But doing everything for us? Rebuilding the world with armies of robots? Why? I know that's not what happens on other worlds that nearly kill themselves. You give every other homicidal species just enough help to let them scuttle by. But not here."

Mik didn't answer. She shot Kah a look that I thought carried more than annoyance at a young human. And frankly, gave me a case of the willies. I'd never considered just how much effort the Galactic Congress had put into Earth. Considering they rebuilt nearly every major city in a few decades, restarted economies, cured diseases. If what Alice said was right, and I'd bet my life it was, why did they coddle Earth so much? Did it have something to do with this door?

"We should go inside. Caesar is right. Maybe you are hiding something from us in there," Alice said. "Eugene?"

"I hate it when you call me that."

Alice looked at me and tilted her head to one side. This was the kinda moment where you have to back your partner's play or there wouldn't be a partnership the next day. Alice backed me into a corner, and I had to come out swinging. Which, frankly, was okay by me. She was more than just my secretary, and we were way more than mere partners. Though, honestly, her choice of shoe color was abysmal.

I stepped in front of Alice and gave Kah a shrug. "Let's go inside and take a look around." Behind me, Alice took a deep breath I sensed was filled with pride. Made me smile.

"Not going to happen, Jack," Kah said.

"That's why you came, isn't it? Not only to prevent Yut, but also to stop us from getting inside. What's in there then? What's so secret?" I asked.

Kah sighed. "I don't know, Jack. Honestly, the Galactic Congress knows nothing about this door. Which is impossible. We have been looking at your world for millennia, and there's no record of anything on this mountain. I submitted a request when we were in the cafeteria. Which means this could be very old. And if it's hidden from the Galactic Congress, then it could very well have been put here by a class ten species. And they are not the kind of aliens to toy with."

I whistled. "Class ten, eh? Heavy hitter. So, what happens when the Galactic Congress gets wind of this place?"

Kah shrugged. "All access will be restricted of course."

"Which means we'll never get to come back," Alice said.

"And we'll never find out what's inside," Caesar said.

"Why do you care, Artificial? This is a matter for corporeal life. Go back to your electrical pathways and leave these matters to the flesh and blooded."

"There's the Ranz hatred of our kind."

Ms. Mik snarled at the bionoid but didn't approach.

"This is getting out of hand. Why aren't the Sentinels monitoring this location now? I'm sure you alerted them to what was going on. Why aren't they here?" I asked, glancing around.

"Yut probably has something interfering with their scans. Or they would have been here by now," Kah said.

"Which is exactly why we need to go inside and see what's there," Alice said.

"I kinda agree with the kid," I said.

"Not my name," Alice said.

I nodded.

Kah looked at Mik. She nodded and took one giant leap to land in front of the door. She shook her head no but did it with a smile. Had to admire her flair. Especially considering her powered armor could probably vaporize us in seconds.

A loud crackle of electricity rose around us, and Kah and Mik grabbed their eyes and screamed. I looked at Alice, but she merely shrugged. In seconds, both Ranz fell over onto the snow and slipped into an uneasy sleep.

I ran up to Kah to make sure he was okay, and the big guy took a few breaths and snored.

"What was that?"

"Okay, let's do this. I want to see it, too," Eddie said.

"Eddie? What are you thinking? These are official diplomats with the Galactic Congress!"

"Sorry boss, I didn't do it."

"Pepper?" I asked.

"Try again, brainiac. Call us even," Virtual-Jack said.

"Oh, you gotta be kidding me. Pepper, why didn't you stop him?"

Eddie's body shrugged. "Eh, we argued about it for several thousand microseconds. Frankly, I was getting sick talking about it," Pepper said.

"They'll be fine, Jack. The Ranz's physiology can't handle certain high-pitched frequencies, it causes them to go unconscious."

A dozen loud snorts sounded to our right. Eddie

stood in front of us as protection, but it wasn't required. All of Yut's cousins jumped up and ran back around the bend from where they came. Only Yut remained, still snarling in rage at not only our little group but also his fleeing relatives. I swear I heard him shout a few obscenities at them.

"Well, I guess that's that," I said.

"Let's open this thing up and see what's there. Yeah?" Alice said.

I nodded and turned toward the door.

****

We walked around Ms. Mik, whose prone and unconscious body took up a large area in front of the door and approached the side of the mountain. My first reaction was the oddity of the surface of the metal entrance. Strange symbols, that honestly looked like doodles from first graders, covered the door. Swirls of birds and insects crawled along the surface, and tiny stick men that oddly resembled the Zun. I wondered if that was the connection to those strange aliens from the core.

"Any idea what any of this says?"

"None. I'm interfacing with the Galactic Library and not a thing," Eddie said.

"Caesar has no idea either. He has back door channels to off-world AIs, and no one knows."

"Swell." I turned back to the door. It stood nearly twelve feet tall and about five feet wide. Whatever walked through this was big. The symbols adorned the edges of the door while carvings of swirls and spheres adorned the center.

"Are these supposed to be planets?" I asked.

"Most likely, but no one has yet to discern a pattern

or location," Eddie said.

"Does anyone have any idea what's inside?" I asked.

"No, Jack. That's part of the curiosity."

I sighed. I guess it was a stupid question. "Alice?"

"What?"

"Ask me what's inside."

"No."

"What? I thought you were onboard here?"

"I am. Still cheating."

"Jack," Yut said from the valley floor. I turned to look at him and he said, "What's on the other side of this door?"

I grabbed my head and waited for the deluge. But nothing happened. Nothing. No answer. Not even a hint. I felt a shiver spike its way up my spine at the silence in my mind. I couldn't even recall the last time I was asked a question that wasn't answered.

"Well?" Eddie said.

"Nothing. I got nothing. Silence."

"You've never not had an answer," Alice said.

I frowned and realized my gift never answered Yut's question. Kah had sent me to unconsciousness before the answer had bubbled into my mind. "I don't know how to get in."

"I hope you're joking," Alice said.

"Just need to ask me again, I think. Yut's answer never came to me because I was knocked out."

"Okay, how do we open this door?" Alice said.

Thankfully, images and answers bubbled into my mind after a few brief seconds of pause. Odd, actually, to be thankful for something being there that I had grown to hate. You've no idea what living is like with a constant crutch to lean on. Was anything I ever did solely done on my own? Was I just a pawn in a larger battle between species that had got godlike status? Well, that's what it felt like, and I can tell you it didn't feel so peachy.

"Well, any answers?"

I nodded, Alice smiled, Kah snored, and Eddie did nothing. Granted, a little anti-climactic, but my day could use a few snoozers. "I'll need all of you to open this. Alice, put your hand here and there. Eddie, you on those two spheres at top."

"These don't move, Jack. None of them do."

"By themselves, no. But have you ever seen anything in the universe move by itself?"

I stepped back and realized we were short a pair of hands. Kah and Mik were still fast asleep, but we needed one more pair of hands on the two spheres at the bottom of the swirls. I sighed and looked over at the only free pair of hands there were currently tied up behind his back.

"Yut, you ready to play nice?" I asked.

The Puntini ambassador growled once but nodded. I walked toward him but felt Eddie's hand on my shoulder, holding me back. His eyes held worry, and I thought I could see myself in his expression. Talk about creepy.

"What are you doing, Jack? He doesn't have our best interests in mind."

"Well, we need another set of hands," I said.

"What about the ghost? Is she still around?" Alice asked.

Melanie forced herself into view with psychic effort and shook her head no. Sure, she could toss a few snowballs and or rattle some chains but doing complex manipulation of a physical item? Let alone two items at once? No chance.

"Sorry, if we want in, we need his help." I walked over to the ambassador, took off his hand binders from a key I found in Mik's belt.

"At least my retainer was good for something," Yut said.

"Sorry but having your army of long-toothed inbred cousins wave guns at me violates the don't-shoot-me clause."

"Well, fine. How do we open the door? Can we do this, please? I want to see what's in there as much as you do."

I nodded. "One thing, see that guy?" I pointed to Eddie. "That's an AI in a full bionoid, he can kill you in a dozen ways, so just remember to play on the good guy's team and don't go all alien rogue on me, deal?"

Yut nodded. That would have to be good enough.

"Okay, here and there, Ambassador."

I took a step back to make sure everyone's hands were on the right spots. At precisely 6:03 and twenty-seven seconds eastern time, I gave the word for everyone to shift of all of their spheres clockwise. Nothing happened.

After coaching everyone on clockwise vs. counterclockwise, can't blame them, what clocks aren't digital, we reset and got ready to try again. Once again, everyone's hands were placed on the correct spheres, including my own, at 6:10 p.m., and within thirty-three seconds we all spun the spheres. Nothing happened.

I frowned. "Everyone, step back."

As soon as everyone released their spheres and

took a step backward, we all sighed a breath of success as the spheres continued to rotate on their own. Other spheres we didn't touch joined in the spin, and soon the entire face of the door moved in a coordinated way.

"It's a solar system," Yut said.

"Not one we have on record. It may be extragalactic. Beyond the local group," Eddie replied.

"Does the galaxy even have relationships outside the Milky Way?" I asked.

"The local galactic cluster, yes. But beyond that it's very rare. The cafeteria extends across the cosmos, but who wants to walk that far? I'm sure class ten species can do it, but they don't like to share their toys," Yut said.

His eyes shined with a hunger to see what was on the other side of the door. I thought it may have been a mistake to let him get this close.

Small rocks fell from the surrounding wall as the door moved. We all took an instinctive step backward and watched the spinning solar system on the door continue to swirl. In seconds, the door creaked outward and slammed into the rock wall beside it. A dark cavern stretched into the depths of the mountain, and Yut made a squealing noise and jumped forward. Fortunately, Eddie was faster and yanked at him by the collar.

"Just hang on, Yut. We'll go in together."

I turned to check on Kah and Mik, both still unconscious on the snowy embankment. "Someone has to stay with them," I said.

"I'm going in," Alice said. The look on her face made it clear she was not to be argued with.

"You need me to keep an eye on him," Eddie said.

"You could both stay out here," I said.

Eddie shrugged, "Yeah, but if Kah or Mik needs me for something, then what?"

"Well, I'm not staying out here." I shook my head and let out a sigh of frustration.

A gray form solidified between us, and we both took a step backward. Melanie's form came into focus, and she smiled once and nodded.

"Thanks, Mel. We won't be long."

She nodded and smiled. I approached the opening to the cavern, gulped a huge ball of fear down my throat, and took a step into the darkness. If this really was the reason I'd been given my gift, then it was high time to find some answers.

Chapter 22

We walked into darkness. Twin beams of light turned on from Eddie's shoulders. His new bionoid body really was coming in handy. Symbols and designs, more than were on the door, decorated the walls. Alice practically buried her face in the wall, her eyes darting over and between each of the symbols.

A dot of light from a source that wasn't Eddie came into view further down the cave. We jogged down the rocky path, leaving Alice with her face glued to the indecipherable language on the walls. More symbols and designs covered the rock the closer we got to the dot of light. Some of them looked familiar, but in what way I wasn't sure.

The dot of light grew into a circle with a table sitting in the middle. A glass jar sat on the table. We fanned out around the odd display, a perplex look plastered on everyone's face, including mine. Sitting beneath the glass jar was a round porcelain plate with the, admittedly, most delicious looking peanut butter and jelly sandwich resting on top.

"Is this a joke?" I asked.

"Tell me what you see," Yut said.

"I see a sandwich. A peanut butter and jelly sandwich. Is this all just a practical joke? Is this what you people do for kicks?" Anger boiled under my skin as I felt the answers to all my questions floating away down the cave and out into the world. Everything was a cosmic joke, and I was the punchline. I felt an uncontrollably strong desire to visit the Queen Vic and drink away the last few days of trouble.

"I don't see a sandwich, but I see food. A bucket of rotten vegetables."

"Rotten?"

Yut glared at me. "Don't judge my race on our eating habits, simian."

I nodded. "Right."

Silence stretched into minutes. "Well, who's going to eat it?" I asked.

Yut shook his head. He frowned, spat on the ground, and stomped one of his feet. "Wasted. Years wasted. Do you have any idea how much time and money I have invested in this? From whispered rumors of your people, of a hidden door to ancient lore of the galaxy. And this is all I have to show."

"I take it you're not hungry?"

Yut raised his eyes to mine, I could practically feel the heat coming off his anger. "You're fired."

"You can't fire me after I delivered on the goods," I said in protest. The only thing to make this day worse was not getting paid.

"Sue me, simian." Yut turned to leave, but nearly fell over as Alice pushed past him.

"I know what this is!" Alice's excitement sent a shiver down my spine. When a genius gets this excited, you need to decide quick if you are going to share in her jubilance or be scared out of your wits.

"An experimental food stall for the cafeteria?" I said.

"A Hesiean evolution chamber." Alice stared at the

sandwich with wild curiosity.

Yut stood up, his eyes fixated on Alice, and walked to the glass jar. "Are you certain, girl? How do you know?"

"The symbols. The reason we can't decipher them is that it's not a language. Not a single language anyway. The Hesiean were a class nine species from the galactic core. They played with time-dilation, probabilities, concepts, and combinations from a million species. They force-evolved themselves by using other species as a template. This chamber is the culmination of their technology."

"How do you know?" Yut said.

"I've spent thousands of hours in the Galactic Library. One of these was found before, but not behind a door on a mountain, which is why no one recognized it."

"Wait, how did the Zun know this was here?" I asked.

"The Zun were force-evolved by the Hesieans. An experimental species," Alice said. "They must want to continue the treatments."

"What happened to the Hesieans?" Eddie said.

Alice shrugged. "No one really knows."

"Someone want to share what an evolution chamber does?" I asked.

"Exactly what the name suggests." Yut placed his hands on the glass jar, his eyes wild and wide.

"What does this have to do with me and my gift? Did the Hesian evolve me in here without my knowledge?"

Yut laughed. "Nothing, you imbecile. I have no idea how omniscience grew in your pea sized brain."

"But you said I was given this gift to open the door?"

"I lied. I have no idea why you're psychic" Yut snorted, his eyes locked onto the food in front of him.

My heart fell into my chest as I realized I was just a pawn. Strike two for being a good private eye. Or was it strike twenty by now? How can a great detective get everything so wrong? Throughout this entire ordeal, from the moment I sat in Kah's office with the young prince wrapped in his warm shell to now, standing in an alien evolution chamber, I had been dead wrong. Neither Kah nor Yut cared one iota about my gift, and there wasn't some great alien conspiracy involving Earth with me in the middle. I had come into this whole thing from the wrong angle and nearly got half of the people I care about killed. Any confidence I had in myself fell through my soul into the ground and walked out the cave with my self-esteem carried in a rucksack over its shoulder.

"Put that back, you have no idea what it will do!" Alice's voice woke me up from my self-pity party. Yut had removed the glass jar from above the sandwich, or in his case rotten veggies.

I choked my own feelings down my throat and felt the tingly sensation of something bad about to happen replace it. "Easy, Yut, I thought you said you weren't hungry?"

"Puntini are always hungry." Yut snorted once at whatever was under the glass jar and moved his hands to grab it.

"Eddie, would you mind?" I said.

Eddie's hand curled into a ball, and he threw his fist at the ambassador. Just before the bionoid's hand reached Yut's chin, some kind of yellow glow came to life around Yut's body. Eddie's fist impacted the yellow glow and stopped dead in mid-air.

"I'm still the representative of a class five species. Our technology is far superior to a simple bionoid from Earth." Yut winked at us and dove his mouth into the center of the food pile.

"We should leave," Alice said.

"Why? Aren't evolved beings smarter and nicer?"

Alice shook her head. "It depends on the individual being evolved. Humans aren't close enough to being able to handle the experience. If the Puntini aren't either, then he could go mad from the process."

I looked at Alice and frowned. "You probably should have led with that."

Alice shrugged. "I'm a genius, not a psychologist."

The ambassador chewed on whatever the evolution chamber gave him for a snack. Within just seconds, he bolted upright and stared at the wall. His body shook without his control, and he let out a terrible scream somewhere between pain and bliss. Before either Alice or I could react, Eddie picked us both up in his arms and ran toward the exit.

"Shouldn't we do something besides run away?" I asked.

"Absolutely not," Alice said.

That was good enough for me.

****

Outside, Kah and Mik were just getting to their feet from Eddie's stun when we ran out of the cave. Behind us, guttural snorts and loud cries echoed out of the cave's walls. I heard Yut's voice cry out in pain and also scream in triumph as the Hesiean chamber rearranged his essence into something that I was sure I didn't want to see.

"What is happening?" Kah said. Mik reached her arm around his shoulder and lifted him to his feet.

"We opened the door," I said.

"It's a Hesiean evolution chamber," Alice said.

"You're joking," Kah said.

"I'm not."

"This isn't possible. This world has been scanned, poked, and prodded a million times over. How could this have been missed?" Mik said.

"The Hesiean, it would appear, have additional tricks up their sleeves. Though they didn't have arms," Alice said.

"Where is Yut?" Kah said.

I had to give him credit for not seeing the ambassador. Who said dinosaurs don't have good vision? "He ate the sandwich."

"What does that mean?"

"He engaged the chamber. He's being force-evolved." Alice walked to a large boulder, sat down, and pulled out her immersion rig.

"Shouldn't you be a little more concerned?" I asked her.

Alice shrugged.

"Didn't you just say he could go mad?"

"Yeah, it's a chance. But small. In the end, this doesn't really help me."

"Not help you?"

"I don't need to be force-evolved," Alice said.

"And the pig-man being force-evolved?"

Alice looked at me and tilted her head to one side. "He's being evolved, not weaponized. He'll probably become a being of pure light and leave our plane of existence. So, bottom line, who cares? This trip is just a waste of time now."

"At some point we should have a talk," I said.

Alice ignored me and activated her immersion rig. Teenagers.

Kah let out a grunt as he rubbed his shoulder where he hit the ground. "She may be right, but also wrong. I need to alert the Sentinels."

Bright yellow light burst out of the cave entrance. Yut's voice echoed off every surface on the mountaintop. Whatever the chamber did, I had a hunch it was over now, but I also had the feeling that Alice was wrong. This blast of light wasn't about to send Yut to any kind of higher plane of anything.

"I have become," Yut's voice boomed, each word exploding like a cannonball over a battlefield.

Alice tilted her immersion rig down, and her eyebrows shot up. Mik took a large step toward the cave with Eddie beside her. I had a sudden fear that we may not be near any upload towers for Eddie, Pepper, or the virtual me. If something happened to them, this could be the end of the road.

"Maybe we should run away?" I suggested.

"That is what I said in the cave," Alice said.

"You also just said everything is fine."

"Well, I'm not the psychic one, am I?"

A thick pale white tendril the size of an oak tree shot out of the cave entrance. Everyone except Mik took a step backward. The ground shook as if an earthquake had just passed through the area. Two more large tendrils shot out from the entrance of the chamber. They dug into the ground and wrapped around rocky outcrops around us. Whatever Yut had become, it looked like he was pulling himself out of the chamber.

"Did you call for help?" I asked.

"No, I can't get a signal. He must have blocked all signals."

"How can he do that?" I asked.

"Because I am a god." Yut's voice felt like it would push into my brain and squeeze the gray matter out of my ears. Everyone clutched their heads just as I did.

"Alice, what about the immersion rig?"

She shook her head. "It's dead. The signal died as soon as he started coming out of the cave."

"Jack, how do we stop Yut?" Kah asked.

Nothing happened. No answer, no flash of images, nothing. I only shook my head in response.

"Can we reverse the chamber's effects and devolve him?" Alice asked.

Nothing.

"How do we make it off the mountain alive?" Alice asked.

Again, nothing. I don't know what scared me more, that the power I hated and wanted gone was actually no longer working, or that Alice had abandoned all of her ethical complaints about using my gift and fired off questions like a soldier on the rifle-range.

"Why aren't you able to answer any of my questions?" Alice asked.

I had to give the kid credit. She wasn't speaking rhetorically; she was asking my gift why the gift wasn't working. But the only answer I received was the same silence. Which meant my gift was gone.

"It's gone. It's not working."

"You don't deserve omniscience." Yut's voice cut through the air like a knife. "I have severed your connection to the cosmic stream."

I felt my back stiffen and the hairs on my neck stand on end. How dare Yut take my gift from me? Sure, I never wanted it, and frankly wouldn't miss it once it was gone, but it wasn't his to take. I took a step toward the tentacles protruding from the cave entrance.

"That wasn't your choice to make, Ambassador. You had no right to take anything from me. Mind stepping out here so we can chat about it?"

A mass of tentacles oozed out of the cave doorway. My nose wrinkled, and my stomach grumbled at the distinct smell of tomatoes and basil. I had no idea where the smell emanated from. My mind felt like breaking at the sight of the mass of tentacles as it lifted off the ground and floated in the air.

"A deity may do as he pleases. Behold, I come to you in the visage of your own god. I shall lay waste to this world, and the Puntini shall rise to rule this universe."

"He's insane. He wasn't ready for the chamber," Alice said.

"What kind of god do you humans worship, exactly?" Mik said.

The floating mass of tentacles shifted and swirled into itself. Part of one of the arms broke off from a sharp rock and landed in front of us. Two large round meaty spheres pushed outward from the mass of swarming tentacles. Red chunky liquid spilled out from the thing and covered the ground over which Yut hovered. I shook my head and blinked my eyes, my mind not letting me realize what I was seeing.

"Is that what I think it is?" Alice said.

I shrugged. "What can I say, I'm an atheist."

"I shall devour your souls. You will become part of my essence and you shall witness every atrocity I commit to this backward planet," Yut said.

I bent down to the piece of tentacle near me and poked it once with my finger, a piece of Yut's new arm stuck into my skin. I lifted the piece up and gave it a sniff.

"Pasta with a primavera sauce," I said.

"I truly can't fathom how much I hate you," Alice said.

Yut roared, a dozen tentacles shot out from his body, several racing in our direction. Ms. Mik let loose her own battle cry, unsheathed a three-foot-long dagger I didn't know she had, and charged. Lasers shot out from Eddie's body as the bionoid leaped onto a rock outcropping.

I looked at Alice and Kah. As we were all the non-combatant types, none of us had any idea what to do next.

Chapter 23

A ball of pasta floated above the rocky terrain. Twin meatball eyes swiveled and rotated within swirls of foot-thick woven strands. The new god, or old Yut, smiled a large noodle grin. Arms of capellini waved in the air and struck the mountainside with force. Snow blasted off the surface of the mountain at Yut's newfound strength.

"Humans. Such a pitiful species. They worship their own food," Yut said.

I couldn't help but laugh. Maybe he had a point, honestly.

A loud battle cry erupted behind me. Ms. Mik screamed something unintelligible and leapt over Alice to charge at the floating Yut. Her battle suit glowed a faint golden hue as twin daggers sprouted out from her wrists. She struck one of Yut's flailing arms, severing the large piece of pasta to fall to the ground.

"She's going to get killed," I said.

"Aren't we all?" Alice said.

"She'll be fine," Kah said. He grabbed Alice and I by the waist, easily lifting us up into his arms, and hefted us behind a large boulder on the plateau.

"Where are the AIs?" Just as I started looking for them, blasts of red light illuminated the area. Eddie's bionoid stood a dozen feet from Yut, the lasers in his shoulder's painting Yut's body with a bloody color.

"Atta boy, Eddie!" I said.

"Zip it meat-maggot," Pepper said. "We're busy."

I nodded and ducked back behind the boulder. "One thing I don't get from all this—"

"Just one thing?" Alice said.

"Why did you tell Yut about my gift, Kah? Why give him that piece of information? Why is it so important to you, what I can do?"

"What are you talking about, Jack?" Kah said.

"Come on, we're about to die by a carb loaded Italian dinner. We can at least be honest in death," I said.

"The entire galaxy knows about your gift and most governments of Earth. It's not a secret."

A shock wave hit me like a boulder made of meatballs. "What?"

"Oh, you're well known. The human with omniscience. Quite the curiosity."

"That's not true. It can't be true," I said.

"Very true. There's a Saturday morning cartoon about you on the opposite side of the galaxy," Kah made the statement as if he recounted yesterday's soccer scores.

I shook my head as my world crashed around me. "If that's true then why aren't more people trying to kidnap me? Use me?"

"Not worth the trouble, I imagine. So, you can answer any question. Who cares? So can the Galactic Library."

"I can see the future too, Kah."

Kah shrugged. "Probable futures. You've never tested it."

"You're lying," I said.

"He's not," Alice said.

My head spun, and my eyes nearly popped out of my head. "What did you say?"

"I've seen the cartoon. It's funny. Supposed to be hidden from general Earth population, like a state secret, but I found it. You would have found it too if you'd visit a Galactic Library once in a while instead of depending on the gift you hate so much."

"Now, for your second question, why the Zun want the door. Honestly, I don't know. The Zun became interested in my investigation. We were partners for a time. They never told me what they suspected this was, so I abandoned them. But whatever they were looking for, the answer is on the other side. And I'd like to hurry before they arrive and make things difficult."

The feeling of betrayal coursed through my veins. "Alice, you knew that everyone in the galaxy knew about me?"

Alice nodded, and a corner of her mouth lifted in a smile.

"Why the hell didn't you tell me? I've been running around the city, the world, the entire galaxy, thinking everyone is trying to poke and prod me into a laboratory, and you knew my gift wasn't even a secret?"

"Yeah," Alice said.

"Alice!" My voice raised to a shout. "Same team!"

Alice looked at me with her deadpan stare. "And in any other situation, without an insane force-evolved Puntini in the shape of a flying spaghetti monster about to kill us, this would have been an ultimate moment of humor and revenge."

"Revenge for what?"

"Secretary? Really? You treat me like I'm a college dropout."

"I mean, technically you are."

Alice's eyes focused into tight daggers, and she ground her teeth.

"Oh, come on, kid. I know you're not my secretary, I just liked teasing you about it."

"Because you thought it was funny?" Alice said.

"Yeah, sure."

"Well, ha-ha. Now we're even."

I sighed. "That's just great." I turned from Alice, anger boiling through my veins. I wasn't so angry at her. She really was just a kid, after all. Sometimes we expect too much from smart teenagers and forget they still have growing up to do. But for me, this was strike three. Here I had been playing cowboys and Indians with Kah and the entire galaxy when all along everyone knew. They probably sat in smoke-filled rooms sipping whiskey and laughing at the human looking over his shoulder for something that wasn't there. Just a swell way to end the day, especially the day I was probably going to get swallowed by the great pasta god.

"Good one, Alice. You're a lot meaner than I gave you credit for." I shouldn't have said it and immediately regretted it, but hey, I'm human too. "You can check off that revenge box now."

Alice shrugged. "Not the only reason."

"Oh yeah? Other surprises for me?"

Alice shook her head and looked away. She slouched against the boulder and lowered her head. Several long, quiet seconds passed between us. Alice took a deep breath and finally said, "I guess I just wanted someone else to know what it felt like."

I knew what she meant without having to ask. She was unique on Earth. Someone who believed she'd made some big scientific breakthrough, but in reality, she hadn't. In some strange way, I felt closer to Alice in that moment than at any other time. We really were just two peas in a pod.

A loud gargled scream sounded behind us, followed by something massive slamming to the rocky ground. Several gallons of sauce flew over our heads and coated the mountainside just beyond our boulder. I assumed Mik got a good hit on Yut.

"How long do you think they'll last?"

"Minutes," Alice said. She rested her head against the rock and breathed heavily.

"Easy, kid. We'll be okay," I said.

Alice tried to brush me off but failed miserably. "I never found them. All my friends from that night. I'll never discover something new."

"Sorry, Alice." I looked away. I realized in that second she couldn't even ask me where they went as Yut had taken away my gift.

Alice laughed and shook her head, tears forming in the corners of her eyes. "I think I may have found something, too. It was just a sliver of an idea, a hint, probably wrong. But I didn't even get to try."

Behind us, Mik screamed again, but this time it wasn't a battle cry. Her body flew to our left and smacked into the rock wall next to the door. To the credit of her military training, she bounced off the ground, a stream of mini missiles firing from her chest, and charged Yut again.

Alice turned to me, a mix of fear and rage in her eyes. "Do you have any idea what it's like to be smarter than Einstein in a universe where everything is already discovered? Tom made an alternative universe, and Yut just became a god. Every technology you can imagine is already invented, catalogued, and ready to be downloaded if you have the permission."

"What does that have to do with anything?" I asked.

"Is this really the right time for this discussion?" Kah said.

"Shouldn't you be helping Mik and Eddie?"

"Why because I look like an extinct three-ton dinosaur from Earth? I'm a pacificist, Jack."

I huffed and ignored him. "Tell me, Alice. Is that what you've been working on since Tom's?"

She nodded. "Yes." Her eyes lit up, and the fear melted away as her mind spun up in a thousand directions. "I checked the library, talked to the brightest minds on Earth and the ones I could reach in the galaxy. I really had a new idea, a new concept. Something no one has tried or even thought of. Do you have any idea what it feels like to have something new in a universe where everything is old? Something that could change life as we know it."

I gulped as I realized that Yut may not be the scariest thing on the mountaintop. "Look, when we get out of here, and we will, I'll make sure we do your thing. Okay? I promise."

Alice smiled. Perhaps for the first time since I met her, she smiled. "Thanks."

"Jack!" Eddie's voice cut through the air, and I jumped up from behind the boulder to see Eddie wrapped up in Yut's grasp.

"Before we get to tackle your idea from the god on

the beach, we really need to deal with the god at hand."

"Any idea on how we do that?" Kah said.

I looked up from Alice to Kah and finally let my eyes rest on Yut. I channeled Pablo Ramsey's great scene from It Only Takes Two to Tango and demanded to know from my memories of his movies what he would do. Confidence coursed through my bones. I felt the confidence of a gumshoe. I smiled and gave Kah a wink. "Sure, I know exactly what to do."

****

I had no idea what to do.

Relying on a gift that could make you nearly omniscient for so long, can give a guy a real complex. Relying on a gift that makes you nearly omniscient for so long can give a guy a real complex. To think nearly all of my troubles would never have been troubles if I'd just done some research was a hard pill to swallow. Not only had my confidence been shattered just moments before, but I also didn't fathom any way to delay Yut, let alone save Eddie from the pasta squeezing his insides into cybernetic stew.

"Okay, I got nothing," I said.

"I might be able to rig something up. A shield or something. Buy me a few minutes, Jack. Yeah?" Alice said.

"Distract him, perhaps?" Kah said.

"How?"

Kah shrugged. "Give him a bill for services rendered?"

I shrugged back. Why not? I stood up from behind the boulder to see Eddie wrapped up tight and Ms. Mik shoved against the wall of rock above the mouth of the cave. She still had one arm free and used it to slice the pasta from around her torso. Lasers continued to fire from Eddie's left shoulder, his right having been mangled into a mess of wires and twisted bio-metal.

"Hey, Yut," I said.

The ambassador-god rotated in the air toward my voice, his twin meatball eyes rolling in their pasta sockets in my direction. Any other day this would be quite the humorous event. Too bad we were all about to be eaten by an ancient Italian carb.

"Yes, human? Don't worry, I shall consume your essence once I have dispatched your servants."

"About that. We have some unfinished business, yeah? I led you to the cave, opened the door, the way I see things, that's a job well done. I think there's the matter of my paycheck?"

Without warning, Yut dropped Ms. Mik and Eddie onto the ground and floated in my direction. The thick stench of tomatoes and olives almost made me gag. Whatever recipe Yut was using for his internal chemistry would never fly in any Little Italy on Earth. I could just see the army of Italian chefs quitting over the sight.

"Payment?" Yut asked.

"Yeah, I opened your door, now you pay me. Simple." I gulped hard. Somehow, with Kah's help, I distracted Yut. I felt the sting of self-judgment as I hadn't thought of the idea myself. Still, I had carried out the plan. That had to be worth something. From the corner of my eye, I could see Kah helping Ms. Mik up and away from Yut's swinging arms. Eddie had gotten to his feet and scrambled back. Now I just had to keep him talking long enough for Alice to do whatever she was doing.

"You're a curious species. My evolved state grants me a unique perspective into your history. Though interesting, it is also odd. Unusual gaps in your evolution suggest tampering. Still, this is a matter for another time. Payment? I grant you the payment of exploration. To the afterworld."

I held up my hands quickly and took a step backward. "Hey, easy, Yut. Didn't I get you everything you wanted? Doesn't being evolved mean being over petty concerns?"

With that statement, Yut stopped moving and hovered. His meatballs rolled in his head as he chewed on what I said. I took the moment to glance over at Alice. She stood up from the boulder, ran her hands through her hair, threw something on the ground, and shook her head. Great. Guess I had to figure out a Plan B.

"Interesting. Perhaps I should no longer concern myself with such petty things. And yet, I do. As I now have access to millions of streams of consciousness and history in the universal maelstrom of thought, I shall consider this over the next eon. Until then, I see no harm in indulgence of pre-evolved desires. I shall roast your flesh and the lizards' together into a stew and meld them into myself. Those that come after shall witness my creation and be envious."

"Are you expecting company?"

"All Puntini shall partake of the sacred bucket. The universe shall fill with the images of your god, and all shall bow to the power and glory of our evolved race!"

The image of a million, floating bowls of primavera gave me goosebumps. Surely one of the big class ten species could deal with Yut, but his entire race of evolved beings? What if the sandwich I saw, or the bucket that Yut ate from, deep in the cave was special? Perhaps the purpose of the thing was to end civilization as we know it throughout the universe by creating super god-like soldiers, and Yut just fell into their trap? My mind swam with the possibilities and let them wash over me a thousand ways like ocean waves over a beached whale.

Then it happened.

An idea leapt out of the river of my mind and landed in my lap like a lead weight. There it was. The answer to this whole fiasco. How to stop Yut, save my friends, and make it back to DC in time for cornflakes. A feeling I'd never felt before filled my soul. I'd figured it out. Sure, I didn't solve a case, but I figured out a solution to the problem in front of me, without my gift or help from Alice or anyone. Just me. Eugene Joseph McGillicuddy. Private Detective for hire. I felt my back straighten and a newfound confidence grow in my chest. On the ground, just a few feet away, I spied my fedora. I trudged to my beloved hat, snatched it from the ground, and gave it just the right tug onto my head.

"Hey, Melanie, still around?" I whispered under my breath.

A tickle of air on the back of my neck sent my hairs into a tizzy, a clear sign of ghost presence.

"I need a little help. Got a poltergeist blast in you?"

I felt her nod.

"Swell. Wait for my signal." I turned back to Yut and gave him a grin. "Hey, Yut, let's wrap this up, shall we?"

"Are you ready to face your doom?" Yut had

moved to just within inches of me. He wanted to gloat. Which played in my favor.

"I have just one last thing to say. But it's the most important thing I will tell you. Perhaps the most important thing you have ever heard in your life. Evolved and not."

A line of pasta above one of the meatballs shifted upward. Yut floated closer to me. I could smell the pepper and tomato wafting on the air with hints of garlic and sage. I know it wasn't the right time to think about it, but boy that evolution chamber did cook up a good pasta.

"Tell me, human," Yut said.

My hand rifled through my pants pocket, my fingers curling around the one item in all the universe that I could use to fight a god. I held the object tight as I looked up from beneath my fedora straight into Yut's eyes.

"Sally sells seashells by the seashore." I pulled my hand out of my pocket and flicked the seashell from Tom's beach into the air. "MThey also maintained a sizableelanie!"

Wisps of white and gray formed around the seashell as Melanie summoned all the ectoplasm at her disposal. She screamed a banshee cry and forced the seashell forward into Yut's unsuspecting maw.

Yut floated backward a few steps before shaking his head. "Do you think a trinket can stop me?"

Before I could answer Yut's eyes stopped rolling. His body shook in an odd manner and shifted a dozen ways, parts of his pasta-self swinging wildly in the air.

"Take cover!" I yelled. I ran to Eddie and helped him to his feet before throwing us both behind the nearest boulder.

Cracks of light erupted around Yut. The spaghetti god screamed and wrapped his pasta arms around boulders and rocks, but the light seemed to infect every inch of his being regardless of where he moved. A thunderous clap erupted on the plateau, followed by a torrent of wind. Snow and dust swirled into a tiny maelstrom of a tornado before everything settled down. I waited a moment before standing. When I got to my feet, Yut was nowhere in sight, and the door to the chamber had closed and resealed itself.

"What did you do?" Alice said.

"Sent him to Tom."

"Are you insane?"

Eddie limped forward and nodded.

"Haven't you been watching him? Of course, he's insane," Pepper said. At least, the tone sounded like hers.

I shrugged. "Figured Tom controls his universe. If anyone can deal with an angry god, it'd be Tom on his beach."

Kah walked up to me panting with Ms. Mik leaning on his shoulder. "Who is Tom?"

I sighed with my back was still straight. "Just a friend." I thrust my hands into my pockets and let the moment wash over me. My fedora was tilted at the perfect angle and bent my head to the side just a smidge. I'd never felt anything like I did in that moment. I'd beaten the bad guy. Not with some superpower but with a thought from my own noggin. Sure, maybe the idea was small—throw a seashell in the air and send a god to a pocket universe—but it was mine. And no one, not Kah, or Alice, or the entire

Galactic Congress could take that away from me. Maybe ninety-nine percent of the time I was a two-bit, fake gumshoe who got lucky and had good friends. But right now, on this mountain, I truly felt like a class A private eye that I pretended to be. And it felt good.

My stomach grumbled as the smell of Yut lingered in the air. "Anyone hungry for Italian? We could make it to Rome in thirty."

Chapter 24

Hot air blasted my face as I stepped into the desert of middle-of-nowhere, Arizona. this time Alice didn't join me, instead she threw herself into a new discovery of something probably very terrifying. Something I was sure would haunt me soon enough. Cacti and rocks were my only companions as I made my way to the entrance of the cave that would transport me to Tom's beach world—a trip I didn't want to make, but knew I had to. When you deposit a newly evolved, and probably furious, god on someone's doorstep, it's best to stop by a few days later with cookies.

Once inside the cave, I took a few deep breaths. Partially to catch my breath, but also to help my stress levels, as I was uncertain exactly what I was going to be walking into. Either the portal was closed—which could mean Tom had no more desire to speak with me—or Yut had won and shut it down. Or the portal was open, and I'd either find Tom not thrilled with me, or Yut going on a spaghetti rampage. None of the possibilities looked very appealing.

Though I was fairly sure I was facing either a severe talking to or being dismantled at the cellular level by Tom. I took solace that otherwise things had turned out not so bad. Yut had lost on the mountain. The entrance to the evolve-o-matic in Tibet had been sealed off, and all access was now restricted by the

Sentinels. Not one of our little band of devolved freedom fighters were much worse for the wear. Though Ms. Mik suffered a few broken bones and Eddie's bionoid needed serious repair, everyone made it out still able to take a deep breath.

As for me and my confidence levels, let's just say I now walk with a not-so-slight bounce in my step. Yes, my gift has often been more of a curse, but for reasons that turned out to be non-factual. According to Kah, he'd reported my gift to the galactic authorities after he'd found out. They had already informed the human governments, and everyone came to roughly the same conclusion of, "that's neat but we have work to do." Apparently, being omniscient in today's universe isn't such a big deal. Granted, Yut used my gift for ill purposes, but only because he was hiding something from the universe. Though I suppose there's some danger to it, I decided to be out and proud of my gift, and everything else in my life.

And as far as my gift is concerned, it came back with a vengeance. Not any more powerful, but just as receptive to answer questions of the answerable kind. I suppose Yut had quieted the voice, but not shut it out completely.

Why go through all of this in my mind while sweating through my clothes? It's simple. I was stalling while I debated with myself about whether I should stay or turn around and let Tom send me a card.

"Are you coming in or not?" Tom's voice echoed off the cave walls.

Startled, I looked about the cave and sighed. Of course, Tom's beach was still one piece. Fine. Let's go get my ass chewed out by a class ten species that had collapsed themselves into a man named Tom. What else was there to do on a Friday?

****

Sunshine and salty air greeted me as I walked through the portal. A dozen young people danced along the shoreline. Their laughter and shrieks of joy told me that if Yut had done any damage here, Tom had cleaned it up quickly. I strolled down the beach and enjoyed the sound of the surf for as long as I could before seeing Tom wave me over to sit with him at his table beneath a yellow umbrella. I sighed in relief as I could see a wide smile on his face. Maybe my upcoming chew out wouldn't be so bad.

"Jack, so nice of you to join us," Tom said.

I nodded. "I thought it best to pay you a visit and apologize."

"Apologize for what?" Tom looked at me with genuine curiosity, and I wondered if I'd misjudged the situation. Though, how you judge a situation with beings that could create their own universes is a fair question in my book.

"Did nothing happen that was unusual? Perhaps with a seashell?"

Tom nodded once and laughed. "Oh, yes, we did have an unexpected visitor."

"He didn't cause you any trouble?"

"Trouble? Oh, no. Though we can be overprotective of our guests' privacy, no one can cause much trouble here. No one but us, of course."

"Well, that's good to hear." I smiled and put my hands in my pockets.

From behind Tom, a waiter approached with a small tray of food and two glasses of what looked like beer. The waiter set the beers on the table and followed by a large bowl of pasta with two fairly large meatballs in the center.

"Care for a bite to eat?" Tom gave me an odd grin.

I hesitated a moment as I stared at the plate. "I'm not hungry."

"Sure?" Tom took the fork and stabbed one meatball. He held it up just in front of his mouth. "It's pork."

"Pretty sure."

Tom stuffed the meatball into his maw and slowly chewed, never once taking his eyes off mine. I nodded slowly and tried to convey that I got the message. At least, I think I got it. I refer to my previous statement of trying to figure out what goes on in the mind of a being as complex as Tom.

"You have such an interesting world, Jack. Did you know that?"

I shrugged. "Sure."

"We mean, we have taken up residence here, and you found a Hesiean evolution chamber on Earth. Two class ten species mingling about on your planet is quite rare."

"I thought the Hesieans were class nine?"

Tom winked.

"Okay, how did you know about chamber at all?" I asked.

"We have friends." Tom grabbed his spoon and twirled pasta onto his fork.

"Yeah, I guess new species are interesting."

"Oh, more than interesting. And then there is you after all. Nearly omniscient."

"Yeah, about that. I don't think I'm all that special.

Galaxy doesn't seem to care much about me and neither do Earth governments."

"Oh, they care, they just don't know what to do with you or whose pet project you really are."

I shrugged once and gave him a solid squint of my eyes. "Your friends tell you that?"

"No, that's obvious."

"Then why hasn't anyone thrown a bag over my head and stuffed me in a room to ask me questions a hundred times a day?"

Tom smiled. He jammed the pasta in his mouth and smacked his lips at the taste. "We must compliment the chef," he said. He took the napkin from the table and wiped the corners of his mouth. "No one is going to touch you because everyone is afraid of whoever tied your consciousness to the cosmic stream."

I nodded. If what Tom said were true, and I'd bet money it was, it would explain something that had been gnawing on my mind ever since Tibet. Why hadn't Yut just kidnapped me? Looks like Yut was scared of whoever put this gift in my head. "Is that not common? Putting omniscience into a class three nothing like me?"

Tom laughed. "We couldn't do it, and we can build universes."

I let the weight of what he said rest on my shoulders for a moment before trying to comprehend. Kah made it sound like my gift meant nothing, and now Tom's flipping the script on me again made my nerves jump and filled me with a sense of dread. Just when I thought I'd put this all behind me, it was getting jammed back down my throat. Maybe the fear factor of messing with whoever did what they did to me would be enough to keep my mind at ease.

"Well, glad I didn't cause you any stress the last few days," I said.

Tom nodded. "Oh, none at all. As we were saying, your world is more than interesting enough to make up for any annoyances."

Something at the back of my mind squirmed its way out of my head and gave me a sense of the willies. Tom was hinting at something, and I wasn't sure what it was. "Not any more interesting than any other world out there, new or not. I'm sure there are plenty of worlds folks would like to visit."

Tom put down his fork, folded his hands in front of his face and stared into my eyes. The moment dragged on for longer than I felt comfortable, but he was hinting at something, I wanted to know what. "We have a question for you, Jack."

Here it comes. "Okay, shoot."

Tom locked his eyes onto mine. "As you said, there are other worlds. But then Earth appears to be unique. For instance, how many evolution chambers were created by the Hessians?"

The answer bubbled into my mind and with it a good helping of fear. "Five."

"Exactly right. Five. Next question, how many evolution chambers still exist in the universe?"

I gulped as the number flashed in my mind. "One."

Tom nodded. "Just one. In all the known and unknown universe. One."

"And it's here."

"Last question for you, Jack. What world in the Milky Way galaxy has the largest and most active galactic embassy?"

The fact hit me like a ton of Ranz piled onto a

Puntini parade. "Earth," I said.

"Earth. Your little world."

I let the truth wash over me. No one ever thought Earth was special. Just another planet that almost blew itself up and was saved by friendly aliens. And believe me, on that score, Earth wasn't special by any means. Every year, dozens of planets pop up in need of galactic help. I wondered how many worlds of class three species had a galactic embassy with a thousand races walking its halls.

"Allow us to answer that, Jack. None. There isn't a single class three world in the entire galaxy with an embassy as large as the one on Earth," Tom said.

Figures he could read my mind in his own universe. "Fine, what does it mean?"

"We have absolutely no idea, Jack. But we can tell you, we are here on your world to find out."

Waves crashed into the sandy beach behind us, and I spared a glance at the throngs of people frolicking on the yellow sand. I envied them. Oblivious to the conversation and implications that were just exposed. Whatever was going on, I could be square in the middle of it. Tom thought so, anyway. Which filled me with the strong desire for a stiff drink.

I sighed once and nodded. Below me on the ground, I noticed a collection of seashells like the one I used to send Yut here to be Tom's lunch. I bent over and grabbed a few. "Mind?" I asked.

"Feel free to visit any time, Jack."

I nodded. I had a feeling that I probably would very soon.

****

I landed in my chair at my office with a thud and

opened a drawer on the side of my desk. My half-filled bottle of Irish whiskey smiled back at me with the understanding and compassion that only a distilled spirit from an emerald isle can offer. I grabbed a cup half-filled with day old coffee, threw the contents into the waste bin and poured myself a stiff drink.

So much had happened in the last few days that I could barely process it all. I'd helped to start an AI revolution, found one of only one evolution chambers in the universe, befriended an entire galactic species wrapped in the body of a used car salesman on a beach that could easily pass for the finest in New Jersey, and then discovered that the entire galaxy, and everyone on Earth, are terrified of whoever gave me superpowers.

That at least deserved a four finger pour.

I picked up one of my old business cards on the desk and smiled. After a moment, my grin flipped, and the name of my agency felt more frustrating than normal. I grabbed a pen on my desk, removed the cap with my teeth, I scratched out the world alien and replaced it with omniscient. I nodded and spat out the pen cap.

Eugene J. McGillicuddy's

Omniscient

Detective Agency.

Perfection. Had a nice ring to it. And might just drum up business. If everyone in the cosmos knew anyway, why not embrace the ace up my sleeve. I stared out the window to the great city of Washington D.C., the new and old, center of the world. I didn't know what game Tom was playing or what angle he had. I only knew he had one. Not that I wanted to tangle with him. That was one all-powerful alien I didn't want to anger.

I shook my head and let the thought die. I'll deal with Tom and his weird beach, another time. For now, as I took a sip of whiskey and a puff of a cigarette, I just wanted to bask in the glory of a case solved. Sure, I used my gift along the way, but I still brought it home. It was me that saved the day. Everyone gets a hand up every now and then. Mine is a talking voice in my head with all the answers, but I choose how to use it.

And in the end, after the chips are counted, that's what really matters.

Epilogue

Alice fell into her seat and threw her bag on the ground next to her chair. Eddie had gone to the android repair shop to fix his suit while Eugene folded himself into his office with a tumbler of whiskey. The case was done. And now everyone could unpack the events that just occurred and try to find some meaning in any of it.

Of course, there wasn't any.

Though, in some ways, that wasn't entirely fair. Alice had finally come to the conclusion she could let what happened go. She could dig into the private eye life and have some fun for a while. Returning to academia just didn't feel right. What was the point anyway?

And Eugene got over his constant feeling of ineptitude. Sure, Alice had played into it a bit for kicks over the last year. But sometimes you have to grow up on your own. Face the world as it is and dig deep into your soul. Let past failures slide and accept what you are. Find your path. And that's what Eugene did. He figured out how to neutralize Yut, though it was rather insane and could've really pissed off Tom and saved the day. So, kudos to him.

Alice leaned back in her chair and sighed. It must have been quite the feeling when Eugene figured it out. When he stopped relying on his gift and just trusted his own gut. After all, even if the aliens know everything, it doesn't mean they want to share it. And just like Yut and Puntini, aliens are just as prone to lying as humans.

A tickle burst into Alice's mind as her last thought rifled through her brain. Aliens lie. They lie to humanity, and they lie to each other. She followed the thread of reasoning back to her friends and the events of her lab and the insistence from the Krill that they weren't in the afterlife network. From her own research into the explosion, she knew from the energy signatures, and from Tom's explanations, there was no way her experiments opened a dimensional rift or gateway. Her friends were indeed dead. But what if dying isn't what the Krill say it is?

According to the Krill, energy dissipation at the time of death, on worlds without their afterlife network, accounts for the missing souls across the cosmos. That's why no one's great-grandfather has showed up to say hello. But what if the energy doesn't dissipate?

Alice popped open her computer and threw on her immersion rig. She compared energy signatures of her explosion with tower frequencies of the Krill. But she'd run that scan before and found no match. When she inquired with the Krill, they said all the frequencies of the spectral towers are published. And Alice believed they were telling the truth.

Computational units, measurements of how much computer power can be thrown at any problem, were virtually unlimited on Earth now, thanks to the Galactic Congress. Using them to design weapons was forbidden but using the massive amount of computational power at her fingertips to do research wasn't.

From the archives of the Galactic Library, Alice queried every alien world's initial interaction with the

Krill. It took over twenty minutes, an eternity in modern computer times, to examine a million alien races' interaction. From scientific journals to literature to historical accounts, Alice pored over the data until she found something that she was quite certain she shouldn't have found. On an alien world halfway across the cosmos, a junior scientist from an aquatic species known for being xenophobic and generally suspicious of everyone, attached sensors to the Krill towers as they were being constructed underwater. The junior scientist's readings were meaningless to him. In fact, they were meaningless to anyone that saw them. Except Alice.

The frequency threshold of the spectral tower during construction exactly matched the energy signatures she experienced during her experiment. Which was impossible. There was no way she could possibly have matched something happening from the Krill. Her experiments had nothing to do with spectral towers. But then, some of the greatest discoveries are made by accident.

With a smile on her face, Alice plugged in the frequency profile from her experiment and from the aquatic species into the Galactic Library. It only took seconds for her query to be shut down, her access to be terminated, and her connection severed.

Startled beyond words, Alice jumped back onto the GalNet and used another connection profile to re-access the Galactic Library. All information regarding the aquatic species, the junior scientist, and the frequency they documented were gone.

"Son of a—" Alice's breath came fast. "Got you."

****

She burst into my office, a pile of electronics in her hands and a smile wider than her face was really built for. I gave her a long stare, which she ignored, and watched as she threw all the materials on my desk.

"You know, you can't go around spending your days frowning and suddenly whip up a grin that wide. Doesn't fit."

"What? Whatever. You said you would help," Alice said.

I downed a gulp of my whiskey and nodded. No rest for the omniscient. "Yeah, sure. Help with what again?"

"My new idea. Remember? On the cliff? Before Yut almost ate us?"

Oh, yes. I remembered, but boy, I wish I had forgotten. "All right, we aren't going to blow up the universe, are we?"

"Don't be silly," Alice said. She paused then, looked to the ceiling and mouthed a series of numbers. I couldn't help but gulp. "That's like a point zero zero two percent chance. Almost impossible."

"Oh, good." I downed another drink.

Alice grabbed two wrist cuffs and a collar from the pile of junk on my desk. Without asking, she wrapped the cuffs on my wrists and threw the collar around my neck. She nodded once, her eyes blazing with life and her grin even wider than before. I can honestly say I was genuinely scared.

"Alice," I said, but she turned and ran back to her pile of things.

"It's like this. The entire universe accepts that when we die, we go to the Krill and their spectral nets. They are the de facto rulers of the underworld.

Everyone trusts what they say. That all the dead live around us all the time." She paused for breath before racing off in thought again. "I checked the libraries, corresponded with scientists around the galaxy, and even asked Tom on the beach. Everyone accepts it."

"That so?" I said, nerves in my stomach leaping through my spine and down my legs, urging me to run away. Now.

"Yes, that's so. And then something Tom said. Those that are experts are believed, trusted, and authority is given to them. But then it hit me. What if the experts are lying?" Alice turned and grabbed a device that looked a lot like either a tiny hair dryer or an oversized gun. I looked for signs she'd recently showered, but not a wet drop anywhere.

"Is that a gun?" I said.

"See, the Krill. They had this gift that no one else in the galaxy had evolved. The ability to see the dead. Why not capitalize on that? Why not create a galaxy spanning network and collect fees?" She shook her head and smiled. "It always comes back to economics, am I right?"

"What?"

"You'll be fine, I think. No, you will. I've already tried it on a hamster, and he was, well, okay-sh."

"Alice, what is all this about?" Times like this I wished I could ask my gift questions myself.

"When you get there, your essence will blend and merge with a new particle. Something never captured before." Alice's eyes lit up in a way that sent shivers down my spine.

"A new particle?"

Alice nodded. "The death particle."

"The death—"

"Particle."

I paused for a moment, waiting for Alice to further describe her new discovery. She didn't. "And tell me again how I find this?"

"When you get to the other side, it should, if my theory is correct, bond with your essence. Your soul."

"Get back from where?"

"The other side. The other afterlife. The place the Krill don't want us to know about. Cause if we did, if the galaxy did, then no one would use their network. It's where everyone that has ever lived exists. Where my friends are."

"Other afterlife?"

Alice pointed the gun that turned out wasn't a hair dryer at me and winked. "Thanks so much for doing this," she said, and pulled the trigger.

A bolt of light erupted from the device and slammed into my chest. The collar and cuffs glowed a bright gold color from the impact, and more pain than I'd ever felt coursed through my body. I wasn't sure if this would kill me and then wished it would, or just stop. Either way, fat chance Alice was getting a paycheck after this.

"See you in a few," was the last thing I heard Alice say.

Before I could even fathom what she meant, I died, I think? My last thought on the earthly plane of existence was I didn't even get to finish my whiskey. Maybe they would have something similar on the other "other" side.

A word about the author...

George lives in Washington DC with his wife, children, overly hyper dog and three-legged cat.
http://www.georgeallenmiller.com

Thank you for purchasing
this publication of The Wild Rose Press, Inc.

For questions or more information
contact us at
info@thewildrosepress.com.

The Wild Rose Press, Inc.
www.thewildrosepress.com

Printed in the USA
CPSIA information can be obtained
at www.ICGtesting.com
LVHW020956271123
765022LV00009B/244

9 781509 249909